BAD PRESS. Copyright © 2019 by Candice Franklynn

ISBN # 9781731018519

www.candicefranklynn.com

Cover designed by Nate Johnston

For my husband.
Your love transformed me,
your wisdom inspires me,
and your unyielding support
made this book possible.

BAD PRESS

Candice Franklynn

This above all:
To thine own self be true,
And it must follow, as the night the day,
Thou canst not then be false to any man.

- Hamlet, Shakespeare

ONE

Delilah

No one likes to look bad. We all obsess about what people think of us. Don't believe me? Think you aren't preoccupied with what other people think about you, whether they be friends, coworkers, lovers, or passing strangers? Then tell me the last time you went a whole day without the thought crossing your mind, even once.

I know this obsession lies within all of us, which is why I've built a career around managing it. Just as it is with joy and sadness, embarrassment is a universal human emotion that crosses language barriers, social classes and continents. I'm not just talking about appearance; the human need to look good goes far beyond the embarrassment of spilling soup on your shirt or running into your boss at the market while wearing yoga pants and slippers. We loathe appearing at fault, or vulnerable, or any variation of imperfect. And my skill is that I can work with clients to make sure they never, ever feel that way again. But on this particularly fateful night, I found myself hoping to avoid two specific breeds of looking bad that notoriously come from this exact kind of evil.

I was on a blind date.

Which meant the evening would be spent one of two ways; either trying like hell to conceal the messy parts of myself I didn't want seen by a potentially great guy, or instead, that same guy would be a hopeless dud, and I'd spend the rest of the night trying to figure out how to leave without seeming rude. Either way, it was a minefield. So, there I sat on my date.

Correction, there I sat *waiting* for my date to arrive.

Looking bad scenario number three, I thought. *He never shows up, and I sit here looking more and more pathetic to everyone around me.*

This date was most certainly not my idea. My best friend Jules, and now temporary roommate, had named two blind dates of her choosing to be the contingency of my staying with her when I got to Portland. She wasn't out to torture me, but it was instead her way of recreating some semblance of the life we had years ago as college roommates. I'd teased her relentlessly when she'd left Los Angeles and moved to the Pacific Northwest, specifically to the hipster capital of the west coast. Looking at the two of us, you'd think *I* would be the one to retreat to Portlandia. While Jules stood tall at nearly six feet with long blonde hair, I was struggling to hit five and a half feet in heels and had a mess of wavy black hair. Jules had the clear complexion, striking cheekbones and striking appearance that made people passing her on the street or in an airport think they were spotting a celebrity, which she was, in a way. Meanwhile, I was lathering on concealer to hide freckles and contouring to make my face less round. At least there were my eyes, I did like my blue eyes.

"You've got to jump right into the deep end of the dating pool," she said while helping me get ready earlier that night. "Wait too long, and the water's all murky with theoretical kid urine."

"I'm not wearing this!" I said, interrupting her nonsense, to which I was only half-listening. Jules's theories tended to be committed to a high level of vividness but lacking in any sort of logic. I was also distracted by the outfit she'd picked out for me; my face wrinkled in consternation with every turn I made in front of the mirror.

"Oh, stop whining," she said, rolling her eyes at me in her dramatic, TV persona sort of way. Jules hosted a local television show, which fed into her exaggerated gestures and over-the-top personality, both of which were not always contained to the small screen.

I was in black pants that fell embarrassingly low on my hips and a sleeveless, white silk top with a neckline that plunged far too deep; both items of clothing were out of my comfort zone. My whining was well-earned in my humble, albeit cranky, opinion.

"What's with you?" Jules asked as she crossed to the bed and started sorting through random accessories. "I remember when you used to wear less clothing than this and not even give it a second thought."

"This may shock you," I said as I tried in vain to yank the pants up higher on my hips, "but my preference in wardrobe has changed in the last ten years."

"Sure," she deadpanned. "That's it. It has *nothing* to do with your reinvented persona and commitment to never connecting with anyone, ever."

"Give me the damn belt," I practically shouted, holding my hand out. While I regularly teased Jules over her northern migration, she never let me live down the fact that I'd chosen a career of, in her words, obsessing over what other people thought.

Jules and I were both raised in Southern California, but we might as well have grown up on other planets. She was the child of an investment banker father and pediatric surgeon mother, raised in Santa Monica to believe she could accomplish anything in this world she chose. I was the only daughter of a props and special effects technician mother who taught me two things. The first being that success was dependent on how good you made everyone around you look, and the second was that you can only ever count on yourself in this life. My dad had split on my mom just after I was born, a fact I tried not to dwell on and take personally, and so mom had moved us to Southern California to make a career out of her art hobbies. Admittedly, I'd spent more of my childhood shaking glitter on fairy costumes than doing homework or playing with other kids. It was only because of an art scholarship that I was able to attend USC, and that's where I met Jules. To say we ran in different circles would be a massive understatement. While she was pledging her sorority and attending every party of the year, I was building theater sets for musical productions and drinking overpriced coffee while listening to overindulgent slam poetry in anti-establishment coffee houses. It wasn't until we were both dating the same guy, at the same time, unbeknownst to either of us, that Jules and I finally met. Jules had walked into Miles' apartment one afternoon during one of our passionate necking sessions on his fraying brown tweed couch. That was the first time I ever witnessed her take a door off its hinges in anger.

During her tirade at Miles, she raged about wasting three whole months screwing him when she could have been getting it better somewhere else, which threw me through a loop since

Miles and I had been seeing each other for *five* whole months at that point in time. I don't recall exactly what I shouted, but I do remember punctuating it with a right hook to his eye and tempered stomp. Finding ourselves fuming side-by-side in the parking lot, but both realizing no one could relate to what we were feeling in that moment more than each other, we reluctantly decided to grab a drink. After an initial awkward ten-minute small talk, and then a half hour of laughter and sharing, we both agreed that he'd messed with the wrong couple of ladies and the rest is history.

When I'd called her two weeks ago and told Jules I'd been assigned to a client in Portland, she welcomed me with open arms and a place to stay, with only a couple of strings attached.

"So? Where are you meeting him?" Jules asked as she flopped down on my bed. I smiled sheepishly, not making eye contact. "Oh, fuck me, you told him to meet you at the library or something, didn't you? Christ Dee, what's wrong with you?"

"No. We're meeting at a bar downtown," I said, too quickly.

"Which bar?" Jules was still not convinced I wasn't sabotaging the first of her two mandated dates.

"Boost," I mumbled.

There was a moment of silence before I chanced a look at her and found her staring at me in mild shock.

"You're taking him to the Hotel Monroe?" she asked.

"Well, I need to check the place out, don't I?" I asked feebly.

"Wait, so you're taking a blind date...to work? I stand corrected; the old Dee Sheppard isn't in hiding, she's back!" And with that, she erupted into a fit of laughter.

"I don't officially work there yet," I lamely corrected over her hysterics.

It was technically true. Yes, I had the job, but it was Friday night and I didn't start until the following Monday morning. In the craziness of getting out of LA and settling in with Jules, I hadn't had a chance to check the hotel out yet and was extremely curious. If I had to go on this date, I'd at least do a little reconnaissance at the same time.

I grabbed a hairbrush off my dresser and hurled it a
Jules. "Knock it off!" I yelled, trying not to laugh, but Jules just
fell further into her fit of laughter.

Thirty minutes later I was walking through the lobby of
the Monroe, an elite upscale hotel in downtown Portland.
Manhattan had the Waldorf Astoria. Los Angeles had the Four
Seasons. Portland had the Hotel Monroe. Beyond being a
prestigious hotel, Monroe now housed Boost, which had
replaced a dying restaurant with the trendiest nightclub in
Portland at the moment, without being *so* fashionable no one
wanted to be seen there. There was a delicate balance that had to
be struck in this town.

My mouth fell open when I entered and took in the dark,
vibrant colors and expansive thirty-foot ceiling. To the left, the
entire wall was floor to ceiling windows that opened to the lights
and movement of downtown. High-top bistro tables lined the
window and the opposite wall, which was decorated in black and
white canvas paintings of vintage car blueprints. The floors were
dark mahogany wood, just like the expansive bar lining the front
wall of the club and the small stage at the opposite end of the
room.

I pushed my way through the dance floor and was lucky
enough to grab a table in front of the window just as a couple
was getting up to leave. I'd purposefully arrived early to make
sure I didn't have to wander around asking strangers if they were
Louis. Let him find me.

And that's how I found myself waiting for Jules's
agent's brother's roommate to arrive. He was supposed to be
quite a catch, but this was fourth-hand information and I wasn't
holding my breath.

Open mind. Keep an open mind.

Outside, the eclectic streets of Portland bustled, and I
was engrossed in people-watching when a high-pitched voice
startled me.

"Hi!"

I jumped and looked next to me to see a strikingly
beautiful woman standing at my table with a captivating
presence and yet genuine smile. She had a bob of hair so blonde
it almost appeared white and wore a pink satin dress that hugged
her body with a small black apron tied around her hips.

"Sorry," she laughed. "I didn't mean to startle you." I found myself smiling back at her despite my uneasiness.

"That's alright," I replied.

"Great shoes!" she said looking at my feet and admiring the black heels Jules had put on me after hiding all my flats.

"Oh. Thanks, I-"

"I have the ones just like that," she cut me off, "but in the peep toe and red."

So, then they're nothing *like these.*

She slid onto the stool next to me and continued speaking so fast that I unconsciously leaned forward to follow along.

"You know, the other day I found the new Louboutin's that would match that top perfectly. They resemble the pica, but with picot-trim and satin."

"Wow. You just said a ton of shit I don't understand," I admitted.

She gave me a confused look and popped a pretzel in her mouth from the bowl on the table.

"My roommate put me in these," I explained, pointing to my foot. "I'm not really fashion forward or trend-savvy."

It was true. I knew what I liked and what I didn't, but good luck holding a conversation with me about any of it. I was fashion illiterate, and it drove Jules crazy, even back in college. She was always up-to-date on the latest Vogue, both US and French versions, whereas the best I could do was point at things I thought were pretty.

Like a child.

Or a monkey.

Jules and I had found other things to bond over. However, I currently felt as though I was disappointing this stranger and hated it.

"She has great taste," the waitress said. "Or he!" she said, correcting herself quickly.

I laughed. "No, you're right. *She* has great taste. In fact, she put this whole outfit together. Even though I'm fashion illiterate, I still like to look good."

"Oh!" The waitress surprised me by clapping her hands together. "We'll be great friends then!"

"Oh, we will?" I asked with a chuckle.

"Completely," she said with a confident nod. "Fashion morons are always in expert hands with me."

Well, at least we're the same brand of crazy.

"So, what'll you have?" she asked, hopping off her stool and landing on her own pair of three-inch heels.

"Dirty martini, please."

"Is anyone joining you?"

"I'm waiting for…. someone. I'm waiting for a date. A blind one," I stammered. "Not a blind *person*, it's just a blind *date.*"

"I'll keep 'em coming sweetie," she said with a wink.

As I watched her walk away, through the crowd came a man that resembled an extra from a lost episode of Miami Vice. He looked as though he was ready to offer anyone he spoke with a great deal on life insurance, or zero percent financing on a dining room set and sofa-bed. His too large, gray suit jacket was slightly wrinkled, and his black hair was oiled to the point of looking thoroughly wet. With determination, he was making his way to my table.

Oh, no. Please don't be Louis.

And because God has a sense of humor, he walked right up to me and said, "Hi, I'm Louis."

Maybe I could pretend I wasn't Dee. I could say I was here with friends or married or I could rattle off what little Spanish I remembered and make him think I didn't speak English. Anything to get him thinking I wasn't Dee Sheppard.

"Your picture did *not* do you justice," he said.

Son of a bitch.

"Oh. Thanks." I said meekly, fidgeting in my seat and already trying to figure out how to escape. The thought briefly crossed my mind that I was being incredibly superficial and should give Louis a chance. Maybe under all that grease and false bravado, he was a great guy. After all, I'd been dressed and groomed for the occasion by someone else, perhaps he didn't have that luxury and made incredibly poor grooming choices. He took my hand and planted a sloppy kiss on it before taking the stool the waitress had been sitting on; I immediately missed her.

As if on cue, she reappeared with my drink, eyeing my date as she approached. She looked at me wearily, and I could swear I saw her fighting back a smile. Before she could even set the glass down, I snatched it up for a huge swallow, tossing the olives to the table.

"And what can I get you, sir?" she asked in a professional voice I hadn't been privy to before.

"Hmm. Do you have a drink menu I could look at?" Louis asked with a furrowed brow.

"I have a wine list and signature cocktail menu right here."

"No wine," he cut her off. "I'd like a menu of all mixed drinks, with all ingredients listed, please."

"Er…Any drink in particular?"

"All of them," he replied simply.

And we're keeping the crazy coming tonight.

The waitress stifled a laugh, took in my look of pleading, and said, "Let me see what I can find." As she walked away, Louis blatantly eyed her ass before turning back to me.

"I hear you're in public relations," he said as he leaned across the table and I could smell his breath from my seat. I turned my head to take in clean air and answer.

"Yes. I actually-"

He interrupted me before I could finish and launched into a story about his adventures as a CPA and how that was *similar* to PR, but not really. He continued at length, and I fought to keep my eyes open until he finally stopped and began scanning the room.

Please let him be even more bored than I am. Maybe we can end this now.

"You know, I'm not sure if our waitress is going to bring me that menu," he said.

I had no idea a grown man could be incapable of ordering a drink without a damn menu. I swallowed the last of my martini and prayed for death.

"Maybe she got sidetracked," I offered. "The place is busy, and they seem short-staffed." I wasn't about to let this douche bag insult my new friend. I may have only known her less than an hour, but I sure as hell liked her more than I did this guy.

"Let's sit at the bar. I'd prefer to order from the bartender myself if possible; cut out the middleman." With a shrug and a nod, I stood up in agreement to the change of seating; at least I was inching my way closer to the door. "I'm going to hit the head. I'll meet you there," Louis said, pounding his fist on the table in a ridiculous move that made the bowl of pretzels bounce before he disappeared into the crowd. He was man enough to say 'hit the head' but still needed assistance in ordering a drink. I shook my head and headed for the bar, lucky enough to find two empty stools off to the right side of the long mahogany bar. I took a seat, planted my head in my hands and began planning Jules' painful death as repayment for this setup. And that's when I saw him for the first time.

He was behind the bar, pouring a drink and laughing at something a customer had said. My chest tightened as my breath hitched in my throat as I took him in. He had a body that would make any red-blooded woman stand up and beg for mercy. Standing just over six feet tall, his frame was muscular without being overbearing but still gave me thoughts of being thrown across a mattress. His dark jeans hugged him just enough to showcase his muscled thighs and a great ass, while the sleeves on his black button up shirt were rolled to his elbows. The lights of the bar almost looked blue as they played off his dark brown hair, which was just long enough to allow an errant curl to brush across his forehead once and a while. I watched as his skilled hands worked at making drinks and his forearms flexed as he reached across the bar. He turned to meet my stare and I found myself staring into the most brilliantly piercing hazel eyes I'd ever seen.

A small smile flashed across his luscious lips and he started to make his way toward my end of the bar. Several sexy bartender fantasies began quickly playing through my mind, but I remembered why I was sitting at the bar and that I only had a small window of opportunity. And so, while I wanted nothing more than to flirt with this man, I instead resigned myself to the fact that he was my best chance of escape at this point and it was time to pull out some old punches.

He stood in front of me and leaned on both palms.

"What can I get you?" His voice was like silk.

Here goes nothing.

"Do you have something that will make me sick?"

TWO

Samuel

I sent the last email of the day and sank back into my desk chair with an exhausted sigh. Since Dominic, our VP of Sales, had begun his mission to market the hotel on a national scale, our business had picked up tremendously. We were quickly going from a high-end local Portland spot, to a West Coast destination hotel. Naming him as our sales and marketing guru was one of the best decisions my father had ever made; business was booming, and we were gaining the national exposure that we needed.

As General Manager, the weight of the hotel business fell to me on a day-to-day basis so that my father didn't have to be involved. Not only did he have one foot out the door into retirement, but I was also anxious to have the reigns all to myself finally. I'd come back to Portland after getting my MBA in New York and interning in Tokyo, still high on the rush of investment deals and hedge fund management. I'd been reluctant to step away from that life and manage the family business back in Portland, but it was my birthright and a future I'd always known I was destined for, even as a small child. I could still remember the pride in my father's voice when we would stand in the backyard, looking down the hill at our view of the city, and dad would always point out the hotel in the skyline and say, "There's your future, son."

I had no idea why Charles hadn't retired yet. It had always been the plan that I would take over, and it was apparent that he and my mother wanted to slow down and enjoy some time together. Not to mention, I was practically running this show all by myself as it was. But Charles still found excuses to stay. I went to the window behind my desk and stared out over the river and the lights of the city.

"Good, you're still here," Dominic said as he came into my office.

Dominic had made a career out of taking businesses to the next level. There were salespeople, and then there were people like Dominic. He'd taken a small boutique in the Midwest and turned it into a huge retailer, later to be hired by a tech company to build their European market share. There was even a rumor that after having a memorable meal in a restaurant, he'd marketed the chef to several networks and gotten her a television show before she could even put her house on the market. And then suddenly, as quickly as I'd come back to the Monroe, my father made the decision to snatch up Dominic to grow the hotel into a national brand.

"Are you kidding? Our VP of Sales would kill me if I didn't get in my twelve hours each day," I laughed.

He threw himself into one of the chairs in front of my desk, crossing his blue jean-clad legs and kicking his sneakers up onto my desk. Dominic shared a stylist with the late Steve Jobs.

"I didn't hear you complaining when last quarter's profits came in. How was Mexico with Christi, by the way?" he asked arching an eyebrow at me.

"Touché, jackass."

I sat down again at my desk and leaned back in my chair.

"Are you ready for Monday?" he asked, getting back to business.

"For the new PR monster to come in? Not even a little bit," I said, rubbing my eyes in frustration.

"She's supposed to be the best," Dominic said matter-of-factly.

I shot him a suspicious smirk. I was still annoyed at Charles's decision to bring in someone to basically babysit us. Logically I knew why a PR person was necessary for a company that was growing like we were. But we were already getting plenty of press, why bring in someone to do what was already happening? Simply put, she was going to put a muzzle on all of us, stifle our personalities in the local press, and become a babysitter to the Monroe brothers.

Granted, we weren't saints.

Ok, we were far from it.

But whatever happened to the philosophy that even bad press was at least *press*? We'd been running the shit out of this hotel, and despite what we did on our own time we were making all of us a lot of money. Last year had been phenomenal, and I was guessing this year would beat it. And while Charles typically let me take the reins on most matters for the hotel, he'd made it clear that this decision was most certainly not open for discussion.

"Admit it," Dominic said laughing, "you're just mad because of the probable interruption to your dating game. Some publicist coming in and telling you to keep it on the DL must really piss you off."

"She can tell me which events she'd like me to attend, but that's it," I replied defiantly. That earned me an irritating smirk from Dominic, which he followed with a deep yawn.

"Head home man, you look exhausted," I said. "Emma isn't working tonight, right?"

Dominic and my sister Emma had finally admitted to the family that they were dating. And while she was boisterous about their relationship, Dominic remained restrained about discussing their relationship. Maybe it was because he was a private person, perhaps it was because it was the boss' daughter, but the fact remained that Dominic didn't want it advertised that he and Emma were a couple.

"She's waitressing for Paxton tonight," he replied with a shrug. Before I could ask him for an explanation, there was a knock on my open door as Pax walked in.

"Got a minute?" my younger brother asked in his booming voice as he leaned on the back of the chair next to Dominic. "I have an issue," he said. Pax was manager and creator of the bar and nightclub attached to the hotel, Boost.

"Just one?" I asked.

"Funny, asshat," he said. "Remember how we talked about me taking the team out to celebrate?"

Boost had earned the coveted spot of being the hottest bar in Portland, which had led to a feature in multiple entertainment magazines last month. Dominic and I had suggested Pax take his best crew out for a night on the hotel's dime.

"Well, I'm taking them out tonight and coming up a little short on staffing the place while we're out," he explained sheepishly.

I looked at Dominic. "This explains Emma working tonight?"

He nodded.

"I've got the wait staff covered and most of the restaurant," Pax quickly explained. "But I need another bartender. Adam can't handle it by himself."

"What happened to Brian?" I asked.

"He's sick," Pax said, shrugging. Then his wicked smile spread across his face and I internally groaned. "I was wondering if Slick Sammy could come out for tonight," he laughed.

"Slick Sammy?" Dominic asked with a scoff. "Why haven't I heard that before?"

"That's what we called him in college when-"

"Enough," I cut him off. "So many lines being crossed right now..." I mumbled.

"Come on!" he whined with a smile. "This was your idea. Plus, you owe me! Boost is the hottest spot within a fifty-mile radius. You should dance on the bar if I asked you at this point. I'm sure the ladies would love it. Plus, think of the booty you'll get bartending tonight!"

"You do realize how lucky you are that your boss is also your brother, right?" Dominic laughed. "I don't know if you could work for anyone else."

Pax gave a noncommittal shrug and then turned back to me for my reply.

"Fine," I relented. "I'm only agreeing to this so you can take your crew out. Let me go home and change."

I slid behind the bar just after eight as Adam was pouring a round of shots for a party at the bar. He looked up at me as I was rolling up my shirt sleeves and proceeded to pour the final shot of tequila onto the bar. I chuckled to myself and handed him a towel.

"Hey, Adam."

He finished his order and shuffled over to me, looking like a deer caught in headlights. I assumed by his shocked expression Pax hadn't let him know I'd be helping out tonight.

"Looks like it's you and me tonight," I said, lightly slapping his shoulder.

"You…you? And me?" he stumbled out. I guess I couldn't blame the poor guy. He'd been bartending at Boost for a little over a month, and tonight he found himself working next to the General Manager. Truth be told, it would have thrown me through a loop once upon a time as well.

"Would you like me to take these orders?" I asked, pointing to the waitress' tickets that were sitting on the bar.

"I'm sorry, Mr. Monroe!" he sped out. "I was getting right on those after I finished the group at the end there."

I laughed openly this time.

"Call me Sam. And I was only asking because I wanted to know where you needed me tonight. I'm sure you have a system. I don't want to slow you down, so let's have some fun, ok?"

A slow smile spread across Adam's face as he thought this over.

An hour later, the two of us had fallen into our own groove behind the bar. We glided back and forth from one end to the other filling orders and keeping the crowd happy. When the waitresses had large orders to fill, one of us would make the mixed drinks while the other would pour beers or shots. For having never worked together, we ran the place quite seamlessly.

Emma bounded up to the bar as I was pouring shots for an obnoxious, yet well-tipping, bachelorette party at the end of the bar.

"Fancy seeing you here!" she said in her musical voice.

"I should say the same," I replied. "Pax suckered you into this as well, huh?"

"Yeah, I owed him. Although I'm surprised he got Slick Sammy to come out tonight," she deadpanned before instantly bursting into giggles.

"Seriously?" I asked. "You too?" She just laughed and hopped up on a stool. "Do you have an order for me?" I asked. "Or are you on one of the many breaks I'm certain you're taking tonight?"

"I need a dirty martini, and make it a *good* one," she barked out, pointing a hot pink nail at me.

I arched an eyebrow at her as I reached for the shaker.

"Got a big tipper out there, do you?"

"No, it's for my new best friend. I just met her, and she rocks," Emma said, as though it was no big deal to have made a new best friend it the last ten minutes. Well, for Emma it really wasn't that uncommon. "She's on a blind date, and I want to keep her well-nourished."

"I don't think a martini counts as nourishment, Emma," I said.

"Clearly, you've never been on a blind date," she said earnestly. I placed the drink on her tray and held up an extra olive.

"For vitamin E," I said as I dropped it in the glass. Emma took off through the crowd while Adam and I continued our coverage of the bar. I was finishing an order for a couple of college guys when I saw her for the first time. She was sitting at the end of the bar running a hand through her dark hair. Her silk top clung to her body, and the color of her exposed skin made my mouth water. A silver chain hung around her neck with a pendant hanging from it that she toyed with absently. Our eyes met and I stared into her deep blue eyes and felt my pulse quicken. She was gorgeous. Before Adam could reach her, I made my way down the bar and stood in front of her.

"What can I get you?" I asked. I could smell the faint wisp of her perfume from where I stood and fought the urge to lean into her further and bury my nose in the crook of her neck.

"Do you have something that will make me sick?" she frantically asked.

Huh.

I searched her face, not sure what to think. She seemed to be serious.

"I'm sorry?" I asked.

"Look, I don't have much time," she rushed out. "The blind date from hell will be coming over here any minute. I need a way out of here! I'd make something up, but I'm a horrible liar and *always* get caught. I was thinking that if you had a way to make me sick, I could convincingly get the fuck out of Dodge; know what I mean? You've *got* to have some bartender tricks up your sleeve. Use your 'what *not* to do' drink advice, but in reverse."

I gaped at her, trying to catch up and make sure I was grasping the rushing waterfall of nonsense coming out of her mouth. She stared back at me and then her eyes went wide again.

"Oh, oh! Oh!" she said excitedly. "I'm lactose intolerant! Do you have some milk back there you could throw in a drink?" She gripped the edge of the bar, stood on the rung of her stool, and leaned deeply over to peruse the bar inventory. I laughed at her enthusiasm as she sat back on her stool. She was strangely intoxicating and so adorable, even if she was a little bit nuts.

"I'm not making you sick," I said, shaking my head. Sure, I knew some drinks that would probably have all one hundred and twenty pounds of her feeling miserable soon, but there was no way I was doing that. For one, I didn't want her to leave. And secondly, if I made her feel anything, it was going to be pure pleasure.

Nice Sam. Try to think more *like a fifteen-year-old.*

"What are you drinking?" I asked again, clearing my throat.

She sighed in defeat.

"Dirty martini," she mumbled out.

I started to make her drink as something occurred to me. The blind date. The dirty martini. Could this be Emma's new best friend?

"How bad of a liar are you that you'd subject yourself to projectile vomiting as an alternative?" I asked.

"Bad. Very bad. Evasive? Coy? Mysterious? Sure, I can try to pull those off. But looking someone in the eye and lying? Man. My face gets bright red, and I get all shifty. I look like an embarrassed Chihuahua. It's always been that way, I can't help it."

"Well, I guess that rules out the possibility of striking it rich at professional poker playing then."

"True. But if I can figure out how to harness the heat from my blush, then we may have an alternate energy source, and I'll make a mint," she said with a confident nod.

"What's your name?"

"Dee."

Adam appeared next to me, asking about a large order, and when he was gone I went back to Dee's martini. Her eyes followed me as I worked and I had to catch myself from staring back at her. There was no denying the attraction I felt for her, she was a beautiful woman. But there was something more; something electric.

"Well Dee, it's been a while since I met a woman whose drink of choice was a dirty martini," I said, reaching for a fresh glass.

"It's not usually my drink of choice," she said. "My drink is usually a mojito."

I paused briefly as she shrugged her shoulders, giving me a weak smile at her admission.

"You know, when I'm with friends, having fun... That's what I like to have," she said with a bigger smile. "But when I need extra courage, or in this case a painkiller, I go for the martini."

She shifted on her stool and kept glancing nervously toward the restrooms.

"That bad?" I asked skeptically, jutting my chin toward the men's room.

Dee met my gaze intently and pursed her lips. I had to force myself to look away from them and concentrate on pouring.

"You have no idea," she said closing her eyes and shaking her head.

I placed the martini on the bar and just before I could reach out to lift her face to look into those beautiful eyes again, her head snapped up. She had a devious smile on her face.

"But don't take my word for it," she said. "Since you won't help me, you'll get to see for yourself."

I smiled back and placed a hand over hers.

"I said I wouldn't make you sick, not that I wouldn't help you."

THREE

Delilah

As soon as his hand touched mine, I felt every nerve ending in my body stand up at attention and my heart start to pound, to the point where I had to focus on not actually panting out loud. What can I say, I'm cool under pressure like that.

"I said I wouldn't make you sick, not that I wouldn't help you." He chuckled and gave me a wink. I was suddenly thankful I was sitting down since my knees would have most certainly given out. Before I could say anything, he ran a hand over the stubble on his chin and made his way to the couple just a little bit down the bar waiting to order.

I wasn't bluffing. I really did want him to give me a believable excuse to leave. What I hadn't expected was for him to give me a justifiable reason to stay. The more he spoke and smiled and moved, the more I wanted to grab onto him and never let go.

"Sorry to keep you waiting," Louis said sliding onto the stool on my right.

"Oh, it's ok, I was just-" I mumbled.

"I ran into an old buddy from school in the men's room, and we got to chatting. Where did you say you went to college?" he asked.

"I-" he quickly cut me off. Again.

"I know that everyone thinks their alma mater is the best, but can you honestly name a better institution than the University of Washington? It is by *far* the best school out there," he said waving his hand in front of him as if to dismiss all points to the contrary. He wasn't going to hear any from me, only because I didn't have the energy to force myself into his one-man conversation. Louis hadn't given me a single chance to tell him about myself, and I was secretly thankful for it. I felt like I was getting a small reprieve; rather than having to join in on this horrible date, I was merely watching it. But eventually, that task became painful, too.

As Louis was starting another story about the wacky hijinks he and the chess club had gotten into at *crazy* "U-dub," the sexy bartender answered my prayers and interrupted.

"Hey man," he said to Louis, giving me a quick glance. "What can I get you?"

That's it? So much for his help.

Louis turned his full attention on him.

"Well, I was hoping you could tell me which alcohol has the lowest calorie count," Louis said.

I looked at Louis certain I would see him smiling, desperately hoping he was making his first joke of the night, even if it was a shitty one.

"Calorie count?" the bartender asked. I could have sworn I caught a smile forming on his perfect lips.

"Yes, I'd like something that won't throw me too far over my calorie intake for the day. I'd like it mixed with something that's equally low-cal," Louis said, as though it as the most natural way to order a drink.

I stared at him with my mouth open. Jules' agent's brother was going to get a phone call from me tomorrow.

"I'm training for the Hood-to-Coast relay and would like to keep it light tonight," Louis said and then turned to me. "That's a marathon that starts in Mt. Hood and continues out to the Oregon coast," he explained, full of himself indeed.

"Yes, I'm aware," I deadpanned.

"You do realize that Hood-to-Coast is in August, which was last month?" the bartender asked slowly, as though he was speaking to a mental patient.

"I'm training for next years' event," Louis said, shaking his head in exaggerated awe as though he'd been asked which way is up. "Look, man, if you're uneducated in such things we call in the Bar Manager; I'm sure he'd know."

The bartender glanced a look at me, and I couldn't help but smirk back at him.

Told you.

"Well," the sexy beast said, "vodka is pretty basic, and I can mix it with cranberry juice, which is… good, I guess. And there's always light beer." His smile was becoming harder to hide and this point.

"Let's do the vodka and cranberry," Louis said slapping his hand on the bar as though he'd just decided to order the best bottle of champagne in the joint.

Gorgeous started mixing the drink, and Louis turned his attention back to me.

"You see, alcohol is one of the worst things you can add to your diet," he lectured.

Clearly, I hadn't got drunk enough at the *beginning* of this date.

"Not only does it have empty calories, but it's usually paired with high-calorie mixers," Louis rambled on.

"Thank God *my* drink is all booze and no mixer then," I said sarcastically with a smile, raising my glass in mock cheers and taking a huge swallow.

"Yes," Louis said, his somber tone unyielding, "but it will still contribute to the existing fat on your body."

I snorted martini and felt my nose burn as I did so. Louis caught what he had said, and his eyes went wide.

"Not that you're fat!" he shouted, catching the attention of a few people around us.

I gaped at Louis, dumbfounded. He wasn't telling me something I didn't already know; I wasn't a model, but I certainly wasn't fat. In fact, the word 'ordinary' regularly sprung to mind. But while not being attention-grabbing in any way, I at least knew that I wasn't *un*attractive. I was more shocked that Louis had found a way to scream about body fat on a first date. Honestly, this man should be studied by social anthropologists.

"I just meant the small amount of fat that *is* on your body... because everyone has fat on their body... some more than others... not you though!" he stammered out. I let him flail about, not interested in offering any help; I wouldn't have even known where to start. A chuckle caught my attention, and I looked up to see the beautiful bartender laughing quietly to himself as he put Louis's drink in front of him. I opened my mouth to unleash the first snide comment that occurred to me, but before I could say anything he set a second drink down in front of me, even though more than half of my current martini remained in the glass. I looked down and couldn't stop the wide smile that spread across my face when I saw the tall mojito. He winked again when I met his gaze and then made his way back down the bar.

⌗

Samuel

It killed me to leave her sitting there with that guy, but I knew I needed to do this just right. I wanted nothing more than to help her tonight and make her smile, and that took patience. And Emma.

When he'd made the comment about Dee's body, I almost dropped the bottle in my hand. It was apparent he hadn't meant any harm, but that didn't stop my frustration, as well as awe, with his complete obliviousness. She was gorgeous; every man around Dee was ogling her, while her date was busy talking about body fat. For a moment, I worried that this moron had offended her and almost interjected. But the look on her face had been priceless and stopped me in my tracks. She'd snorted her martini and looked at him with a sexy brow arched, going so far as to pop an olive from her drink into her luscious mouth while he tripped all over himself. I quickly went from annoyance at him, to being impressed with her. Clearly, she couldn't believe what a dipshit he was, and she was simply amusement, rather than indignant.

I busied myself behind the bar, filling orders and waiting for Emma to show up again. Whenever I could, I would look over at Dee and each time was the same. Her date was talking nonstop while her eyes were glazed over. At one point I had to reach under the bar in front of them for a bottle of whiskey and heard him talking about Boost.

"You said you were interested in checking this place out," he said dismissively. "But I don't really see why everyone makes such a fuss about it."

"Well, the scenery is nice," Dee said quietly. I glanced up and caught her staring down at me. She blushed furiously and looked away, leaving me with the confidence that I was going to make this woman mine, as planned. There was something about her that brought out the desire to buy her flowers as well as fuck her senseless; it was an odd dichotomy for me. Finally, as I was finishing an order at the opposite end of the bar, Emma made her way to me.

"I need your help," I told her. I knew I was going to owe her big for this and was hoping she'd do it, no questions asked.

⬿⬾

Delilah

When Louis started another story about golf, I was ready to fake a phone call from Jules or feign symptoms from some strange African virus. But I knew what would happen. My inability to lie in situations like these would give me away and I'd end up either caving or beating myself up all night for being rude. Why couldn't I get 'Work Dee' to rub off on 'Personal Dee' once and a while?

It was during times like this that I envied Jules' strength. I wished I could find the courage to tell Louis what a horrible time I was having and just leave. But god only knows what he would think, and my crippling people-pleasing tendencies left me not willing to risk it. Thankfully, before I could berate myself any further, my waitress friend reappeared next to me. She was balancing a tray on one hand while her other was perched on her hip. She didn't even toss a glance my way as she slid between Louis and myself, reaching for a small stack of napkins on the bar. Her body pressed up against him, and his eyes went wide with shock and pleasure.

"Excuse me, honey," she said seductively to Louis, emphasizing the 'honey' and positioning her mouth inches from his neck. His jaw went slightly slack and his eyes roamed her body up and down. Just as she turned to leave, she gave me a coy smile.

What...the fuck?

Tonight was getting stranger and stranger. Horrible first date. Sex god tending bar. Bipolar waitress professing friendship and then flirting with my loser of a date. I knew Portland was supposed to be weird, but holy shit this was odd.

Maybe I'm on one of those reality prank shows...

"What was I talking about?" Louis asked as I turned back and forth in my seat, examining the ceiling and walls for hidden cameras.

"Yourself," I said flatly. "Does that painting look like it has a camera in it?"

Louis looked confused and started to speak again but was cut off by our bartender.

"Hey, either of you live over in Camas?" he asked.

I squinted at him in frustration.

Seriously man. Just forget helping me if that's all you've got.

"Sure do," Louis said proudly, giving no attention whatsoever to the oddity of the question.

"Well, there's something on the news about a huge fire over there. It's taken out a few houses already. We're letting everyone know," he replied. "Sad, they look like really nice places."

"Oh man," Louis said, rising off his stool. "Do you know where?"

"Somewhere near the lake," he said, reaching for a glass.

"They're ALL near the lake, jackass," Louis screeched out in a high-pitched panic.

"Something lack... Lackglenn? Lackmead?"

"LacaMAS?!" Louis shouted.

"Yeah, that's it."

"Oh Jesus, that's my street!" he said, turning to me and frantically leaping completely off his stool. I caught a small smile on the bartender's face.

I will be damned.

⚬⚬⚬

Samuel

"Fine, I'll do it," Emma said. "But *only* because I like her!"

She stalked off toward Dee and her date. I watched as she wedged herself between them and went in for the kill. I chuckled at Dee's look of confusion as she watched Emma do her magic. The look of satisfaction on my sister's face was enough to tell me that she'd accomplished her part of the plan.

"Here," she said dismissively, handing me the loser's wallet. I glanced at the address listed on his license.

"Of course this asshole lives in Washington," I mumbled before turning to my sister. "I owe you," I said as I made my way back down the bar.

As I told captain dipshit that his house was burning to the ground, I watched as Dee's face went from shock to confusion and finally to realization. She looked at me and I smiled quickly at her.

"I need to go," he said in a rush to her.

Mission accomplished. See ya never, sucker.

"Of course," she said, playing along. "I understand completely!" Her enthusiasm was over-the-top, but he didn't seem to catch it. I grinned even wider, despite myself, happy to be rid of the date so I could have her to myself.

"I should text my neighbor and see what's happening," he said, patting his pockets for his phone.

Fucking Christ.

I almost groaned out loud. Not only was he going to figure out this was all complete bullshit, more importantly, he was going to realize his wallet was gone. I looked at Dee and her face had gone red as her mouth opened and closed a couple of times as the same thoughts occurred to her. She shifted in her seat while mindlessly shaking her head and I recognized the embarrassed Chihuahua immediately. Before I could respond, Emma appeared.

"Hey, did you hear," she all but shouted at me as she shoved herself up to the bar next to the guy, "half of Camas is burning to the ground!"

Dee's blind date did an anxious hop up and down as he received all the confirmation he needed that the worst was happening, and he needed to go. He turned to Emma to clarify, which meant turning his back to Dee. She looked at me wide-eyed and I quickly held up his wallet and shrugged sheepishly, making her jaw go slaw with panicked shock.

Guess I didn't think this all the way through.

He turned back to Dee and started offering invitations for a raincheck and hopes that she would see him again once he'd sorted everything out. As he did so, I slid the wallet to Emma who then slipped it into his coat pocket and disappeared. Mr. Marathon sprinted for the door as though his life depended on it, leaving Dee gaping at me in surprise.

೦೫೦

Delilah

I was ecstatic to be rid of Louis. More than that, I was also excited to be left alone with the sexy bartender. I'd been fantasizing about wrapping my legs around him the whole time Louis had yammered on and on about golf and investment plans for the last thirty minutes.

"Well, that was interesting," I said.

"Interesting?" he said incredulously, leaning in front of me with a smirk. "I'd venture to say that that was fucking brilliant. Spectacular, even."

I couldn't suppress my smile at his comment but quickly tried to recover.

"That was above and beyond the fake emergency call. Pull that trick often?" I asked in as much of a serious tone as I could muster.

"Actually, no. In fact, I may owe her a kidney for getting her to do that," he said gesturing over his shoulder at our waitress friend.

The traffic in the bar had slowed down, and we were able to keep our conversation going with minimal interruption. We talked about random things and continued getting to know each other as he sporadically had his attention diverted by the occasional customer. When he'd have to step away to tend to an order, I would nurse my mojito and watch him work. Not only was he skilled behind the bar, but he was confident with the customers as well. There didn't seem to be a person he couldn't charm. I marveled at his ability to work any sort of crowd and wondered what would happen if he harnessed that ability; a man like this could accomplish so much more than being a successful bartender.

"Who set you up with that guy?" he asked after finishing an order and returning to my corner of the bar.

"My best friend."

"Hmm. And by 'best friend' I'm inferring that this person has *met* you before?" he asked, furrowing his brows. I smiled and nodded. "And she still set you up with him?" he continued with his faux contemplation, tapping his chin. "So that must mean that she just doesn't *like* you!"

"Hey, she loves me, thank you very much. It's the calorie-counter weirdo that she's never met before," I said, gesturing toward the door. "It was a friend of a friend sort of thing. I just went along with it."

"In that case, you must be a very trusting person."

I pursed my lips, not sure what to say. Call it a professional hazard, the result of seeing the underbelly of society and far too many people doing the bad shit they were capable of, I wasn't trusting at all. After being in PR for nearly a decade now, starting from the bottom after college and working my way up to Senior Associate, I'd seen everything from politicians with underaged girlfriends, musicians with debilitating drug problems or vile fetishes, and my personal favorite, the internet and social media stars so hungry for attention it was depraved what they would do to get ahead. It wasn't just for the title and office in New York that I was fighting so hard for this promotion; it also meant I could finally handle corporate clients exclusively.

In my quest to get here over the years, I'd become guarded and a touch cynical, and it was only recently that I was starting to make peace with it. However, the strange thing was that all of that seemed to disappear as I talked to this mysterious man and found myself wanting to share my secrets, simply so that I didn't have to carry them alone any longer. I felt like I could trust him with my issue of losing *trust*, and the idea made me wince at its strangeness.

"You ok?" he asked, pulling me from my internal dribbling monologue.

I most certainly decided against launching into my story of self-pity and decided to keep the conversation light instead.

"Jules is hard to argue with when she sets her mind to something," I said, returning to the topic of my blind date. "And since I just moved to Portland, she's decided that I need to be thrust out into the social scene. She's only trying to help, and I let her since it's pretty futile to try to fight her off anyways."

A sexy smile played at the corners of his mouth and he leaned across the bar, stopping inches from my face. I was frozen in place as I stared into his hazel eyes.

"Well, I'm glad," he said in almost a whisper. "And as a Portland native, born and raised, I offer my services to *thrust* you even farther."

My mouth fell open and I gaped at him dumbly. Did he really just say that? I swallowed hard, trying to think of a witty remark. Trying to think of *something* to say. Trying to remember my name. Thankfully I didn't have to.

"Hey, can I get some service over here?" someone called out, and I was shaken from my trance. He chuckled quietly as he made his way over, and while he took care of his customer, I tried to steady myself as best I could. Granted, I hadn't been on the dating scene in the last couple of years, but could it have really changed this much? Since when was flirting *this* intense? I needed to regain some control.

He made his way back over to me, still smiling that damn sexy smile.

"Ok," I said as I crossed my arms on the bar. "Beyond witnessing me on a horrible date, you also know about my random drink preferences and lack of fibbing skills. Time to even the playing field."

"Hey, you shared that all by yourself," he said, holding his hands out, palms toward me in a sign of innocence. I squinted at him and he let out a resigned sigh.

"Well, you did tell me about the Chihuahua, so I guess I can share," he said. He leaned on the bar with his left elbow and right palm while staring at me.

"I'm a horrible speller," he said seriously. "I can't even write a letter by hand without typing it out and using spellcheck first."

I continued to squint at him. "Not good enough."

"My brother thinks I hate golf because it's a boring sport, but I actually hate it because it's the one sport I absolutely suck at, miserably."

I wanted to laugh, but my squint didn't falter.

"Ok," he said, leaning on both elbows, silently acknowledging that I needed more dirt to feel like we were on equal ground. He leaned in further and I could feel his sweet breath as he lowered his voice to almost a whisper and said, "I have a hard time trusting people, too."

For what seemed like the hundredth time tonight my breath was taken away, but this time my chest tightened, and I felt tears sting at my eyes. The walls around my heart started to quake and it scared the shit out of me. Despite all logic, I felt the urge to reach out and place a hand on his cheek, but he stood up before I could do so, almost as though he was trying to extract himself from this hold as well.

"What kind of work do you do?" he asked casually, although the tone didn't reach his eyes. His question jerked me back to reality so suddenly I heard a rushing noise in my ears. Instantly I remembered where I was, and that in two days I'd be back here at the hotel to start my new job. What the hell was I doing? I was finally getting a shot at this promotion, and before it even began, I was already messing it up. I had to get out of the bar and fast.

"I uh… I need to go," I mumbled, gathering my things and trying my best not to look at him. The last thing I wanted to do was leave, but I couldn't risk this chance at getting my life together by letting my heart take over.

"Thank you for helping me," I said as I pulled cash from my clutch. "I would have been stuck here until last call with him otherwise, I'm sure." I flipped a couple of bills onto the bar and avoided his gaze, fearing that if I looked at him I'd stay as long as he asked. His hand fell on mine and I looked up into his eyes before I could stop myself.

Huge mistake.

"Stay," he said quietly.

Nothing in my thirty-two years alive had been as difficult as refusing that simple request. I channeled all of my energy, remembered New York, thought about letting this opportunity slip through my fingers, focused on the job and somehow found just enough strength to leave.

"Thanks for the mojito," I mumbled as I snatched up my jacket and made my way outside as quickly as I could, pulling in a deep breath of air as I did so.

❦

Samuel

I finished the night with Adam in silence, trying to figure out how I'd misjudged my interaction with Dee so badly. Beyond a mutual physical attraction, I also thought there was a connection I'd never felt before. Within an hour of meeting her, I'd been as honest and open with her than I'd been with a woman in a very long time. It instantly occurred to me how sad that was, considering the fact that it all took place across a bar in a busy nightclub, but I'd never had the desire to bare myself like that to a woman so quickly, even in my most euphoric, post-coital hazes. But when she bolted for the exit, I was left questioning every word and wondering if the connection was even real. I wasn't bold enough to think I'd be rounding all the bases with her tonight, but I thought I'd at the very least get her phone number.

"Don't worry, it's not you," Adam said, pulling me from my thoughts as we were cleaning up after closing.

"What?" I asked.

"It's not you," he said again, loading glasses into a dishwashing tray. "Women who come here are usually looking for status or power. And they never look *behind* the bar for that. It's not personal, trust me. Don't let it get to you."

I watched as Adam finished his work and felt suddenly irritated. He was a good kid, and any woman that walked into this place would be lucky to leave with him.

"You should have told her who you are," he said laughing.

I thought back to Dee and her blind date. Is that what she was looking for? Was she a status junky? No doubt I could blow her standards out of the water; I practically owned the club she was trolling. And I'd fucked my share of status junkies in the past and knew that all it took was for me to drop my name for them to drop their panties. But Dee had seemed different, and I was hoping there was something more to her than that. In fact, if I was being honest with myself, she'd struck me as the sort of woman worth chasing for once.

And I was ready to do just that.

She hadn't come across as an easy lay and had even admitted to needing a push from her friends to go out on a date.

When I commented on "thrusting" her myself, I could practically hear the sexual tension crackle between us. I'd almost kissed her right then if I hadn't had been distracted by a customer. But what was more surprising was the partial baring of souls we'd done with one another.

That is, right before she sprinted for the exit.

In the end, Adam's comments made the most sense and I realized he must be right. I felt like a spoiled child being denied a toy at the thought of missing my chance with her simply because she thought I was *just* a bartender. But I decided it was her loss since she was a materialistic snob and hoped I saw her one day when I was in my element.

As we finished closing Boost, I thought about seeing Dee on the street as she waited for another potential sugar daddy to show up for a date. I'd wave an Armani clad arm at her, hop into my sports car and leave her standing there feeling like the shallow temptress she was.

During my agitated pettiness, I also felt a strange sense of vindication. Charles had more than once brought up my penchant for a "certain type" of woman and pressed me to meet a "nice girl." If you decode those conversations, he was basically saying that he was annoyed with me for fucking easy women that only wanted me for my money. What he didn't understand, and tonight had proven, was that those easy women were refreshingly real. It was the nice girls that played the games. At least you knew right up front what the slutty gold-diggers were looking for, and since I wasn't looking for a serious relationship, I felt no remorse in deciding my low-maintenance sexual practices were justified.

"Nice work tonight," I said extending my closed fist to Adam. He bumped his to mine and smiled before turning to leave.

As I drove home, I fought off any more thoughts of Dee and instead tried to focus on how I was going to deal with the pain in the ass PR woman who would soon be joining our team. I sighed in frustration thinking that I would gladly deal with a dozen Dees rather than the one woman planning on telling me how to live my life from now on.

FOUR

Samuel

As Monday morning dawned, I poured all my resolve into putting on my game face and heading into the office for what would most likely be a *challenging* day, to say the least. I was unclear as to how much of a headache the new PR monster would be, only certain that she would definitely be one, and that life was also going to be different for a while at the hotel. But not for too long; this nonsense would only last for as long as she did, and I was going to make damn sure my opposition was hard and clear, to both her and my father. The goal was to have her vacating her office before she even unpacked her knickknacks or hung a single motivational cat poster.

Of all mornings to be struggling to gain focus, this was not the best. Over the weekend, on more than one occasion, I'd found my thoughts drifting back to Dee. They ranged from revenge fantasies to thoughts of her moaning my name and writhing beneath me. It wasn't like me to be hung up on a woman, let alone one I'd only known for the span of a couple hours.

I drove to the hotel in a haze, vacillating between the two women who were vexing me, one personally and the other professionally. Before I could make it to the elevators, my phone buzzed with a text message from Pax: Breakfast!

I chuckled and turned toward the restaurant. At a table in the back, I found my brother spread out and hugging a mug of coffee with one hand, while rubbing his temple with the other.

"Long night?" I asked louder than necessary as I sat down.

"Shit!" Pax muttered at the table. "Take the volume down."

I laughed and signaled to the waitress for coffee.

"Thanks for the invite, at 10PM, on a Sunday night," I said. Pax's text had simply read, "Tacos, tequila, tits." Which was Pax's eloquent way of inviting me to dinner, drinking, and finally a strip club. "Sorry I couldn't join. How was the night?"

I sipped my coffee as he mumbled about shots and lap dances and a waitress he was *definitely* going to go back and hit on, once she'd forgotten about the ass he'd made of himself when they met. My mind frustratingly wandered back to Dee. Once again, her skin and smell were on the forefront of my mind and I wondered how soft her lips felt.

"...shitty pool playing aside, they can definitely hold their shots! Hey, are you even listening to me?"

Pax's question broke through my thoughts, and I scrambled to catch up with his story before he caught on that I was preoccupied with my own stupid shit.

"Uh, yeah. Waitress," I said lamely, taking another drink of my coffee.

Pax narrowed his eyes at me in a display of irritation with my audience skills.

"Sorry brother, I'm just thinking about today-"

"Don't even try to play this off like you were thinking about work," Pax interrupted. "I know your work face, and that was definitely not it. Who is she?" he asked, wiggling his eyebrows at me. With a resigned sigh, I launched into the story of Dee before I could even stop myself.

Pax was the last person I thought I'd be confiding in, but I couldn't shut up as I went on to tell him about the blind date and saving her from the calorie-counting asshole. I left Emma out of it, ashamed at myself for asking her to pick up old habits, but I told him about the flirting and her running away and my inability to stop thinking about her. I finished by sharing the inevitable conclusion of her being a gold-digging pain in the ass.

"Let me get this straight," he said. "You think that because she took off, she's only interested in men with money? Her goal was to get to your wallet through your cock? And when she assumed your wallet was empty, she no longer craved your cock?"

Pax was looking at me like I was a child, and to be honest, I sort of felt like one at that moment. He was vulgar but accurate.

I nodded slightly.

"If she was only interested in men with money," he said slowly, as though he was speaking to a small child, "and she thought you were just a bartender, then why would she have talked to your ass at all? Let alone for over an hour? I thought you went to college. That shit just isn't logical, bro. If I was a betting man, and I am, I would wager you said something stupid and scared her off."

My brain started to swim for a moment and then froze. The guy had a point; it didn't make sense. And between the newly minted philosophical version of my brother and my observations on Friday night being turned upside down, I couldn't seem to formulate a coherent thought.

"Well..." I started. "I guess I just took what Adam said, clearly something based on his own experience, and ran with it..."

"Fascinating," Pax said, rolling his eyes. "Look, I don't know why your Juliet ran for the hills, but I seriously doubt it has anything to do with this bullshit money-grubbing theory of yours."

"Then why-"

"Shit, I don't know! Women are fucking confusing."

"That's very helpful Pax, thank you."

"Look, who cares what her issue was; you obviously need to get this chick out of your system. I say you find her and fuck her brains out."

And the philosopher has left the building.

"Oh yeah?" I asked sarcastically. "How do I find her? I don't even know her last name."

"Remember the name of her date?"

I nodded.

"Well, then we find him and get her name." I opened my mouth to interject, but Pax put a hand up to stop me. "We'll call him up and give him some bullshit story about how his date left something at the bar, but there was no reservation and the bartender remembered him from the 'emergency' and boom! We get her name and find her."

Leave it to Pax to be the Sherlock Holmes of pussy.

And he had somewhat of a point; maybe if I found her and had the chance to talk to her in the light of day, put some reality on the whole situation, she'd tumble off the pedestal I was placing her on. Then again, fucking her out of my system didn't seem like the worst plan in the world. Nothing like making a woman purr like a kitten to absolve your insecurities about her feelings for you, right?

"She's new to town; it'll probably make her harder to find," I said skeptically.

"Never doubt the internet, my brother," Pax said waving his phone at me. "Plus, this will give me something to do during this bullshit meeting," he mumbled, which elicited a groan from me.

"Right," I said, glancing at my watch. "We should head up. I have a couple of things I need to take care of before the big introduction to the manipulative, fun destroying shrew."

"Jesus. You think it's going to be that bad?"

"I think she's coming in to babysit us. And I think she's going to make things miserable for as long as dad lets her."

I didn't care that I sounded like a spoiled child. I was tired, annoyed and sexually frustrated to boot. Pax slapped a large hand on my back as we made our way through to the elevators.

"Well then, we'll present a unified line of resistance, bro. No one is going to tell me I can't party."

∽∾

Delilah

Monday morning, I found myself back at the Hotel Monroe, rushing frantically into the coffee shop next door. My assistant Mae was already sitting at a table near the front and I plopped down in front of her in a huff.

"Sorry I'm late," I panted, letting my purse and laptop bag slide off my shoulder.

She gave me a friendly smile and pushed a to-go cup at me. "I got your latte and don't worry, we still have a few minutes," she said.

Mae was the best and I was eternally grateful I was able to bring her with me to Portland.

When I was offered the assignment at the Monroe, I was allowed an assistant and Mae was my first choice. The PR world can be tricky; it's a profession based on manipulation and illusion, and we're artists working with smoke and mirrors. When you work in a field where you can never let your guard down, the only way to stay sane is to have someone with you that you can trust and rely on 100% of the time. I'd been mentoring Mae since she was an intern and hoped that if the Monroe assignment went well, and I was offered the role in New York, I'd be able to convince Mae to come along, too.

She handed me a leather-bound portfolio. "All the highlights are in here," she said, "just in case you need them."

Mae had compiled extensive research on the hotel and Monroe family; I'd only wanted the crucial information since I was coming in to do immediate and massive damage control for the hotel's image. Some PR jobs were simply a matter of managing events or press releases, but this was *not* one of them. Over the last week, Mae had sifted through endless internet searches and tabloid nonsense in order to feed me only what I needed to know to formulate a game plan. In this early stage of the project, her job was research, whereas mine was strategy. And the clock was ticking; less than two weeks ago my boss had called me into his office and told me I was being eyed for the Corporate Liaison position in our New York office. This would be my chance to work with Fortune 500 companies on their branding and communications; no more press releases on behalf of boy bands about Instagram pictures girls had posted backstage. But before I could be offered such a role, I had to prove I could handle corporate PR.

The Hotel Monroe, unbeknownst to most of their employees, was being positioned for sale. The owner, Charles Monroe, had approached a business broker a few months back about getting a valuation for the business. One of the first things he was told was that he'd have a better chance of selling, or at the very least would get a higher price, if he could get his PR problems under control. They'd introduced him to JPL Relations, the firm I worked for, and the assignment was sent to me as a test of my abilities. And because the sale hinged on the branding, I had to get to Portland immediately, wrap this up successfully, and with less than two months at my disposal. The timeline was rushed, but the assignment was going to be a softball, mostly.

"We're thinking Samuel and Paxton are the priorities, right?" I asked as I flipped through the abbreviated clippings.

Mae knew me well; for each employee, she'd condensed all media points and articles into essential documents and highlighted the important portions in yellow. There were no puff pieces, pictures, or information generated by their own marketing department. I was focused instead on a highly condensed collection of information in bulleted form. I had information on the Monroe family and hotel executive employees that could rival the FBI's.

"Yes, they're the ones getting most of the press these days," Mae replied.

"Ok, we start there."

We started to make our way to the hotel and I felt the butterflies rise in my stomach like it was the first day of school. I'd finally reached a point in my career where I was actually sought out as an expert, but I still wasn't outwardly and overly confident.

You can do this. You've been waiting to run a show like this.

"How was your weekend?" Mae asked, interrupting my internal pep talk.

"Oh…er…"

My thoughts immediately went to the bartender and the hot dreams I'd had about him last night. Truth be told, I was late this morning because I'd hit the snooze several times, hoping to get back to the amazing sex we'd been having in my subconscious.

He was intoxicating.

He was calming.

And I had to see him again.

"Whoa! That good?" Mae asked, eyeing the blush that crept across my face.

"No. Actually, it was probably the worst blind date I've ever been on."

I recapped the horror that was Louis, leaving out the sexpot serving us drinks and the whole pick-pocketing incident. For some unknown reason, I wasn't ready to share that story yet.

"Holy crap!" Mae said. "Did you kill Jules?"

Mae had met Jules when we first arrived in town and had spent our first night here on Jules' couch since her studio apartment wasn't ready yet. We had been given an extremely thin housing budget, and since Jules had offered me her guest room, I'd let Mae use the whole sum to find something livable for a couple of months.

"She was already in bed when I got home, although I considered smothering her with her Egyptian cotton covered pillow in the middle of the night. And then she left early Saturday morning for a shoot on the coast. But trust me, when I see her tonight, I'll be informing her of what constitutes a sound set-up."

We reached the hotel and I let my smile fall and squared my shoulders.

I can do this. I can do this. I can do this.

The executive offices took up the tenth floor of the eleven-story building. I gave our names to a receptionist and she led us to a large conference room with expansive windows. Standing at one end of the long table looking over a spreadsheet was Charles and a tall dark-haired man.

When people speak of men that age well, they are usually talking about men like Charles Monroe. His salt and peppered hair cut in a youthful style made him look distinguished, rather than old. He was leaning on the table with both palms, his shoulders flexed. Beneath his dress shirt you could make out a body that was well maintained and probably smoking hot once-upon-a-time. He looked up at me and the wrinkles that creased around his eyes only seemed to make them sparkle more. I tried to place what was so familiar about them this time.

"Delilah!" Charles said, making his way over to me. We shook hands and I couldn't help but smile at his enthusiasm.

Charles had traveled to LA to meet with our firm a couple of weeks ago, when I was first assigned his case. Over lunch, he had explained his press nightmare, his situation in detail, and his guilt at deciding to sell the hotel rather than give it to his children, most of whom were running it into the ground. There was the *special assignment* involved with his case, but the gist of the position was to shake things up while controlling the chaos. To the best of my knowledge, no one knew Charles was selling, or what else he and I had planned for the staff, or his eldest son.

The relief on his face when I walked into the conference room made me chuckle.

"Hi Charles, it's good to see you again. And again, please call me Dee. This is Mae Livingston."

"Pleasure to meet you," he said, reaching for her hand and then motioned to the man next to him.

"This is Dominic Aiello, our VP of sales. He's on *our* team," he said with a wink, and I tensed slightly with surprise. Until I had a chance to confer with Charles in private, I was not going to assume the extent to which Dominic knew of my job duties. Charles hadn't sugarcoated the situation I'd be walking into at the hotel, and a substantial portion of our strategy had been around secretive plans he had for his son and GM. Dominic may have been in favor of the rebrand and press control, but until Charles said so, I was going to assume no one was in-the-know of our plans when it came to Samuel.

I looked at Dominic and took in his appearance. He was wearing a crisp white dress shirt and blue blazer with faded jeans and sneakers. I went through the information in my head that Mae had provided on him. Dominic came from a competitor in Dallas and was a strategic genius. He was a bit reclusive, rarely making it into the press. He was also recruited by Charles in the last year.

"Too true," he said extending his hand. "You weren't expecting *everyone* to hate you, were you?"

"I was prepared for it," I said honestly, shaking hands with him.

"Well, I understand the need for what you're going to do. And I don't want any setbacks in our plan for expansion," he said smiling at Charles. "Besides," he continued, leaning toward me conspiratorially, "I know what it's like to be brought in by Charles under the guise of cloak and dagger."

He winked, but there was no humor in it; it was as though he was letting me know that *he* knew I was here to do more than just get PR and communications under control. He was *right*, but I couldn't let him know that. Dominic Aiello was a slippery one, and while he may be the most put-together and

low maintenance of the executives when it came to PR, I still
didn't trust him.

Today's meeting was meant to seem as a meet-and-greet
with everyone, but Charles had let me know that he expected me
to lay down the law right from the start. He was at a loss when it
came to regaining control of the hotel's image and press, and
admitted that an outside professional would probably fare better
than he had. Charles needed me to strong-arm the wild children.
Draw a line in the sand. Shut this shit down. Basically, he
needed me to be the bad guy. And for him, I would. This was
where I earned my salary.

A giggle behind me made me turn, and I saw the
receptionist walk in carrying a tray with coffee and pastries
while a large man whispered in her ear. He was barrel-chested
with a full head of black curls. His navy-blue silk shirt was only
buttoned halfway up his chest, and his sleeves were sloppily
pushed up to the elbow, showing off muscled arms that were just
as eye-catching as his impressive stature. This guy was a brick
wall of muscle.

I smirked, thinking about the noise Jules would make as
she hit the floor from fainting, should she ever see this guy. He
was the type of steroid-induced, glorified jock she coveted.

Around his neck were several glow-in-the-dark
necklaces that had turned a dull color, losing their smolder hours
ago. He held a mug of coffee and I noticed a collection of
random club stamps printed on top of his left hand; one appeared
to be a decapitated grizzly bear.

"Christ," Dominic said next to me, addressing the giant.
"You couldn't have at least gone home to change?"

"Didn't see the need since we had this meeting at the
crack of fucking dawn," he replied in a booming voice.

"It's ten. Dawn was at six," Dominic deadpanned.

Charles cleared his throat and came up next to me.

"Paxton this is Delilah Sheppard, our new head of PR
and Communications," he said gesturing a hand at me. He was
using my full name with Paxton, allowing me to decide when,
and if, I wanted to be casual with him. He hadn't done so with
Dominic, and I quickly made a mental note. "Delilah this is
Paxton Monroe, he manages the bar and restaurant, and is my
youngest son."

His disheveled appearance clearly indicated that he'd spent all of last night partying, and that combined with the blatant flirting with the receptionist, I was certain this was Samuel, the playboy of the family. The information Mae had compiled told me that Paxton may be the most reckless of the Monroe family and had many vices, but partying and women weren't included in them.

Paxton extended his right hand to shake mine and I saw more club stamps making their way up his forearm.

"You're not what I was expecting a manipulative, fun destroying, shrew to look like," he said as he looked me up and down.

And so it begins.

"And you're not what I was expecting the brilliant, cutting-edge, innovator of Portland entertainment to look like," I replied, earning a hint of a grin from him. "Is that the Club 52 bunny stamp?" I asked as I tilted his hand and gestured to one of his many stamps, grateful for the research I'd done on the city. We stared at one another for a moment and then his eyes darted to the collage on his skin. I steadied my breathing, quickly preparing myself for our next round of sparing. Surprisingly, a huge smile spread across his face and he let out a loud guffaw. I felt myself relax, slightly.

"Hell yeah, it is!" he said. "Your job may be complete bullshit, but I think I might actually *like* you," he said, patting me roughly on the shoulder. Paxton plopped into a chair and began typing determinedly on his smartphone after his introduction to Mae, which was thankfully short and to the point. I started setting up my things on the table when Charles appeared next to me again.

"Dee, I'd like you to meet some more members of the team," he said gesturing behind me. For the next few minutes, I was touted around the conference room, shaking hands with middle management and far too many people with a VP title. Most folks I met had a timid approach to being in the conference room, leading me to believe that strategy meetings weren't a common occurrence for the hotel. I was finishing making pleasantries with a finance executive named Robert when a familiar, albeit surprising, face caught my eye.

Emma, waitress at Boost and my new best friend, flitted into the conference room with the same air of enthusiasm she'd had last night. I almost dropped the file in my hand with surprise.

Granted, I knew I'd see her from time to time, now that we worked for the same company. But what was she doing *here*?

"Emma!" Charles said next to me.

Her eyes met mine and went wide; clearly, she was just as surprised to see me as I was to see her.

"This is my daughter, Emma Monroe," Charles said.

"Event Manager and Guest Liaison," I finished for him automatically.

Shit, she was Emma *Monroe*.

I knew all about her from Mae's research. At 28 she was the youngest of the Monroe kids. Emma had attended the University of Washington and earned degrees in both Hospitality and Fashion. She'd had every opportunity to become the next irrelevant heiress, but instead graduated college and gone to work for the same hotel that made her family wealthy. She oversaw major events for the hotel and personally handled the high-end clients. If a million-dollar guest needed someone to be a personal shopper, plan a wedding reception, get box seats to a Trailblazer's game, or even help plan the perfect marriage proposal, Emma was the one they went to.

What the fuck was she doing serving me dirty martinis this weekend!?

"Um...yes," Charlie said, obviously taken aback by my interjection. "Emma, this is Dee Sheppard."

We shook hands silently, holding our stare. I silently prayed she wouldn't say anything. I didn't like the idea of a member of the Monroe family having blackmail rights over me, but I definitely didn't want to lose ground so soon in the game.

"Nice to meet you," Emma said in the chipper voice I recognized.

This is your punishment for mixing work with pleasure.

"I'm sure you'll love it here," she said, repeating the employee mantra as I stood frozen in place. Her smile didn't falter as she started to tell me about the hotel, but her gaze quickly darted between her father and me more than once.

Finally, he wandered over to say something to Dominic, leaving Emma and me alone.

"Oh my God!" she exclaimed in a whisper, eyes still wide with excitement. "You're *Delilah Sheppard!*"

"You're Emma Monroe!" I accused back, pointing at her.

A quiet giggle escaped her, she seemed to be *enjoying* this!

Thoughts of her announcing details of my blind date to the boardroom, or suddenly yelling, "This girl can't dress herself!" ran quickly through my mind and I started to panic.

"Please," I started to beg, "please don't say anything about the other night. This job is really important to me and the last thing I need after-"

She cut me off with a frantic wave of her hand and a fierce shake of her head.

"You don't tell anyone about the pick-pocketing thing, and my lips are sealed about the other night," she said with a decisive nod. I had no idea what she was talking about, but if she was willing to strike a deal, I was more than willing to take it.

"Done!" I said in a frantic whisper and rapid head nod. I turned back to organizing my things on the table, trying to recompose myself. The only one left to arrive was Samuel Monroe.

Last one to show up. He wants me to know he's in charge. Jackass.

"There's something you *really* should know," Emma said in a low voice next to me.

I cocked my head at her, but before I could ask what she meant by that, Charles interrupted us.

"Ah, there you are Samuel," he said, looking over my shoulder.

I braced myself in preparation for meeting Hotel Monroe's GM and Portland's most notorious playboy. He would *not* break me, no matter what sort of nonsense he threw at me. He would be my biggest accomplishment. Samuel Monroe would be the accomplishment that would catapult me into my promotion. One way or another, I would put this PR nightmare in his place. With a determined expression and squared shoulders, I turned to meet the nightmare and instead entered my own.

Standing before me was the bartender from Boost, who was none other than Samuel fucking Monroe.

This time, I actually did drop the file I was holding.

FIVE

Delilah

"Samuel, this is Delilah Sheppard."

Charles continued with introductions, but I couldn't hear him over the loud ringing and crashing sounds going on inside my brain. For a brief moment, I was elated; standing in front of me was the charming man I thought I'd have to seek out and explain my strange behavior to, if I ever got the courage and circumstances worked out just right with this assignment. But now I didn't have to, he was here! And in a nanosecond, just as that thought occurred to me, I quickly remembered that this was *Samuel Monroe*. Introductions weren't necessary.

I knew all about Samuel.

He graduated top of his MBA class at NYU, before heading off to Tokyo to intern and work for some of the largest investment and hedge fund firms in the world. He'd been groomed since birth to take over the family hotel, which is why he'd returned to Portland a few years ago. And oh yeah, did I mentioned that he was also a complete man-whore who coveted public attention on a regular basis?

An irrational side of my brain allowed my ego swell at the idea of playboy Samuel Monroe flirting with me for most of the night. But professional Dee, and the self-respecting majority of my brain, swiftly knocked her unconscious with a theoretical baseball bat, remembering that this was, after all, Samuel Monroe.

I was shocked he hadn't dropped his name the other night, being the arrogant asshole that I was led to believe he was. It was illogical he wasn't slinging around some sort of an 'I'm the owner' shtick with women. But maybe that was his angle or one of his games; perhaps he challenged himself to charm the pants off of any woman, no identity needed. Or maybe he really knew who I was at the bar the other night.

Fuuuuuck. Please don't let it be that.

If his angle was to screw me the other night only to be able to screw me at work today, I didn't stand a chance in this meeting.

A million questions kept swarming in my head, making me dizzy. I silenced them all with the resolution that whatever game he was playing would be irrelevant in the end. What mattered was that we were playing *my* game now, and I would *not* lose. Despite what had gone on at Boost, or how gorgeous he was, or that my hands screamed to tangle themselves in that mess of dark hair, by god I would remain professional.

Samuel knelt to retrieve my dropped papers while smiling up at me. He stood and started to speak, but I cut him off.

"Mr. Monroe. Nice to meet you," I said coldly, extending a stiff hand to him and hoping that he would respect my covert plea for discretion. In what felt like a moment that stretched for an eternity, he seemed taken aback and slightly recoiled with a look I couldn't quite place. But a second later his posture shifted to match mine, and he narrowed his eyes at me.

"Ms. Sheppard," he said in a low voice. As we shook hands I tried to maintain composure as his hand enveloped my own. I irrationally fought the urge to lace my fingers between his and not break the connection. Unfortunately, my reaction didn't escape his attention at all and a small smile danced across his face.

Sweet Jesus, this is not good.

"Let's get started, shall we?" Charles said, motioning toward the conference table.

I quickly withdrew my hand from Samuel's and went to my seat, counting down from ten and trying to regulate my breathing.

Charles took his seat at the head of the table with Dominic on his left and me on his right. Emma took a seat next to Mae while the rest of the room shuffled into chairs on either side along the length of the table. Samuel took his place at the opposite end of the table as his father and Paxton collapsed into a seat on his left. Both brothers leaned casually in their chairs, staring at me with smug expressions, while the rest of the group fidgeted nervously, clearly in tune with the tension in the

room. The tableau was crystal clear and indicative of what lay
before me for the next two months.

"Alright everyone, as you know, I've brought Ms.
Sheppard onboard to oversee press and communications for the
hotel," Charles began. "As we're expanding as a company,
public relations and corporate communications have become a
priority. Our image will be crucial moving forward, and Ms.
Sheppard's an expert in her field. She has my complete trust
when it comes to matters of PR, corporate communications and
advertising. I'd like you all to welcome her to the team, and
more importantly, listen to what she has to say."

I caught Samuel and Paxton exchange a quick look. I
assumed they'd join forces against me but worried how strong of
a front they'd actually be.

"Delilah, the floor is yours," Charlie finished with a
solemn nod toward me and a warning glace across the table.

"Thank you, Charles," I said with a steadying
breath. "The Hotel Monroe has a ton of potential, and I can see
why Charles and Dominic think it's possible to expand to such a
grand scale. You've done a great job." The men on the opposite
end of the table all slightly nodded, privately praising
themselves. "But I also see how all this success and revenue is
built on a house of cards, ready to implode on itself," I paused to
reach for our prepared documents from Mae while trying to
ignore the tension that filled the room.

"Let's talk about the last six months," I began, slipping
on my glasses, "the Monroe has been mentioned in thirty-one
Associated Press stories during that time," I said referencing my
notes. "Twelve of them have been stories about inner-city street
racing and high-speed chases. Nine of those articles revolved
around sexual escapades and playboy antics. An impressive six
articles in six months were about cocaine busts and drug
possession. And then we have one massive bar brawl story, as a
cherry on top."

I swept a glance around the table, reminding myself of
exactly whom I was dealing with, but I couldn't bring myself to
look at Samuel, knowing that I'd lose my nerve. Instead, I
settled my stare back on Dominic and felt my expression relax
when I took in his despair and was reminded of why I was here.
Regardless of what he was playing at, this guy was fighting to

grow the hotel and knew that it would all bow under the weight of bad press like this.

"Two of the articles were about businesses on the rise," I said encouragingly with a small smile at him, earning a sad grin in return. I knew I had everyone's attention by the deafening silence that filled the room.

"No matter how brilliant your business strategies, or how much customers rave in their reviews on travel sites, the Monroe *will* fail if we can't reconstruct its image and prevent these negative stories," I said. "And that's what I'm here to do."

"Excuse me," Samuel drawled. He was staring at me with a determination and defiance that lit a fire in my gut professionally but also ignited a desire within me. The confusion was already making me dizzy.

"Can't it be argued that all of those stories succeeded in getting the Hotel Monroe *into* the national press at the very least? Which are twenty-nine more instances than we'd be in the press in the first place?" he asked, raising an eyebrow at me.

Paxton snickered at his comment while the corners of Samuel's mouth played at a smile.

"Of course," I said, enjoying his visible shock at my admission and not denying the smug smile that begged to come out.

"Well then, that seems to be good news to me," he said, equally smug. He looked at Charles and sat up straighter when he saw his dad's frown. "I'm not saying that we should *plan* for bad press to be our strategy," he clarified quickly. There was enough non-verbal communication going on between them for me to deduce what I needed to know about their relationship. Samuel may be a cocky son of a bitch, but he was also Charles' son and reported to him in more than one way.

"All I'm saying," he continued. "Is that this proves what I've been saying all along. We're getting attention! The hotel is in the press. This isn't necessary," he said, gesturing a hand at me but not taking his eyes off Charles.

"Let's talk about your market research," I interjected, extending my hand to Mae before Charles could respond. She handed me the file, and Samuel's eyes snapped from his father to me.

"In those same six months, preference for the Monroe has dropped 34% among businesses and their travel agents. There's been a 15% drop among conference coordinators, and a whole 20% loss of sales has happened on travel websites." I chanced a glance at Samuel and almost shivered at his cold, dead stare. Across from me, Dominic was rubbing his temples with his eyes closed, clearly frustrated with this research.

I knew what was coming next and wished I could prepare Dominic for it; I had to go in for the kill vehemently. Regardless of my understanding of the role I'd been hired to play, I still had a moment of hesitation before doing so. Charles had been explicitly clear when he'd offered me the position. My job was to shake things up and clean house, no matter what it took. And it was true that everyone in this room wouldn't be here in two months. I suspected that it had taken a certain level of desperation for a man like Charles to realize he was at his wits-end and lacked any form of a solution to his current press problem, let alone to sell the family business he'd built from scratch. When I took the assignment, I knew I would be helping Charles through a tough time, holding his hand as he made some tough calls. But it was only now, literally sitting between father and son, that I realized how deep these cuts were going to go.

When I finally did what I was hired to do, what Charles and I had agreed needed to be done, I would ultimately become the PR monster everyone in this room was expecting. And it would more than likely crush the budding relationship that had blossomed with Samuel, let alone what it would do with a potential friendship with Emma. If I did my job correctly, there would be no going back, and I hesitated for a second longer than I thought I would.

It's not personal, it's business. He's not your soulmate, he's your assignment.

I squared my shoulders in preparation for the hatred he'd have for me and decided to deal with that pain later. This job was my life, this promotion was mine to win, and I had to protect it all.

"Here's your good news, Mr. Monroe," I said, staring Samuel down. "Among women 18 to 25, your hotel has become *the* spot to frequent in hopes of winning one of the

Monroe men as either a conquest, or sugar daddy. There's even a Twitter hashtag for it and Reddit board."

"What the fuck is a reddit?" Paxton asked his brother loudly, who glanced at him in warning.

I shoved the report down the table at Samuel with more force than I'd intended. "Too bad those girls never book your suites or plan elaborate parties in your ballroom or conferences in your meeting rooms. Otherwise, you'd have a brilliant business plan on your hands."

I barely took a breath before continuing; I had to keep going because if he spoke before I finished, I knew I'd be lost.

"Several Instagram hashtags and Snap Chat accounts have been created with the single purpose of following Paxton Monroe's movements in hopes of anticipating his next illegal street racing event," I said, shoving the printed pages down the table.

"And next month, Forbes is planning on printing an article about the top-ten emerging businesses in America that are expected to fail, despite their initial hype," I said in a low voice. To me, this was the most depressing piece of research. "Hotel Monroe will be listed as number six."

The effect was achieved. I'd shut Samuel and the rest of them up, except for Dominic who let out a muffled groan.

"Organizations don't want to plan their conferences here because of the hotel's reputation. Business professionals don't want to stay here when they come to Portland because of your reputation. Local companies don't want to hold meetings here because of the hotel's *reputation*. Are you starting to understand the *mess* I've been hired to clean up, Mr. Monroe?"

I stared back when Samuel glowered at me, daring him to contradict what I was saying and praying I didn't break under his angry stare. A quick peek at Charles reminded me once again why my job was important. He looked like someone had run over his puppy and I wanted nothing more than to tell him that this would all go away tomorrow.

"How are we going to fix this?" Charles asked quietly.

"Well, first things first," I said, taking off my glasses and looking at him reassuringly. "We're going to get Hotel Monroe pulled out of this Forbes article." I heard a disbelieving snort from down the table but couldn't place where it came from. "The issue hasn't hit press yet," I said in a louder voice, addressing the room again. "I've called in some favors, and we'll start by stopping the bad press that's already coming our way. We've also made a round of calls to some contacts in the blogging world. This is Mae Livingston. She'll be handling press releases and daily operations for me."

Mae gave a small wave, clearly not appreciating the spotlight in this hostile environment.

"As for our strategy," I began. "We're going to reconstruct the image of several members of the Monroe staff and ultimately the hotel itself. We'll be working closely with Emma and Dominic to coordinate events that will provide heavy media coverage for the new *personas* we've created and-"

"Are you a good liar, Ms. Sheppard?" My head snapped up at Samuel's interruption.

"Excuse me?" I asked louder than necessary. He slowly leaned forward on his elbows and gave me a quick, devious smile.

"It just seems to me," he continued, "that to carry out these *strategies*, you'd need to be a good liar." Paxton snuck out another chuckle despite Charles stiffening in his seat, but Samuel continued. "I mean seriously, anyone that can convince the media that we're all saints would need to be a damn fine fibber, wouldn't you say?"

My mouth fell slightly agape while he arched a menacing brow at me. I couldn't seem to find any words, but Samuel appeared to have many.

"I'd imagine a PR pro without adequate lying skills would come across as, oh gee I don't know, a shaky chihuahua, perhaps?"

Oh shit.

Within seconds I shifted through shock, hurt and then blind rage. With a deep, steadying breath and fists clenched under the table, I stared back at him.

"My job isn't to be a liar, Mr. Monroe," I said in the evenest voice I could muster. "My job is to create an appropriate image in the press, of you and all the other members of the hotel's executive team that screw off on a regular basis and act a fool."

Sam's smile fell, and he narrowed his beautiful eyes. Next to me, Mae fidgeted, probably caught off guard by the sudden intensity of Samuel.

"Let's cut the bullshit," he said. "You're going to give us personality make-overs and parade us in front of the press at parties. Doesn't that seem so contrived that everyone in the world would see right through it?"

I opened my mouth to respond, but he kept going.

"Are you telling me that if we start dressing Paxton in pastel colors, have him take a few pictures with sick children, and make him walk the red carpet at benefits to save tree squirrels or some shit, our sales will go up? Really? The way I spend my weekend, or how Pax lets off steam, both have a direct line to the P&L?"

Paxton barked out a laugh and looked at me in defiance. "Fuck the squirrels," he said.

"Not quite, Samuel," I said, not taking my eyes off him. "There's actually a subtle science to what I do. But that was a nice try." We glared at each other and I could feel the irritation crackle in the air between us. "As you said, let's cut the bullshit. Since you mentioned him, let's start with Paxton," I said with a smile.

Mae shifted some papers my way as Paxton sat up straighter in his chair.

"We all know that your propensity for racing has made you appear, first and foremost, as a lawbreaker with the press and public. We need to return the focus, instead, to your genius for nightlife entertainment-"

"Oh, hell no!" Paxton said, cutting me off. "You're telling me I can't race cars anymore?"

"That's what you heard?" Dominic asked, exasperated. "Not the genius for entertainment business part, just the racing crap?"

I sighed at the interruption. Seriously, they were like children.

"No," I said directly to Pax. "We're going to use your racing reputation to our advantage."

He looked lost. Perhaps a different approach was necessary.

"Here's the deal Paxton, we're going to take your pseudo-Fast-and-the-Furious bullshit antics and turn them into a constructive hobby. I've contacted some folks at IndyCar, and you'll be the Grand Marshal for an upcoming race. You'll also be driving a car in a charity race in a few weeks at the Expo, so we'll need to get you professional training, which will all be covered by the press. Mae's working to make sure you also have the best pit crew for the race so hopefully, you'll end up winning the whole thing and get even *more* positive attention."

Paxton's eyes started to bug out of his head, but I kept going.

"I'll be working with Emma to put together a charity benefit at Boost for a local chapter of MADD. Drunk driving isn't really an issue with you, but it gets close enough to the whole 'road safety' thing to show your concern for the community. For each event, you'll be introduced as 'Paxton Monroe, up-and-coming Entertainment Innovator.' The title is a bit overkill, but it'll earn us some ground and most likely lead to some puff pieces in trade journals."

I looked up from my notes to see Paxton grinning at me; even though his mouth was hanging open and he was dumbstruck, his expression was clearly amused.

"I may be a shrew, Paxton," I said, winking at him and hating myself for using their term to make my point. "But I'm definitely not a fun destroyer."

Paxton went practically catatonic; mumbling something about racecars and checkered flags while Dominic snickered into his fist. Samuel, however, was now seething at me. Either he didn't like that I'd one-upped him, or he still thought I was full of shit.

"As for everyone else," I said addressing the room but returning my eyes to Samuel. "I'll be discussing our strategies for them on an individual basis."

Samuel balled a fist and leaned back in his chair, closing his eyes. The material of his shirt stretched across his chest and I could see that every muscle in his body was tense.

Every hard, sexy, strong muscle in his chest…

He ran a hand down his torso to straighten his tie, and my traitor eyes followed every millimeter of the movement. I was lusting after, as well as alienating, the hottest man I'd ever met. When my eyes snapped up to his I realized that I'd been caught ogling him.

Please don't let there be drool on my chin because it would completely negate everything I just said.

He licked his lips minutely, smirked smugly at me, and suddenly I was irritated. Here I had been worrying about destroying the 'chemistry' I'd felt with Samuel while doing my job but had completely ignored the fact that the other night had most likely been nothing more than a near-miss in the realm of casual hook-ups for him.

I resolved myself to no longer worry about being Charles' PR monster, or the shrew, or whatever ridiculous name they called me. Because in the end, I had to remember that this was Samuel Monroe, and all the bad press about him couldn't be wrong.

SIX

Samuel

I was in hell. I sat listening to Dee, or Delilah Sheppard as I now knew her to be, rattle on about details for upcoming events and image strategies and thinly veiled jabs at my social life, all while wearing those damn glasses and black suit, which made her somehow even more desirable than she'd been in the bar. She was smart and sexy and infuriating and brilliant and definitely going to make my life a living hell. To say I was conflicted would be an understatement. I wanted to thank my father for bringing this woman into my life, while also wanting to rage at him for putting this chain of events in motion.

When I first saw her in the conference room, my heart almost leaped out of my chest. Standing in front of me was Dee, the woman that had bewitched my mind for the past two days without even knowing her for more than two hours. As I'd picked up her dropped papers and looked up into the bright blue eyes of the woman I'd been waiting for, I went through every thought I'd had about her, trying to pick the most appropriate thing to say to her at that moment.

"Mr. Monroe, nice to meet you," she said, offering her hand stoically and giving me a stern look. I rocked back slightly at her tone and cold greeting. Her face was stone and her posture rigid. She obviously didn't want anyone to know about Friday night, but there was more to it than that. I took in everything I could observe about her, just as I had before, and realized that this wasn't the woman I'd met in the bar.

I was shaking hands with a shrew disguised in Dee clothing. Or was it Dee dressed as a shrew? Either way, this wasn't who I met before, and I was confused.

We exchanged pleasantries and I took my seat, still having a hard time deciphering which version of the woman was real. When she blushed slightly at my father's introduction to the group or bit her bottom lip, she resembled the woman I wanted to wrap my arms around Friday night. But when she would look

at me, her eyes were cold, and her shoulders were set. There was
no doubt that Friday was a distant memory for her, and I was
now in her crosshairs.

    Bring it on, Dee.

    And oh, how she brought it. For the next half hour, I was
assaulted with examples of how she was way ahead of us, knew
more than I thought possible by an outside contractor, and was
going to dig in her heels *deep*. Dad was right, she was a shark.
My feeble attempts to discredit her only made Dee's case that
much stronger. Despite my fierce resistance and internal
struggle, I couldn't help but admit to myself that she was
amazing. The more she talked and chastised us, the more I
realized how intelligent she was; and although I hated to think it,
she was fucking right. Her plan was a good one.

    This was *not* how I'd envisioned this meeting going.

    But it was clear to me that I had walked into a gunfight
armed with a yo-yo. Little did I know that Dee would have a
handful of trump cards already waiting and be several paces
ahead of all of us. Who the hell was this woman? She was
poised and precise and determined. Nowhere could I see the
uncalculating and thoughtful woman from two days ago. How
could one person be *so* different? It was practically night and
day. She was eloquent and resourceful and intimidating, not to
mention fucking adorable when she was serious in her wire-
rimmed glasses.

    At the first opportunity I could find, I threw out a
comment about her shaky Chihuahua complex. I knew I was
goading her and felt a little guilty, but I needed to know what
was real. I prayed for a smile or some sort of recognition of the
conversation we'd had at the bar. I waited to see what would
happen and which woman would emerge as the conqueror, but I
was left just as confused as I'd started. For a moment, there was
the same deer-in-headlights behavior that had made her so
endearing before. But in an instant, that fire was back in her
eyes, and I realized I'd awoken her beast within.

    My further attempts to bait the 'real Dee' to come out
only dug my hole deeper. Before I knew what had happened, I
looked like a moron while Pax bowed at her feet with visions of
race cars dancing in his eyes.

    Thanks a lot, brother.

By the time the meeting had moved on from individual PR strategies to event planning, I'd resigned myself to having lost the battle of getting rid of the shrew. I'd also realized that no matter how attracted I was to the woman I'd met at Boost, she'd been an illusion and I would only be chasing shadows by pursuing Delilah Sheppard. The real version was before me, and she was fucking ruthless. I leaned back in my chair and mentally prepared myself for what was to come with the rest of this meeting.

And that's when I noticed Emma for the first time. She was nervously bouncing in her seat, tapping her pen on her pink day-planner. Excessive energy was normal for her, but this was a bit shiftier than she usually looked. I caught her eye and raised an eyebrow at her, silently questioning her about this strange turn of events. With a fierce glare, she implored me to stay quiet, causing me to wonder what her game was with keeping Dee's secret.

I sighed and looked back at Dee to find her staring at me, or should I say staring at my body. Was she checking me out?

Couldn't be...

She'd been nothing but a cold wall of fierce professionalism since I'd walked into the conference room. But there was no mistaking the look on her face, subtle as it may be. I experimentally ran a hand down my torso in the apparent act of smoothing my tie and watched as her eyes followed. As I swiveled my chair her eyes snapped up to mine quickly. I gave her a small smile, and a pink blush spread across her cheeks at being caught.

There she is.

I'd found the sexy and shy woman I'd met before. But in an instant, she was once again gone.

"I'd like to address our policies for public events," she said with an uneven voice, looking down at her paperwork. Her subtle appraisal of my body confirmed what I thought, which was that she was attracted to me. Her quick shift back into her professional persona confirmed what I feared, which was that I'd imagined the entire connection we'd shared Friday night. The woman sitting in front of me was the real Dee, whether I liked it or not.

I watched as she straightened her suit jacket, squared her shoulders again, and looked back up with the same fire as before.

"When it comes to major events, we'll be walking the red carpets and attending meet-and-greets with members of the hotel staff," she continued, gesturing to her assistant. Mae Livingston looked utterly caught off guard. Either she was way out of her league, or this meeting wasn't going the way she thought it would. Perhaps she assumed we'd all be welcoming them with open arms.

"What can we expect from that?" Charles asked, prodding her on like the traitor he was.

"We'll be there to assist in answering difficult questions and mediate tense press situations," she said, smiling back.

"You're going to tell us what to say," I translated in a deadpan voice. That earned me a glare.

"I'll be *helping* you with crafting statements," she said back, trying to maintain her smile. My frustration at being fooled by her ridiculously faux-naïve and endearing routine before was blending with my initial irritation at a PR overhaul in general, and the resulting combination was simply making me more willing to be an outright asshole.

"Right, because I need help answering questions about which designer I'm wearing, or where I'll be spending my next summer vacation?"

"I assumed you could answer those questions all by yourself, Mr. Monroe. But I'll be sure to write the designer's name on your palm as a cheat sheet, just in case."

"While you're at it, why don't you tie a house key around my neck and pin your business card to my shirt, just in case I get lost?"

By now we were leaning across the table, staring each other down.

"Don't worry. If you get lost, I'll just search the local socialites' beds and sorority houses. I'm sure I'll find you at some point. I wouldn't waste the business card," she said with aggravating sarcasm.

"Do I have a curfew, too?"

And then her tone and demeanor got frigidly serious.

"Your curfew is just *before* you say something that will hurt this hotel."

I was pissed she'd assume I'd be reckless enough to hurt the hotel. Furthermore, I was furious that she somehow thought she cared more about the Monroe than *I* did.

"News flash, I don't say things that hurt this hotel," I sneered at her.

"Of course you don't, Mr. Monroe," she said with a condescending smile. "You *do* things that hurt this hotel. My stopping you from *saying* something foolish is only a small portion of my job description."

By now I couldn't give a damn that we had an audience or that dad would kick my ass for this later. The more she rallied back at me, the more she confirmed what a farce the other night had been. I heard Dominic clear his throat and start to speak.

"So, Ms. Sheppard, do you think-"

"What are the other parts of your job?" I asked, cutting Dominic off. "Being judge and jury to what's acceptable behavior? Tell me, which college did you attend that teaches that?"

Dee's eyes never left mine, but the fire in them grew excruciatingly strong.

"I went to USC. And the class you're referring to is Organizational Behavior, to say the least."

"Behavior? Or control? Because it seems to me that you're using the terms interchangeably."

"Don't use words you *can't spell*, Mr. Monroe," she said in a low, venomous voice.

Oh, fuck no.

A small part of my brain registered that I deserved that, based on my Chihuahua comment earlier, but the rest of me wanted to inflict as much damage as possible and figuratively light the conference room table on fire.

"Alright," dad said, snapping me out of my death gaze. "I think we've covered enough here. I'd like to show Dee around, and I'm sure the rest of you have things to do." He was addressing the room, but his stare fell on me alone. I straightened back up and noticed the rest of the table for the first time since my battle with Dee had begun. Everyone was sitting in shocked silence, eyes dancing back and forth between us.

Dominic was clearly pissed that I'd taken my opposition to her so far. Emma, the only one aware of what was *really* going on, was shooting daggers at me and cautious glances at Dee.

The room emptied as dad escorted Dee and Mae down the hall. Emma followed Dominic out, but not before turning to point a small, scary finger at me. I knew my sister well enough to know that I was in for one hell of a lecture from her later.

Guess that answers whose side she's *on.*

Finally, it was just Pax and me, sitting side-by-side in silence. After a few moments, I sighed and pinched the bridge of my nose, squinting at the oncoming headache.

"I think it's safe to say," I said quietly, "that she's not going to be that easy to get rid of, and this is worse than we thought."

Pax chuckled as he stood.

"Speak for yourself, bro. I'm going to race a fucking stockcar."

His fist pumped in the air as he walked out, and my head thumped against the back of my chair.

SEVEN

Delilah

Charles escorted me through the offices for a tour, but because my head was still in a fog, I barely heard a word he said. I was shown the corporate gym to which I had a key, the suites on the top floor which were at my disposal, as was the executive lounge. He gave me a tour of Boost and the restaurant, but instead of listening to his ideas for potential future events, I couldn't stop staring at the stool I'd been perched on a few nights before.

My thoughts were stuck on those hazel eyes and cocky smile. Samuel Monroe was the most frustrating asshole but damn if he wasn't the sexiest man I'd ever met. Logically I went through my mental notes of the meeting and tried to focus on things I could use in the future. I knew I needed to sort out the personality traits and behaviors of everyone that would either be helpful or a hindrance.

Like Emma's exuberance. That could be beneficial in a liaison capacity with organizations. Or Dominic's tenacity to make the hotel Portland's top location could be helpful in getting the sales and operations team onboard with my vision. And Samuel's bottom lip; I was sure it tasted better than it even looked and *that* was going to be a definite bonus.

Fuck!

I could feel my already shaky confidence wavering and that all-too-familiar feeling of being in over my head, trying to keep afloat. With a deep breath, I tried to remember what my mentor had taught me.

It doesn't matter what is real, it matters what is seen.

I could fake it until I made it.

As we made our way back up to the executive floor, I squared my shoulders in the small elevator. I wouldn't let Samuel win. I could do this. I would be the epitome of professionalism and make Charles praise the day he came to our firm for help.

"Dee," he said softly next to me, thankfully bringing me out of my internal pep talk before I started humming 'Eye of the Tiger' to myself. "I should apologize for Samuel this morning."

I held a hand up to stop him.

"No, you shouldn't Charles. It's all part of the job, remember? You told me what I was walking into."

"I don't think I prepared you adequately since even *I* was a bit surprised by how… intense he was. Rest assured, I'll be having a word with him. That was unprofessional and childish, not to mention an example of how *not* to speak to a lady."

I smiled warmly at the contradictions in Charles's personality. He'd asked me to come in and strong arm his team into behaving, something he admitted he wasn't able to do himself. He wanted me to be the bad guy that he couldn't be to drive good press, but here he was, bristling when someone spoke to me harshly. Businessman or not, I guess Charles was a gentleman first, and I tried not to let it offend my inner feminist.

"Charles, that would actually be counter-productive. Please, just let me do my job; I promise you, I can handle it."

The elevator dinged and the doors opened. Charles motioned for me to go ahead of him and I placed a confident Kate Someone-or-another heel out and strode through the hall. I could feel everyone's eyes on me and tried to ignore the whispers as I maneuvered my way through the cubicles. The shrew had arrived, and everyone was standing to get a good look at her. I raised my chin and smiled.

Mae was already settling into her desk outside my office. She saw me approach and stood with the files she already knew I'd want, and her capable attention made my confidence rise. I scooped the papers from her with a wink and strode into my new office. As soon as the door clicked behind me, I sighed in relief and practically doubled over in fatigue. Appearances, while necessary, could also be a bitch to keep up.

Once I'd regained myself, I finally took a glance around the office. The walls were painted in a warm coffee color, and the lush cream carpet was freshly cleaned. The L-shaped mahogany desk sat in front of a floor-to-ceiling window with a view of the city that took my breath away. Every wall was bare, and the bookshelves were sparse. I hated this part, the settling in and decorating, all to make an effort to look as though I planned on being here a while.

I only made it two paces toward the desk when the door flew open behind me. Turning I saw an irate Samuel stride in and a flustered Mae running in behind him.

"I'm sorry Dee, I tried to stop him," she panted.

"It's fine, Mae." I gave her a small smile as she nodded and closed the door, looking at the back of him with wide-eyed fear. Samuel's stare hadn't left my eyes since he walked in. His fists were clenched, and his nostrils flared; he was pissed.

I stood my ground and just stared right back, ready for whatever he threw at me. He was probably upset about the changes I was going to be making, not to mention the verbal sparring we'd engaged in during the meeting. *And* the fact that Charles was obviously on my side rather than his. Not to mention, the jab about him not knowing how to spell probably didn't go over too well. Honestly, I had no idea what he was more pissed about at that moment in time.

"Who was that guy Friday night?" he growled at me.

Okay. Wasn't prepared for that.

"What?" I asked, rocking back a bit and trying to catch up.

"Was he a friend you roped into your little plan? Or was he an actor? How much did you pay him to put on that show?"

"I don't know what-"

"Were you there doing recon? Watching the 'problem child' in action before coming in today to put the reins on? I've met some manipulative women in my day, but sweetie you take the cake. I hope your little charade gave you everything you were looking for. Get enough ammo to add to your already ridiculous amount of power around here?"

"You have *got* to be kidding me!" I said, with wide-eyes I was trying desperately not to roll. "You think I was there to *spy* on you? How in the hell would I have even known you'd be there, let alone bartending? Last time I checked, there wasn't anything in my research that said making mojitos was in the GM's job description."

That earned me a confused look and shut him up for a minute.

"I thought you were the smart brother," I said, crossing my arms and cocking my head to the side inquisitively. I knew I was baiting him, but I just couldn't resist.

"I thought I was too," he said rubbing his eyes in frustration and rolling his neck. "What the fuck is happening to me?" he asked so quietly I wasn't even sure I was meant to hear it.

"You were the only one pulling off charades that night," I said, "so you can take that finger and just turn it around."

"Oh, come on, you were *begging* me to get rid of that guy for you. Had I known who you were, I might have let you suffer all night with that witless moron. I'm sure he had plenty more country club stories for you, or maybe more to say on the subject of the size of your ass."

I saw red, and the line between personal and professional got even fuzzier.

"Fuck you, Samuel."

Yes, very *professional Dee, well done.*

"Sorry, but I don't think you're going to be around long enough for that to happen. I give it a week before you're back on a plane to wherever you came from," he said with a wry smile.

"California," I drawled with pleasure, remembering my research and the disdain locals had for Californians and their consistent migration north and driving up of housing prices and their propensity to generally fuck Portlandian's lives over. I enjoyed the look on his face at that moment and added, "Los Angeles, to be exact."

Sam's right eye twitched, and I could tell he was struggling with a litany of personal and professional battles, just as I was, so I decided to give him a reprieve.

"I know you don't want me here," I said as calmly as I could muster, "but Charles hired me to do a job and I'm going to do it. Just because you don't like it, doesn't make me manipulative or evil. The more you rage against this, the more you sound like a spoiled child who isn't getting his way. So how about we just-"

"You think you know me? Or any of us? Well, I've got news for you. Your research may have helped you make a couple of snap judgments, but you have no idea who I am, what you're dealing with here, or what you're getting in the middle of right now."

I didn't have to prod to know that he was referencing the tension between him and Charles for ownership. I controlled my reaction and thankfully didn't give away the fact that I knew more than he thought. He was now standing so close, that I had to tilt my head slightly to maintain my stare at him. Regardless of how pissed off I was at his arrogance, I still couldn't help but notice how amazing he smelled. It was like cedar and lemons and man.

Good god woman, will you just focus!

"I know exactly who you are," I said in a whisper, which is all I could get out until I built up enough steam. "You're the heir to one of the most impressive hotels and businesses on the West Coast, and you use that power and title to get into women's pants, rather than grow your empire. Your birthright isn't a privilege to you; it's a goddamn pickup line."

"And you are so obsessed with appearances that you've made a career out of forcing people to be something they're not, all in the name of looking good."

Ouch.

"Whatever your opinions are of me or my job, you need to get used to the idea that you don't have a choice here. You *will* do what I say, Samuel."

His eyes were positively smoldering, and I could feel his breath on my face when he leaned forward and spoke next.

"I don't take orders well," he said in a low husky voice.

"Yes, I've been told. Trust me, I've heard that before, Mr. Monroe."

"I can make things very difficult for you."

"I assumed you were already planning on doing that," I said with a smirk of my own. "But I expect you'll come around, sooner or later."

"I hope you're used to failure."

"And I hope you like a challenge," I countered, still not backing down.

"You are absolutely infuriating," he grumbled.

"And you're an absolute ass."

Before I could even register what was happening, Samuel slipped a hand behind my head and brought my lips to meet his. It wasn't a gentle kiss; it was full of frustration, passion and raw want; just as the two of us were, as well.

As if they had a mind of their own, my hands latched into his beautiful mess of hair and I pulled him even closer. I answered his kiss with reckless abandon and sucked his bottom lip between my own. My eyes were closed but still rolled into the back of my head when I realized that he *did*, in fact, taste better than he looked.

He slipped an arm around my waist and the other wrapped around my shoulders, completely engulfing me in his embrace. I felt his hand weave through my hair as my tongue swept across his lip. Granting me what I wanted, he opened his mouth and met my tongue with his. If I could have formed a conscious thought, I might have been embarrassed at the soft moan that escaped me in that moment, but as it turns out when Samuel Monroe sticks his tongue in your mouth, your brain effectively shuts down.

Our kissing grew more and more urgent. Hands grasping at one another and bodies pressed together. It was hard to say which one of us had a tighter grip on the other's hair. I didn't realize we were moving until my back slammed into the wall. Samuel's mouth moved from my lips to behind my ear and I gasped out for breath. I tilted my head to the side as he licked and kissed his way down my neck, earning another deep moan from me as I pressed myself into him deeper and he nipped at my collarbone.

I'd be lying if I said I hadn't wanted this all along. Yes, he'd pissed me off something fierce in the meeting this morning. And yes, I'd wanted to claw his eyes out at some point today. But none of it eclipsed how strongly I was pulled toward this god of a man and how badly I needed him to touch me. Consume me. Own me.

His hands slid down my back and roughly grabbed my ass. He lifted me slightly, and I wrapped my legs around his waist while sucking his neck and still fisting his wild hair. My ankles crossed around his waist as I gripped tightly at his hair and the collar of his dress shirt, pulling his face back to mine. Our lips met frantically again just as the buzzer on my intercom went off.

We pulled apart slightly and our eyes met, his shining with the same excitement I'm sure mine mirrored. And then a darkness passed over his face that I was sure traversed my own as the realization dawn on both of us what just happened. Suddenly the conscious thought entered my brain that I was making out with my assignment, five hours into my first day. I untangled myself and we exchanged awkward glances as I made my way to the desk.

"Yes?" I said in a shaky voice after pressing the button to reply to Mae.

"Mr. Fitzgerald is on line one for you," Mae said through the intercom. When I didn't respond right away, she added, "Your scheduled call?" I quickly let Mae know that I needed a minute. With a steadying breath, I turned to face him and was halted by the icy stare he was shooting at me.

"Fitzgerald. As in the talent manager for the bar?" he asked in a cold tone that actually made me shiver slightly.

"That's right," I hedged. I was confused, not only by his detached tone but also by the subject matter in general. Carl Fitzgerald was the talent booker for Boost and responsible for the has-been performers making appearances at various Monroe events. How could *this* be the thing that gets us back to sparing?

"Are you firing him?" He spat out the question as he took a step backward, clearly irritated. The wall was slowly going back up between us again. and I wasn't entirely certain as to why.

"No," I said evenly, leaning back on my heels and crossing my arms, defiantly giving him nothing in the way of additional information on the matter. Once again, he was rallying against my job, and I was getting sick of his mood swings. Samuel ran a hand through his already messy hair and let out a low breath. He closed his eyes for a moment before giving me a determined stare.

"Then I'm assuming you'll be discussing firing the handful of performers he books at Boost, instead?"

"It's certainly where *I* would like to see the discussion going, yes."

"And do you have plans to meet with any of these people?"

"No, but I don't see how-"

"Of course not," he cut me off. "Naturally you couldn't be bothered to actually meet with the people you plan on taking jobs away from; that would be too personal."

"This isn't personal, it's business," I replied evenly back. "I'm not here to dote on friends and punish the wicked. I'm here to *do a job*!"

Man, I'm getting tired of having to say that.

He was gorgeous, and my body gravitated toward him, but damn if he wasn't dense enough to make me want to shake the shit out of him. For a moment, I wondered if this was yet another reason why Charles hesitated in giving the business to him; Sam was clearly someone that acted from the heart and was reckless with his decision making.

"How about the fact that you're stepping in and managing an employee that reports to Pax?" he asked with an exasperated shrug.

"What did you expect, Samuel? You've got washed-up pop singers with a penchant for nose candy, or grunge singers with a habit of stumbling through the lobby, drunk off their ass at random times of the day. Is it such a huge stretch of the imagination that I wouldn't want paparazzi bait like that associated with the hotel? Or that it isn't the kind of message we want to send to customers about the experience they'll have here? 'Oh hey, ever wonder what happened to that douche from the '90s with one hit that was arrested for illegally breeding ferrets? He's playing at Boost this weekend, score!' I fail to see where terminating these entertainment contract lands as *shocking* for you."

A small smile played at the corners of his mouth as though I'd inadvertently made a joke and he was struggling not to laugh. Would I ever be able to anticipate Samuel's responses correctly?

"Look," he said quietly, taking a deep breath before continuing. "I get where you're coming from, but I'm actually asking for a favor here." In one step, Samuel was directly in front of me again, and I could feel the heat radiating off his body. We stared at each other without words for a moment before he spoke again. "I was told that you were the best, but I was also told that you were here to help the Monroe team overall. All I'm asking is that you don't circumvent Pax altogether and let him be a part of the conversation. Help him be a better manager and empower him to make these decisions and have these discussions." He reached out and took my hand, rubbing his thumb along my palm and looking imploringly into my eyes.

"Fine," I muttered, with an exasperated huff. "I'll talk with Pax and let him decide how to handle this." I immediately regretted acquiescing to his request; the smug smile on his face told me everything I needed to know.

He's playing me.

"I'm glad you see it my way," Samuel said soothingly. My eyes went wide, and I batted his hand away from me with more force than I'd intended; it was as though he'd slapped me. In less than a day on the job, I'd managed to have an inappropriate liaison with an employee of my client, and just as horrifying I'd changed my strategy on his request. I felt used and played and hated myself for thinking that kiss had been anything more than a tactic. He looked at me in defensive curiosity, like one would look at an animal they thought may strike at any moment. I looked up into his eyes still shining in confusion from my rejection to his touch, and I realized that the best thing for both of us would be if I kept playing my part, and we both kept our distance.

"I've agreed to talk to Pax, but please don't think that insinuates any sort of change in my plans when it comes to eradicating the problems from this place," I said as I stepped away from him, putting the desk between us. "And this kind of inappropriate behavior will not happen again, I promise you that, Mr. Monroe."

I jutted my jaw out and squared my shoulders to emphasize my point but knew I couldn't do anything about the way my eyes gave me away. My mother had always told me that they were the actual reason I was a crappy liar, not the shaky chihuahua nonsense friends had fed me growing up. Mom would say that in times of stress my eyes had a more extensive vocabulary than my brain, which was really saying something. I prayed they didn't give me away now.

Samuel searched my expression, not giving anything away until his jaw tightened and his nostrils flared slightly.

"Let my assistant know if you need a meeting with me, Ms. Sheppard," he said as he crossed to the door, leaving me crestfallen in the confines of my new office.

I sank into the leather desk chair and took a couple of steadying breaths. In less than an hour, I had managed to span quite the emotional spectrum with Samuel, ranging from irritation to ecstasy and back to blind fury. He was quick to judge and rash to act, which made him dangerous. He was also intelligent and loyal and not off the mark when it came to grooming Pax to be the leader he needed to be; a small part of my irritation was that I secretly conceded that Samuel's management approach should have been mine from the start. My pulse raced in a slight panic at the loss of confidence I was experiencing. Closing my eyes, I let myself indulge in one brief moment of remembering how his lips felt on my neck, how his hair curled around my fingertips, how his tongue tasted on my own.

The buzzer going off again on my desk practically caused me to jump out of my skin.

"Sorry, Mae," I said guiltily into the intercom, before picking up the waiting call. "Thanks for holding," I said, kicking off a short call with Mr. Fitzgerald in which I explained who I was and that I'd be meeting with him and Pax about contract negotiations in the coming weeks. Surely, he wondered why the minimal information I was giving him couldn't have been sent in an email. God knows I would have wondered that if I were in his shoes.

Thankfully, the rest of the day passed without much fanfare.

I received several invitations to come meet-n-greet with different departments as a thinly veiled attempt to stave off terminations. Clearly, everyone in the company thought that rather than being here to polish the company's image and manage PR, I was brought onboard to weed out employees and issue mass terminations. Which was ironic since I was actually only here to help with the firing of one person.

By seven o'clock, I was packing up my things as Mae ducked her head in to say that she was taking off unless I needed anything else.

"No, go home. I'll be in around ten tomorrow, I have a breakfast meeting," I said.

"Right, Mr. Garcia called to confirm your meeting. Twice," she said before turning to leave.

I rolled my eyes at Levi, not surprised at all. I rode the elevator down alone, leaning against the wall and willing myself to get home without crumbling under the mental and emotional exhaustion of the day. Halfway to the front doors of the lobby, a booming voice echoed off of the marble.

"Hey, Sheppard!" I turned to see Paxton jogging over from the direction of Boost. I prayed this wouldn't be any form of a sparring match; it had been a long day, and I was in no shape to battle wits with anyone, even if was Paxton.

"What's up, Paxton?"

"Whoa," he said, solemnly holding up a hand. "First things first, the name is *Pax*; only my parents and arresting officers call me Paxton."

"Lovely."

"Sounds like you had a bang-up first day. The fireworks were pretty entertaining in the meeting this morning, and I heard you made Lisa in HR cry!" His huge grin was infectious, and I had to laugh at the ridiculous rumor since I hadn't even met anyone in HR as of yet. Although it wasn't worth correcting since there were bound to be more rumors like it on a regular basis; if I started chasing them down one by one, I'd never get anything done. "Look, I just wanted to let you know that Sam can be a hardheaded bastard, but he's actually a great guy once you get to know him."

"Why are you telling me this?" I asked.

"I get that you're here for a reason, and I'm sure it's going to be very entertaining to watch the two of you," he chuckled before getting suddenly serious. "But never doubt Sam's loyalty to this place or his commitment to the business. Yes, he's quick to jump to conclusions and is reckless with his personal life, but if you operate under the assumption that he doesn't give a flying fuck about the hotel, then you're in for a rough ride."

"Again, why are you telling me this, Pax?" I couldn't figure out why he'd bother to improve my opinion of Samuel.

His grin was back, and he was chuckling in a conspiratorial way that made me think I wasn't in on the joke.

"I've *never* seen someone get under that guy's skin the way you do. Like I said, this is going to be damn entertaining, and I hope you two don't end up killing each other. In the process, though, I don't want you to jump to the wrong conclusions either. Because you see, you have dad's ear." He said the last part with a knowing look, and I understood. He didn't want me jeopardizing Samuel being handed the business someday. He held a hand up to stop me when I started to reply. "Just give the guy a chance."

"Fair enough," I said with a sharp nod, feeling a slight pang of guilt for misleading Pax when it came to my intentions with his brother.

"Well, if you'll excuse me, I have waitresses to sexually harass," he said as he turned back toward the club.

"I didn't hear that!" I could hear his bark of a laugh as he rounded the corner and I made my way out to the warm Portland night. Jules' loft was in walking distance of the hotel, in the Pearl District of downtown and thankfully it wasn't raining tonight as I trekked the five blocks and didn't have to wait for the streetcar. As I rode the elevator up to the sixth floor, I could feel the emotions from the last twelve hours bubbling to the surface. Now that I was almost home, and my guard was coming down, I felt raw and exposed. My hand shook slightly as I put the key in the lock and by the time I made it into the entryway the tears were starting to form.

"Hey, Dee," Jules called from her room when the door closed behind me. "Let me get the wine; you have a lot of spilling to do! First date this weekend, and then the first day at the new job today!" She rounded the corner and took in the sight of me, leaning against the door with tears in my eyes while my laptop bag, keys, and purse lay in a pile at my feet.

"Ah shit," she mumbled. "I'll get the ice cream, too."

Samuel

I'd been staring at the same email for almost twenty minutes and still didn't have a clue as to what it said. However, with remarkable clarity, I could recall how soft Delilah's skin was and how sweet she had tasted and how badly I wanted her in my arms again. I shook my head violently and tried to get back to work. No matter how hard I tried, I couldn't shake her from my thoughts or stop replaying the afternoon in my mind.

My unannounced visit this morning was intended to be a warning. I barged into her office planning on telling Delilah how ridiculous her plans were and that I wouldn't lay down to her schemes. Instead, I'd started asking her about her blind date and couldn't stop inhaling her intoxicating scent. She'd spun me in circles and I couldn't keep my head straight. Delilah's raw feistiness had been like a magnet, and when I'd planned on countering her insults with one of my own, I'd shocked myself by kissing her instead. And while kissing her had been a surprise to both of us, it had also felt like the one thing I needed to do that day. Everything about her drew me further in. Once I touched her, felt her, tasted her, groped her ass and pressed into her body, I knew I needed more.

That is, right up until Fitzgerald's call. If left unchecked, I would have taken her on that uncluttered desk without a care as to who heard us. I wanted Delilah so bad, but when I realized she was effectively making Pax into a show-pony and eliminating his limited number of responsibilities, I suddenly saw the shrew standing before me and second-guessed everything I felt. Up until that point, I'd selfishly been thinking the worst she could do was create a hassle for me on a daily basis, making me walk a tight-rope of good behavior. But now I understood the power she had, the power Charles had given her, to render someone like Pax unnecessary and elbow him out of his role in the business. Despite how I felt about her personally, I couldn't let her do that to my brother.

My head fell into my hands as I moaned in frustration just before the door to my office opened. Emma stormed in looking pissed with my assistant Leslie fast on her heels.

"I'm sorry-" Leslie said with a huff but stopped when I waved her off.

"It's ok, Leslie. Apparently, this runs in the family." With a confused expression, Leslie closed the door behind Emma, and I faced my irritated sister. We stared at each other for a moment, her expression angry and mine blank, until she finally spoke.

"Are you really such a tool that you'd question which is the 'real' Dee?"

Way to cut to the chase Emma!

"Emma I-"

"No," she cut me off. "I don't want to hear it! I watched you in that meeting. You can't decide if you want to hate the woman in the conference room this morning or fall for the woman you met in the bar, which makes you a complete moron."

She always had a knack for reading between the lines, as well as reading me like an open book. Although now it was more frustrating than it was endearing since I had no clue how to respond to her.

And my silence only pissed her off more.

"Seriously Sam, are you honestly questioning her character?"

I took a moment to think about the question, and the answer was 'yes.' I still had no idea who this woman was; she was fearless and determined in her job, capable of starting a companywide shit-storm, while Charles just smiled on from the sidelines.

"Look, I have no idea. Even you have to admit that she was one person the other night and another this-"

"No shit!" she cut me off in a frantic shriek. "And if you can't reconcile that in your pea-brain then you're more dimwitted then I thought."

"Emma I don't see how-"

"Sam," she said in a low, serious tone that shut me up quickly. "Don't you think that *I* can recognize when someone is trying to reinvent their personality for the sake of self-preservation. Trust me when I tell you that Dee is protecting herself. I know you think that I only like her because of a connection over shoes or cocktails or some other stupid shit, but that's not it. She's real, and this image she's created of herself isn't who she really is; it's what she uses to get by in her profession."

I swiftly made my way around the desk and hugged my sister. It was easy to forget how far she'd come and how intuitive she could be.

"I'm sorry," I mumbled into the top of her head.

"It's okay," she said. "Just be nice to her."

I held my tiny sister and thought over her words.

What if she was right and Dee was only hiding behind the shrew?

EIGHT

Delilah

The next morning, I was flicking a sugar packet between my fingers, nursing my second coffee and staring mindlessly out the window while I waited for Levi to join me at the bistro he'd chosen for breakfast. He was already fifteen minutes late, which wasn't a shock. In the five years I'd known Levi, he was rarely, if ever, on time.

"Oh em gee, it's Dee Sheppard!"

I heard Levi before I saw him, and a smile spread across my face before I even clapped eyes on him at the door. He was easily a foot taller than most of the people around him and beaming at me, his trademark unending enthusiasm coming through. His rail-thin frame was dressed in dark designer jeans and a salmon colored dress shirt and cream wool scarf, and as usual, his messy blonde hair was styled in a just-rolled-out-of-bed look that no doubt took half an hour to achieve. I was in a simple black suit with a blue dress shirt and black heels. A glance at his shoes confirmed what I already knew to be true, that he was always the better dressed of the two of us. But what else would you expect from a fashion and lifestyle reporter?

I stood and hugged my old friend, my feet leaving the ground for a moment as he wrapped me in his embrace.

"Christ child, it has been too long," he said as he set me back down, smiling his ear-to-ear grin at me. "I'm sorry I'm late; had a rough night. Break-ups just suck, don't they? Ugh, the *drama*!" He signaled the waitress for coffee with a flourish of his hand.

"Oh no! Did you and Jonathan split up?" I asked.

"Baby girl, Jonathan and I ended months ago when he took that job in Chicago. You might know that if you called more," he pursed his lips as our waitress poured his coffee.

I looked at my hands shamefully; it was true that I'd been a bit of a fly-by-night friend lately. Levi's work took him up and down the west coast; however, he spent the majority of

each month in Los Angeles, so I couldn't really blame our lack
of contact on his traveling. He'd had an independent blog that
focused on style, nightlife and culture on the "Left Coast" as he
liked to call it. In an average month, he would cover everything
from nightclubs in Seattle, the food scene in Portland, pride
weekend in San Francisco, all before ending with LA style
pieces. It had originally been his way to subsidize his nomad
lifestyle, traveling from one of his tribes to another, friends and
boyfriends scattered across three states. But as he built up a
name for himself, and quite the following, a large trade
magazine finally bought him out. These days, he not only kept
up the blog via their site but also wrote articles for the print
magazine as well.

"Egg white omelet and wheat toast," he said to the
waitress before she could ask for his order.

"Um, same," I muttered as she left without a word. "I'm
sorry Levi, I should have called more." My guilt wasn't just that
I'd been incommunicado as of late, but what's worse, when I
finally reached out a couple of weeks ago, it was to ask a favor.
I'd needed a crash course in Portland culture and lifestyle, and
Levi was hands down the best person for the job. We'd had
dinner in LA before I took off for Portland, and I'd spent a
shameful amount of time peppering him with questions and
talking about my potential promotion. This breakfast was my
pitiful way of apologizing.

He waved his hand dismissively in front of him while
taking a sip of coffee, throwing out the thread of conversation as
quickly as he'd started it.

"Please, I don't have a leg to stand on when it comes to
being flighty. How about we cut this small talk bullshit and you
tell me why you're here."

"You know already," I said, grasping my coffee mug in
two hands. "I'm here doing a quick rebrand for the Hotel
Monroe. I told you all about it when we talked about the
corporate promotion."

"Right, yes, I remember. But since this particular meal
you're letting me get a word in edgewise and ask questions, I
have one in mind. Charles Monroe just up and decided to hire a
PR firm from LA to handle his rebrand?" he asked, looking
skeptically at me.

"Yup," I said, sipping coffee and avoiding his eye line.

"Good lord child, you are shit at lying," he said with a laugh. "Well, it makes sense that he would want to get the Monroe kids under control; they've been some serious fun to cover and low-hanging fruit when it comes to gossip in the PDX. But still," he said eyeing me carefully with a squint, "something's not right."

"I don't know what you're talking about," I stammered out.

"Oh, come on, Dee. I know you, and I know the kind of shit you do. You're a badass bitch when it comes to getting shit under control. But hiring Delilah Shepard from JPL to smack around a couple of Portland executives for a hotel rebrand is kind of like hiring Frank Lloyd Wright to organize your pantry."

"Shit, I don't know if I deserve quite that big of a compliment."

"Yes, you do, and yes you know it," he said with a dramatic eye roll. "Cut the shit girl, is the reason you're here why I think you're here?" he asked conspiratorially, leaning forward and practically hissing out the question in a whisper.

With a sigh and the realization that I wouldn't be able to avoid this conversation, I leaned on the table to mirror his conspiratorial posture. Either he had put together that Charles was looking to sell the hotel, or god forbid, the *other* reason I was here. Or both.

"Off. The. Record," I said pointing at him and narrowing my eyes.

"Of course," he said, impatiently motioning for me to spill.

"No, I mean it Levi, this can't get out. I'm trusting you here, this gets out not only is it my ass, but you better believe that I'm coming for you with everything I've got."

"Holy shits and giggles," Levi said with wide eyes. "This must be *good!*"

"I'm not afraid to use the Cabo story if I have to," I whispered, threating Levi with the darkest secret of his I could think of.

"Christ! We're just two girlfriends talking here!" he exclaimed at my threat. "Off the record! Damn, do you need it in writing? Excuse me," he asked a waitress as she passed by, "can you please bring me a knife? It appears I have a blood oath to swear."

She looked back and forth between us, clearly confused.

"He's kidding," I said as she furrowed her brow and stalked off. "Ok," I said, turning back to Levi, "Charles wants to sell the hotel. But they need to clean up the PR first. Otherwise they'll be a discount 'business in trouble' purchase."

"Whoa," Levi said, raising his eyebrows. "That's big. They're practically one of the last places still family-owned in this town. Kind of sad to think about the Monroe becoming yet another Hilton or Kimpton property." I nodded and shrugged. He was right, I supposed, but that wasn't really my problem or concern. Levi took a sip of coffee as his eyes narrowed sharply at me over the top of the mug.

"And?" he asked.

"And what?" I said, already feeling the heat in my face. Levi sighed dramatically.

"Let me go ahead and speed this up. 'What are you talking about, Levi?' C'mon Dee, I can tell there's something else. 'No there isn't.' Yes, there is. 'No, I can't.' Just spill it already. 'Ok, Levi, you know I can't keep anything from you; you're just too gorgeous to deceive.' Thank you, Dee, I think so too." He punctuated his one-man show with a gesture for me to go ahead and take the floor. With a deep breath, I leaned in whispered the last thing I was here to do for Charles.

Levi let out a low whistle. I automatically looked around for prying eyes or eavesdroppers out of habit. I couldn't believe Levi had put this together so easily; I hoped no one else had. We stared at each other in silence for a long minute, as he took in the news and most likely processed that he must now keep it all off the record, and I tried to convey with my expression that I was done talking about this topic.

"So, how is Ms. Blonde Ambition? Didn't you say you're living with her now?" he asked, blessedly changing the subject and giving me a bit of air.

"She's great. Don't tell me you don't watch her show! She'll be crushed," I said sarcastically.

Levi and I had become friends after our paths continued to cross on red carpets and press junkets. He was usually at whatever movie premiere, awards show, or press conference I was attending. However, while I escorted my clients and helped them navigate the press and intrusive questions, Levi was in the throng of reporters hurling questions as inappropriate as he could come up with at anyone that walked by. It was his shtick when it came to covering celebrities; he didn't give a crap if publicists blacklisted him, seeing as how he was never striving for a cover story or feature interview, his topics were far too varied to invest that much time on one famous person. That unique point-of-view allowed him the freedom other journalists didn't have. It was at one premiere in particular that our friendship started; I'd known about Levi, met him once or twice, but he really made an impression when he asked my client how many of the actresses in the movie he'd slept with during filming.

Rather than vilify Levi and make an enemy out of him, I decided to befriend him and use his particular voice strategically. Over the years, I'd reach out to Levi when it was advantageous to have a particular story leaked, and as a byproduct, we'd become pretty good friends. One night, over drinks, as we were sharing stories it had come to light that he and Jules knew one another. He'd covered an event her production company was hosting and naturally Levi had offended the shit out her with how much of a dramatic attention-whore he was. She did not seem to see the irony in that description.

"Thirty minutes of television watching a half-naked woman working on cars? Honey, what the hell do you think I'd find entertaining about that?"

I laughed with him and lifted my coffee mug to make way for our arriving breakfast.

"Now on to the bigger and better question for you. How is it at Hotel Monroe?" Levi asked, raising both eyebrows while he speared his omelet.

"Still off the record?" I asked. Levi mimed slicing his palm with his butter knife and nodded.

"Well, it's off to a rocky start, but for the most part, it's what I expected. Some members of the staff are going to be more... *challenging* than others."

I was, of course, thinking of Samuel. He was undoubtedly going to be difficult, but I suspected it was going to be more of a challenge for me to keep my hands off of him.

"Dear Jesus, you're such a PR goody-two-shoes. I told you we were off the record. Come on Dee, it's *me*! Would you cut the bullshit please?"

"I fooled around with one of the Monroe men," I blurted out before realizing what I'd said. And once I did, I took a deep inhale in shock and started to choke on my toast. Levi slid a water glass toward me.

"No one ever accused you of being boring," he mumbled as I took a drink and swallowed the offending piece of bread. Once I settled down, we were silent for a moment before Levi once again leaned conspiratorially across the table.

"Is it Pax Monroe? I would *not* blame you if it were. I've only seen pictures of that beast of a man, and I want to spread him on a cracker." When I didn't say anything, he continued. "Oh God, is it Samuel? The man-whore? Honey, I know he's sexy and has that whole 'I-just-had-sex-so-look-at-how-messy-and-hot-my-hair-is' thing going on, but that's just masochistic! Unless," he gasped dramatically, "it's Charles? DeeDee, you're barking up a *very* married tree with that one. The silver fox would never leave his wife-"

"Would you stop talking?!" I blurted loudly. "My god, your knowledge of the Monroe men is frightening."

Levi scoffed. "They're high society, *and* they live in Portland; naturally, I know them. Now dish. Which Monroe man has your panties twisted?"

"Samuel," I grumbled reluctantly. Our waitress chose that moment to check on our table.

"We're going to each need two very large Bloody Mary's," he said.

"Levi, it's nine in the morning on a Tuesday."

"And you're crushing on one of the West Coast's biggest man-whores. Vodka is in order."

"None for me," I told the waitress.

I only gave Levi the highlights while he drank his Bloody Mary and nodded dramatically along with my story. I told him how Samuel and I had met before the job even started, and about our connection and flirting, and how we then met *on* the job and felt the same connection plus, some additional tension. The make-out session was explained in detail because come on, he'd understand my inclination to dry hump Samuel. When the story was finished, Levi just stared at me over his drink, playing with his celery stick and looking coy.

"What?" I asked.

"I'm just impressed," he said, slightly shrugging his shoulders and looking out the window.

"Impressed?"

"I'm impressed that someone got you to turn the robot off." He held a hand up to stop my interruption. "It's not a bad thing, don't get me wrong. You're amazing at what you do, and no one's questioning that. But you've become a bit of a force, and this is such a monumental fuck-up. This guy must have really gotten to you."

"Can we talk about something else now?" I asked, not wanting to dwell on my huge gaffe at the one thing I was confident about.

Levi was turning out to be just as useless as Jules had been in the guidance department regarding Samuel. Don't get me wrong, they were two of the best friends I could ever ask for, but I just wanted someone to tell me what in the hell I should do. Even though Jules had held my hand last night, listened to me rant and get the whole story out, she still didn't have any insight as to how I should handle the situation.

When asked, she replied, "Fuck if I know. I never shit where I eat, which *you* taught me, by the way, and now you seem to have set up a buffet at this new job."

Helpful.

I was brought up to speed on Levi's dating drama, which required a flowchart to keep straight, and we filled each other in on other work news. He told me about the art exhibit he was heading to Seattle to cover, while I told him more what I was planning over the new two months to lock this promotion in for myself. When the check arrived, we both threw down cash, knowing that neither would allow the other to pay. We made our way outside and Levi began walking me to the Monroe.

"So," he said while we were waiting to cross the street, "you're the new shark for the Monroe family, and you've yet to lay down any ground rules for me on coverage."

"I'm not going to ask you to look the other way, if that's what you're assuming," I said with a sigh, hoping Levi didn't think I'd become *that* cutthroat.

"I didn't assume anything DeeDee," he said, smiling down at me with the same expression that always made me want to hug him.

"The only favor I ask is for you to share with me what you hear in the rumor mill. I'm going to be working night and day to combat bullshit media hype, present company excluded of course," I said with an exaggerated bat of my eyelashes, to which Levi tipped his head at me in a grand gesture.

"Say no more," he said. "I'll let you know what I hear. Plus, I have an inside source at the Monroe. I'll probably know what you had for lunch today before you even finish eating it."

My eyes went wide and I slapped his chest, causing him to laugh.

"I hope that's a joke, Mr. Garcia!"

"You'll never know," he said, wiggling his eyebrows. "I'll be swinging back through town in a week or so; let me know if anything is going on you'd like me to cover," he said, gesturing up at the hotel behind me.

"Definitely." I gave Levi a tight hug and promised to call him soon.

Levi whispered into my ear, "Now go have sex with Samuel on his desk." He turned to leave but not before swatting me on the ass, making me yelp and laugh. As I turned to enter the lobby, I was stopped in my tracks by two piercing hazel eyes glaring at me from the other side of the glass.

NINE

Delilah

As I approached the hotel's door, Samuel's face came further into view on the other side of the lobby, our stare never breaking. His hands were in his pockets, and he watched me carefully as I opened the glass door. Try as I might, I couldn't read his expression as his eyes danced around my face. A ringing sound brought him back to attention, and he pulled his cell phone from his pocket. Samuel's eyes stayed on mine even after he began his conversation and I made my way to the elevators, confused as ever on the evolving topic of Samuel.

I spent the better part of the morning checking and re-checking my outlines and project plans, knowing I needed to have my ducks perfectly in a row to pull everything off within the two-month deadline. It was a robust event and communication plan, to say the least, but with the added operational goals Charles had thrown in, it was going to be down to the wire.

Mae popped her head into my office and shook me from my cloud of planning.

"Emma's here," she said with a smile. Shamefully, I'd scheduled the easiest of the Monroe family members as my first meeting, easing myself into the convoluted family battle that lay ahead of us. But truth be told I was excited to meet with her right away, particularly since I hadn't had a chance to speak with Emma since our rushed exchange before yesterday's introductions.

"Great, send her in please."

Emma bounced into my office wearing a white pencil skirt with a black and white pinstriped shirt and black heels, which made me laugh.

"What?" she asked, her grin slipping in confusion. I stood and came around my desk, jutting a foot out at her. She let out a cute squeak when she saw that we were wearing the exact same shoes. "I told you we were going to be friends!"

I laughed with her. Emma's cryptic musings were already growing on me.

"Before we get into everything, I just wanted to thank you for your discretion yesterday."

"Please," she scoffed. "It's nobody's business what you do on your off time. Although I find it interesting that you chose Boost for a first date."

"Would you believe that I actually thought scoping the place out beforehand would make me slightly more relaxed on my first day?" I asked in a defeated huff.

"Wow, that worked out well, didn't it?" Emma said through her musical laughter. We moved on and began discussing events already booked on the calendar as well as a few I wanted to add. For over an hour, Emma and I went over the details for the Portland Art Museum's fundraiser dinner the Monroe family would be attending this Friday, Pax's racing events I had planned, as well as the annual fall gala coming up. Emma was amazing. Her mind ran at warp speed, because no sooner would I vocalize an event and an idea, she would have a dozen suggestions for location, décor and color schemes, entertainment choices and menu options. This woman could undoubtedly plan a wedding from start to finish in the time it takes most people to make out a grocery list.

"Ok, I think that covers everything that's coming up soon," I said, leaning back in my chair and rubbing my tired eyes. "Let's go over the details for the holiday and winter calendars another time; I don't think I have it in me today."

Emma chuckled and began gathering up our notes.

"Um," she said quietly. "Are we moving into the part of the meeting where we talk about how I appear in the press?"

I looked up as she was sitting back in her chair and eyeing me speculatively.

"Honestly Emma, you're clean. Mae didn't find much on you when she did her research, other than the obvious stuff about your graduation a few years ago and the clothing line you did for fashion week when you were in college. Everything else was just a collection of blurbs for Monroe events."

You're the least of my worries when it comes to the Monroe's.

I felt the last part was better left unsaid, for fear of her thinking I was insulting her brothers.

"Yeah, I tend to keep a lower profile than my brothers," she said with a nervous smile.

She pressed her thumbs together and rolled her shoulders back twice in a purposeful movement. For a moment, I thought she may just be stretching, having spent the better part of an hour at my desk, but there was just something off about her entire demeanor that was different than before. All at once Emma appeared rigid and tense, but not in a typical anxious way, but rather fearful, as though dreading something. Honestly, she looked like she was being held at gunpoint.

She pressed her thumbs together again, rolled her shoulders twice more, and then pressed her lips together. That's when I realized what it was, they were tics.

"Emma, is there something I should know?"

She looked behind her to confirm that the office door was closed before continuing. It was unnerving to see her so timid when she was usually so exuberant.

"Emma, I won't tell anyone, if that's what you're worried about. Not even Mae."

"Oh, I know," she said, meeting my eyes again. "There's something you should be aware of, just in case."

Once again, she checked to see if the door to my office was closed and her energy was starting to make me feel uneasy and anxious. She leaned her forearms on the edge of my desk, and I mirrored her posture.

"I have a medical condition," she practically whispered.

Suddenly my heart began to race as my mind flooded with all sorts of horrible scenarios. How sick was she? Was it life threatening? I'd only just met this person, but I was already pretty attached to her.

"A *psychiatric* condition, to be precise," she continued.

I tried to reevaluate everything I had come to know and observe of Emma. My public relations experience prepared me for the most common conditions in my field, depression and bipolar disorder. But Emma didn't seem to exhibit either, which left me both curious and on alert.

"What sort of condition?" I asked.

"I'm a recovering kleptomaniac."

My mind went completely blank for a moment as I stared at Emma in shock.

"As in... you steal things?" I asked, unable to stop the ridiculous question once it had started.

"As in, I have the compulsion to take things whether they belong to me or not," she said and then gave me a small smile. "That's how my shrink prefers I explain it."

"I don't... I mean... Do you...How..."

I was babbling and had no idea how to approach this topic.

"It's technically a form of OCD, and I haven't had an episode in over three years," she explained calmly, probably deciding she should probably just take over the conversation for now. "I have a therapist that I see regularly, and I'm on medication that helps me immensely."

I finally broke out of my mental fog, relieved that it'd been a while since she'd had an episode, if for no other reason than the look of sheer pride on her face when she said that. We may not have known each other for long, but I was proud of Emma for having the strength to conquer something like this.

"They make medication for kleptomania?" I asked, trying to understand as best I could.

"Well, at first they wanted to put me on a heavy regimen of mood stabilizers and tranquilizers."

"I'm going to go out on a limb and say that you're *not* on any of those."

"No," she continued with a smile. "I'm just on one dosage, which technically is designed to control alcohol dependency but actually works for a lot of compulsive behaviors. I'm lucky, it works wonders for me. I also drive to Seattle once a month for a support group meeting."

"Wow," I breathed out. In my head, I was reconciling the fact that this upbeat, charismatic woman was also running a gambit of treatment to keep a condition like this under control. Emma truly was amazing.

"Who knows about this?" I asked.

"Only my immediate family."

"You've kept this from everyone in your life, outside your immediate family, and you confided this secret in *me*?"

"I thought you should know, that way you'd be prepared if I ever have a relapse and pull a Winona Ryder."

I inadvertently let a laugh escape and instantly clapped a hand over my mouth, looking at Emma in wide-eyed horror.

"It's ok, you can laugh. I've gotten to the point where I can, too."

"Thank you for trusting me with this Emma. And I doubt I'll ever need the information," I said with a wink. Her infectious grin relaxed me, and we both leaned back in our chairs.

"Dee, can I ask you something?"

"Of course."

"Are you planning on staying here long?"

I was really hoping it was going to be a question I could answer. If for no other reason than I could repay her gesture of honesty. But I wasn't sure how to answer that honestly without breaking my word to Charles.

"I'm going to be here as long as you guys need me." It was the truth, sort of.

"I'm not going to ask about the details of why my dad hired you; I'm sure there's a lot of layers as to why you're here, and there are some things you just don't want to know, you know?" She gave me a tight smile and I nodded in return. "But if you're only going to be here a short time, and you know that to be the case, please don't start something with my brother that will leave him heartbroken when you leave."

I wanted to feign confusion, ask her 'whatever do you mean?' But it would honestly be insulting to her at this point. Based on my slack jaw and wide eyes, I was sure Emma could tell *something* was going on between Samuel and me, something beyond what she saw at Boost the other night. I cleared my throat and regained my composure as best I could.

"I think *heartbroken* may be a bit of a stretch," I said, more sarcastically than I'd intended. The idea of Samuel being heartbroken over any woman, let alone me, was ridiculous. Emma arched a brow at me. "What I mean," I clarified, "is that you have nothing to worry about. Regardless of how long I'm here, nothing can ever happen between us, not that I would even want it to. It's unethical and frankly against my own rules."

"Hmm," Emma said, eyeing me closely. "Ok, I guess we'll have this conversation another time. There's been too much emotion in here today anyhow."

In a flurry, she stood and gathered her things to leave. I put a hand over hers as she reached for a stack of invitation designs.

"Thank you for trusting me."

"Oh!" she said, bouncing on the balls of her feet, "I almost forgot to tell you, I have one last secret. Dominic and I have been a couple for almost a year now."

Emma gave me a blinding grin before turning with a flourish and bounding out the door. I ignored the fact that she'd taken my pen with her.

After Emma had left my office on Tuesday, I buried myself in press releases and correspondence for hours, only to reemerge for coffee and bathroom breaks. On one such trek to the employee lounge, I came across Samuel as he was grabbing a bottle of water from the fridge. He was in a black suit and white shirt, sans tie, and looking absolutely mouthwatering. As I approached the counter and our eyes met, I considered making a peace offering. Despite whatever confusing sexual tension was happening between us, there was still the fact that we'd be working together and should try to get along.

But Samuel spoke first.

"Your boyfriend sure knows how to make an exit. Guess round two of the blind dates really paid off," he said with a smirk as he brushed past me and walked away.

For a moment I was at a loss for what in the hell he was talking about, blindsided by the topic. And then I remembered he'd been downstairs when Levi and I had said goodbye that morning. I had to bite my lip to stop from laughing at his assumption of Levi and I being on a date. But as funny as the assumption was, it was also coupled with an obnoxious remark and Samuel's own version of a hissy fit.

When I returned to my desk, Mae informed me that the executive photoshoot happening the next day had to be bumped to a 5AM start time in order for the photographer to be in Seattle by afternoon. I let her know that Samuel was to be scheduled first.

Petty? Maybe.

Amusing? Hell yes.

Pax's strategy meeting kicked off my Wednesday. He'd asked that we move it from midmorning to just after lunch, and still managed to come into my office looking half asleep, smelling of cigarette smoke and sickeningly sweet perfume. His jeans and dress shirt were wrinkled from being out all night, just as they'd been the first time we'd met; but this time his personality was completely different. I'd spent the better part of twenty minutes attempting to discuss interviews and events lined up for him, but Pax had other things on his mind.

Well, *one* thing, to be exact.

"I'll be driving an *actual* IndyCar, right? Not some bullshit pace car, but a *real* racecar?"

"Yes," I said impatiently. "But like I was trying to say, there are a couple of magazines that I'd like-"

"Can I pick my colors? Or my number?!" he asked animatedly, bouncing slightly in his seat.

"I don't know, Pax. I'm sure we can arrange a number or color choice for you. So Forbes Magazine-"

"I want red!" he practically yelled at me.

My resistance at this point had given out to his constant string of interruptions.

"I'll tell you what, Pax," I said, rubbing my temples. "You give me a list of requirements you have for your racing experience, and I'll give you a list of requirements I have for you regarding media appearances and behavior. We'll match each other, *point for point*. Deal?"

His enthusiasm was palpable as he jotted down the details of his car design, helmet size and lord only knew what else. He handed it to me, and I made a grand showing of placing it with the other notes I had in his file on my desk.

"Ok, I'll handle *that*," I said, waving a hand over the file like a magician, "I need you to handle something for me, now." Pax raised an eyebrow in question and cocked his head to the side, waiting for instruction. "We need to talk about the talent you have appearing at Boost."

"Yes," he said diligently, as though waiting for the test questions to start.

"They're a mess, Pax. You must know that," I implored, hoping that he at least saw this conversation coming.

"For sure. Total d-bags and has-beens." Another decisive nod and expectant stare.

"Ok, so what are you planning on doing about it?"

"That's Fitzgerald's gig, not mine." This time I let Pax's expectant stare and silence last as long as it took for him to keep speaking and offer some sort of explanation. "See, he's the dude that books that stuff. He like, organizes their calendars and stuff, and decides who plays when."

"Thank you," I deadpanned. "I'm aware of his job description. Are you aware he *reports* to you?"

"Well yeah," he said, with a confused shrug, "but I don't know how to do that shit. I mean, I could fire a bartender and take over until I hired another one. But managing talent is all that dude, it's his jam, not mine."

"Huh." I cocked my head to the side and took in this 'innovator' and member of the executive team that didn't know his ass from a performance evaluation.

Nepotism at its finest, ladies and gentlemen.

"Alright," I said, leaning forward and taking a deep breath. "God help me, but let's back up a couple of steps and talk about your management style."

Almost an hour later, Pax gathered his things to leave my office with the confidence to have a meeting with Carl Fitzgerald about what he expected from him, for Boost, going forward. And while I was pleased and proud of the work Pax put in when it came to management and performance evaluation, I couldn't help the nagging irritation I felt with myself. I'd more or less resorted to holding a meeting with Pax that should have been done by human resources. I was holding extra meetings and enabling managers like *Pax* to execute things I needed done immediately.

So much for cleaning house.

But I had to admit, the coaching had felt good, and it was great to see his confidence grow the more we talked.

"I'll have Mae send you the details for your first interview as soon as I have them, and we'll meet again just beforehand to prep. In the meantime, drive the speed limit," I told him as he made his way to the door.

"Thanks, Dee!" he called out as he left.

Later that day, I was rushing to a meeting with a local journalist and barely caught the elevator in time. When the doors closed, I looked to my left and realized that I was alone with Samuel. Today he was in dark gray pants and black dress shirt with the sleeves rolled up to his elbows, hands once again in his pockets. His appearance would have been overwhelmingly tempting if it wasn't for the look of contempt he quickly shot my way before giving me the cold shoulder.

"Samuel," I greeted him quietly, only to get a grumble in return.

We rode in silence for a bit until he finally spoke.

"I suppose I have you to thank for being scheduled in the 5AM time slot for the photo shoot this morning," he said quietly, staring at the descending numbers above the door.

Looking down at my shoes I swallowed a laugh.

"I know what a dedicated team member you are. I figured you wouldn't mind," I replied, smiling to myself as I looked up at the same numbers, trying to ignore the stifling tension sucking the air out of the elevator.

"I didn't mind at all. Although it was a bit early considering I had the Knight Social last night."

Ah shit.

How could I have forgotten about the damn meeting of Pacific Northwest business leaders? I felt remorseful for one brief moment until I remembered his snide comments and general disdain for my presence, and suddenly I was over it.

"The shift in my schedule means we'll have to pick another time for our one-on-one meeting," he said without giving me so much as a glance. "Maybe next week sometime?"

His patronizing tone caused my jaw to clench.

"Well that's sweet of you, considering you told me I wouldn't last a week," I said with a sniff. "I've put off getting settled or even decorating my office; I don't have so much as a plant. I must have gotten into your good graces by starting your day so early."

In my peripheral vision, I could see him turn toward me and I looked up into his piercing stare.

"Oh. You did," he deadpanned. "And I plan on getting into *yours*."

I couldn't tell if he'd intended his words to be an innuendo, a threat, or both.

TEN

Samuel

The entire week had been nothing more than an antagonistic shoving contest between Delilah and me. On Tuesday morning, I'd walked into the hotel with a completely different frame of mind than the day before. My feelings of amped anticipation were replaced with determined resolve. While I was no closer to answering my questions about Delilah's apparent split personality, I *had* come to a decision regarding how I would interact with her going forward.

There was a large part of me that wanted to bend her over my desk and consume every inch of her body. But there was also the reality that I didn't do romantic relationships or fuck women I worked with. Both of those facts eliminated anything other than a working relationship with Delilah. I needed to find a way to put my feelings of lust for her aside. She wasn't going anywhere soon; Pax and Emma's blaring stamp of approval on her had been the final nail in *that* coffin. Regardless of my thoughts about her ridiculous job, she was now a member of the team, whether I liked it or not.

Entering the lobby, I caught our concierge Peter's eye, and he made his way over.

"Mr. Kuroda's flight was delayed," he explained, answering my silent question. "The driver will let us know when they're in the garage." I nodded in reply and Peter made his way back to the concierge desk.

Aki Kuroda was a Japanese chef I'd befriended during my time in Tokyo. His restaurant was highly acclaimed and practically the only place I ate for a solid week once I'd discovered it. But as I'd gotten to know the man behind the Michelin star eatery, I learned he also had a passion for street food as well. He'd taken me to some of the most amazing places to eat, all of which I would never have found as an American intern in the city. I'd gotten wind that he was considering moving to the States to start a new restaurant, and I was determined to recruit him for our soon-to-be remodeled restaurant.

As I was waiting in the lobby, a familiar streak of black hair outside caught my attention, and I turned just as Delilah stepped onto the curb in front of the hotel. I couldn't help but smile as I watched her gracefully hop up on the sidewalk and throw her head back in laughter; her beauty was palpable, even from this distance. For a brief moment, I disregarded everything I'd decided about never being with Delilah sexually and let myself drink in her image. She was gorgeous and charismatic to everyone around her, but it was the little things that made her stand out to me. Like the way she tilted her neck when she tucked her hair behind her ear, or the dimples in her chin when she laughed, or the way her eyes squinted when she smiled.

Way to put those feelings aside.

I shook my head and jammed my hands in my pockets in frustration. How the hell was I going to work with her?

Just as I was beginning to give in to my craving for her, a beanpole of a man stepped onto the sidewalk behind Delilah and scooped her up in an embrace. I itched to cross the lobby, storm through the double doors and rip his arms off at the sockets. But I was stopped in place when I realized that she seemed genuinely happy. I watched as he whispered in her ear and smacked her on the ass, all of which earning a schoolgirl giggle from Delilah.

A flash of anger rose up in me when I realized that she'd had a boyfriend all the while her legs had been wrapped around me the day before.

Wait, that doesn't make any sense.

She'd just been set up on a blind date a few days ago; perhaps this was another one? It was completely within the realm of reason that her friend would still be setting her up after the failed calorie-counter from the other night. But this looked more intimate than a first date.

The silver lining was that Delilah being off the market meant we could move past this ridiculous *thing* between us and work together, which is what needed to happen. Maybe this goofy pretty-boy outside was the solution and hitting him with my car wasn't the best idea. It finally registered that I'd been staring at them when Delilah walked into the lobby and her eyes were locked with mine. One look into those eyes and a traitor part of me said a prayer that the guy outside was just a friend.

My phone rang out through the fog my thoughts, alerting me to Mr. Kuroda's arrival in the underground garage. I watched Delilah step onto the elevator before making my way to the private entrance that led up from the garage.

"Konnichiwa Kuroda-San," I said, bowing slightly to my friend as he emerged.

"Konnichiwa, Monroe-San."

He spoke fluent English, but I wanted to make an effort while he was a guest in my city. We continued to make small talk in Japanese the entire ride up to the executive floor while I continued to push Delilah to the back recesses of my mind in an attempt to focus. Once Mr. Kuroda was settled in his suite and his itinerary for the next couple of days was confirmed with Peter, who would manage all his transportation and reservations, I returned downstairs to prepare myself for the networking meeting I had that evening.

Later, when my eyes began to blur from reading dozens of emails, I decided to take a break. I'd been in the lounge for less than a minute when I was joined by Delilah. Her scent of coconut combined with flowers consumed the room, and I had to concentrate on blocking out the inappropriate thoughts I was having about her. I reminded myself quickly that both of us wanted to keep things civil and professional. I would politely comment on her date, let her see that I was fine with it, platonic to the core, and we'd both be on the same page.

"Your boyfriend sure knows how to make an exit. Guess round two of the blind dates really paid off," I spat at her before I could stop myself.

Smooth, asshole.

I froze for a moment when I realized what I'd actually said and then made a hasty exit before Delilah could ask me to clarify what I meant, mainly because I didn't have a fucking clue. Somehow, I'd come across as a jealous asshole, rather than a curious coworker. I was actually a bit surprised she didn't throw something at me or shout a remark back.

I should have known better with Delilah.

As I was leaving at the end of the day, Leslie let me know that my noon appointment with the photographer the next day had been rescheduled for five in the goddamn morning. Delilah had access to my entire schedule, so she knew about my dinner tonight as well as the budget meeting I had tomorrow afternoon, which would now be done on about three hours of sleep.

"That seems a bit extreme for retaliation," I mumbled as Leslie passed me the directions to the photo shoot.

"I'm sorry, what?" she asked, confused at my rambling. I shook my head in response and made my way to the elevator, making the mental note that it seemed Delilah didn't like to play fair.

Wednesday morning, or what still felt like Tuesday night to me, came around and I was hurting. Not only was the photo shoot at an ungodly hour, but it also entailed me changing into three different suits for promotional pictures that would be used for press kits, the website and god knows what else. The makeup woman had to work at covering up the shadows under my eyes from a lack of sleep and a slight hangover. Thankfully things moved along quickly, and I was already changing back into my clothes when Pax showed up for his session.

"You want to explain to me why you *had* to have the first time slot?" he asked incredulously, tossing his jacket over a chair in the wardrobe room.

"What are you talking about?"

"When I found out this thing was moved up, I asked to have the first appointment, so I could just come straight here after closing the club. But I was told that you just *had* to have it, so I've been dicking around for the past three hours. What the fuck man?"

"You could have gone home and cleaned up," I said, noting the club smell coming from his general direction.

"Once I go home, I can't resist my beautiful bed, and I'll be out for the rest of the day. You know this. Now, why are you here so early?"

"I pissed Delilah off," I said.

"What'd you do now?"

"I'm pretty sure I insulted the guy she went on a date with yesterday."

"Was it the same guy from the bar?"

"No it was-" I stopped and turned quickly to look at Pax in shock.

"What? You didn't think I would put it together that Dee is the mystery babe from the other night?" he said, sitting on the leather sofa and smiling his goofy grin.

"How did you know?" He was right, I didn't think he'd put it together.

"Give me some credit man. I may not be an expert in a lot of things, but sexual tension is definitely one of them. From the way you two were carrying on the other day in that meeting, I would say you're at stage three on the sexual tension scale. And there's no way you could be there after only knowing each other for five minutes, just not possible."

"Stage three?" I asked, confused.

"Yep, stage three. There are five stages of sexual tension," he said, holding up his huge hand for effect. "But once you hit stage five, it's only a matter of time before you end up naked and sweaty together. And you guys are at stage three for sure. Stage four will happen directly after she sticks her tongue in your mouth for the first time."

I was suddenly reminded of slamming Delilah into the wall of her office and grinding myself into her.

"Busted!" Pax said, pointing a finger at me and grinning like an idiot again. "Damn bro, you didn't even make it a week before playing grab ass with her?"

"I just kissed her, we didn't sleep together," I said with a sigh, flopping down next to him and running both hands through my hair.

"No shit. If you'd fucked her, you wouldn't be this worked up. But there's no turning back from stage four, you'll either be fucking like bunnies soon, or you'll kill each other in an attempt to fight it."

"It certainly looks like we're erring on the side of the later. I don't know what to do," I sighed. "I still think Delilah's whole purpose here is complete bullshit. Plus, she's completely irritating and frustrating and..."

"Hot," Pax interjected.

"Yes," I growled out. "Extremely. The whole thing is maddening. Pax, I can't fuck her if we work together; that just won't work out and you know it. Not to mention dad is already pissed I disagree with her being here, how do you think he'd take it if he found out I was nailing her, too? Probably wouldn't help my chances with him very much. What would you do in my shoes?"

"Fuck if I know. I never shit where I eat, so I can't help you, bro."

"Thanks."

I spent my drive to the hotel convincing myself that Pax's theory was utterly incorrect where Delilah and I were concerned. Yes, we'd crossed a line the other day. But she'd obviously seen it as a mistake, and I was doing everything I could to make sure we never reached that point again. She was dating other men, and I definitely had plenty of women that I could call to satisfy my needs.

Stage four be damned.

Later that day I was still repeating my anti-Delilah mantra and heading out to grab lunch when she slipped into the elevator with me. As she brushed past me, I was once again engulfed in her warm scent and had the intense urge to touch her. In that brief moment, I hated her for being so alluring and tempting me the way she did.

We greeted each other briefly before I took several steadying breaths to gather my wits while I watched the floor numbers countdown.

Has this elevator always been this damn slow?

I focused all of my mental energy on remembering why Delilah and I should avoid each other and the many reasons why I shouldn't give in to my lust. But just like in the lounge yesterday, her presence was assaulting, and her hair was begging to be touched. Surely it was only because I was exhausted that I found her so hard to resist when no other woman had haunted me like this. It was then that I remembered my morning, and once again lashed out like a child before I could stop myself. In the moment, I decided to tell her I couldn't meet with her when the truth was that I could probably make our meeting work in my calendar after all. But I needed more time to clear my head since I'd become such a basket case where she was concerned.

She may be calm and calculating during our exchanges, but everything up until this moment had taught me that I couldn't trust myself around Delilah.

Our exchange turned tenser as I distractedly listened to the beeps of each floor, counting down to my exit. If she wanted to play, we could play. I too could fight dirty. And later that day, my moment arrived. I was sitting in my office after a budget meeting when Leslie buzzed on the intercom.

"There's a Mr. Wilcox from the Portland Daily on line one for you." I took a moment to wonder at what the local paper would be calling for and then smiled to myself.

Please be calling for a quote.

"Sure," I said into the intercom and picked up my phone. "Samuel Monroe."

"Mr. Monroe, this is Jason Wilcox from the Portland Daily."

"What can I do for you, Mr. Wilcox?"

"Well, we have a press release here for the Hotel Monroe's involvement in the museum's fundraiser this weekend, and I was hoping to get a quote from you regarding your company's involvement." My smile grew at the fortuitousness of his call. Here was my chance to send Dee a message.

✺

Delilah

Thursday morning, I was once again dreaming of Samuel. His powerful hands were gripping my naked hips as his tongue snaked along my collarbone, and just before he finally slipped inside of me, the potent smell of coffee overtook my senses and my eyes fluttered open of their own accord.

"Wakey, wakey," Jules sang, waving a steaming mug in front of me.

"Ugh, what time is it?" I groaned. Jules was never cheerful this early in the day.

"Just after eight," she said, stepping away from my bed quickly as she anticipated the panic induced flailing that began.

"Holy mother of god!" I screamed, bolting for my closet. "How the hell did I sleep this late?!"

"Well you've been *very* busy this past couple of nights," she called from my room while I hopped up and down into a pair of slacks in the walk-in closet and ripped the first shirt I saw off of a hanger.

"What are you talking about?" I asked as I jammed myself into the blouse, not paying attention to whether or not it was on backward.

"You've been extremely vocal in your sleep, more so than I remember you being when we were roommates." I stopped midstride on my way to the adjoining bathroom, shirt pulled halfway down my torso, and gaped at Jules.

"What have I been saying?" I asked quietly, knowing and dreading the answer.

"It's actually just been a lot of moaning and screaming of the word 'yes.' Although I did catch the word 'elevator' last night..." she trailed off, tapping her chin in thought. I rushed into the bathroom in an effort to hide my spreading blush from Jules.

"Oh, and there have been several screams of 'Sam' I might add," she called after me. My head poked back out to look at her, toothbrush dangling from my mouth and comb in hand. Jules laughed at my frozen state. "I'm only kidding, I just wanted to see your face. But Dee, have there been more make-out sessions with that asshole?" She was still smiling, but there was no missing the tension in her voice.

"Wo! Wot ah awl!" I said through toothpaste. Jules just stared at me until I removed the toothbrush. "No, not at all," I repeated. She examined my face carefully for a moment before crossing the room to hand me the coffee.

"Alright," she said with a sigh. "Well, I may not like the real version, but kudos to Dream Sam for making you scream like a banshee."

The more she heard about our interactions during the week, the more Jules-the-protector had made it clear that she didn't like Samuel. She couldn't figure out his angle, and our game of pushing each other's buttons made her nervous, especially knowing why I was hired by Charles. I had to agree with that last part; I couldn't tell if I was relieved or depressed at the thought Samuel hated me. We were a bit volatile, and I was still on edge waiting for his next move. Something had slowly shifted during the week, and I realized that a part of me was enjoying the challenge that Samuel presented. We were still scowling at one another when we crossed paths, but the hostility never reached Samuel's eyes and I knew it was the same for me. Our torment was slowly starting to feel like a game.

Such as last night; while I was waiting for the elevator, Samuel passed by and greeted me with a low "shrew," but did so with his sexy smirk. I replied with an equally quiet "whore" and heard a chuckle come from his retreating form. Each day I walked into the office with no clue as to what to expect from him next. And at the same time, each day my anticipation to see him grew.

By some miracle, I was walking into my office twenty minutes later.

"Sorry I'm late," I said to Mae for the second time this week.

"Um, Dee?" she said nervously, following me into my office and eyeing me warily.

"What's up?"

"I was sorting through the daily press and thought you should see this," she said handing me the Life & Style section of the Portland Daily newspaper. The feature article was on the museum's weekend-long fundraiser, kicking off with the black-tie dinner the Monroe family would be attending tomorrow evening. Throughout the city there would be scattered events all designed to raise money for businesses in the arts and community organizations. There was a community festival on the waterfront, a youth fair at the zoo, and an expanded Farmer's Market at Portland State on Sunday.

I skimmed the beginning of the article before looking back up at Mae with a confused shrug.

"Third paragraph," she said. I returned to the article and read.

The emerging Hotel Monroe has contributed heavily to the weekend's events, buying a table at the benefit dinner as well as sponsoring a booth at both the Youth Fair and Community Festival.

I smiled at that. Dominic had let me know earlier in the week that he'd pulled together both sponsorships at the last minute. We worked together to get that information out to the press as soon as possible; I still couldn't figure him out and sensed he didn't really like me, but we worked well together at least.

"Keep reading," Mae mumbled when I smiled.

When asked about the hotel's involvement, General Manager Samuel Monroe said, "It's great to be giving back to the community and helping smaller businesses get their start. It turns out, we're sponsoring the artists' booth at the festival, but I was really hoping we would get the Free Clinic's booth. Keeping the community as STD free as possible truly enhances my social life."

BANG

"Delilah!" Mae screamed when my forehead slammed onto the desk.

"Ugh," I groaned. "Why didn't we *know* they were contacting him for a quote?"

I looked up at a sheepish looking Mae.

"I haven't been able to get the editor on the phone yet," she said. This first week we were frantically contacting publications to let them know that all press would be running through our department. It wasn't a foolproof system, but it had the potential to avoid things like this. Leave it to Samuel to follow through on his promise to get back at me, ten-fold. He told me that he'd be returning the favor and getting into my 'good graces' for the early photo shoot, and my instincts had been right to suspect it would be outlandish.

"But THIS," I shouted, shaking the newspaper violently and continuing the inner diatribe out loud, "is *overkill* compared to the 5AM start time I gave him! He's fighting fire with napalm!"

Mae stared at me in confused shock.

"I can call the paper and try-"

"No," I cut her off and sighed. "It's too late to undo any of the real damage."

I groaned again thinking about what Charles would think when he read this. Day four into my new position and the local paper had quoted Samuel regarding his continued evasion of gonorrhea. He wasn't just messing with me; whether he knew it or not, he was messing with my reputation, career, and future. Samuel had taken our game to a whole new playing field.

And then inspiration struck.

I laughed a bit maniacally, causing Mae to take a slow step backward.

Fine. He wanted to play? I could *play*.

ELEVEN

Samuel

"SHE SIGNED ME UP FOR A FUCKING GOLF TOURNAMENT!"

Pax replied to my announcement with his booming laughter that bounced off the walls of his small office. I slammed the door behind me and sank into the leather chair in front of his desk, my forehead falling into my right palm. I couldn't help but chuckle in defeat.

Touché, Delilah Sheppard. You win this round.

From the moment I read the Portland Daily article that morning, I'd been waiting on pins and needles for her response. When I'd gotten to my office earlier, I flipped through my messages and made a few phone calls before picking up the Life & Style section of the paper Leslie had left on my desk for me. I scanned the pages, looking for the hotel's name; I didn't have to look far.

"Oh, shit!" I hadn't realized that I'd actually screamed out loud until Leslie came rushing into my office in a panic.

"Are you ok?" she asked as her eyes danced around the office, trying to find the fire. I groaned at the knot in my stomach, which grew with each realization of what was to come of this blatant misquote. Not only from Dee, but from my father.

"Can you get Jason Wilcox at the Portland Daily on the phone?"

This was bad.

Delilah was going to be pissed. Charles was going to read me the riot act. And I was going to murder that piece of shit reporter. He had taken what I'd said completely out of context; I had been shooting for a cloak and dagger sort of dig at Delilah's assessment of my character, and what he'd printed was more of a grenade tossed over a fence.

After monotonous small talk about the weekend's events, the reporter had asked if I was planning on visiting the festival and supporting any of the organizations personally. I hadn't planned on attending any of the festivals this weekend, but I obviously couldn't say *that*, so instead I replied, "As a fan of the arts, I support all of these organizations. And as for the community outreach groups and resources, I think we can't have enough of that kind of thing for folks. Like the downtown clinic that's opening up; let's face it, STD testing is important in everyone's social life these days, am I right?"

Being taken out of context didn't even cover the creative liberties this jackass had taken with my remarks.

"I'm still trying to reach Mr. Wilcox," Leslie said as she reentered my office. "But Ms. Sheppard's office just delivered this for you."

I took the envelope from her carefully and listened for a ticking noise. When it appeared that I wasn't holding a letter bomb, I opened it to read Delilah's response to my STD quote.

Dear Mr. Samuel Monroe,

Pumpkin Ridge Golf Club welcomes you to this year's charity golf tournament.

Thirty minutes later, I was in Pax's office and internally admitting defeat while he laughed his ass off at the latest round in my game with Delilah.

"Bro, did you tell her how much you hate golf? Is that why she set this up?" Pax asked, flipping through the information packet for the golf tournament happening later this month. I couldn't help but smile. It appeared that Delilah also remembered the conversation we'd had before the war had begun.

"Yes. She knows I hate the game," I said.

"I have to hand it to her, she's got spunk. I like her."

"I know you do, you've said that a dozen times this week."

"You must have pissed her off something fierce. What did you do?" Pax asked, wiggling his eyebrows.

"I made an STD comment to the paper that was taken *completely* out of context. No doubt she assumed that I did that shit on purpose and went overboard when she reacted."

"Wow," Pax said with a laugh. "Talk about the pot calling the kettle black."

"What are you talking about?"

"I'm talking about you two being so similar it's frightening."

"How the fuck can you say that?" I asked incredulously.

"You guys are so much in sync in your miscommunication, that you're *actually* speaking the same language whether you realize it or not." Pax laughed at his own comment, but the humor fell on deaf ears with me.

"We're not in sync at all. In fact, she drives me insane if you must know," I said sitting forward. "Let me tell you what a clusterfuck this woman is."

And then I told him everything, illustrating in detail the nightmare I'd fallen into since Monday. I told Pax about pressing Delilah into her office wall and our subdued fight in the elevator days later. I told him about her plans to fire Carl and the talent without even meeting with them, and about Emma violently defending Delilah to the point of tears. He heard all about me having no clue as to whether Delilah was the real version of herself or if she was actually the shrew. I told him about the preppy asshole that grabbed her ass and how he'd simultaneously been a beacon of hope as well as a call to violence for me. And finally, I explained to Pax that no matter how hard Delilah and I tried to undermine and infuriate one another, our game still entertained the shit out of me. He listened to every detail in silence, and when I sank back into my chair with a resigned sigh, he finally spoke.

"Are you finished?" he asked calmly and then leaned forward onto his elbows resting on the desk between us when I nodded in reply.

"Has it ever occurred to you, that all of this bipolar chatter going on in your head would shut the fuck up if you would just *talk* to her?" He leaned back and chuckled to himself, returning to the golf tournament brochure on his desk. I went back to rubbing my temples and wondering why I thought my little brother was going to have any more insight and advice than that.

I'd been in a silent funk since leaving Pax's office earlier in the day. It's not that his advice had been illogical; it was simply improbable. How the hell was I supposed to strike up a conversation with Delilah about how she was driving me insane

without it turning into a fight? Let alone, an argument that my
father would hear about?

That afternoon, I was pouring myself a cup of coffee in
the lounge when I heard the approaching click of heels on tile. It
stopped suddenly before turning to see Delilah standing in the
doorway with the cutest smirk on her face. Her expression was
both timid and smug, and despite myself, I smiled back.

"I thought I was the only one around here that drank
coffee in the afternoon," I said, turning back toward the counter.
For a moment I thought she may leave, but the sound of her
heels resumed, and she approached behind me.

"What can I say, I'm a caffeine junky." I looked down at
her as she came to stand next to me, tilting her head aside and
fighting a smile.

"You're dying to laugh about it, so I'll let you know that
I got the information packet for the golf tournament," I said,
turning toward her. "Well played."

She let a snicker escaped as she tried to cover up her
laughter as a cough, quite unsuccessfully.

"Oh good. I'm glad you got everything so quickly," she
replied, her words dripping with sarcasm and causing Pax's
words to surface involuntarily. I set my mug on the counter as
she was pouring one of her own.

"I'm assuming that was payback for the Portland Daily
article?"

That got her attention. She set her coffee down loudly
and turned quickly to face me, finally making eye contact.

"What the hell were you thinking? Were you *that* pissed
off about the photo shoot? Do you have any idea how much of
an idiot you make me look like when you say shit like that? Not
to mention how asinine *you* look? I can't even begin to-"

"I was misquoted," I interrupted loudly over her rant.

Delilah blinked at me a couple of times before speaking
again. Apparently, she *had* assumed I said those things on
purpose.

"How badly were you misquoted?" she asked slowly,
eying me carefully.

"That asshole listed off a bunch of booths and asked my
opinion of them," I explained while gesticulating a bit wildly.
"When it came to the free clinic, I said something about STD

testing being important for everyone. He *completely* twisted my words around."

She sighed and squinted as she rubbed her temple roughly. It occurred to me that it was the exact same move I did when I was frustrated.

Damn it Pax, you seed-planting mother fucker.

"Wilcox is new at the paper, which probably makes him a bit overzealous to get his first big article noticed. I'm actually not that surprised, now that I think about it," she said quietly.

"How do you know that?" I was a bit surprised at her knowledge of the soon-to-be-dead Jason Wilcox.

"Because it's my job!" she exclaimed and punctuated it with a frustrated stomp of her foot. "How many times do I have to tell you that I know what I'm doing?" She took a slow breath and continued, "I'm sorry for assuming you said all that stuff on purpose. The possibility of a misquote probably should have occurred to me. No, it definitely should have occurred to me."

"Damn straight," I gloated and laughed when she rolled her eyes.

"But Samuel, you really should avoid the phrase 'sexually transmitted disease' at all costs in the press. You know that, right?"

"Well, *that* part may have been on purpose," I said sheepishly, wishing we could go back to the part of the conversation where I was right, and she was wrong.

"Seriously? Just because I made you get up early?" she asked, rolling her eyes.

"Oh, come on! You knew I had that networking meeting the night before, *and* the budget meeting the next afternoon, which by the way, was tons of fun on three hours of sleep."

Delilah gasped quietly, her hand covering her mouth for a second.

"Shit! You had a budget meeting the next day?"

"I…er... wait, you knew that."

"Of course I didn't know that! I wouldn't mess around with something like that! You thought I did that on purpose?" she asked, raising both eyebrows in shock.

"Well, I… Yeah," I admitted lamely with a shrug. "You have access to my schedule."

"You jackass. Just because I have access doesn't mean I checked it and did that intentionally. I may have wanted to goad you, but I'm not that unprofessional."

"I'm sorry," I said, feeling slightly stupid. "I just assumed you were upset because of what I said about your...that guy."

"Well that *was* a rather rash assumption you made there," she said, obviously trying not to laugh.

"Not a boyfriend?" I asked before I could stop myself.

"Not a boyfriend. He's an old friend."

I was annoyed at the spike of relief I felt, but it was overshadowed by the clarity this conversation was giving me. Pax was right; talking to Delilah was silencing the roar of confusion in my head.

"Man, this is sad. I used to be so poised and logical," Delilah mumbled, breaking me from my thoughts. She laughed and turned back to her coffee, emptying a sugar packet as I slid the soy milk toward her.

"Just so you know, I'm not usually this bad with people," I told her.

"I'd believe that," she replied, sucking her thumb into her mouth to catch some errant soy milk. I almost groaned out loud. "You were right about Pax. He took to the management coaching really well and will probably get better results from Carl than I would."

"You talked with him about that?" I had to admit that I was a bit surprised she had followed through on my favor.

"Yep, I'm having him meet with human resources once a week to get training on his management style. Should help him get better over time," she said.

I examined Delilah's face while she took a sip of coffee. There wasn't a trace of sarcasm in her words; she appeared sincere.

"What?" she asked when I continued to stare.

"Nothing. I'm just... surprised."

Delilah smirked at me. "You were right; he deserves the chance to manage his own people."

"Can you say that first part again?" I asked, giving her a lazy smile.

"Not a chance," she said, turning to leave. "Oh, and by the way." Delilah spun back around and took a step closer so that her body was almost touching mine; a couple of random strands of her hair brushed my shoulder. I almost put a hand on her hip to pull her in and close the small distance between us, but she spoke first.

"Asking Emma to do that pick-pocketing stunt, with her condition? Not cool, Samuel," she said in a low whisper. Delilah shook her head in disappointment and made her way out of the lounge, leaving me staring after her wide-eyed and mouth agape.

Emma had told Delilah about her condition.

The gravity of that fact struck me like a ton of bricks. That combined with Delilah's apparent sensitivity for my little sister's secret destroyed any remaining shred of resistance I had for her joining our team. I still had misgivings about her job, and I was sure at some point I would battle the shrew again. But all of that took a backseat to my growing respect for the woman.

Later that night, I had just walked out of Delilah's empty office when she emerged from a conference room down the hall and started toward me. We passed in the hallway and traded smirks.

"Goodnight, Samuel."

"Night, Delilah."

Just before I turned the corner, I could hear her musical laughter coming from her office, and I smiled.

◦◦◦

Delilah

Thursday had been a long and surprising day. I'd started the workday enraged at Samuel and was now ending it wondering if we were becoming *friends*. I was still riding the high that had come from clearing the air with him that afternoon when I passed him in the hallway at the end of the day. We greeted each other, and the scowls were thankfully absent, as were the terms of offense.

I stepped into my office and gasped at the sight in front of me.

There on my desk, in a large ceramic pot, was the ugliest plant I had ever seen. The spindly leaves had a shredded look to them and alternated in color between pea soup green and baby poop brown.

I couldn't help the laughter that erupted from me.

Samuel's message was loud and clear. He was still going to be a pain in my ass, but at least now, I was welcome.

TWELVE

Delilah

"Miss Sheppard? Your party has already arrived. This way please."

I followed the hostess through the restaurant to meet Charles for our lunch meeting. We'd agreed that every Friday we would have touch base meetings, during which I would fill him in on the week's activities. This first meeting would be happening over lunch so that I would finally be able to meet his wife, Rachel Monroe.

As I reached the back of the restaurant, I spotted Charles at a table by the window overlooking Pioneer Square. Next to him was a stunning woman with long auburn hair and striking green eyes.

"Ah, Dee," Charles said, standing to greet me and motioning me toward the chair across from them. "Dee Sheppard, allow me to introduce my beautiful wife, and the brains behind the operation, Rachel Monroe." Rachel playfully swatted his chest at his boastful introduction but gave him a loving smile in return.

"It's wonderful to meet you finally," she said, sitting back in her chair as Charles draped his arm over the back of it. Her accent was barely detectable, just as you would expect from a British woman that had moved to the States when she was a young teenager.

"Likewise," I said. "I've heard so many wonderful things about you, and your reputation in the non-profit community is impressive."

"I've heard great things about you as well; not only from Charles but also from my children. Emma is quite taken with you, and I'm not sure what you've done to Pax, but he seems to revere you," she said with a laugh. I smiled politely and tried to ignore the fact that she hadn't said anything about Samuel. I decided that it was probably best if he hadn't mentioned me to his mother during the past week; god only knew what kind of horrible impression she might have of me by now.

"How was your first week?" Charles asked.

"Eventful," I said, trying not to sound too surprised that this assignment was taking some actual work. "Everything seems to be on track with the press we've lined up. I managed to rework that negative article in the Daily and may be able to get some feature interviews in major publications earlier than I thought possible. I was worried about pulling off Pax's charity event so quickly, but Emma has been amazing."

Rachel snorted softly. "You should have seen that child plan her birthday parties every year. She gets her extravagance from Charles's side of the family."

Charles hailed from a long line of entertainers. His father had been a movie star in the 1950s, and his brother was now a Broadway producer. Charles had broken with tradition by going into the hospitality industry rather than entertainment.

"Well, she's been a great asset. In fact, everyone's been very…welcoming."

"You've met with everyone individually then?" Charles asked.

"Nearly. Samuel's meeting had to be rescheduled for next week, and I'm meeting with Dominic this afternoon."

Charles and Rachel exchanged a thoughtful look.

"How are things going with Samuel?" Rachel asked. "Charles told me that your first meeting was a bit strained."

If only she knew how strained we'd really been in that meeting, not to mention since then.

"We're finding our way," I said, trying my best to sound confident. Truth be told, I had no idea how Samuel and I would get along from one day to the next. For now, we seemed to be in a mutual cease-fire, but I wasn't getting too comfortable in that just yet.

"Based on his comments in the Portland Daily yesterday, I'd say that he's testing your limits," Charles said, raising both eyebrows at me.

Damn.

I was worried that Charles would take Samuel's quote to mean that I was slacking on the job, and it appeared as though that may be the case.

"He was misquoted," I insisted. "Regardless, I've already spoken to him about the article, as well as directing press to me in the future. We've reached an understanding- "

Rachel's laughter cut me off while Charles raised his water glass to his lips in a poor attempt to hide a smile of his own.

"I don't doubt that you cracked the whip on Samuel," Rachel said. "I've heard about what you do to clients that misbehave like that, misquote or not."

Confusion set in and I'm sure my face reflected as much.

"Didn't you once make a client attend University simply because he mocked education in an interview?" she asked.

The story wasn't false. Early in my career, I'd represented a pop singer that had been quoted in an article as saying that he felt his years in high school had been, "like, a total waste of time, man," because he was making millions of dollars now without the assistance of his diploma. Before the anticipated outcry of his fans' parents, I registered him for online classes at a University that he could complete from the road. In a follow-up interview, he advocated education because you never know when a back-up plan will be needed. I was surprised that Rachel even knew about that; it had been ages ago, and it's not like my name was attached to it in the press.

"I didn't know you were so knowledgeable of my resume," I said.

"Dee, darling, do you think I would have agreed to this plan without learning everything available about you?" Rachel asked earnestly.

"Agreed to this plan?" I was stuck in this conversation. On the one hand, I had no idea how much she knew of the strategy we had laid out. But I also didn't want to get my boss in trouble with his wife by letting on that he really hadn't mentioned her in the early planning stages. It was clear the mixing of family and business started at the top, but what else could you expect from a family business.

"Of course I-" Rachel stopped herself and turned sharply to eye Charles. "You cheeky bastard!"

Despite my confusion at the situation, I couldn't help but laugh as Rachel playfully shoved Charles, who looked at the table with a shameful expression.

"He told you this was all his idea, didn't he?" Rachel asked while pointing at Charles.

I pursed my lips and looked between them silently, unsure what the smart move would be in this conversation. Both of them may have been smiling, but I still wasn't planning on getting between Mr. & Mrs. Boss in an argument.

"I didn't credit *anyone* with the idea, love. I just told Dee about the position and..." Charles stopped talking when Rachel gave him a pointed look that reminded me of Emma. Her daughter may have gotten her extravagance from her father, but she certainly inherited her mother's ability to cripple the male sex.

"Dee," Rachel said, turning to me with a gentle expression. "I was the one to agree to the PR piece of the hotel's sale, but not before approving of the person they sent to whip my children into shape."

I opened my mouth to respond but thought twice of it. I had questions, but I didn't want to say too much.

"Is it safe to assume," I started slowly, clearing my throat more than once, trying to buy myself some time to find right the words. "I'm assuming, even though you weren't a part of our planning process, that you share my...and Charles' specific...goals?"

Rachel arched an eyebrow and shook her head with confusion.

"Are you in...alignment with the strategy he and I talked about?"

Please don't make me spell it out.

"Aha," Rachel said with a smile, placing a hand on Charles' arm, "I do believe Delilah is subtly asking if I know why you *actually* hired her and what you have planned for Samuel."

Charles smiled sadly and nodded; I had learned by now that this was not his favorite topic and whenever we had discussed it our planning and strategy meetings, it was clear that sadness blanketed his motives.

"Yes, Dee," Charles said solemnly. "Rachel knows you're here to help us fire Sam."

A little over an hour later, Dominic strolled into my office for our meeting. He was wearing his typical uniform of faded jeans, sneakers and a dress shirt, although his standard lazy grin was missing.

"Dee," he said mechanically as he dropped into the chair in front of my desk.

"Hi, Dominic," I replied. It had been a long week, and I didn't really have it in me to spar with anyone else. Thankfully, Dominic wasn't a PR priority or problem; I only had logistics to work out with our VP of Sales. "I don't have anything to go over with you other than the confirmed VIP's attending our upcoming events, as well as some marketing pieces that I'm adding to the schedule." I slid the appropriate reports across the desk to him. "Pax's racing event will be up first."

Dominic flipped absentmindedly through the paperwork I handed him, looking impatient and annoyed.

"If there's a problem-"

"No, it's all fine," Dominic interrupted. "These marketing reports have actually already been approved."

With a shove, the papers were sent forcefully back me across the desk, which I caught with a slap of my palm. I stared at Dominic with my unspoken questions about his hostility while he glared back with his own animosity and silent accusations.

"Dominic? Do *we* have a problem?"

He turned in his chair, gripped the door behind him and flung it shut with a slam, making me jump at the noise.

"I want to talk about Emma," he seethed.

"Ok," I said with a sharp nod, unsure what he was so upset about and admittedly a little afraid of him.

"I know that you know," he said.

My face gave away nothing. I assumed he was referring to their relationship, but I wouldn't let on about anything that Emma had told me earlier in the week.

"She told me you know about us."

"Ah, yes, she did tell me," I said, trying not give anything away, and instead silently going through everything I knew about Dominic. I knew the story about Charles recruiting him, and his background with building brands and businesses, but not much more than that; pretty much whatever was on his business profile was all I knew of the man. He was a closed book, and for some reason, he made me nervous. I couldn't put my finger on it, but I was never at ease when I was with Dominic, regardless of whether or not we were actually conversing, if he was in the room, I was unsettled. And now more than ever, he had me unsettled; his anger was confusing.

"I want to be abundantly clear," he said in a low, even tone, "that no one outside of the Monroe family knows about us being romantically involved. And more importantly, that's how it's going to stay. Are we clear?"

"Dominic, there's no need to get aggressive-"

"This isn't aggressive." It was a cold, deadpanned statement, but the steel in his eyes read like a threat. "I know your type. Unlike these guys around here, I've worked with publicists running communications for an entire business before. These guys may be worried about you bossing them around or telling them what to say, but I know what you're capable of, I know there's an agenda. There's always an agenda."

He was right, and trying to argue that he was wrong was a waste of time.

"Regardless of whatever my strategy with Charles may be," I hedged, "there's no reason for you to feel threatened by it, at all."

"It's not your strategy with Charles that concerns me, it's how you choose to get there that has my attention, now that you know my biggest secret." He leaned forward and put his elbows on his knees, pointing a single finger at me. "If it came down to it, I wouldn't put it past you to leak a story to help drive whatever narrative you're trying to achieve here."

Fuck.

That landed on the bullseye with a thud. He was absolutely right; if needed, I would run with any story that might make things play out faster and better in the press. I'd done it before, and I wouldn't hesitate to do it again. But there *was* a line.

"Certain stories go into the metaphorical vault and are never to be leaked," I said, looking at him pointedly. "Ethically"

"Right," he said, nodding and clearly catching my meaning. "Emma's condition. Yes, I would think that her condition qualifies for your vault," he said sardonically. "So, let me put it this way, my relationship with Emma, gets bundled with that fact, and it's all locked away in there as well."

I studied Dominic's face and demeanor, trying to deduce where this seriousness and intensity was coming from. It felt like overkill to me, but to Dominic, this was clearly a secret so private and sacred, he'd all but threaten me if I ever exposed it. I'd have to play things carefully with Dominic, gaining his trust and getting to the root of why this was so important to him.

"If it gets out that I'm with Emma, there's no scenario in which I don't look like the guy nailing the boss's daughter to get ahead. It'll appear as though I'm trying to circumvent Sam, and that Emma is a hapless pawn. Any way you shake it, her and I both look bad."

Holy shit, that was blunt. And correct.

No psychological warfare needed here, no corporate espionage required to uncover Dominic's true motivations, he'd laid them all out on the table for me in a stunning display. And it was in that moment I suddenly realized why Dominic always made me uneasy.

There was no subtext with Dominic; he said what he meant and meant what he said. It was unnerving.

"I'm not going to say anything about you and Emma," I said, swallowing hard and trying to remember that this was *my* meeting, after all. "I understand your hesitation and trepidation about my line of work, but take solace in the fact that, at the *very least*, outing his daughter as having a relationship with a VP really wouldn't make my boss very happy. If you don't trust my morals, at least trust my motivations. I'm here to execute on Charles' priorities. Period."

"Good," he said, leaning back in his chair and taking on an air of nonchalance that made my head spin. "Anything else we need to go over?"

I blinked at him a couple of times, but he just stared back.

"No. As I said, I only had those marketing reports and VIP lists for you," I said, eyeing him cautiously.

"Good," he repeated as he stood and made his way to the door. "Let me know if you need anything else from me." He walked out without so much as a glance over his shoulder.

Pax, Samuel, and a handful of executive employees had been attempting to manipulate and beat the 'shrew' all week, trying to show me who was really boss around here. I'd seen them all coming with their typical complaints and their usual behaviors. But without even being detected on my radar, Dominic had swept in and knocked me on my ass.

Mae and I wrapped up the day early so we could go home and get ready for the fundraiser dinner. We'd both be walking the press line with the Monroe group and needed to be dressed accordingly. She'd left an hour earlier, but I'd been stuck catching up on paperwork after my long lunch with Charles and then expanded, confusing meeting with Dominic.

When I finally made my way to the elevator, I found Samuel already waiting for it. A part of me wanted to tell him all about my meeting with Dominic and ask him what the hell was going on with that guy, but then I remembered myself, and that a connection with Samuel would only make firing him that much harder in the end.

"Hello, Samuel," I said, stopping next to him. He turned to me and smiled.

"Delilah."

The elevator opened with a ding and he motioned me ahead of him. The doors closed and once again I found myself trapped within this small space with him, both of us staring up at the descending floor numbers in silence.

"Did you like the elkhorn fern?" he asked, turning to look at me.

I snorted involuntarily and looked up at him. "Is that what that hideous thing is called?" Samuel laughed and shook his head. "Thank you," I said quietly, smirking up at him and acknowledging his kind, albeit odd, gesture.

"Working a half day?" he asked, motioning toward my laptop bag.

"No, I'm heading off to nag at people, destroy some fun, you know…random acts of shrewery. And you?"

"Judging a wet t-shirt contest and then raiding a sorority house."

The elevator opened to the lobby and I turned to look at Samuel, but he was already staring down at me.

"I'm sure I'll being seeing you in a couple of hours," he said with a wink.

"Oh, you can count on it."

We exited the elevators and set off in opposite directions. As I reached the front entrance, I turned to look over my shoulder and discovered Samuel looking back at me the same way. We traded smiles just before he disappeared into the restaurant and I pushed through the door. The weather was still warm and sunny, despite being September in Portland, and I started the six-block walk to Jules' apartment with a spring in my step and a smile I couldn't shake. What had started as a truce and reprieve from the battle, was turning into something felt like friendship. Well, if I was being honest with myself, a friendship with a healthy dose of flirting. And I let myself swim in the warm emotional waters of that new connection with Samuel for all of one block's walk before I felt the weight of the whole situation slip down over me and extract all the joy I was feeling in that moment.

The reality was that in less than a month, I would have to sit down with Samuel and tell him he was fired. I'd have to say to him that his father would rather sell the business than give it to him. The fact that Samuel and I were getting closer and friendlier only meant that my job was getting harder, not easier. Hating each other would have made this so much simpler.

Despite all the reasons and logic, however, a little voice inside of me said that I would never be able to hate Samuel Monroe. In fact, I was actually at risk of falling for him. But sooner rather than later, he was going to hate me. I'd see to that.

THIRTEEN

Delilah

Jules' show, *Ultimate Torque*, was currently filming its fourth season and had already been renewed for a fifth. The show, which centered around her rebuilding and restoring vintage cars while dressed immodestly, to say the least, was never really a career aspiration for her. It had been the result of Jules finally embracing a stereotype she'd been bumping up against since college. She'd been one of only a handful of female engineering majors in school, which leant itself to a whole cluster of challenges, but it wasn't until she graduated and landed a job at a tech company in Portland as an engineer that she really dealt with adversity. Working on cars was supposed to be an outlet, a hobby that used her skills, let her get her hands dirty, and took her mind off of everyone telling her she could make so much more money if she went into modeling. Instead, Jules dealt with just as much misogyny at auto part stores, car auctions, and junkyards. Even in her hobbies, she was told she was 'too pretty' to be good at something like that.

Then one fateful night, after a bottle of wine and Jules reaching her chauvinistic limit, she opened her webcam and filmed a transmission rebuild tutorial, in a bikini. She uploaded it to YouTube, and the rest is history. Not only did Jules end up with an unbelievable number of followers, for obvious reasons, she also developed a large group of car enthusiasts that acknowledged she really knew what she was talking about. Jules was getting just as much respect as she was getting ogles. Well, almost as much.

When her YouTube channel hit a pinnacle of followers, a local station reached out and offered her a time slot to do her show weekly. The bikinis were swapped out for revealing clothing by designers, and her garage was replaced with a sound stage. Originally, doing the show in Portland was a requirement because of her position at the tech company, but as her popularity grew and the show took off, she eventually left her job to be a local celebrity full time. *Ultimate Torque* filmed every Thursday morning and aired on Saturday afternoons. This meant Jules was typically unseen and unavailable for most of the week with her prep work until Thursday night rolled around. At that point, she became blissfully available for each weekend starting Friday morning.

Which meant that on this particular Friday evening, while she was perched on my bathroom counter watching me get ready for the museum event, I was getting caught up on everything going on in her world. She'd been listening to me vent about all the goings on at work every chance I had with her; now, it was Jules' turn.

"Let me get this straight," I said as she handed me another bobby pin. "You haven't been on a date in *three* months? How is that even possible?"

"I've only been meeting blues and greens lately. Hell, I'd even settle for a yellow at this point," she said with a sigh as she pulled hairs from my brush.

"Holy shit, you're still using the *scale*?"

Jules had developed a scale for rating men when we were in college that determined whether or not she would date them based on a color-coding scale. Blues were cringe-worthy and not to be spoken to, while greens were a waste of time due to a large flaw of some sort. Yellows were to be placed in the friend-zone and booty called only in cases of emergency. Oranges were allowed access to Jules's phone number and one date over drinks to prove themselves.

Red was the highest rating, but I'm not sure why it existed in the first place since no man had ever managed to earn the honor. I wondered if it was an unobtainable level of expectation that kept Jules from ever truly committing. The possibility of a 'red' gave Jules an out with men since she could convince herself that there was something better out there. But I still mused at the idea of what would happen if she actually met one in the flesh. I imagined spontaneous panty combustion.

"Hell yes, I'm still using the scale," she scoffed. "That shit is more important now than it was in college because there are factors like career choice and net worth to take into consideration." I'd never been able to wrap my brain around how Jules doled out her ratings, mainly because she'd always said the biggest factor was "just a feeling" she got when she met someone.

"Wait, what about that body shop guy you had on your show last week?" I asked. "He was so sexy."

"Green."

"No, really?"

"He had bad teeth," Jules said with a dramatic shudder.

"It didn't look like it on TV," I said.

"Trust me, in person they were bad. Total deal breaker."

"Jules, don't you think you're being a *little* too harsh? For all you know, he could have been a lot of fun, or at least great in bed."

"It's irrelevant because the thought of a guy with a bad grill kissing me or, worse yet, feasting on my girly bits makes me dry up like the Sahara. Like I said, deal breaker."

"We should go out tomorrow night and hunt for some oranges," I said with a laugh.

"I agree; god knows I need to get laid. Plus, we need to find a nice guy to distract you from Samuel-the-asshole," she said as she hopped down and disappeared into my room. Jules was still anti-Samuel despite hearing about our current cease-fire, so I didn't bother to tell her what color I secretly ranked him.

"Dee? Every dress in your closet is black," she called in a muffled voice from the recesses of my walk-in. I don't think I'd ever seen Jules in anything other than a vibrantly colored dress, and who could blame her? The woman was made to stand out.

"Comes with the job," I yelled out to her as I sifted through the jewelry drawer for my lucky bracelet. Jules appeared in the doorway to the bathroom holding a hanger in each hand at arm's length.

"Seriously, the only deviations from basic black are this one with the beads down the back, and this one with the stones on the sleeves," she said, holding up two of the ugliest dresses in my wardrobe making a face that resembled her reaction to having just smelled a rotten egg. With a laugh, I gestured to the bedroom door behind her.

"I'm wearing that one."

Jules turned to the recently dry-cleaned, floor-length dress hanging from the back of my bedroom door. It was solid black like the rest but had a high soft cowl neck in the front with a deep V in the back. It was my favorite.

"Jesus, it's just as boring as the rest of them!"

"Publicist on the red carpet," I said, pointing at my own chest.

"And?" she asked incredulously.

"And I'm supposed to blend in, Jules. Be invisible."

Jules looked at me like I'd just told her I'd peed on the living room floor, before finally shaking her head and turning to leave.

"Well since the dress is boring, we're putting the accessories on steroids," she said, disappearing into the hallway. I finally found my silver bracelet and shoved it on before crossing the room to take the dress off the hanger and slip into it. Jules reappeared a moment later with an armful of accessories and dropped them onto my bed.

"First the shoes," she said, handing me a beautiful pair of jeweled heels that practically blinded me when the light hit them. The rest of the accessories were variations of the jeweled shoes and sparkled on the outskirts of my dress.

Once the look was complete, I did a small twirl for Jules. "What do you think?"

"I think you're going to have a hard time pulling off that whole 'invisible' thing," she said with a self-satisfied smirk.

The charity dinner was taking place in the ballroom of the Portland Art Museum. The location couldn't have been better since the street blissfully allowed for only thirty-feet of a press-line leading into the entrance. This would be a dry-run on rapid press interviews with the Monroe family, since the press tonight only consisted of regional news stations, a handful of travel journalists and a few celebrity bloggers. By the looks of things, I estimated the carpet to take less than a half an hour to walk.

The museum was a short walk from the loft, but I still took a cab to save my feet additional stress since I'd be on them all night. I pulled a few bills from the clasp on my garter and handed them to the cab driver before stepping onto the curb across the street from the gathering media circus. A purse was impractical on the red carpet for those of us actually working it, and so I kept everything in a satin pouch strapped to the garter around my thigh.

"Dee!"

I turned and saw Mae crossing the street to meet me. She was dressed in a basic black cocktail dress that hit just above her knees and was gorgeous in her simplicity. Mae held out my half of our walkie-talkie system with hands shaking so bad I thought she might drop them. I smiled at her carefully as I put the small bud in my ear and turned on the handset.

"You ready for this?" I asked slowly with raised eyebrows as Mae jammed her earpiece damn near into her brain.

"Yeah... I got this..." she mumbled, fiddling with her phone as she connected it to the device. I snatched it from her with one hand and put the other on her shoulder.

"It's thirty-feet of press-line with Charles and Rachel," I said in the most soothing voice I could muster.

Mae and I were dividing up the red-carpet responsibility, and I'd coordinated the event down to the minute. A car would be showing up with Dominic and Pax first, and I would walk them down the press line, while Mae waited for the car with Charles and Rachel. She would escort the couple while I circled back to meet the final car with Samuel and Emma. The headsets were simply a precaution in case any issues arose.

I handed her an access pass and her copy of the note cards detailing facts about the hotel like revenue numbers or event dates and locations. I'd learned the hard way that the night you didn't bring your cheat sheets, would be the night a reporter would ask the most obscure question imaginable.

"Remind Charles and Rachel to mention Pax's racing event and benefit. We need as much press as we can get for that since it's coming up so soon." Mae only responded with a stiff nod of her head while she eyed the growing throng of reporters. "Hey," I jerked on her hand to get her attention. "If you need me, I'll only be a few feet away."

She gave me a stiff smile and gripped her phone tightly. Knowing that was probably all I would get out of her for a response, I led Mae across the street to wait. A couple of minutes later, a black town car stopped at the curb and Dominic stepped out while smoothing down his tie. I pushed my way through the crowd to meet him just as Pax emerged from the car, buttoning his suit jacket and grinning as he stood upright. Both of them were in black suits; I was surprised at Dominic's lack of jeans, as well as Pax's lack of wrinkles. They looked sharp and sexy standing next to one another and scanning the crowd. Somewhere in the distance, a female voice screamed a loud 'woo' and I laughed.

"Gentlemen," I smirked with mock seriousness when I reached them.

"Hey, Dee!" Pax said, as though surprised to see me there.

"I'll be with you guys the whole walk, but I'll only step in if needed. If you're uncomfortable answering a question just say, 'no comment' and I'll take it from there. Also, if you're unsure how to handle a question just ask me." They both nodded in reply. "Most of the reporters are going to be from different business publications and regional newspapers and magazines. You'll be getting a lot of questions about the hotel," I said to Dominic, "and Boost." I finished, looking at Pax.

"And when I do, I will talk about the upcoming benefit and Boost's ranking in Portland Monthly's list of hot spots," Pax recited automatically, rolling his neck and cracking his knuckles.

"Right, Pax," I said, trying to hide my smile. He resembled a football player ready to take the field. "As for the gossip columnists, bloggers and everyone else, just remember what we talked about ok? Any questions about your street racing deflect back to the IndyCar event and MADD benefit. Dominic, the only foreseeable question you'll need to navigate is why you're the only member of the staff out with the Monroe Family tonight."

"I was actually curious how you wanted me to handle that one," Dominic said, acknowledging that he couldn't tell the truth, which was that he was here as Emma's date.

"Just say that the family invited you to join them at their table as a thank you for all the work you've been doing for the hotel. It'll give you a great lead-in for the expansion plans."

I looked them both over one more time, straightened Pax's tie and winked at him.

"Ok, let's do this," I said.

As we made our way to the start of the press line, I caught Mae's eye while she was bouncing on the balls of her feet waiting for Charles and Rachel. I held up my phone in a show of camaraderie, to which she nodded in reply. Dominic and Pax approached the group of reporters, the first of which seeming a bit overzealous for a fundraiser event. He eyed my press badge, phone and index card, the publicist's uniform, and smiled.

"Bill Meyers, Oregon Magazine," he said, introducing himself.

"Dominic Aiello and Pax Monroe of the Hotel Monroe," I said with a nod as I stepped aside and let them approach the rope dividing the press from the carpet.

"How are you guys tonight?" Bill asked, reaching out to shake their hands.

"Great, how are you, Bill?" Dominic said shaking his hand, while Pax stood rigid next to him.

"I'm well, and from what I've been hearing these days, so is the Hotel Monroe. Tell me, are the rumors of a second hotel in the works true?" he asked Dominic, thrusting his recorder toward him.

"Yes, actually, a plan has been set in motion for expansion." Dominic launched into his explanation of the hotel's growth, and while my ears were listening to his answer, my eyes were drawn toward Pax. His hands were fisted at his side, and his jaw was set firmly. If it weren't for his eyes darting between the reporter and Dominic, his stance would greatly resemble a wax statue.

"And I'm assuming a big part of all this success is attributed to Boost." Bill turned his attention to Pax, who stared back at him like a deer in headlights. Determined to get a quote on the subject, Bill continued, "How do you feel about the bar's success?"

Pax snapped his head over his shoulder to look at me questioningly. My eyes went wide in surprise for a moment before nodding vigorously for him to respond.

"Boost is currently number one on Portland Monthly's 'Hot Spot' list," Pax said robotically, and a bit too loud, to Bill.

"Um, right. Ok, and what's your response to all that attention?" I had to hand it to the guy, he was trying like hell to get an interview from Pax, whether he was willing to give it or not. I just couldn't figure out what had made Pax so timid. My curiosity peaked when Pax once again looked to me before answering.

"Answer the question," I hissed at him.

"I'm happy!" Pax yelled exuberantly with a frightening fake smile plastered across his face.

"Alright, thanks," Bill said, eyeing Pax carefully before turning his attention to the next person in line. Dominic looked at me in silent question, and I quickly shook my head in dismissal, trying to convey that I assumed Pax was just nervous while I quickly sidestepped to the next reporter.

"Cindy McFarley, from Glam Gal," she said while smacking gum and I groaned internally. I was hoping that Pax would have worked out his stage fright issues before we made it to a gossip reporter. I introduced the guys and wasn't surprised in the least when her full attention fell on Pax.

"Who are you wearing tonight?" she asked with a giggle.

Once again Pax turned to me with a questioning look and I wanted to smack him since this was the easiest fucking question the guy could get tonight. I rolled my eyes and jutted my chin at the reporter as another signal for him to answer.

"Hugo Boss," he stated in a monotone voice.

"Mmm, very nice. And are you a boxer or briefs kind of guy?" she asked, dipping her chin in a sickening attempt to flirt. This time I wasn't surprised when Pax looked back at me for confirmation that he was allowed to answer, but I was getting more and more annoyed.

"We're actually both boxer men," Dominic said, gripping Pax's shoulder tightly and causing Cindy to break out into a fit of giggles. Once she had taken a handful of photos, they turned to move down the carpet. But before they could reach the next reporter, I stopped them both by gripping their wrists and yanking them out of the processional line.

"What the hell is going on, Pax?" I whispered harshly.

"What? What did I do?" he asked in a panic.

"You're asking her if you can answer each question like you're a goddamn puppet!" Dominic said.

"Fuck you, man!" Pax growled back. "If I screw *any* of this up, she'll take away my racecar. And I'm *not* having that!"

Apparently, I'd dangled a carrot so large in front of Pax it had paralyzed the poor bastard.

"Pax, he's right. You're starting to look like a show-dog out there waiting for commands. Relax, I trust you're not going to mess up questions about the club, or who you're wearing," I laughed. "Tell you what, unless the question has the words 'street racing' or 'illegal' in it, you're free to answer."

Things got a little smoother from there. As predicted, the majority of the questions for them were about the hotel business and Boost. Only one reporter got our scripted answer when she inquired about Dominic's attendance. She also earned herself a 'no comment' from Pax when she asked about his status with underground racing circuits. I made a mental note to be on guard when Samuel made his way to her later on.

Two journalists later and I looked to my left to see Levi grinning like an idiot at me from the other side of the velvet rope.

"Levi Garcia," he said, extending his hand to Dominic and Pax for an enthusiastic shake.

"Dominic Aiello and Pax Monroe from the Hotel Monroe," I said, giving him a warning look. *"Behave,"* I mouthed. Levi's eyes lit up at the mention of Pax's name, and he looked him up and down several times before licking his lips and starting the interview.

"Well Pax, I hear you're driving in the IndyCar event coming up. Were you a fan of the sport before getting the spot in the charity event?"

"Yeah I was, I'm a fan of speed in general," Pax beamed. Thank god he'd made that comment to Levi because any other reporter would have used it as a lead-in for discussing his street racing. I trusted Levi not to let the interview turn to Pax's indiscretions and get awkward.

"I tend to like it fast myself," Levi said in a breathy voice.

Ok, so we just have a different *kind of awkwardness to deal with.*

"Do you play any sports?" Levi continued, completely ignoring Dominic and eye-fucking Pax.

"I played football in high school, but these days the only time I get a chance to play is with the guys on Thanksgiving in the park. Which in Portland typically turns into a rainy and wet mess of guys in the mud," Pax said with a chuckle.

"Oh, sweet Jesus," Levi moaned as his eyes rolled slightly into the back of his head. I cleared my throat loudly, snapping him back to attention. "Well, I'm not surprised football's your game; you *look* like a football player. So strong. Can I feel your bicep?"

"Ok! I think we're done here," I said, ushering a confused Pax and Dominic down the line.

"Cock block," Levi hissed at me.

"Creeper," I whispered back.

We finished up with the last reporter from a local news station and stepped off the carpet and through the open doorway leading into the ballroom. Once inside, and out of earshot of the press, Pax turned to me.

"That wasn't too bad. I'd say that I rocked the shit out of that red carpet!"

"Yeah, once you snapped out of your Tin Man impression, you totally nailed the grueling task of composing sentences to half a dozen local area journalist," Dominic quipped, patting him on the back.

"You both did great," I said, checking my watch. Emma and Samuel's car would be pulling up to the curb in less than two minutes. "I have to run back out there. You boys have fun."

I slipped back outside and began to snake my way back to the start of the press line, scanning the crowd for Charles and Rachel, spotting them near the center of the processional. I stopped in my tracks and chuckled in surprise for a moment. I didn't know how she'd done it, but Mae had managed to get Charles and Rachel in line behind the Mayor and his wife. At the moment, she was orchestrating a group photo for the crowd of photographers. The girl was a natural.

I snapped out of my reverie and rushed back to the street, and no sooner had I reached the edge of the carpet when a car pulled up, and Emma stepped out of the back seat. She was in a floor-length canary yellow gown with blue accessories and shoes; she looked like sunshine personified. Her face lit up with her beautiful smile when she saw me approaching and stepped onto the sidewalk, but mid-step my breath hitched and I almost stumbled when Samuel climbed out of the backseat behind her.

He was dressed in a black suit with a charcoal dress shirt and pewter tie, looking like pure sex. As my eyes roamed across his body, I was involuntarily flooded with images of things I wanted to do to Samuel while his amazing suit lay on my bedroom floor. Our eyes finally met, and Samuel gave me a sexy smirk, effectively letting me know that I'd been caught checking him out, again. Trying my best to snap out of it and be professional, I closed the distance between us and smiled at the pair of them.

"Are you guys ready for this?" I asked in a shaky breath.

"Are you?" Samuel asked, arching a brow at me and still smirking. He had to know that he was affecting me, and furthermore, he was beginning to play with me because of it.

"Here's how this is going to work," I said, outlining all the rules I'd explained to Pax and Dominic earlier. "Emma, I have all the details here for dates, venues and other specifics on the hotel's events, just in case you get stuck." I waved my cheat sheet in the air before turning back to Samuel. He was the PR wildcard tonight, and even though I was prepared, my stomach still had butterflies at the possibilities of how tonight would go. We may be in a cease-fire, but that was just between us as individuals; it did nothing to quiet the thought that he could easily go rouge just to prove a point about my position here. I secretly prayed that Samuel would suddenly develop Pax's case of stage-fright. "Just don't…be *you* tonight. Ok?"

Great coaching Dee. Expert work.

An unrecognizable emotion flashed across Samuel's face and before I could even blink it was gone. His smirk returned as he looked over my head and scanned the crowd behind me.

"Just tell me that I'll get a moment with that asshole from the paper," he mumbled.

"Sorry, no can do." His head snapped down as he scowled at me. "He was demoted to classifieds this morning." I gave him a wink and tried my damnedest to ignore the heart-stopping smile that followed. "Let's go."

I stepped back onto the red carpet, this time considerably tenser. Bill Meyer was still only interested in the operations of the hotel, and we navigated through his interview quickly. And predictably, Cindy McFarley was still a tease and giggled maniacally when I introduced Emma and Samuel.

"Mr. Monroe, it's such an honor," she cooed, making me want to smack the shit out of her. "I have to ask, are you a boxer or a briefs kind of guy?" I involuntarily snorted at her bypassing of the question regarding Samuel's suit and going straight for the underwear. Emma shot me a quick look and smirked before turning back to Cindy.

"I'm actually the kind of guy that doesn't discuss his underwear with strangers," Samuel said matter-of-factly, but still in his sexy velvet voice.

Holy shit, that was pretty good.

I couldn't have given him a better answer to that question; it was evasive and tactful and pissed Cindy right the hell off. My silent rejoicing was cut short when Cindy turned her frustration on Emma.

"Emma, you're looking gorgeous tonight. Whose gown are you wearing?" Cindy's words were dripping with venom, but no one else seemed to notice. I inched my way closer, practically wedging myself between Samuel and Emma.

Emma answered the question as she gripped the skirt of her dress and twirled a bit, her smile radiating. Based on her expression, it was clear that Cindy didn't give a shit about Emma's response and was merely setting herself for a follow-up question. The hair on the back of my neck stood up, and I instinctually placed a hand on Emma's back for support. Out of the corner of my eye, I saw Samuel look down at me questioningly.

"You designed a line for Fashion Week your senior year in college, which failed miserably. Since you never sold a single piece of your collection, and they're probably all sitting in your closet at home, why wouldn't you wear one of your own designs on nights like this?"

You bitch.

I wanted to hit Cindy at that moment. Mae's phenomenal research had included every detail possible regarding the failed clothing line Emma had designed in college. I'd assumed it was a sore subject, but with all the event planning, secret relationships and kleptomaniac discussions we'd had this week, I hadn't had the chance to ask her about it. And based on how quickly Emma's expression had fallen and her shoulders had slumped at the question, I gathered that this was an *extremely* sore subject for her.

"I'm sorry," I interjected loudly, lowering my hand from her back and grabbing Emma's elbow while leaning past her to stare Cindy in the eye. "The European owner of Ms. Monroe's entire fashion line chooses to remain anonymous. We can't discuss the details at this time."

Cindy's eyes went wide, and she began typing frantically on her phone while I ushered Emma and Samuel to the next reporter. Emma gave me a look of gratitude while Samuel eyed me as if I'd been caught stealing the last cookie in the jar.

"You just lied. I thought the shaky chihuahua would make an appearance when you lied," Samuel whispered into my ear as we walked, causing goose-bumps down my neck. I turned to look at him over my shoulder and inhaled his scent as I did so.

"Isn't your mother European?" I asked in a whisper. Samuel gave me a quick nod as I couldn't help but notice that he was staring at my lips while he did so. "Well, she's the one that has Emma's clothing line, so I wasn't lying. Move along," I said, quickly turning away before I did something embarrassing involuntary, like jam my nose in his chest and inhale loudly.

Samuel scoffed and joined his sister for the next interview. The next ten feet of the red carpet went by uneventfully. Samuel was asked several times about the hotel's growth, while Emma was grilled on the details for upcoming events. One journalist for a financial magazine asked Samuel if he was ever going to take over the hotel and his body visibly tensed. I considered jumping in since I *knew* this question was hitting on a sore subject, and I had no idea how Samuel would handle it. But before I could say anything, he surprised me with his answer.

"You know, we really haven't talked about it since we're all so focused on our plans for a second hotel."

I had to clamp my jaw shut to keep it from falling open. What the hell was going on? As he went on to talk about Dominic's plan for expansion, Emma turned and quirked an eyebrow at me in question. I gave her a look that said that I was just as confused as she was; Samuel was navigating the press like a fucking pro. Just as I was starting to think I'd wandered into the Twilight Zone, we moved on to Amanda Luften, the reporter that had brought up Pax's street racing.

"Hello, Emma. Mmm, and hello again Samuel. I haven't heard from you in a while," she cooed at him. Samuel shifted uncomfortably from one foot to the other with his hand in his pockets.

"Hello, Mandie," he answered quietly. It didn't take a genius to figure out that these two had been intimate at some point. I quickly went from professional irritation to blinding jealousy and then finally landing on petty humiliation. Standing there, looking at this tall, beautiful, clearly 20-something woman, who had obviously slept with Samuel, I suddenly felt foolish for thinking our game of cat-and-mouse was anything other than that, a professional dance. I couldn't compete with these kinds of women, blatantly throwing themselves at him. God knew how many of them were out there, a number I probably did not want to know myself.

"You haven't called in a while, I was starting to think you'd forgotten about me," she pouted.

"Can you get on with your actual interview questions?" I seethed. "We have a schedule to keep." Amanda finally took notice of me standing just behind Samuel and looked down at me in disdain.

"I see you got yourself a publicist," she said, the title coming out like a dirty word. We stared each other down, both scowling and silently acknowledging our dislike for one another.

"We did," Samuel said, shooting me a worried look that made me wonder how crazy I appeared at that moment. "And you should probably ask your questions now," he said in a warning tone, making me feel like the chaperone interrupting their date.

"Well, I saw in the Portland Daily that you're still an advocate for safe sex," she said, turning her nauseating pout back to Samuel. "Good to know, I suppose. Are you still single?"

I will cut a bitch.

She was not only bringing up the one article I was hoping to avoid tonight, but she was also doing it in a way that made me want to shove her nose into her brain with my palm. Emma reached a hand back and squeezed my own; the gesture both calmed my nerves momentarily and snapped me out of my red haze. If Emma was calming *me* down, then I needed to get my head out of my ass and back in the game. I couldn't let the nonsense with Samuel cloud my professional responsibilities, but I also couldn't help but think back to Samuel's hands on my body as this woman made innuendos about their sexual relationship.

"Actually, that quote was taken completely out of context," Samuel said matter-of-factly. "I was simply trying to praise the work the clinic does in our community. As for my relationship status, I'd prefer to keep my private life, well, *private*."

Amanda froze in shock at Samuel's evasive answer, and I'm ashamed to admit that I did the same. Later I would deal with the fact that, whether or not he knew it, he'd made the insinuation that he was in a relationship. More than anything, I was shocked at his impressive sidestep of the misquote question. Taking advantage of Amanda's sudden speechlessness, I ushered the pair of them down the carpet and away from her inevitable follow-up questions.

I was able to catch my breath and collect my wits while a reporter talked to Emma about whether or not she used local vendors when planning an event. During her discussion about florists, Samuel looked over his shoulder and caught my eye. In that moment, I felt like he could see right through me; because instead of a cocky wink or a smug smirk I got a nothing more than a warm smile. His expression wasn't arrogant or antagonistic or playful. It was genuine.

"Thank you, Ms. Monroe."

With the ending of Emma's interview, I broke eye contact with Samuel and moved them a couple of feet to the next reporter and almost groaned out loud when I saw Levi bouncing on the balls of his feet in anticipation. As if this night hadn't been confusing enough, Samuel and Levi would meet each other *now*.

"Levi Garcia with The Advocate," he announced with his shit-eating grin.

"Emma and Samuel Monroe," I grumbled, trying to convey to him that I wasn't in the mood for his games. However, based on the way his expression hardened into a big-brother version of protective, it was safe to say that Levi assumed I was trying to convey some sort of distress. He looked at Samuel sternly, to which Samuel replied with a sharp look of his own. For a short red carpet, this had turned into one of the longest in my career.

"You're Dee's *friend*," Samuel said coldly, stepping in front of me before I could say anything.

"I am," he responded in a baritone voice that I'd never heard come out of Levi before.

The pair of them gripped hands in a showdown-style handshake and stared each other down. Emma racked her eyes up and down Levi's body, taking in his outfit and manicured appearance and then Samuel's hostile stance. She brought her hand to her mouth to hide her laughter and turned slightly away from the display of blatant male dominance toward me.

"I don't think Sam knows what 'The Advocate' is," she whispered.

It was clear that Levi wasn't going to ask a single question and the staring match would continue indefinitely, so I cut in.

"Ok then, we need to get moving along!"

I'd introduce them properly some other time, if necessary. The press line was certainly not the place to clear up whatever issues were going on. Levi gave me a protective look as the three of us walked away, and I made a mental note to call him in the morning. The last reporter on the carpet was thankfully from a hospitality blog and only asked Emma about the fall gala and Samuel about high-end clientele. And yet again, he answered questions better than I could have scripted for him and left me wondering if he was a pod-person.

The three of us stepped through the entryway of the museum and Emma hugged me tightly.

"Thank you," she said pointedly, and I knew she was referring to the interview about her clothing line. I gave her a shrug and a wave in an attempt to play it off, and she flittered into the lobby and headed for the ballroom.

"I'd say that went well," Samuel said casually.

"That was... I can't..." I was frustratingly at a loss for words. His gaze shifted from my eyes to my mouth and back to my eyes as he smirked and lifted his finger to my chin to shut my agape jaw. "You were perfect?" I hadn't meant for it to be a question, but I couldn't believe what was happening.

Samuel chuckled and leaned down, his breath tickling my neck as he spoke. "I'm not a moron, Dee," he said as his hand ghosted on my hip. "Just because I never play it, doesn't mean that don't know the rules of this bullshit PR game."

The stubble on his jaw scratched lightly on my cheek as he leaned back to look down at me, and it was almost enough of intimate contact to distract me from the light bulb going off in my mind with such brilliance I almost winced at its sheer wattage.

Samuel knew how to behave in the press, which meant that all along when he said and did those ridiculous things it had been *on purpose*? He'd said it himself, he wasn't a moron and knew how to act expertly with the press. So why would he hurt the hotel or his career like that intentionally? Was this part of some sort of rebellion against the establishment for him? If so, the fact that I was the spokesperson for said establishment would certainly explain his attitude toward me. A large part of me was livid that all this time his behavior could have been nothing more than a tantrum of sorts; a spoiled brat acting out simply because he didn't want to be told how to behave. But that didn't explain tonight. Was tonight some sort of gesture? Or was tonight some sort of message?

"Aren't you coming?" he asked, breaking me from my thoughts.

"Afraid not; I'm not off the clock yet," I said, gesturing over my shoulder at the reporters. "I have follow-up questions to answer. Enjoy your steak dinner."

I tried my best to keep my expression blank as I turned to go meet Mae and address the waiting reporters. My head was swimming with questions and emotions about Samuel and his actions, and I wanted to stand there and get some answers, not just for myself, but for Charles and our plans. But if this week had taught me anything, it was that I needed to clear my head and think before talking to Samuel.

FOURTEEN

Samuel

I watched from the back-seat of the town car as people began filling up the sidewalks of downtown Portland, rushing to get to their Friday night plans at local bars and restaurants. Next to me, Emma was rapidly typing away on her cell phone.

"Stop Twittering," I teased with a poke to her ribs.

"Tweeting," she corrected without looking up.

"I don't understand the fascination with telling people what you're doing at all times."

"It's called social networking, grandpa. You should try it."

"I have my own way of networking socially," I replied with a chuckle. Damn it, where was Pax when you needed him? That would have earned me a high five for sure.

"Yeah you do, although it hasn't escaped my attention that you haven't been networking socially lately," she said, still typing on her phone. I frowned at her comment; it hadn't escaped my attention either that I'd broken with my routine and become a bit anti-social. But to be fair, it had been a particularly grueling work week. And it wasn't as though I wasn't getting laid. In fact, I'd just been out with Shayla.

Jesus, was that over two weeks ago?

"You told Delilah," I said quietly, changing the subject to something I'd wanted to ask her about for days. There was no need to elaborate; Emma knew what I was referring to. She slipped her phone into the small purse on her lap and met my eye line with a firm expression.

"I did," she said, raising an eyebrow and giving me an expectant look. "Let's hear it. I'm sure you have an issue with me telling her," she said.

"I'm just surprised, Emma. You keep this so close to the chest, and then you go and tell someone you've known for only a couple of days. Forgive me for being a little taken aback here."

"Sam," she said, her tone softening. "If I were ever to slip up and have an episode." I started to protest, but Emma just shook her head to stop me. I had complete faith in my baby sister; if anyone could beat this condition without a relapse, it was her. "It's possible, Sam. And *if* that ever happens, someone like Dee would be the biggest ally I'd have in that situation. My family will be there for love and support, but Dee? Dee will have the power to *protect* me. I know you think her job is to make your life miserable, but it's actually to shield us, protect us from intrusions into private things like this. If you would stop and pay attention once in a while, you may notice that she's extremely skilled at it."

This I knew. The fact that Pax was practically walking around with an 'I heart Delilah' t-shirt these days was proof enough that she knew how to do her job well.

"It wasn't that you told a publicist, or even Delilah specifically. I'm just nervous-"

"About me telling *anyone*," she finished for me. I nodded solemnly, trying to swallow the big brother reaction continuing to boil within me. "It's my secret to tell, Sam. And I *trust* Dee."

I cleared my throat, "I owe you such an apology, Emma. I can't believe I asked you to lift that guy's wallet the other night. I don't know what came over me; I was so focused on the task at hand, I didn't even stop to consider what it meant for you. I'm never an asshole like that, I hope you can forgive me."

"It's fine, I could have said no. And plus, that's how I know you love her."

"Excuse me?"

"Oh, never mind," Emma said exasperated, shaking her head and waving a dismissive hand at me. "You two, I swear."

"Emma, what are you-"

"Forget, another time. And yes, it was an asshole move to ask, but I'm a big girl. You're forgiven. I understood then, and still do now; you were *distracted*." She giggled, and before I could question her further, she exclaimed, "We're here!"

Our car queued up about a dozen feet from the museum and we inched our way to the start of the red carpet.

"Are you going to at least tone it down tonight?" Emma asked, and I looked at her questioningly before shrinking back under her scrutinizing stare. "I have to imagine that Dee has enough to do tonight without you making her job ten times harder." My sister was scary when she wanted to be.

"I'll be good," I said.

Actually, I'll be great.

Delilah had done me a favor this week when it came to giving Pax a chance, regardless of the fact that we'd been at each other's throats at the time. She was also protecting my sister *and* her secrets as though they were both her own. I owed Delilah, and there was only one thing I could think of to do as repayment that would be worthwhile and meaningful. I would play her game tonight and give her the faux-Sam performance she would want from me.

We approached the curb and Emma jumped out. I slid across the back seat, and that's when I saw her through the window of Emma's open door. Delilah came through the crowd looking like an angel and the image made my gut clench. Her dress was simple in both color and style, but the way it hugged every inch of her in just the right way made her mouthwatering in black. On her feet were the sexiest pair of heels I'd ever seen and as I dragged my eyes up her body, I noticed the simplicity of her jewelry and scarcity of accessories. Her hair was up loosely on the crown of her head, exposing her neck and the spot on her collarbone that I'd drug my tongue across days earlier. It wasn't a surprise that her makeup was simple, nor was it a surprise that she was still beautiful without it. Delilah outshone every woman around her.

My eyes were still set on her face when I climbed out of the car, and I watched in amusement as her gaze snaked its way up my body, just as mine had done to hers. Her tongue swept across her bottom lip just before she pulled it between her teeth. Holy hell, Delilah was blatantly ogling me, and I couldn't help my smug smile at the knowledge that we affected one another in all the same ways. On top of infuriation, antagonism, and frustration, there was also attraction and undeterred lust.

Now I had two reasons to be on my best behavior tonight, one being in appreciation and gratitude to Delilah, but the second being that I increasingly wanted her to be happy. Happy with me, specifically. Our truce had made me hungry for more when it came to her; I was done being an asshole in her eyes.

"Just don't... be *you* tonight. Ok?" she said as she finished her instructions to us for the press line.

So much for her not thinking I'm always an asshole.

I wasn't deterred, though. Reporter after reporter, I stayed the course and played the press game like I was back at the investment firms I'd interned with years ago. I was evasive and yet informative, charming while still being aloof. Essentially, spending nearly an hour talking while not really saying anything of substance at all. It was mind-numbing, but if it made Delilah's life easier, I could do it for one night.

When we finally reached the doors to the museum, I was feeling pretty proud of myself. I had wanted to give Delilah a gesture of goodwill and appreciation, and I felt like I'd done just that. But I hadn't realized I was expecting a huge show of appreciation for my performance until I didn't get it from Delilah. She fumbled a bit and sounded completely surprised that I'd behaved accordingly. I guess it wasn't glaringly obvious that I possessed the wherewithal to navigate nights like this, but a 'thank you' from the woman would have been nice. Remembering that I had some work ahead of me in showing Delilah that I wasn't a bad guy, I was anxious to get into the ballroom and sit with her during dinner. Neutral territory would do us a world of good tonight.

"Afraid not; I'm not off the clock yet. I have follow-up questions to answer. Enjoy your steak dinner," Delilah said in a flat voice, barely looking at me. She turned quickly back toward the door and hurried outside.

What just happened here?

Had I pissed her off? I know I didn't mess up a single question tonight because she'd used the word 'perfect' specifically. With a sigh, I turned toward the ballroom to meet up with my family, grumbling to myself. Delilah was easily the most difficult woman to figure out.

When I made it to the table, the last open seat was thankfully between Dominic and Pax. I hadn't had a chance to talk to my father about the Portland Daily article and was sure he had something to say about it. There was also a chance that my mother had heard about the mini-war raging between Delilah and myself this week; she would *definitely* have something to say about that.

"Gentlemen," I said, sliding into my seat.

"Bro, I made that red carpet my bitch!" Pax said on my left.

"Make him shut up about it before I kill him," Dominic grumbled on my right.

"Scotch, neat," I said to the waitress behind me.

Dinner consisted of Emma and my parents discussing Delilah's brilliance, Pax explaining what an interviewing genius he was and Dominic threatening to kill Pax. I sat in silence until the speeches finally started and gave me a reprieve from Dominic and Pax's bickering, as well as the curious glances I was getting from my sister and mother.

Once the Mayor wrapped up his ode to the arts and the crowd began to mingle, I stood up from our table and made my way to the bar. As the bartender turned to make my drink, I spotted Delilah over his shoulder. She was sitting alone on the opposite side of the round bar with a glass of red wine in front of her, typing away on her phone.

"Ok, a martini is for courage and a mojito is for fun. What's red wine?" I asked, sitting on the stool next to her. Delilah turned to eye me quickly before smiling and setting her phone on the bar, shaking her head as she did so.

"You know, I can't keep track of all the things I told you that night," she said, bringing her wineglass to her lips.

"Well, I remember them all," I told her, mirroring the motion and taking a drink of my scotch while waiting for her answer.

"Contemplation," she said with a nod toward her glass. I cocked an eyebrow at her, but she spoke before I could ask further. "I suppose you're going to put that excellent memory of yours to good use and continue to torture me," she mused with a smirk and arched eyebrow.

"Says the woman who signed me up for a golf tournament."

Delilah's head fell back as she let out her beautiful laughter. I committed the sound to memory and vowed to make her do it again as soon as possible. The music in the ballroom changed to a soft melody, and as I looked over my shoulder at the couples on the dance floor, inspiration struck.

"Dance with me," I said, turning back to Delilah. I needed her undivided attention, and this was the perfect opportunity.

"I don't know if-"

"Oh, come on. The press isn't in here so we won't be starting rumors. It's just one dance, Delilah."

She eyed my outstretched hand and starting chewing on the inside of her lip.

"You do know *how* to dance, don't you?" I taunted. Delilah's eyes snapped up to mine and narrowed just before she slapped her hand forcefully into mine, unable to resist the dare.

We reached the dance floor and I pulled her into my arms. All musings in my head stopped when her arm slipped delicately around my shoulder. Delilah's body was warm against mine; I felt electricity where my hand touched the small of her back and our hands met. We started to move to the music, and she went back to chewing her lip while not making eye contact.

"What's on your mind?" I asked, wiggling our clasped hands to get her attention.

"I'm just confused," she said quietly, looking up at me and then away again.

"Well, then just follow my lead," I said, smirking down at her while she swatted my shoulder.

"Not about the dancing, I'm confused about you."

Finally, I had Delilah cornered and the opportunity to let her know that I wasn't the asshole she probably assumed.

"You navigated that red carpet perfectly without my help, which means you know how to do this. I've been mulling this over," she said methodically, "and I don't think you would hurt the hotel intentionally, but it *appears* that you've been acting the way you have on purpose. Tonight has just left me...well, confused!"

Damn, so much for my grand gesture. All I'd managed to do tonight was muddle our understanding of one another even further.

"You're right, I would never hurt the hotel on purpose," I said, grimacing when she looked relieved. "But you need to know that I never really believed I *was* hurting the business in the first place. I was just being myself, trying to enjoy the situation. I say the things I do in interviews because I find most of the questions to be ridiculous; it's my way of having fun with it. The alternative, well it just makes my skin crawl."

"The alternative?" Delilah interjected with raised eyebrows. "What, acting like a responsible businessman?"

"Hey, I *am* a responsible businessman. Just because I make jokes in interviews and get photographed with multiple women doesn't mean I don't know how to do my job." She furrowed her brow and started to interrupt, but I didn't let her this time. "No, wait. There's been nothing but talk about how great *you* are at *your* job. Well, Delilah, I'm pretty fucking awesome at what I do as well. My negotiation skills with vendors and unions *alone* have saved the hotel hundreds of thousands, if not millions, of dollars. I bring in clientele from all over the world without ever leaving my office. I think it's time you give me a little credit, too."

"I never said you were a bad GM, Samuel."

"No, you just said that I hurt the hotel and now you think that I possibly do it on purpose."

"Please try to see things from my perspective, from a PR perspective. No matter how brilliant you are in the boardroom, if you come across like an ass in public people assume the behavior translates to your work. And let me tell you something I should have said from the beginning; I *know* that it's all bullshit. I *know* that it's absurd that Pax's racing would make people think he was incapable of creating the best club in town. Or that your social life means you don't know how to operate the hotel business better than any other GM in the industry. But it's the reality of the media and the way the public responds, whether we like it or not."

I twirled Delilah to the music in an attempt to give myself a moment to think over what she'd said and watched as her dress spun around her body. Part of me felt like a moron for trying to fight against something I had zero chances of fixing or even changing. Delilah was right, no matter what any of us did or said, the media machine and its effect on public perception would remain unchanged. She'd accepted the system and made a career out of playing it, whereas I was jeopardizing my career by trying to buck the same system. I knew she had a point, but I still cringed at what that meant.

"The alternative," I said when she was back in my arms, "is so hard to stomach."

"You said that already. What are you talking about?"

"Not being myself. Putting on this plastic, boy-scout persona and pretending to be someone I'm not. I still contest that my behavior doesn't always hurt the hotel, but if we did things your way, I don't know how I'd stand it."

"Samuel, you told a reporter once that you don't wear underwear because they don't make a package big enough to hold your package."

I laughed at the memory as I revolved us across the dance floor.

"That was in response to the overused 'boxers or briefs' question. And admit it, Delilah, it was funny."

Delilah was trying desperately not to smile, biting her bottom lip so severely it was turning white under the pressure. The action made me laugh even harder.

"Ok," she relented. "It was funny, albeit juvenile, and you *know* it was wrong. I'm convinced, now more than ever, that you do actually know that."

"What was I supposed to say? What I said tonight? Some sterile answer that doesn't even point out the absurdity of the question? That's not me, Delilah. And I hate the idea that I might have to be some false version of myself in order to be successful."

I looked around the ballroom and drew in a steadying breath to settle my nerves. When I looked back down, Delilah's confident look had returned.

"What about saying that only lucky ladies get to find out what you wear?" she said, arching that sexy brow at me and looking coy. I opened and closed my mouth a couple of times in shock before speaking.

"But that's not-"

"It's not a boy-scout response, I know. But you're not a boy scout or a monk, and I don't want you to be," she said with certainty. I smiled when she blushed with the realization of the innuendo she'd unintentionally made. "It's also not a blatantly oversexualized answer that when taken out of context makes you sound like a complete perv."

"You never stop surprising me," I said, so quietly I wasn't sure she heard me.

"Samuel, if you'd work *with* me, I know we can come up with a compromise. You don't want to pretend to be someone you're not. I get that, I really do. I don't want that either, but I also don't want you to give the press a handful of things to talk about *other* than the success of the hotel when your name is mentioned. Take a minute to look at what I'm doing with Pax. I know you're pissed off that he's been converted to the PR team all of a sudden, but just think about it. I didn't ask him to buy a mini-van or talk about how against speed and adrenaline he's suddenly become. I'm still letting him race cars, just in a more controlled way. In fact, I'm adding about a hundred extra miles per hour to his average speed," she said with a chuckle.

"So you're saying," I said, with a conspiratorial grin, "that you'd like to come up with a way for me to be myself in the press-"

"While playing by my rules," she finished, nodding her head. "Yes, exactly. Why do you think I wanted to meet with everyone individually, Sam? This isn't a one-size-fits-all kind of science."

I thought about Delilah making my big brother smile at the reality of living a completely legit lifestyle. And then about the image of Delilah's hand falling supportively on my little sister's back in a time of need tonight. Four days ago, I was ready to toss her out of the building for bringing nothing but a carpetbag full of bullshit to our door. Now, I was holding her in my arms and not only respecting her for loving the hotel as fiercely as I did but also allowing myself to be tamed.

"You're a rare bird, Delilah Sheppard," I whispered, looking at her lips and then back into her eyes just in time to see her complete the same circuit with her stare.

"The music stopped," she said quietly. We continued to stare at one another, our faces close together and her sweet breath washing over my face.

"What music?" I asked, leaning down further. I hadn't made the decision to kiss her; my body naturally gravitated to hers like it was the most basic force in the universe. But before I made contact, Delilah turned her head and pulled out of my arms to walk away. I tightened my grip on her hand and pulled her back to me, causing her chest to slam into mine. I had no idea what I was doing; I just knew that I couldn't let her walk away.

"One more song," I said as a soft piano melody started to play out in the ballroom.

"Only if you don't try to kiss me again," she whispered, looking up at me shyly through her lashes.

"Did you not like it when I kissed you before?"

"No. I didn't," she said, jutting out her chin defiantly. Her cheeks blushed with the prettiest shade of red and shoulders trembled a bit as she shook her head more times than she probably realized.

"That's going to come in handy," I said, taking in her momentarily cartoonish appearance and running a knuckle across her cheek. Delilah pulled her head back slightly away from my hand and closed her eyes.

"Samuel, please."

"Why?" I asked. Was she pulling away from me because we weren't alone tonight? Was it because of the things she'd heard about me? She wanted to stay professional just as I did, but at some point, we had to acknowledge that there was something kinetic between us. I didn't know what I wanted from Delilah, but after having her close to me like this, I knew that I didn't have the strength to stop myself from giving into it whatever it was.

"We work together," she said. I sighed at what was becoming a flimsy excuse for us to not give in to what we both clearly wanted. "We're finally getting to a place where we can enjoy working together," she said, gripping my shoulder and interrupting my thoughts. "Let's not mess that up. Friends? Please?"

"Friends," I said with a reassuring smile. I wasn't in the practice of the slow play with women, but that didn't mean I was incapable. "So, Pax tells me that he's the teacher's pet and made the red carpet his bitch tonight."

Once again, I earned myself one of her genuine guffaws and the tension was effectively cut short.

"Oh, did he? Well, did he tell you about the first couple of interviews?"

We spent the rest of the dance laughing at Pax's expense and swapping insults about the reporter that had cornered Emma. When the song finally ended she excused herself to say hello to my parents, and I watched as my new friend disappeared into the crowd.

Friends.

I'd never been friends with a woman before, and apparently, I'm one sick masochist because I'd chosen Dee as my first. And while the thought of being friends with Dee left a dry, bland taste in my mouth, I didn't let it get me down. We wouldn't be just friends for too long, not if I had my way.

FIFTEEN

Delilah

My Sunday morning routine had been the same for years. A mushroom omelet and pot of French press coffee, both of which I enjoyed during recorded episodes of bad reality TV and cooking shows from the previous week. To this day, I can't recall how the ritual began, but I still found the same comfort in it, especially after college when I got into a career that had me out at events most Friday and Saturday nights, talking and managing people nonstop. The solitary and brain break were welcome every week.

Moving in with Jules hadn't put a damper on my Sundays since she rarely got out of bed before ten on the weekends anyhow. This particular Sunday wouldn't be an exception, based on the amount of alcohol she'd consumed the night before.

I'd kept my promise and went hunting for code orange bachelors with Jules Saturday night. She'd begun the night hopeful, but after three bars and countless men deemed 'unworthy,' Jules had decided to forfeit her man-hunting and spend the night with Jose Cuervo instead. When it became clear that getting blitzed was her new plan, I'd switched from mojitos to club soda so that I'd be capable of dealing with the belligerence that was inevitably coming. Jules rarely drank hard alcohol, but when she did, it was an adventure since it was due to her being either extremely happy or extremely pissed off.

Around midnight she'd started telling me how much she loved me, and that she was considering lesbianism since men were all ridiculous. When said decision was made, she'd prefer me to be her first lover since I was such a "gentle soul." This was clue number one that it was time for her to be cut the hell off. After a quick trip to the restroom so she could vomit, Jules had agreed to accompany me back to the loft. While I was paying the incredibly patient ride-share driver that had endured over ten minutes of being yelled at for his gender being completely inept, Jules decided to explain to the doorman why he would remain a "green" as long as he also remained a doorman. The poor kid wasn't a day over nineteen and looked scared out of his mind while my best friend had an arm around his shoulder explaining the definition of net-worth.

Yes, I was certain that this particular Sunday I would *definitely* be uninterrupted in my morning routine. However, I'd just started my second episode when Levi's number showed up on my vibrating phone.

"Good morning, Levi."

"Jesus Christ, Dee. Could you not yell?" he groaned.

"This is my normal speaking voice, Levi." I paused the TV and crossed my ankles on the edge of the coffee table.

"You're still yelling," he whimpered.

"Someone sounds hungover," I said, chuckling at Levi's pain, just as he would surely do at mine.

"Someone sounds too chipper to have enjoyed themselves last night," he replied.

"Well played, Garcia. If you must know, my attention was required to tend to another inebriated friend last night."

"You and Jules go man hunting last night in her never-ending quest to find a code red?" Levi asked in a bored tone. I could picture him rubbing his forehead in an attempt to erase his headache.

"I find it hilarious that you claim to hate her but can still recall the many facets of her personality," I teased.

"She's hard to shake," Levi mumbled. "Like a fungus."

"One day, you'll realize that she's your sister from another mother, or however that phrase goes."

"Is this why you called me twice yesterday? To tell me that I secretly yearn to paint Jules's toenails?"

"No. I called you yesterday to find out what the hell was going on Friday night."

With the chaos of the red carpet and the entire evening behind me, I'd fallen asleep as soon as my head hit the pillow Friday night. Saturday morning, however, I'd awoken cringing at two separate thoughts. One was that I'd asked Samuel if we could just be friends, which was great for my professional life but sure to kill me slowly on a personal level. The second had

been that Levi had taken a strange disliking to Samuel and I
needed to know why.

"Oh, come on," Levi said. "I didn't even get to *touch*
him!"

"I'm not talking about Pax," I said, rolling my eyes and
laughing to myself at Levi's predictability. "Although, your
crush on Pax *does* make me worry, honey. I'm actually talking
about your gunslinger standoff with Samuel."

"You gave me the signal!" Levi exclaimed.

"What signal?"

"The 'this guy just hurt and or offended me' signal. I
may be an unlikely source, but I'll unleash an ass-kicking on
him if I have to."

"Stand down," I said, shaking my head at the mental
image of Levi trying to defend my honor by strangling Samuel
viciously with his cashmere scarf. "It wasn't a distress signal,
Levi."

"Then what?"

"It was the 'please don't make this red carpet any
weirder than it already has been' signal."

"That bad?" he asked, adding a tsk-tsk noise.

"No, it went okay. It definitely could have been worse;
there could have been *multiple* members of the Samuel Pussy
Club there, rather than just the one," I grumbled.

"Damn sweetie, you've got it bad. Jealous much?"

"I do not. And I *am* not," I insisted. "We kissed once,
that's it. We're just friends now."

Levi let out a bark of laughter before whimpering again.
"Holy Jesus, that hurt my head," he said under his breath. "Good
luck with that DeeDee."

"You're a pain in my ass, Garcia. But regardless, I'd still
like you to come for dinner. Mae's boyfriend is in town visiting
her from LA this weekend, so I thought I'd make Sunday dinner.
Care to join us?"

"At Jules' house? Pass"

"Come on, Levi. Who knows when you'll be in town
again, and when I get this promotion, I'll be on the 'wrong
coast' as you like to call it and we'll never get to see each other.
Please?"

"Ok," Levi said, with a resigned sigh. "Count me in. What should I bring?"

"I'm not even sure what we're having yet, but wine always works."

A distinct gagging sound came from the other end of the line.

"Fine. Erm… ugh, shit. I'll see you tonight," Levi garbled out. I started to respond, but the line went dead before I could get a word out. I tossed the phone onto the coffee table and reached for the remote. Before I could hit play, Jules' door swung wildly open with a bang. She shuffled out of her room and I had to choke down my laughter at her appearance. Her typically immaculate blonde hair was a tangled rat's nest on top of her head, and her face was marred with the makeup she'd neglected to wash off last night. Her hands were fisted in the hem of her pink tank-top, and the matching pajama bottoms appeared to be on backward. In an erratic zigzag path, Jules shuffled her way to the living room with her eyes practically closed and then flopped dramatically onto the couch, her head falling into my lap.

"Never, ever let me drink that much again," she said as her arms wrapped around my knees. I chuckled softly and brushed her bangs out of her eyes. "I didn't do anything stupid, did I?"

"You woke up alone, didn't you?" I teased quietly. Jules pinched my calf in response without even bothering to open her eyes. "Ouch! No, you didn't do anything stupid. Although you may want to apologize to Brian."

"Brian?" she asked, looking up at me timidly.

"The night doorman."

"Dear God, what did I do? I didn't traumatize the kid, did I?" she asked.

"No, you just educated him on the finer points of why he will *never* have a chance with you," I said, laughing at the memory of Jules' rant.

"Wow, I'm such a bitch," she said with a yawn as she closed her eyes again and nuzzled her face into my thighs. "Is it still hangover's choice?"

"Of course, what do you want tonight?" I asked. Our Sunday dinner was a tradition born in college, and as such, custom was that the menu was always to be chosen by the person with the worst hangover from Saturday night, and therefore the most particular palette.

"I want gumbo."

"Gumbo?" I asked loudly, Jules winced at the volume.

"What? Your gumbo is amazing," she said. "And your garden salad concoction thingy..."

"Why can't you crave burgers like normal hung-over people?" I said, tugging on a strand of her hair and moving to get up. Jules stretched out and took over the entire couch.

"Because burgers are bad for you," Jules mumbled into a throw pillow.

"Whereas pints of tequila can be considered health food," I tossed back before closing the door to my room to shower.

An hour later, I left the loft to buy groceries for dinner, giving Jules the time she needed to recover. Knowing what I did about her, she would be spending the afternoon making a protein shake and taking the longest bath known to man. Needless to say, I had plenty of time to kill before she'd be coherent, let alone social.

With that thought in mind, I turned left down the street rather than right. Typically, I'd make a quick run to the market on the corner, but the expanded farmer's market would be stretching all the way from Portland State, through the South Park blocks, and ending with a festival in Director's Park. If I wanted to kill some time, the market would surely do it. The sounds of different genres of music could be heard, and my senses were assaulted by the food smells coming from dozens of tent-covered tables. Vendors selling produce, flowers, bread and every assortment of specialty foods stretched out as far as I could see. I'd never experienced a Farmer's Market like this. We had them in LA, and I was definitely a fan, but this was incredible. It would take me all afternoon to get through the market, which was just fine.

I spotted a booth selling honeydew and started sorting through the fruit, looking for one ripe and not too large to carry around with me. I'd narrowed my selection to two when a velvety voice whispered into my ear, "Nice melons."

Fighting the shiver that threatened to snake through my body, I closed my eyes momentarily and took in the familiar smell and voice that I recognized immediately as Samuel's. With slightly more composure, I turned around and had to start the whole calming process all over again. He was standing in front of me looking positively, mouth-wateringly, delectable. He wasn't dressed for the board room, or the red carpet, or the bar. Instead, he was dressed casually in jeans and a black t-shirt that showed off the impressive biceps I'd been missing out on. I always thought of Pax as the buff one, but Samuel clearly held his own. His arms were toned and, unlike the dress shirts I'd only seen him in before, the snug t-shirt gave a hint of his abs and the six-pack begging to be touched. And as if the wardrobe wasn't enough, the man was looking down at me over the top of a pair of sunglasses with his signature smirk.

"Thank you. Which do you think is riper?" I asked, holding them suggestively in front of me.

Not helping the 'just friends' thing with the flirting, Dee.

Samuel chuckled lightly and surprised me by flicking them both with his finger, causing me to jump twice in my already wound-up state.

"That one," he said, pointing to the honeydew in my left hand and never taking his eyes from my own. I turned to pay and take another moment to steady my breathing. When I turned back, Samuel's glasses were back in place, and his hands were in his pocket.

"I'm surprised to see you here," I said as we stepped away from the booth and started walking down the busy path together.

"I'm surprised to be here, myself," he said. "I wasn't planning on checking this out, but I was walking back from brunch with my mom and saw the signs. Figured I was already here and had nothing else going on today."

"Not a fan of farmers' markets, huh?"

"Never actually *been* to one." He shrugged and continued looking around at the booths on either side of us.

"Are you serious?" I shrieked, unable to contain my surprise.

"Jesus," he said, whipping his head around and indicating with his hand the people near us that were all now looking at me in slight alarm.

"I'm sorry," I laughed. "Not to sound like a typical Californian, but how can you be from Portland and have *never* been to a Farmer's Market?"

"Right, because we all drink kale juice with every meal, have at least three dogs, and ride bikes everywhere."

"Well, yeah. And where's your beard, by the way?"

"And I'm assuming you live at the beach, like everyone else in LA?"

"Point taken," I laughed. "I'm just saying, if we had markets like this in LA, I'd probably be there every week. Don't get me wrong, we have them, and they're fine, but nothing like this."

"I'm guessing you have a soft spot for them."

"I do, and they're a bit addicting. You picked a great market as your first."

"Fine, let's pop my farmers' market cherry," he said, rubbing his hands together and clearly mocking my enthusiasm.

"God, you're so crude," I said, laughing. "But you'll see."

Samuel followed me as I haphazardly meandered from booth to booth, browsing produce and collecting ingredients for dinner. We talked about cooking, and I found out that his lack of experience with a fresh market made complete sense when you combined it with his apparent lack of culinary skills. To hear him describe it, I imaged his apartment to be scattered with takeout containers and old pizza boxes. He'd scoffed at this admission and made a jab back at me for reverting to our assumptive tendencies, all after teasing me for picturing his apartment, of course.

We moved on to the subject of music and I admitted to my love of jazz. Samuel seemed genuinely shocked. When I asked about his reaction, he confessed that he'd taken me to be a pop music fan, which I laughed wholeheartedly at and took my turn at ribbing him for assumptions.

Conversation flowed smoothly, and we bounced from topics like childhood vacations to our shared love for old movie marathons when we were sick. Nearly half an hour later, I found myself sorting through a basket of carrots and thinking about our night in the bar a week earlier. Samuel was so easy to talk to, and time passed quickly when we were together; well, when we weren't trying to kill one another, that is. On the one hand, our new friendship seemed more comfortable than ever since I was coming to the realization that it was second nature to be around Samuel when we were being ourselves. But on the other hand, it made me dejected that I'd found this sort of chemistry with someone I could never be with.

"This is fun and all," Samuel said next to me as he sorted through bean sprouts, "but you *do* realize that the stuff on your list is all located within twenty feet of each other at a grocery store, right? Ten minutes, tops. That's all the time you'd need."

"It's more about quality, and the experience, than the speed," I said, refocusing on the task at hand. I saw him turn slightly toward me and I cut him off just as his mouth opened to speak. "If you say, 'that's what she said,' I'm throwing a carrot at you."

Samuel let out a belly laugh and nudged my shoulder playfully.

"Do you normally spend most of your Sunday shopping for food one pop-tent at a time?"

"Well, today I'm not in much of a hurry," I told him offhandedly. "My roommate is nursing an impressive hangover, and I'd like to be out of the loft until she's feeling better. Jules is volatile when she feels like shit."

"Ah, the infamous Jules." Samuel held up a sprout and tossed it in the bag when I nodded in approval. He had taken to digging through the barrel and seemed determined to select the best of the group; I didn't have the heart to tell him I didn't actually need sprouts. "I'm assuming this is the same Jules that set you up with Mr. Calorie Counter the other night?"

"One and the same," I chuckled as we made our way to the vendor, and I all but threw cash at her before Samuel could pay for the produce. We'd been having this battle at every booth we visited; he kept insisting on paying for things, and I kept telling him that was ridiculous. What I knew of his father led me to think that he was being chivalrous, but it was annoying as all get out. Plus, we're just friends and friends didn't do that sort of thing.

"Is she suffering from the after-effects of a horrible blind date of her own?" he asked, sliding his sunglasses back in place as we turned the corner and continued our stroll through the market.

"No, she's recovering from our girls' night out," I said absentmindedly, rooting through one of my bags in search of the raspberries. I found them and popped one in my mouth before offering the container to Samuel. He accepted my offering while chuckling lightly under his breath.

"What?" I asked.

"I find it incredibly ironic that you went bar hopping last night, and *I* didn't," he said smugly, chewing on a mouthful of berries.

"Since when does Samuel Monroe spend a Saturday night alone?" I mumbled.

"I didn't say I was alone, I was just commenting on you hitting the social scene you admonish me for loving so much."

"Ah, where did you meet her then? The grocery store?" I was surprised by how quickly my frustration spiked at his mention of being with someone else last night.

Son of a bitch; I am jealous!

"Green's a sexy color on you, Sheppard," he said, and I knew he wasn't referring to my blouse. I stopped in my tracks and turned to retort, but before I could, Samuel turned as well and pressed my lips together with his thumb and forefinger. "I was having dinner with Emma."

If I was surprised at my jealousy, I was more shocked at how relieved I felt that Samuel was with his sister last night. His eyes searched mine, and no matter how hard I tried to appear passive, I was sure he could see the tornado of emotions swirling in my head. He released my lips and his hand slightly cupped my chin before falling to his side.

"You really think I sleep with every woman I meet, don't you?" he said sadly, taking a step back from me. I sighed and forced myself to swallow my nonsensical possessiveness and act like a sane person.

"No, if that were true I would have been under you already," I quipped in an attempt to lighten the mood.

"Or on top of me," he said with his smirk, clearly not requiring much prodding to get back to easy going.

"Actually," I said, skipping over his comment and resuming our walk, "I subscribe to the PR rule-of-thumb that a celebrity's public persona is an exaggeration of their true self."

"Ah ha! So that means… wait, what the hell does that mean, exactly?"

"It means that I don't believe you *literally* sleep with a different woman every night. According to the theory, you aren't as much of a man-whore as you appear to be." His smug smile started to make another appearance, and I quickly continued before he could speak. "Don't get me wrong," I said, holding up a finger and smirking at him, "I still think you're a player, and the adjective 'promiscuous' wouldn't necessarily be misplaced on you. But, I would guess that the 'true self' portion of the theory implies that you act the way you do because of some other issue. It wouldn't surprise me if 'reckless man-whore' in the press translated into 'wounded commitment-phobe' in real life."

The next few feet were walked in silence, and I suddenly realized how harsh all of that had probably sounded. I'd started spouting communications theory and lost sight of the *person* I was not only talking about but also talking *to*. Samuel had shown a glimpse of vulnerability regarding my opinion of him, and I'd responded by telling him that rather than thinking he was a complete whore, I instead thought he was a broken man. Damn, maybe the guy just likes women and doesn't want to be tied down! And instead of simply asking, I started psychologically profiling him in the middle of the farmers market.

How in God's name have I created a career for myself in publicity when I am so bad with people on a personal level?

I knew the answer to that question as soon as I'd thought it. I was great with people; it was *Samuel* that I was always a mess around. Never in my life, personal or professional, had I been so erratic. I wouldn't blame him for walking in the opposite direction at any moment. In fact, I could have just obliterated our ceasefire with my word vomit.

"Stop pulling on your lip, Dee. I'm not mad at you," Samuel said, and my eyes darted up to his face. He looked back down and gave me a small smile. "Oh, come on, you think you're the first person to tell me they have a theory as to why I live my life the way I do?"

I felt like a complete asshole at that moment. He'd said it so lighthearted and jovial, but his words made me feel so judgmental and ignorant. I was one of countless others who passed judgment on Samuel without even knowing the real man. And what made it worse, was that I felt a real connection with him unlike anyone else I'd ever met, and I'd *still* spewed my stupid theories on him.

"Well, if we're going to be friends we might as well do it right. C'mon, let's take a break from your farming fun, and talk," he said, leading me to the park benches in the center of the market.

"We're not actually farming-"

"I'll get us some coffee," he said with a laugh, cutting me off. As he disappeared into the crowd, I buried my head in my hands and groaned. Up was down, right was left, Samuel was the rational one, and I had no idea how to act. He reappeared moments later with two drinks and slid onto the bench across from me.

"Ok. Your theory, let's have it," he said, sipping his coffee.

"I...No, I..."

"You've told me that you don't believe I'm as vile as I appear to be in the press, but you think there's an underlying reason for why I am the way I am. Honestly, Delilah, I'm just repeating what you've said. Out with it, ask your question."

"Someone broke your heart, didn't they?" As soon as the question left my lips, I winced. The thought had occurred to me in bits and pieces since Mae had given me his file. I hadn't planned on asking him outright, but apparently the open invitation was far too much for my inner filter.

"Ah," he said with a wry smile, "the assumption that a woman destroyed me and now I can no longer bring myself to love. Therefore, I fuck everything that comes my way." His eyes were glued to the table and his expression was blank. I wanted to fill the silence but had no idea what to say. "I'll tell you what," he said, snapping his head back up. Our eyes met, and I was surprised to see them without a trace of anger or annoyance. Instead, Samuel looked relieved. "I'll make you a deal. I'll give you the whole story, but only if you promise to give me an honest answer to a question of my own."

"Deal," I said, without even thinking about the terms. I just wanted to know every inch of his heart, and if it required a compromise, I'd give it gladly.

"I didn't have my heart broken," he said quietly, looking down at the straw wrapper in his hands. "I broke a heart."

I inhaled loudly, not expecting his admission, but his hand hit mine on the table before I could react. "Yvonne Bloom; we dated in college and had lived together for almost a year. One night during our senior year we got into this huge fight; she was pre-med and heading off to Stanford for medical school, while I was taking off for grad school in New York. It was an issue we'd avoided and danced around before it finally all blew up one night. Neither of us wanted to relent, and finally, I just stormed out, and like an idiot, went straight to a party some friends were throwing," Samuel said with a sigh. "There was this girl, I had some drinks, and I'm sure you see where I'm going with this. I didn't even like her, and to this day I can't recall why I did what I did when Yvonne was home waiting for me." Samuel rolled his eyes and sat up straighter, stretching his back before leaning on his elbows on the picnic table between us. "I know it was years ago and it shouldn't really still affect me," he said looking up at me, the sadness behind his eyes apparent. "But I couldn't lie to her; I told her what I'd done, and I'll never forget the look on her face, how hurt she was. I started questioning what kind of person I was and how I could do something like that to someone I really loved. I came to the conclusion that I'm just not capable of that sort of commitment; I'm a guy that can love but doesn't do well with being someone's person. I decided the best thing to do was be honest about myself, always. Let people know what they're getting into from the start."

"You were just a kid," I said.

"I know," he laughed. "And Yvonne's totally over it. She's married and has a kid, lives in San Francisco now."

"But you're still living your life by the rule a 19-year-old version of yourself made up?"

He laughed and shook his head. "Well, it sounds ridiculous when you put it like that."

"I'm sorry, you're confiding in me a painful story, it's not my place to commentate on it," I said, shaking my head at my own impulsiveness.

"Ok then," he said, smiling ruefully at me and quickly shaking off any semblance of the emotional man that'd just been talking. "It's your turn. You agreed; I get a question now."

I was suddenly regretting my agreement to this conversation.

"Why is this assignment so important to you?" he asked casually, sipping his coffee again as though he'd just asked my favorite food.

I opened and closed my mouth a couple of times to respond but found myself at a loss. I had been preparing for so many different questions to come out of his mouth, this one actually took me by surprise.

"I'm enjoying your goldfish impression, but I was really hoping for an answer," Samuel said.

"Why do you ask that?" I shrugged. "I was assigned the hotel, and I go where I'm assigned."

"True," he said with a nod, "But I looked you up. You've handled some major celebrities and big stars in LA, and I'd imagine that if someone with a resume such as yours were sent to Portland to handle a hotel rebrand, they would probably be phoning it in a bit. Not attacking it with this much gumption."

"Maybe I just have integrity and take a lot of pride in my work."

"I think there's something else," he said, casually taking a sip of coffee and waiting for me to speak.

At this point, what could the truth about this particular point hurt?

"I have a chance to be promoted," I said. "I've been wanting to get into corporate communications and PR for a long time. And if I can execute the Monroe assignment perfectly, and impress my bosses, I have a real shot at the job in-" I stopped myself, suddenly remembering Emma's warning about getting close to Samuel and then skipping town. "In New York," I finished solemnly.

"New York," he said with eyebrows raised. "Great city, you'll love it there." I couldn't quite distinguish his expression as he took another sip of coffee while looking off into the crowd of people around us. For a man that prided himself on being an open book, I suddenly couldn't read him at all. "That's it then, you'll be leaving," he said, turning to look back at me, "probably sooner than later, I'm guessing."

I nodded, unsure what to say.

"Hmm." Samuel tilted his head back and looked at me carefully. "I know what we need."

Before I could ask, Samuel was on his feet and on my side of the table, grabbing my hand to pull me off the bench. I scooped up my bags quickly as he started to lead us away from the lawn and toward a grouping of booths at the edge of the plaza.

"What are you doing?" I asked, trying to keep hold of my things as he held my hand and led us into the crowd.

"Putting the knowledge that comes with having a sister to good use," he said as we stopped in front of a table that smelled absolutely divine. Laid out before us was a collection of chocolate concoctions of every variety, and I realized that we were standing at the booth of a leading Portland confectioner. Truffles were next to candies which were next to a dozen different flavors of fudge. My mouth fell open just after filling with saliva, and I absently put a hand to my jaw to check for drool.

"Deep conversations and the sharing of secrets are to be followed with chocolate," Samuel said in a monotone voice, and I knew he was quoting Emma. I couldn't stop the giggle that erupted as he waved his hand exaggeratedly over the product selection like Willy Wonka. I pointed at a dark chocolate truffle and he held up two fingers to the owner. He paid for our chocolate before we made our way back out into the crowd of people walking the market, leaving the conversation about my promotion and moving to New York behind us.

"Wow, you might just be the best friend I've ever had," I said with a moan after swallowing a bite of chocolate goodness.

"Glad to know I'm succeeding, since being friends with a woman is *completely* new to me. What's next? Do I braid your hair?" he asked, tossing the last of the truffle into his mouth.

"No, that doesn't happen until after the pillow fight in our underwear," I said, causing Samuel to start sputtering and choking next to me. I slapped him harshly on the back while laughing at him. "Just kidding. Actually, you're doing great at the friend thing, relax."

"Thank you," he said, clearing his throat. "Makes you wonder why we were ever at war with one another, doesn't it?"

Just as the words left his mouth, we turned the corner, and Samuel stopped dead in his tracks. I looked up at him questioningly and followed his line of sight, my breath catching when I saw what he was staring at.

SIXTEEN

Delilah

Directly in front of us was a booth situated underneath a large sign that read 'Community Clinic: Free STD Testing.' I was grateful to at least see they hadn't made a poster board advertising Samuel's quote from the Portland Daily.

"Please tell me," I said quietly, while still staring at the site in front of us, "that they don't know you by name over there."

"I doubt *all* of them know me," he whispered, looking over the rim of his sunglasses at the table. He seemed relieved when I laughed, clearly not confident in how his joke would land.

"Let's just keep moving, shall we?" he said, pushing his glasses back up the bridge of his nose and wrapping an arm around my waist. I let him lead me down the path and leaned into his side for a moment before pulling back and attempting to think of anything other than his touch.

"What's the matter, Monroe? Afraid I'll find out your dirty little secrets?" I asked as we continued our walk.

"I'm willing to bet that it's pointless to hide any of my secrets from you for long," he said looking down at me. "If you don't find out on your own, I'm sure I'll end up telling you myself."

"I guess I have that effect on people," I said, staring up and losing myself in the intimate, warm gaze he was looking at me with.

"Fuck people," he said with quiet force, pinching my chin between his thumb and forefinger. "You affect *me*."

My traitorous body reacted and started to turn toward him and press our bodies together. I yearned to kiss him, and despite every rational decision I'd made thus far, I wanted nothing more in that moment than to be enveloped in Samuel's embrace and go back to our bad decision from before. I started to lean into him and quickly realized what I was doing.

"I should get home," I said quickly, pulling out of his reach and taking a step back. It was becoming harder and harder to resist him, and the reasons for doing so were getting fuzzier the more time we spent together.

"Another blind date?" he asked, jamming his fists into his pockets and giving me a smile that didn't reach his eyes.

"Actually, I'm making dinner for friends. Hence the groceries," I said, holding up the bags in my hand. I met his stare again and the calm returned to my thoughts. "Why don't you come?"

Wait, what?! Not so calm after all.

As soon as the words left my mouth, I knew I'd made a mistake.

"Really?" he asked, obviously taken aback at the invitation.

"Of course!"

Dee, shut the fuck up!

I'd just invited Samuel to spend the evening with my roommate, who would most definitely not hide her distaste for him, my assistant, her boyfriend, and let's not forget Levi. A dimension did not exist where this was a good idea. But yet I couldn't seem to part ways with the man and therefore had turned Sunday dinner into the most awkward dinner party ever to happen.

"Um, yeah. Yes, great. When should I be there?" he asked.

I looked at my watch and couldn't believe it was already after four in the afternoon. I'd spent the whole damn day at the market, with Samuel.

"Everyone's showing up in about an hour. I need to grab some thyme," I said, gesturing to the booth behind him. "I guess you should just come home with me?" I hadn't meant it to sound like a question, or a pick-up line, but the idea of Samuel in my home left a lump in my throat. His thick hair and newly discovered body and kissable mouth so close to the location in which I slept every night was probably not the best idea in my quest to keep things professional. But the train had left the station and I was riding that thing right off a cliff.

"Ok, grab your thyme; I'll meet you over there." He gave my shoulder a squeeze and took off in the opposite direction. I walked to the booth selling herbs in a haze. I could do this, no big deal. I was making dinner for friends, and Samuel was a friend, my friend.

Friends have dinner together, and spend the day shopping together, and then make-out on the couch together...

I shook my head violently, trying to push away thoughts of his hands on my body and tongue in my mouth. Christ, this friend shit was *hard*. I handed my bag to the young girl behind the table to be weighed and reached for my wallet.

"I'm ready," Samuel said next to me, making me jump slightly in surprise. I turned to hand over my cash, but not before noticing the bouquet of daisies in his other hand. We made our way back through the market, but my eyes had yet to leave the flowers. In fact, I was squinting at them; it was as though they were speaking to me, but I just couldn't make out the words.

"They're your favorite, aren't they?" Samuel asked, noticing my attention to the bouquet.

My brows furrowed as I tried to shift through every conversation I'd had with Samuel in an attempt to figure out how in the *hell* he knew my favorite flower.

"How?" I asked abruptly, at a loss for an explanation.

"At the bar. We were talking about allergies, and you told me you were allergic to lilies, which was sad since you thought they were the most beautiful flower ever. And by default," he said, lifting the bouquet from his side so I could see it clearly, "daisies are your favorite flower."

There was only a whooshing noise in my mind for a moment as I blinked rapidly and stared at the flowers while we walked. I'd had my share of boyfriends over the years, some more serious than others. But my 'friend' Samuel managed in that moment to make my heart swell more than any other man ever had.

"I was always taught that you should bring something to a dinner party," Samuel continued. "You *clearly* have the food list settled, and I've yet to see a damn booth selling liquor in this place, so I figured flowers for the table would be my best bet."

I managed to nod and mumble something incoherent in response, still trying to clear my head. His awareness of my personality, combined with the diligence he paid the manners his mother taught him made my legs itch to wrap themselves around him.

"You're still surprised that I remember everything you told me that night, aren't you?"

"If you could sound *prouder* of yourself, that would be great," I grumbled sarcastically as we turned the corner leaving the market and heading to the loft.

"I can definitely try," he said in mock seriousness, making me smile as he lightened the mood. That was until we reached the entrance of my building.

Here goes nothing.

We rode the elevator in anxious silence; well *I* was anxious, Samuel was whistling softly and jingling the keys in his pocket. I should have been preparing him for Jules and Levi, but we'd need a much longer elevator ride for me to do it right. I opened the front door and heard Mae's laughter coming from the living room, and I smiled at the thought that she was naturally early. Thankfully, she'd met Jules a few times before, so my absence didn't make things awkward for her.

"Hey, Dee," she said when I came around the corner to deposit my bags on the counter of the bar adjoining the kitchen.

"Hello there. Good to see you, Henry."

Before Mae's boyfriend could respond I heard a quiet gasp come from her and turned to see Samuel coming into the living room, flowers still in hand and a smile on his face. "Mae, right? We haven't had much of a chance to really speak at the office yet, other than you trying to keep me from barging into Delilah's office," he said with a chuckle and extending his hand to her. She shook it tentatively, her eyes bouncing between Samuel in surprise and back to me in question. My attention, however, was on Jules. She'd put together who Samuel was based on his comment and was now shooting him a narrow stare, her fists slightly clenched at her side.

Henry and Samuel were introducing themselves since the silence was deafening as the ladies were all having conversations with nothing but pointed looks. It vaguely registered that I was being rude by slacking on the introductions, but there were other priorities at the moment. I went to stand next to Jules and put a hand on her forearm. Her head shot down to look at me and she silently asked, *What is he doing here?* I shook my head minutely and just as mutely implied, *I'll explain later*. Her reply let me know that she wasn't happy with that answer and I'd be explaining in detail later. The whole exchange took less than five seconds.

Henry returned to the couch, seemingly unaware of the crackling tension in the room, and Samuel turned to me before his eyes fell on Jules.

"Samuel Monroe, this is my roommate, Jules Dahl."

He had no idea what he was walking into, or that Jules already had a dislike for him before he'd stepped foot into her home. I quickly imagined all the pithy things Samuel might say that would make this worse, like making a joke about her matchmaking skills, or bringing up her hangover.

Instead, Samuel said the only thing that could have saved him at that moment.

"Oh wow, you're JD from Ultimate Torque! I'm a huge fan." She hated the nickname the network had used to market her show when it first started, but the ice around Jules thawed a bit at being recognized by a fan and she reluctantly grabbed his outstretched hand to shake it. "It's so nice to meet you."

"Mmhmm," was all she offered in return, but I could tell the scales were tipping ever so slightly in Samuel's favor with Jules, and I sighed quietly in relief.

"I keep trying to get my brother Pax to watch your show, I know he'd love it," he said, undeterred by her lack of response.

"Which one's Pax?" Jules asked me.

"IndyCar," I replied.

"Oh," Jules said, turning back to Samuel. "Tell him not to bother. I don't condone street racing, and he'll be waiting until hell freezes over if he wants a segment about NOS."

Samuel's brow furrowed in confusion to Jules's answer and blatant hostility. She was slightly thawed but still chilly.

"Jules actually helped me get a celebrity appearance for Pax's event next week," I told Samuel, trying to mediate the conversation between the two of them.

"Really?" Samuel asked hesitantly, clearly not wanting to say the wrong thing and rile Jules up again.

"Yes," Mae chimed in, "Lex Ross agreed to a meet-and-greet at the last minute."

"Who?" Samuel asked me.

"He's an eight-time IndyCar winner," Jules said with a sigh, clearly annoyed with his ignorance on the subject.

"It's ok, I didn't know who he was either," Mae offered sweetly to Samuel, figuratively placing herself between him and Jules. I gave a silent prayer of thanks for Mae and gave her a grateful glance. Samuel and Jules continued to face-off; she remained antagonistic, and he was getting defensive.

"Hey Dee, do you mind if Sam and I check the score on the Mariners game?" Henry asked.

"Sure!" I said, enthusiastically jumping at the chance to leave the room. "Ladies, care to help me?" I scooped up my bags and the flowers Samuel had set on the counter before making a hasty exit into the kitchen. Once there, I dropped my head after resting my palms on the cool countertop and closing my eyes. I'd taken exactly two deep breaths when Jules and Mae appeared.

"What the hell, Dee?" Jules hissed. "What is he *doing* here?!"

I grumbled an unintelligible answer as I started pulling items out of their bags and throwing them in the sink to be washed, annoyed that I didn't have a spectacular answer as to why Samuel was sitting on our couch at the moment.

"I have to admit I have the same question as Jules," Mae piped in.

"I ran into him at the market, and we got to talking, and I invited him."

"No, that shit doesn't fly. I want an explanation for why the man you're practically at war with, *most* of the time, is here for dinner tonight. I know the two of you *had a moment*," she said, annoyed with speaking in code in front of Mae, "but he's still been an asshole and made your life miserable since then." She crossed her arms over her chest and continued burning holes in the side of my head with her stare.

Mae looked at Jules with a squint, picking up on her blatant code words.

"Yes, we had... a moment," I said carefully "But it's over, and we're just colleagues. *Friends*." I stressed the last word and eyed Jules deliberately, trying to tell her to shut the fuck up. Instead, she threw her head back and scoffed loudly while washing the carrot in her hand.

"Friends?" she asked, turning off the faucet and facing me. "You two are just friends?"

"Y-yes."

"Oh," she said, her expression relaxing and finally looking like my friend again. "Well, in that case, would you mind if I asked him out? He's clearly a fan, and even though I think he's an asshole, you know how I feel about angry sex. Samuel could be the perfect guy to end my slump."

I could feel the heat radiating through my body and I tried, unsuccessfully, to reign in the evil stare I gave Jules. I'd already felt small pangs of jealousy when he'd fawned all over her earlier, but I'd managed to fight them down with the knowledge that Samuel may do many things in this battle of ours, but he would never fuck my best friend. But the idea of Jules using her amazing beauty to lure him to bed, left me with a pit in my stomach since I wasn't naïve or optimistic enough to think that he would resist.

"Whoa," Mae breathed out, eyes wide in surprise.

"What?" I asked, looking around the kitchen for the fire.

"Nothing," Jules said flippantly, tossing a strand of blonde hair over her shoulder as she returned to prepping the food. "You've just proven my point; you have it *bad* for this guy."

It wasn't the first time in a 24-hour period that someone had told me that. Combine it with what I'd felt all afternoon with Samuel, and I was starting to second guess everything and feeling more and more dread about what was to happen in the coming weeks. And then, the doorbell rang.

"Fuck me," I muttered, knowing full well who was on the other side of the door. I could hear Jules snicker as I left the kitchen and headed down the hall.

"Hey sugar!" Levi said, brushing past me. "I had no idea what you'd want, *or* what you were making for dinner, so I brought three different types of white wine and a selection of red. I know it's overkill, but I'm sure your lush of a roommate will drink what we don't," he said, slipping his jacket off and setting the case of wine down on the table with a bang, causing Samuel and Henry to look up from their spot on the couch just as Levi wrapped his arms around me and lifted me off my feet in his signature bear hug. I patted him affectionately on the back and stiffened when I noticed Samuel shoot up from the couch, cross the living room and make his way over to us with a quickness.

"Levi," I said, prodding him to let me down. When my feet hit the floor, I turned so that I was standing between Levi and Samuel, each of my shoulders almost touching a different male chest. Samuel had resumed his stance from the red carpet, while Levi was dragging his eyes luxuriously up and down his body. "Allow me to introduce you two, officially. Samuel Monroe, meet my dear friend Levi Garcia. Levi, meet Samuel, my colleague." The last word was even more strained than it'd been in the kitchen.

"Levi," Samuel said, offering his hand to Levi and eyeing him carefully, clearly expecting a repeat of Friday night's showdown. Levi, however, had other plans now that he knew Samuel wasn't a threat to me at all.

"Oh my God, Samuel, it's so amazing to finally be meeting you 'officially'," he gushed, making air quotes with his hands, mocking my second introduction. "I've read a lot about you, well and *written* a bit about you, and I have to admit that I *did* have a bit of a schoolboy crush on you for a while. When Dee said that she was working with you, well, I couldn't believe it! I'm just really sorry that our first encounter went the way it did. But I thought DeeDee was upset the other night, and the tiger comes out when that happens," he said, capping off his speech with a subdued growl and clawing hand gesture at Samuel's chest.

"Wait, you're... I mean... you're not..." Samuel stammered. The poor guy's head was probably spinning at this point.

"I met Levi in LA, where he lives half the time," I said, interrupting his rambling. "We've worked together and been friends for years."

"Just friends," Samuel said to me, repeating what I'd said to him in the break room the other day. I nodded.

"Yup," Levi added, "mostly because DeeDee has breasts and I love peen."

"Peen?" Samuel's brow was furrowed in confusion again.

"Yeah, peen," Levi said, looking at Samuel like he was slow. "You know, Penis? Cock!"

If Samuel had any doubt as to Levi's sexual orientation before, it was certainly all cleared up now. I was sure my expression matched Samuel's one of surprise, not because of Levi's homosexuality but rather the fact that he'd just yelled cock at Samuel in my living room. This was not how I pictured the afternoon going when I made my omelet this morning.

"Can I help with dinner?" Levi asked as he started to walk toward the kitchen.

"Jules is in there," I warned.

Levi did an immediate about-face and walked into the living room instead.

"In that case, I'll watch baseball," he said, sitting down next to Henry on the couch. "Hey, I'm Levi. Which quarter are we in?"

"You live in a sitcom," Samuel said quietly as we watched Henry explain the finer points of baseball to Levi, which included the difference between quarters and innings.

"It sure feels that way sometimes." I looked up at him. "Overwhelmed yet? Because you've only been getting them in fits and spurts; wait until we get them all at one table."

"Have you met my family?" Samuel said, looking down at me. "I think I can handle it." He gave me a quick wink and went to join the male bonding session in the living room. Well, if you can call Levi raving about the pitcher's ass actual male bonding.

I rejoined the ladies in the kitchen and quickly went to work on getting dinner ready. As we worked, in hushed voices Jules and I caught Mae up on the whole 'Samuel thing,' as Jules referred to it. It occurred to me that sharing the story with my assistant wasn't the most professional thing to do. *Fuck it,* I thought, taking a sip of my wine. The idea of keeping my personal and professional lives separate was becoming highly laughable at this point. I'd signed the death sentence for that line when I walked into the bar a week earlier.

About an hour later we were all seated around Jules's kitchen table, wine bottles and dishes being passed in every direction possible. Samuel and Henry were animatedly discussing Seattle's starting lineup, while Jules and Levi were arguing about casting decisions for the next season of god-knows-what TV show. Beside me, Mae lifted the gumbo dish and held it across the table.

"Gumbo, Samuel?"

He eyed it carefully before giving Mae and then me an apologetic look.

"Thanks, Mae, but I can't-"

"I made it with just chicken and sausage," I said, bringing my wine glass to my lips to hide the smirk threatening to come out.

"Why in God's name would you do that?" Jules huffed.

"Because Samuel's allergic to shrimp." The look on his face was priceless. He blinked quickly in surprise and then smiled to himself as he took the dish from Mae.

Levi made some off-handed comment about being allergic to latex, and just like that conversation and laughter started back up again. Every once and a while during dinner, I'd look up and watch Samuel as he joked with Henry, or talked to Levi about his website, or tried like hell to get Jules to warm up to him. Every time I looked up, the thought kept invading my mind: *he fits here.*

And every time I had that particular thought, a pang of guilt and sadness shot through me.

Before I knew it, and despite myself, I was sad to find the dishes were done and the party was breaking up. Mae and Henry took off first, with Levi not too far behind them, mumbling something about a date downtown as he left. I walked Samuel to the elevator as he continued to praise my cooking.

"This friend thing is kind of fun," he said, pressing the down button for the elevator. "Oh, wait. Is this the part where we go our separate ways and become mortal enemies again tomorrow morning? Or does this friendship survive the threshold into work?"

"No," I said with a laugh. "Don't get me wrong, I'm sure you're still going to piss me off every now and again, and while fighting with you can be fun sometimes, I think I prefer it this way. It's less exhausting, don't you think?"

"I do," he said, looking down at me with a sigh. "Let me take you to dinner this week." He tucked a strand of hair behind my ear as I looked at my feet trying to find the will to decline the invitation to spend more time with him. "What? Friends don't eat together? Hell, we just did! Don't you go out to dinner with your friends?" And while his words were playful and speaking of friendship, his fingers still twirled with a strand of my hair while his other hand reached my hip and pulled my body closer to his.

"Lunch," I offered breathlessly as I dared to look up into his eyes but made no move to separate us.

"Ok, lunch it is," he said giving me a lazy smile. His hand snaked from my hip to the small of my back while he lowered his face to my ear and said, "I'll take whichever hour of your day you're willing to give me."

His words were so genuine and sincere that I had to pull back slightly to take in his eyes and read his face, which told me everything he was saying was honest. With an exhale I relaxed into his embrace and slipped my arms around his neck, never breaking from the stare that held my focus and heart.

"Sam," was all I managed to get out in a whisper.

"Dee," he whispered back in reverence just before lowering his lips to mine. This was different than our first kiss; it wasn't frantic or angry, but rather soft and intimate. Both of his arms wrapped around my waist, tugging me gently against him, while I crossed my arms behind his neck and sank into his embrace. Sam wasn't grabbing me this time; he was holding me. Our bodies weren't crushing against one another, but rather melting into each other.

The elevator dinged and I let out a low, disappointed moan unwittingly before we pulled apart slowly.

"Friends don't do *that*," he teased in a low husky voice.

"No, I suppose they don't," I replied, shifting from one foot to the other nervously. Sam leaned over and kissed me chastely on the lips and then on the tip of my nose.

"We'll make the rules up as we go," he said, smiling triumphantly at me and stepping into the elevator. "And it's about time you start calling me Sam."

The elevator closed and I was left staring at my reflection in the steel doors.

"Hey," Jules called a minute later, poking her head out of our doorway into the hall. "What are you doing out here?"

"I have *no* idea," I answered honestly.

SEVENTEEN

Sam

The smile on my face couldn't be helped as I rode the elevator up to the office the next morning. There was also no keeping Dee out of my thoughts, and I wasn't even trying any longer. Yet again, my mind rolled over our Sunday together and the fun I'd had shopping with her. Well, not the actual *shopping* part of the day. I still held firm in my opinion that the errand of getting food for *one* goddamn dinner would have taken all of twenty minutes in an actual fucking grocery store. But Dee's enthusiasm had been infectious, and I found myself relishing the way her eyes lit up when she saw a booth she'd been looking for, or the intensity on her face while picking through a barrel of vegetables. More often than I cared to admit, the words 'adorable' and 'endearing' had sprung to mind while we shopped.

As I'd wandered through the market with Dee, I was surprised to find myself being turned on while she did innocuous things like close her eyes to smell spices or brush her arm against mine to reach for something. It was as though she had an electric connection to my body and everything she did aroused a reaction. When I finally kissed her, when I finally had her body in my hands again, it was as though a pressure valve was being released and I could breathe a little easier. As for titles, friend, boyfriend, I couldn't give two shits what Dee called me; she was way more concerned with semantics like that than I was. What I cared about was that, little by little, she was giving more of herself to me. More than anything else, I just wanted to be the one she let her hair down with. I knew now that she was leaving soon, and I was guessing that was part of her reluctance to get closer. But the bricks in my defense were quaking when I was around Dee, and I was hoping that I had the same effect on her.

I made it to the office earlier than normal, but despite the time, Leslie was dutifully at her desk, typing away on her computer and making me wondered if she slept here.

"Good morning, Mr. Monroe," she said, looking up from the screen.

"Morning," I replied, grabbing my mail and messages from her. "I'd like you to add a lunch appointment to my-"

"Calendar for today? With Ms. Sheppard?"

"Yes. How did you-"

"She called this morning and asked me to add it to your schedule," she interrupted again. I fought like hell to keep my expression neutral rather than smug when it occurred to me that Dee had jumped so quickly on setting up our lunch date.

"Ms. Sheppard also had me add your one-on-one PR meeting with her to your calendar, just before the lunch appointment today. You meet with her at eleven, assuming that's ok," Leslie added.

Here I'd been solely focused on the fact that I'd coerced Dee into a lunch date and forgotten completely about our conversation on Friday night. Her acquiescence to lunch from yesterday faded away in my memory and was replaced with her insistence on Friday night that I should concede to her professional expertise.

"Eleven works great for me, assuming there are no other pressing matters," I mumbled and walked past her into my office, but not before noticing Leslie's rarely appearing smile as she turned back toward her monitor. Three conference calls, an international sales teleconference and who knows how many emails later, I was on my way to Dee's office for our meeting. When I reached the end of the hall and approached Dee's office, I heard Mae before I turned the corner and actually saw her.

"Well, I can officially deny that Paxton Monroe was in a street race this weekend." My ears perked up at the mention of my brother. I knew he'd spent the weekend in Seattle at a car show, and my blood boiled at the ridiculous claim he was getting into trouble a week before his racing event. It had become clear that Pax would cut off his own arm before doing something to look bad in the media, or more importantly, piss off Dee.

"No, you don't need to confirm that with Ms. Sheppard!" Mae practically yelled, "I'm her Assistant and have the authority to comment on such things, and we deny all claims that Mr. Monroe was involved. Thank you, have a good day."

I heard her slam the phone down in a huff and smiled to myself. Mae initially came across as a wallflower, but Dee was clearly grooming herself another PR bad-ass. I turned the corner and came to a halt in front of Mae's desk with my hands in my pockets, not bothering to hide my amusement at the situation.

"Hello, Mae." Her head jerked up, and she had a brief look of frustration that vanished when she saw me and smiled back.

"Oh, hello Sam-" She pressed her lips together and furrowed her brow, "I mean, good morning, *Mr. Monroe.*"

I couldn't hold back my laughter at her sudden professionalism. She truly was Dee's protégé; Mae was now two-stepping along the line between her personal and professional life.

"You can call me Sam here, too," I said, still chuckling. "Shit, I have a fifty-dollar bet with your boyfriend on the Mariner's game this week. I think we're beyond 'Mr. Monroe' at this point; unless of course, I lose." I gave her a smile to let her know I was kidding, and Mae's entire body relaxed as she smiled in return. "Is she in?"

"Yep. She said to send you in when you got here."

I started toward Dee's office and began readying myself for whatever she may throw at me during this meeting. I quickly cursed myself for not talking to my siblings and getting a read on what to expect. But in all honesty, Emma would have told me to stop playing games and just meet with Dee, while Pax would have said something ridiculous like man-up and grow a pair.

I walked in ready to meet the challenge of succumbing to the PR circus and getting this meeting done and over with, simply so we could head to lunch and back to being comfortable. But I stopped short as soon as I clapped eyes on her. Dee was at her desk, reading something in front of her, and wearing the sexiest pair of glasses imaginable, causing me to want to live out every librarian fantasy I'd ever had right there on her desk. I'd seen Dee in her glasses before. She'd worn them in our first meeting, but since then I'd also seen her throw her head back in pleasure, tasted her pouty lips, cupped her luscious ass, grasped her-

"Are you just going to stand in my doorway the whole time?" Dee's voice broke through my sex-induced thoughts and brought me back to attention. "We can have our meeting that way if you'd prefer, but you may get uncomfortable after a while," she said, smirking at me over the rim of those damn glasses that were sure to give me a heart attack. I crossed the room and sat in one of the chairs in front of her desk, doing so carefully as to hide my hardening cock. I had no idea how I was going to get through this meeting.

"Lose the glasses," I said, before even realizing what I'd said.

"I'm sorry?" Dee asked, giving me a confused and somewhat surprised look.

"I just mean, if we're not going over paperwork or anything…it would, um, make this feel less…" I stopped my rambling when I realized I had no idea where I was going with it. Fuck it, I hadn't figured out exactly where my head was, but I was also losing my patience with holding my tongue. "They're distracting, ok?"

Dee gave me one more smirk before removing her glasses, albeit exceptionally slow and making it clear that she was enjoying the discovery that I had a physical response to her.

"Shall we get started, Mr. Monroe?"

"You can't be serious," I deadpanned. Mae calling me 'Mr. Monroe' I understood, simply because of her precarious status on the corporate ladder. But I'd had my tongue in Dee's mouth and her breasts pressed into my chest sixteen hours ago. While I was prepared for some office awkwardness the next day, I certainly wasn't prepared for us to take two steps back into professional formalities.

"Of course I'm not serious," she said, waving a hand in front of her face dismissively. "You ate my cooking and flirted all night with my best friend, I'd say we're beyond formalities."

Not exactly the same way I'd qualified our progression, but it worked for me.

"I was only trying to get Jules to lower her ice shield," I said defensively at her mention of flirting. "That *hardly* constitutes flirting!"

"I wasn't talking about Jules. I was talking about Levi," Dee said with a coy smile. "He's called me three times this morning to ask for your cell number; I think he's quite taken with you." I laughed at my overcorrection; I'd sought to win over Dee's friend Levi, figuring that his opinion mattered to her, but I hadn't intended on *winning over* her best friend.

"Well, hey. If you're going to keep playing hard to get, I could do way worse than Levi."

"I think so," she said, looking down at her legal pad. "Let's see... 'Break Ice.' Check!" And with a flourish of her pen, she looked back up at me in satisfaction and flashed that unreserved grin that made my heart pound loudly in my ears. Fuck, she was gorgeous and amazingly cool.

"I meant what I said Friday night," she said, jumping right in, "if you let me, I can help you still be yourself, but in a manner that makes you look good for the press, helps the hotel and keeps Charles happy."

And there it was. Dee didn't beat around any bushes and instead went straight to the heart of the matter. Naturally, I wanted to help the hotel in any way possible. I never thought I was hurting the company, but her influence was slowly starting to erode that notion. At the end of the day, I wanted to please Charles, regardless of what it took. I not only wanted to earn his trust so that he'd have the faith to hand over the business one day but also wanted his faith as a father. Somehow, I knew that Dee recognized my need for both.

"OK, let's hear it," I said, tenting my fingers in front of me and preparing for the worst.

"George Clooney," she replied matter-of-factly and punctuated the thought with a sharp nod.

"No, Sam Monroe." I slapped a hand to my chest to illustrate. "Although, I take your confusion as a compliment."

"No. I'm giving you George Clooney as an example of the PR model I'm going to employ with you."

Now she'd lost me.

"Clooney was a well-known ladies' man, committed bachelor and general smart-ass with the press for years," Dee explained without a modicum of condescension. "Sure, he's married now, but for over a decade he personified the confirmed bachelor. He also rarely answers a direct question in the press and tends to make a joke out of most reporters' attempts to get dirt on his personal life."

So then why am I a douchebag?

"What makes him different from you," she continued, answering my silent question, "is that he does *all* of this with sophistication, instead of sleaze. Just like Clooney, you can do whatever the hell you want, Sam. I don't care," she said, a brief grimace flashing across her face. "I just want you to talk about it differently and be slightly more discreet."

"For example?" I prompted.

"For example, you may occasionally read gossips reports that George Clooney left a party with a waitress, or bedded a fan after a movie premiere, or took an Extra back to his trailer. But it is all speculation because you never actually fucking *see* it!" Her voice had risen and was strained at the last bit, giving away the fact that she was just as uncomfortable with us discussing my sex life as I was. A week ago, I wouldn't have balked, but now it just seemed wrong to be talking with Dee about how to behave with other women going forward. "I mean, since no one ever catches him on film, it's just hearsay. And *rumors* of your activities are one thing, Sam; they add to your mystery. Pictures make you trashy. It's just the nature of the beast."

She rubbed her forehead roughly and took a deep breath.

"Got it. Point made," I said, in a rush for the conversation to move on to a new topic.

"Also, we need to talk about your answers to interview questions."

I braced myself for the bait-and-switch that was coming, expecting all of her talk of letting me be myself to turn out to be a ruse designed to get me in here and browbeat me into submission in one form or another.

"Relax, I'm not going to bully you into proper PR behavior. I don't want you to be the teacher's pet that you were on Friday night, not all the time, anyway. But you also can't revert to how you were behaving before. I know you hate this public relations game, and you hate reporters even more. But I have to tell you, Sam, you're a reporter's wet dream."

"Come again?" I asked, shocked.

"Reporters work in sound bites and attention-grabbing quotes, and you hand them over every chance you get. While you may think that the glib and snarky comments you make are an act of defiance against the press machine, the reporter standing in front of you is probably mentally counting the number of copies they're going to sell of their magazine or clicks they're going to get to their site with your quote in their headline."

Suddenly, I felt like a gigantic tool. It was as though I was the last man still shouting that the world was flat, only to realize that I had it all wrong and everyone else knew it. For all of my business experience and education and charisma, it took someone else to point out the glaringly obvious fact that I was my own worst enemy in this arena.

"Ok, what do we do?" I asked, slightly sheepish.

"You let me coach you," Dee said, smiling in triumph. "Give me an honest run for a few weeks, doing things *my* way, and I guarantee you'll have the press eating out of your hand."

"Done," I said, dropping my hands to my lap.

"Ok then, that's the big stuff," she said, visibly relaxing. "Let's talk about what I have on deck for you."

The next hour was spent going over interviews, speaking engagements and appearances Dee was in the process of setting up for me. Her approach was impressive. For every business magazine she lined up, she added a college recruitment conference. There were speeches to be given at both black-tie events and young professional seminars. Somehow, in the week that she'd been here, Dee had managed to get a cover story with Forbes in the works. But based on what I was learning about her, I was sure she'd gotten that ball in motion long before setting a single foot in the Hotel Monroe.

I'd felt a shitload of emotions about Dee since meeting her a week ago. Frustration, confusion, lust and even endearment at times. But when she started explaining to me how she was planning on cross-promoting Pax's racing charity with my speeches at safety conferences with local businesses, I felt a new emotion: respect. Dee Sheppard was an artist.

"Ok, that about covers everything I had," Dee said, breaking me from my thoughts and settling back into her chair. "Did you have any questions for me?"

"Sweet Jesus, no! You've covered it all. I'm on board; sign me up, et cetera. Get up, we're going to eat," I said, standing up quickly. I was ready to practically bolt from her office merely to get us in a new setting and have the opportunity to clear my head. Her look of surprise told me that she'd forgotten about our lunch date, if only momentarily, either because she'd gotten wrapped up in our meeting or just saw lunch as a means to an end for this PR strategy session. I could care less which it was; I was taking her out no matter what.

We made our way through the hotel, and I took a gulping breath of fresh air when we reached the street. Not only was being in Dee's office for so long killing me for numerous reasons, but the elevator ride had been brutal since I'd started to equate elevators with my sexual frustration for her.

"Where are we going?" she asked as we rounded the corner at the end of the block.

"A great little hideaway bistro," I said, pointing down the street to the familiar sign in the distance. "You'll love it, assuming you like French food."

"Naturally," she said.

"Well then, you're in for a treat," I said, settling on throwing an arm around her playfully and smiling to myself when a quiet laugh escaped her.

We walked into the restaurant, and the owner's wife waved at me enthusiastically from the back, motioning me to sit anywhere I chose. I'd been coming here for years and was an honorary member of their family at this point. Mr. and Mrs. Armond were responsible for keeping me well-nourished via takeout during long nights ever since I'd started working at the hotel. Dee sat and took in our surroundings, her eyes falling on Mrs. Armond frantically waving her daughter to our table.

"Come here often, do you?" she asked, smirking as Tia rushed over.

"Oh Dee, sweetheart. You're wittier than that; you can come up with a better pick-up line, can't you?" I said with a solemn shake of my head.

"It's not like I commented on your shoe size," she mumbled into her water glass, causing me to laugh. Before I could lob another pithy remark over the net at her, Tia appeared to take our drink order. In perfect French I ordered us two iced teas, having noticed Dee usually had one in-hand throughout the day.

"Merci," I said, thanking her as she walked away.

Dee stared at me with wide eyes. "You speak French."

I gave her a simple shrug and tried to act casual. I'd never been one to boast, but I'd be lying if I said a large part of the draw of bringing Dee here for lunch was a chance to impress her in any way I could. Whether it be with my connection to the community, or passion about local businesses, or solely my linguistic abilities, I didn't care. She impressed me at every turn, so sue me for trying to keep up.

"Do you speak other languages?" Dee asked.

"I do," I replied, taking a sip from my own glass of water and not meeting her gaze for fear of breaking into a shit-eating grin.

"How many?" she asked, dropping her menu to the table. Composing myself, I looked up at her and made a show of counting them needlessly off on my fingers.

"Four," I said finally.

"Four?!"

"Well, actually five, if you include English." The smug smile was becoming too hard to suppress as Dee's mouth remained agape in surprise.

"You're fluent in four different foreign languages?" she asked disbelievingly.

"Working in globally, it's extremely beneficial; I did my masters work in New York and then an internship in Japan, as you know. Add to that being in the hospitality industry, it's the cornerstone of building solid client relationships."

"Which languages?" she asked quietly, leaning across the table on her forearms.

"Japanese, French, Spanish and Russian. Japanese helps bring in the high-tech and financial clients from Tokyo. French helps build out the luxury side of the business. Spanish and Russian are simply helpful since there's a large community of both groups in the Portland area."

A small shade of pink blushed over Dee's cheeks, and her eyes stared into mine widely as my pulse quickened and started to make me hard. Jesus, I'd learn to speak Swahili or juggle dinner plates if it meant she'd keep looking at me like that.

"Continually surprising me," Dee mumbled, looking back down at her menu on the table.

"And here I thought I was the only one out of the two of us being pleasantly surprised all the time." Dee looked up at me quickly before looking down again. "I don't know what I'll do with myself if we cease all our war activities at the office. I may have to keep finding ways to goad you," I said, enjoying the devilish expression on her face when she looked back up at me.

"Oh really?" Dee asked, snapping into our playful banter. "Is that because you like fighting with me?"

"Not at all," I said, watching her face fall microscopically. "It's because you're sexy as hell when you're angry." I'd thrown it out there, testing the limits of our relationship, specifically while out of the office.

"Well then," she said, smoothing her napkin in her lap but keeping my gaze and smirking again. "You should see me when I'm extremely pissed off."

Before I could reply, our drinks arrived, and we went on to order our lunch. Tension and banter gave away to casual conversation as we started talking about anything and everything, seemingly picking up right where we'd left off at the market yesterday. We discussed books, music, movies and all those subjects that don't seem crucial at first but really tell you a lot about a person. We disagreed on several movies, her professing love for a piece of shit I walked out on and me trying to convince her to give an old western a chance. We had similar tastes in books, in that we were both all over the place with our eclectic style.

The check arrived, and we both looked at our watches in shock; I'd forgotten it was even a weekday and that we had to go back to the office. With one last look at Dee, the sexy woman whose company I was really starting to enjoy, I mentally said goodbye to her and prepared for the return of work-Dee, the cold woman that held my dating history in the forefront of her mind.

The rest of the week passed by in a blur of meetings, conference calls, and paperwork, with the only reprieve being my daily lunches with Dee. I'd yet to get her to agree to dinner or anything that could be construed as a date, but she still agreed to leave the office with me for over an hour every day for lunch. During that time, we left work at the office and never talked about it until we returned. Instead, we talked about Dee, an only child of an eccentric mother, and Sam, a spoiled rich kid that

wanted to prove to the whole world that he was more than his
last name. I told her things I'd never told anyone. Like the fact
that being successful in business was expected of me since birth,
rather than something that would set me apart from the crowd.
Over sushi, I'd explained that getting into my MBA program
hadn't given me the slightest sense of accomplishment but rather
had felt like a natural step in my life, a sentiment I hadn't even
realized I felt until I'd said the words out loud.

Dee told me about growing up without a father and a
mom hell-bent on making everything and everyone look perfect
all the time. At the Italian restaurant near the waterfront, sharing
a plate of ravioli, she'd told me about her art scholarship, that
resulted in a theater major, which then turned into a
Communications degree instead. I was starting to see the
evolution of Dee and where her obsession with appearances and
perfection had come from.

Each lunch ended with us walking back to the office and
me trying to push the envelope. I still had no idea what I was
doing when it came to Dee, nor did I try to think about it very
often. I had a suspicion that if I got too far into my head on the
subject, I would dissect it to the point of deciding to avoid her
altogether. And regardless of how smart *that* move might be, I
was a selfish fuck that just wanted to keep enjoying the fun I
was having with her. Spending time with Dee felt good, and I
liked feeling good. End of story.

Tuesday, I tried to hold her hand, which didn't go over
too well. She did this awkward little sidestep and arm twirl to
get away from me and almost fell off the curb into traffic. I tried
hard not to dwell on the fact that she'd nearly killed herself to
avoid holding my fucking hand. Wednesday, I used stealthier
tactics and grabbed her hand to lead her across the street in a
rush before the light turned, and then just didn't let it go. That
worked better, and she seemed okay with it. Either that or she
just didn't want to repeat her awkward dance and get hurt.
Regardless, it gave me the confidence to hug her before we got
out of the elevator. I say hug *her* because that shit was definitely
one-sided since she froze up like she was trying to evade a
goddamn T-Rex.

My behavior was confusing the shit out of me, but I
couldn't help it. I'd never put much effort into chasing a woman

before, let alone panting after one for the smallest touches or affections. But when I was around Dee, I just *had* to touch her. It was like her body called out to me, and I just needed to have a hand on her every chance I got, even if it was just to hold hers.

Thursday, I was starting to lose my damn mind. As much as I was enjoying spending time with her every day, it was getting harder and harder to play this fucking friend game. And being trapped in that elevator with her was pure torture. I was like a fat kid trapped in a fucking bakery, sweating and panting with the effort of *not* doing something. When the numbers above the elevator doors read seven, I realized I had little time left.

"Dee," I said, turning to face her and finding her eyes already clenched shut tightly. Her face was scrunched up in concentration, and she shook her head minutely.

"Don't," she whispered.

I couldn't stop myself as I gripped her arm and spun her toward me, the quick motion forcing her eyes to open widely and stare up at me in surprise. "How the fuck could I *not*? There's an attraction here, I know you feel it; you can't deny what you're feeling, and you certainly can't expect me not to want to touch you after all this time together," I rushed out, knowing she understood precisely what I meant. I wanted her, and how could she possibly ask me to deny it? She was clearly fighting off the same physical urges I was.

She opened her mouth to answer, but I wouldn't let her. Instead, I fisted both of my hands into her hair and took what I'd been craving all week by bringing her lips to my own, letting that inner fat kid do a swan-dive into a vat of frosting.

Dee stiffened in my grasp for a fraction of a second before she relented and pushed her body into my own. Her hands went to the lapels of my suit jacket and pulled me even closer to her as she whimpered softly into my mouth. Her foot hooked around the back of my knee, throwing me off balance and forcing me to slam a hand against the wall behind her to keep from falling over. We broke away, both gasping for air. Before I could register what she was doing, Dee threw her arms around me and attached her lips to my neck, peppering it with kisses and dragging her tongue along my skin. I stared at the ceiling before my eyes rolled back into my head, enjoying every microscopic touch and feel of her. It was like electricity was

coursing through me, as though when we touched I was
switched on. Jesus, what would happen to me when we finally
had sex?

With that thought, the elevator dinged, and Dee detached
her lips from my neck, launching me back with a swift shove to
my chest. She snatched her purse from the floor where she'd
dropped it and was out the door without even a backward
glance, all before I could even catch my breath. I stood there
panting for a second until Leslie came around the corner and
stopped, looking at me questioningly from the elevator doors, as
I stood there with a hand on the wall.

"Sam?" she asked. "You ok?"

"Yeah. I'm just going to ride one more time," I said with
a twirl of my finger as I punched the button for the lobby and let
out a long breath when the doors closed. Today had been tough,
and tomorrow was going to be even harder.

EIGHTEEN

Sam

The next day, shortly before noon, I swiveled in my desk chair as I stared out the window, not focusing on anything in particular and trying not to check the time yet again. After only a few days of repetitiously seeing Dee midday, I had created a habit so soothing and impactful, I was reduced to an anxious mess at the broken promise of having lunch with her again. She hadn't canceled, but rather we were never scheduled to meet up. And while my brain ached to dwell on what she was doing instead, I knew full well that her day was taken up with finalizing the details for Pax's event that evening. So instead, I chose to focus on whether or not she was as much in her head about our elevator ride from the day before as I was, wondering if she was obsessing about how this game of chess was going to play out.

Thankfully, before I could waste any more of my day on what-ifs and possibilities, my calendar alert went off for the meeting Dee had organized for the executive team down in Boost. Faster than I cared to acknowledge, I launched myself from my desk and took long strides toward the elevator, not even glancing at Leslie's reaction of my near sprint across the office. Despite my haste, I still wasn't the first one to join Dee and Mae at the bistro tables they'd gathered in the middle of the club for the meeting. I slid onto a seat next to Emma as the rest of the executive team came to order and quieted down. Dee stood up and clapped a hand on Pax's shoulder.

"Ok, everyone. Tonight's a big night," she said, taking off her glasses with a slight smirk in my direction.

"WOO!" Pax yelled, accentuating his outburst with a fist pump.

"Or in the words of Pax, 'WOO!'" Dee hollered, getting a round of laughter from the group. "We're not doing a full red carpet tonight, but rather a short press line at the Boost street entrance. So, employees can enter through the back or directly from the lobby, while the rest of the guests will come through the front for photo ops and short interviews. Pax, you'll meet me downstairs at seven, which will give most of the guests a chance to show up and give us plenty of time to do an in-depth round of interviews."

Pax nodded seriously and scribbled, 'be in lobby at seven' on the legal pad in front of him. I fought the desire to smile, not wanting to condescend his newfound business acumen.

"Dominic and Sam both put together lists of potential heavy-hitter clients," Dee continued, looking over a document in front of her. "And we've worked extensively this week on sending the business leaders on the lists an invitation to tonight's event, with the promise of meeting a racing celebrity. That celebrity will be Lex Ross."

A murmur of approval went through the group as everyone muttered praise and expressed their admiration for Dee, acknowledging what I was already aware of, which was that she was a genius at what she did. And that I appeared to be one of the few people in the group with no clue about IndyCar racing.

"Emma has designated a VIP section of Boost for these folks, so Charles, Sam, and Dominic will know where to spend their time schmoozing future customers." Charles chuckled in appreciation and Dominic looked smug, while Dee and I danced glances in each other's direction.

The rest of the meeting was spent going over additional details. All members of the hotel's executive staff would be in attendance and would be 'on the clock' in one way or another. The guest-list was comprised of local business elite and celebrities; however, everyone was basically broken down into two categories: current customers of the hotel that needed and deserved our love, and potential clients of the hotel that required even *more* attention and love. If there were any issues Dee and Mae would be on hand for crisis control; knowing what I did of Dee, it wasn't going to be necessary. All proceeds from the evening would be going to MADD, so members of the local chapter would be at the event and were to be treated like royalty.

I glanced over at my father, and he was leaning back in his chair comfortably, looking at Dee like she'd just turned the table in front of him to gold.

"I think that's it," Dee said, wrapping things up. "Pax, I want to see you afterward to talk about some interview strategies. After that, I'll be working with Emma to get everything prepped. If anyone needs anything, Mae's on hand to answer questions and help out."

Everyone started to disperse, and I was practically vibrating with tension waiting for a moment alone with Dee. I intentionally held back and made a poor showing of gathering my nonexistent things, which basically consisted of my shuffling my phone back and forth between my hands and opening and closing my tablet's case while everyone left the club.

"Give me twenty and I'll be in your office?" Pax offered as he left, to which Dee nodded.

Finally, it was just the two of us.

"I don't think I've ever seen my brother this focused," I said as I made my way around a group of chairs to lean an elbow on the bistro table she was still gathering her things from. "If you'd been around to keep him this motivated back in school, we'd probably be living with a different version of Pax right now."

Dee chuckled quietly as she continued packing her bag, not meeting my eye line. "'Focused' is certainly a word I'd use. 'Giddy' is definitely another one."

"Are we back to awkward and weird?" I asked, not having the desire to play our old game of cat and mouse. Not after the week we'd had together. But rather than shrugging and continuing to avoid my gaze, like I'd assumed she would, Dee surprised me with a warm look and a soft smile.

"Not at all," she said. I grabbed her bag as she started to lift it from the chair onto her shoulder. "Walk with me?" she asked with a head tilt toward the door, not stopping me from carrying her bag and making me slightly nervous with the airiness of her demeanor. I fell into step with her, and we started to make our way out of Boost and back into the lobby.

"I did some thinking last night."

"Let me guess," I interjected, "our kiss in the elevator was a big mistake, and we need to pretend like it never happened." I was trying to keep my voice light, but I was having a hard time hiding my frustration with the stalemate that was our dating game. Sexual tension and courtship were one thing, but this was becoming a bit of a monotonous endeavor. Every step forward with Dee inevitably led to three steps back. And while I wanted to rail against the insanity and futility of it all, I knew damn well that the fatigue in my voice came from the knowledge that for reasons I could not shake out, I would play this game for as long as it took.

"Actually, no," Dee said, interrupting my mental moping, causing me to stumble slightly as we rounded the corner from the corridor leading out of Boost and into the openness of the lobby. She smirked at my reaction and stopped walking, turning to face me directly and look up at me with wide, determined eyes. "I'm done pretending there isn't something here; clearly there is and clearly I'm attracted to you six ways from Sunday. God knows I've been shitty at keeping my distance physically, I might as well stop denying it, full stop. That being said," she continued, clearly wanting to cut off my visible excitement at the prospect of a green light, "we can't do this."

There was a finality in her last statement that hadn't been there before, an absoluteness that told me she'd found a new way to talk herself out of being happy and giving in to how we felt. I arched a brow in feigned patience and waited for her to continue, not sure I had the stamina for the new battery of reasons Dee had concocted for us to remain colleagues and nothing more.

"Don't look at me like that," she said, pursing her lips and furrowing her brow. "I know you think I'm just a glutton for the rules and unnecessarily keeping you at arm's length, but trust me when I tell you that there *is* a reason, ok? There's a reason I don't want to let this go any further. I have my reason's for wanting to *try* and keep this relationship as professional as possible."

"Ok, let's hear them," I said, calling her bluff and asking to see her cards. "What are these grandiose reasons for us to deny this thing between us?"

"You're going to hate me," she said, holding my eye and sighing with a resigned shrug. "Maybe not today, maybe not tomorrow, but sometime soon. Trust me when I tell you, in the not-to-distant future you're going to have every reason to hate me, and us getting close romantically will only make that harder. For both of us."

"Self-deprecation is a weird shade on you, Dee."

"For fuck's sake." She rubbed a hand over her forehead in frustration and narrowed her eyes at me, "Sam, I'm not feigning impurity here. I'm not putting on some lame attempt to convince you of my shortcomings. I'm trying to tell you that this can never work."

"Because one day I'll discover the *real* you, right? One day I'll get a peek behind the curtain and see who you *really* are and not want to be with you any longer. Am I getting this correctly?" She opened her mouth to argue at my sarcastic tone, but I shook my head as I kept talking, "No, no. It's my turn to tell you what I think is going to happen here. I think you're going to eventually give in to that voice inside your head that keeps telling you that, despite all evidence to the contrary, I'm worth a fucking chance." Dee's eyes went wide with my honest declaration, and I took a step closer to her, not wanting to lose my momentum or her captivation. "I think sooner or later, you're going to see that denying this attraction between the two of us is only making it stronger. One day, maybe not today and maybe not tomorrow, but eventually you're going to stop giving a shit about what anyone else thinks and what everyone else wants to happen, and you're just going to focus on you."

Dee closed her eyes and took a breath. "And most importantly," I said, leaning in even further so that she could hear me at a low rasp of a whisper, "you're going to realize that the question isn't whether or not I can make you feel pleasure, but how *much*."

I hadn't intended for the last part to sound sexual and take on the tone of innuendo, but that just seemed to be the breaks with us these days.

"I need you to see that this isn't going to end well," she said in a low, pleading voice.

"And I need *you* to see that I don't give a fuck." She looked at me cockeyed for a moment, which made me laugh, and if we'd been alone at that moment, I wouldn't have been able to resist the urge to caress her wrinkled forehead. "Dee, I hear you that you have reservations about us, about this. But I disagree about our future being written in stone. You may be operating under the assumption that no matter what we do, this won't end well. But I happen to believe that I possess a lot of tools at my disposal that will help you find complete happiness." With a wink and a smile, I handed Dee her bag and made my way to the front doors before my hands could betray me and pull her in for a punctuating kiss. She was trying to convince me that she was no good, and I had no patience for that kind of talk. I didn't know where this new self-abhorrent attitude came from, perhaps it was all simply a new attempt at convincing me that an office romance was doomed from the start. Whatever it was, I didn't care. She wanted this just as much as I did, I could feel it.

Later that night I shut down my computer and changed my outfit for Pax's party. I replaced my shirt, tie, and jacket with a simple black dress shirt from the closet in my office.

Pax walked up just as the elevator arrived, looking stoic and fighting off his nerves. We rode a few floors in silence, stopping occasionally as guests entered and exited on different floors. His tense posture didn't change while he tapped loudly on his phone. He was nervous, making me on-edge just by being near him. Rather than giving into old habits and unleashing a rash of shit on him for being such a basket case, I thought of Dee and tried to distract and calm him.

"Hey, have you checked out that 'Ultimate Torque' show I was telling you about?"

"Nuh-uh," Pax grunted, without even looking up from his cell phone.

"I'm telling you, you'll like it." I couldn't help but smile at the thought of his reaction when he finally saw Jules. She wasn't just his type; Jules was the epitome of what he worshiped in a woman.

"A show about a woman pimping out cars? Hmm, how many episodes are devoted to air freshener choices and floor mat coordination?"

"You might be surprised."

It wasn't a lie; Jules's episode about super chargers had made huge improvements to my sports car a few weeks ago. She may be an ice queen, but the woman knew her shit, that was certain.

"Not interested in some scary, butched-out chick telling me shit I already know."

"She's not butched-out, bro. In fact, she's pretty cute. I met her last weekend, and she's just as good looking in person as she is on TV."

"You hittin' that?" Pax asked, finally diverting his attention from his phone and snapping his head in my direction.

"No, jackass, I'm not," I said, squinting at my brother's vulgarity. "She's Dee's roommate, and I met her when I went over for dinner the other night."

"You had dinner at Dee's?" he asked, turning to face me directly. I reluctantly nodded, cursing the trap I'd just stepped into. "Are you hitting *that*?"

"Again, no. We're just *friends*." I was getting sick and tired of that fucking word. Pax's laughter filled up every inch of the elevator and the volume made me wince.

"Friends? Since when did you become a non-closer, incapable of getting the ass you want? I give it two weeks until your balls turn so blue that they fall off. Friends? Seriously? Have you *actually* convinced yourself that you can just be her friend? Good luck with that Sammy."

Before I could come up with a pithy response, the elevator doors dinged and opened to the lobby.

"You folks have a great night," Pax said over his shoulder to the elderly couple standing in-shock against the back wall of the elevator behind us. "Bro, come on. Enough about manly she-mechanics and Dee; if you're not planning on getting your dick wet tonight, you can at least be my fucking wing-man."

With a sigh, I followed him into the lobby and toward the front doors.

"Dude, can I be frank?" he asked, turning on a dime to face me.

"Sure. Can I still be Sam?"

"Shut up and listen, I have no idea what's *really* going on with you and Dee, but please don't fuck this up for me. Tonight? It's important, and I don't want your pissing match with her to interfere with this." Pax's sincerity was eye-opening. Not only did his words make me realize that people were still observing my relationship with Dee to be hostile, but also that

this racing thing was even more important to him than I'd
initially thought.

I decided right then that I'd make sure this was the best
night possible for Pax.

NINETEEN

Sam

"I promise, no fighting with Dee tonight," I said, giving him an encouraging pat on the shoulder. "It's all about you and Boost."

"Good. Now excuse me while I go meet the press and wow them the way that I do." He flashed a grin before turning to walk away. I followed a few steps behind and turned to make my way to the club as he headed into the lobby.

"Have fun, rock star," I called, to which he replied with his signature fist pump. I had to hand it to the guy; he was nervous as hell but still knew how to turn on the game-face like a pro.

I walked into Boost and stopped short as I took in the transformation of the club. Hanging from the ceiling were several IndyCar team logos and random racing flags. Waitresses were wandering throughout the crowd wearing skimpy versions of pit crew uniforms. On the stage was a large DJ booth and next to it was a standing six-foot poster board of a cover of Car & Driver magazine with my brother posing in a sharp Armani suit.

"Pretty awesome, huh?" I turned to the voice next to me to see Emma smiling at her handiwork in the club.

"Pretty awesome, indeed," I said, nodding. "What's with the life-size cutout?" I asked, pointing toward the magazine cover taking up a third of the stage.

"Dee got a feature story with Pax for next month, and we were able to put a rush on the artwork for tonight. Pax hasn't seen it yet; I'm really hoping I'm there when he does."

"Just what the guy needs," I laughed, "more food for his ego."

Emma let out a huge roar of laughter and clutched her stomach sardonically as I cocked a brow in question at her.

"Because your ego is starving?"

"Maybe not starving, just carb-conscious, I suppose," I said, nudging her with my shoulder.

"The VIP section is over there." I nodded as Emma pointed out the roped off booths against the far wall.

"Got to go to work," I mumbled, taking my leave and making my way to the VIP area to start the schmoozing process. Hands were shaken, drinks were poured, deals were talked about. By the time I needed a second beer, I'd secured a couple of client meetings for next week and had the exec from a local sporting goods company eating out of the palm of my hand. When he excused himself for the restroom, I made a quick dash for the bar to get a refill. I was halfway there when I caught sight of Mae running frantically across the floor. She stopped in her tracks, whipped her head around frantically searching for someone or something, before looking down at her phone with a furrowed brow.

"Everything ok?" I asked when I reached her, causing Mae to jump slightly and turn to me.

"I don't know! I mean, I should probably...but... I don't know what to do!" she blurted out loudly in an incoherent rush.

"Mae," I said calmly and looking at her pointedly. She stilled her shaking and looked up at me wide-eyed. "I'm about this close to closing a deal with a global company looking to hold their annual meetings at the hotel," I said, holding my thumb and forefinger up at her. "And in about thirty seconds he's going to come out of the bathroom behind me and see you in your headset running around white as a ghost, in an absolute panic, and wonder what the fuck is going on." She looked over my shoulder quickly and the panic in her eyes increased. "Now calm down and tell me what the hell is up?"

"Ross canceled," she said so quietly that I barely heard her over the music.

"Shit," I grumbled, running my hand through my hair roughly. We'd gotten over half the potential clients here tonight with the promise of meeting a celebrity.

"Dee told me to get a backup celebrity, but I didn't," Mae said, tears forming in her eyes. "I didn't think he'd cancel, and there was so much else to do I figured it'd be a waste of time getting someone else, so I didn't. And now...now..." her lower lip quivered as she fought off tears. "It's going to be a disaster and look like Dee's fault."

I couldn't help but smile at her last comment. Most people would be worried about getting their ass reamed by their boss in this situation, but Mae was worried about how this would negatively reflect on Dee. It not only spoke to Mae's character but also spoke volumes about Dee as a boss. She inspired loyalty and devotion from her people, and the businessman in me respected the shit out her for that fact.

"Have you called Dee yet?" I asked, going back to the issue at hand and trying to keep my own panic at bay. I'd vowed to make sure this night was perfect for my brother, and that was starting to look like a longshot. She shook her head and began to answer, but Emma walked up before she could speak and put a hand on Mae's shoulder.

"According to my watch, Pax should be finishing up his interviews any minute. Are Ross and his people here yet?"

Mae let out a small squeak and looked even more frantic than I thought possible.

"Well, we have an issue with that," I interjected.

"With what?" Emma asked, narrowing her eyes at me.

"Ross canceled," Mae said.

"What!?" Emma exclaimed.

"Keep it down!" I said, shushing her with a look over my shoulder at folks in the VIP section, who were thankfully unaware of the commotion.

"What's going on?" Dominic said, walking up and looking confused.

"Ross canceled," Mae said, making me worry that she had lost the ability to say anything else. Dominic looked at me with concern, and I gave him a grave nod back. Before anyone could say anything else, a roar went up in the crowd and a spotlight hit the entry of the club. Pax walked in waving his arms and smiling like a hero on parade at the cheers and loud music in his honor. Two steps behind him, Dee walked in shaking her head and smirking in obvious amusement at his grandstanding. Despite the problem at hand, I couldn't help but marvel at her beauty. Her hair was curled and fell down her shoulders, moving with her as she walked into the club. The silver silk top and black pants she had on weren't too dissimilar from what she'd been wearing the first time we met, which had

taken place a whole thirty feet from where she was currently
standing and felt like ages ago.

As Pax started mingling with the crowd surrounding him,
Dee scanned the room and caught sight of our group. She
purposefully made her way toward us.

"What's wrong?" she asked as soon as she was within
ten feet of us.

"I'm sorry! It'll never happen again, I swear," Mae
gushed, leaving out her party line. Dee's eyes widened as she
looked around the group, meeting my eyes last and sighing.

"Ross canceled," I supplied on Mae's behalf. Dee looked
at Mae.

"Family emergency at the last minute. And I know you
said to book backup talent but-"

"You didn't," Dee cut in with a resigned nod. "I know.
We had a ton of things to do in a short amount of time, I didn't
push it either. Shit."

Everyone started talking at the same time. Mae was
apologizing again, Emma panicking about schedules and
Dominic talking loudly about client expectations. I stood
silently, watching as Dee stared off into space and her mind
clearly worked a mile a minute. The noise of the club and the
voices clamoring all around didn't faze her as she drifted away,
lost in thought, her eyes shifting slightly back and forth while
chewing on the inside of her lip.

"Ok," she said, snapping back to attention and silencing
the group. "Thankfully, the marketing materials were all printed
before we had talent booked, so Ross's name isn't on any of it.
No one's said anything to the VIPs about him have they?" she
asked sharply, looking at me.

"Not that I'm aware of," I said, slightly afraid of Dee
when she was on point like this.

"Good. Emma, go take Pax through a hand-shaking
circuit of the club; that'll keep him occupied from noticing
anything is wrong until we fix this."

"Got it," Emma said, running off quickly into the crowd.

"Dominic, go let Charlie and the rest of the team know
what's up and help them with keeping the VIPs busy for a while.
If anyone *has* mentioned Ross, laugh it off and explain we were

able to get someone better." He nodded and left for the back section of the club.

"Mae," Dee said, softening her tone and grabbing her by the shoulders. "Go to the bathroom, or upstairs, or where ever you need to go and collect yourself. It's going to be ok, but I need you to calm down and come back on your A-game. If you need to cry, do it. Just make sure you fix your makeup afterward." She winked and gently pushed Mae toward the door.

"What about me?" I asked.

Dee gripped my forearm and led me across the room forcefully to the side of the bar.

"Nothing yet," she said, taking a steadying breath. "Carry on as normal, but if this goes according to plan, then I'll need you to help me mediate." She pulled a cell phone from her back pocket and said, "Meet me here in ten minutes?" I nodded, and Dee took off quickly through the crowd, leaving me staring after her like a dumbstruck moron. I returned to the VIP table and finished getting my prospective client as close to signed as I could get for the evening, before returning to the bar to order a scotch.

"Can I get a dirty martini?" a sweet voice said from behind me. I looked over as Dee slipped onto the stool next to me and gave me a smile.

"Martini? That shit can't be good. I was *really* hoping you'd order a mojito after calling whomever you just did," I admitted.

She chuckled and shook her head slightly as she leaned her elbows on the bar. "Relax, I have it handled. The martini is for courage, remember? If we were fucked, I'd be ordering shots of tequila."

"Noted," I said with a smirk, tilting my scotch at her.

"I'm sure it is," she said with a smile. "I know I've been acting slightly psychotic and I owe you more of an explanation." I knew exactly what she was talking about; Dee thought it was due to a lack of clarity that I wasn't letting the topic of our involvement go.

"Don't worry about it; I'm not an idiot. I'm assuming you've got some version of 'work relationships are never a good idea' speech finely tuned and coming my way soon."

"Well, no. I mean, yes, they *aren't* a very good idea. But that's not it, not completely anyway. There are other factors at play here, things I just can't talk about. Trust me, ok? It's easier if you do."

I leaned on my crossed arms and tilted my head toward her conspiratorially. "What makes you think I prefer things easy? It's being hard that will make this all worth it."

Dee's eyes bore into mine, not wide with surprise or narrowed with frustration, but instead clear and intense with their focus, almost as if she was considering my offer genuinely. I considered my next words carefully but didn't get to speak them since her phone vibrated on the bar, causing her to jump slightly and break our stare.

"Here we go," she mumbled to herself as she read the message. She dialed a number quickly and brought the phone to her ear. "Bring Pax and meet me in the kitchen," she said, clearly speaking to Mae and slipping back into no-nonsense Dee. With a quick flourish, she hopped off her bar stool and turned to me. "Let's go."

I slammed back the rest of my scotch, guessing by her demeanor that I may need it and praying that this all turned out well. We maneuvered our way through the crowd toward the back of the club and slipped through the double doors leading to the kitchens. The staff was bustling around, busy with the enormity of the night's event and orders needing to go out, too busy to notice our small group huddled off to the side of the pantry. A moment later, Mae walked through the same doors with Pax close behind. He looked confused at the change in plans, but nowhere near as concerned as the rest of the group.

"Ok, here's the deal Pax," Dee rushed out, gripping my brother by the shoulders. "Lex Ross can't make it tonight."

"What?" he shouted as he tensed up. "There's a club full of people waiting for him out there!"

"No, there's a club full of people out there waiting for a celebrity appearance. I've called in a favor. We're still going forward with our plans, the itinerary doesn't change, just a different celebrity." Pax took a steadying breath and relaxed as Dee continued. "Pax, have you ever seen the show 'Ultimate Torque'?"

It was my turn to stiffen in shock, but before I could say anything, I heard the sharp clicking of heels on the tile floor behind me and a familiar voice ring out.

"Here I thought my waitressing days were over, but you have me entering this over-the-top party through the goddamn kitchens?" Jules asked in a huff as she approached us.

Pax's eyes snapped to look up over the top of Dee's head, and I took a steadying breath as I watched events fold out in slow motion. Jules approached our group smirking at Dee, but her eyes quickly fell on my brother and swept an appraising glance over his body, head to toe, before staring questioningly at him. Pax mirrored the same look and appraisal of Jules.

"Pax, this is my friend Jules Dahl. She hosts the show 'Ultimate Torque' and has agreed to step in as the celebrity appearance tonight," Dee said as they continued to stare each other down questioningly. Pax snapped his head to me, eyebrows raised and mouth agape.

"*This* is the butch TV host you were telling me about?!" he asked incredulously, pointing a sideways finger at Jules.

"No! No," I started before being cut off predictably.

"Butch?" Jules shrieked. I rubbed my forehead in frustration just before catching sight of Dee rubbing her temples next to me. "You had the nerve to describe me as *butch*, pretty boy?"

"No," I rushed out again, panicking in the eye of the firestorm of Jules's stare. "I told him you were cute!"

"Cute?" Jules and Dee said in unison. Jules was eyeing me with twice the hatred she'd thrown at me a week ago, which was terrifying, while Dee was looking at me with a somewhat hurt look. If I hadn't been terrified of Jules clawing my eyes out at that moment, I would have found her small hint of jealousy adorable and promising.

"He should have described you as fucking hot, because that's what you are, baby," Pax drawled, finally composing himself and reaching out to shake Jules's hand.

"Baby?" Jules asked, turning the heat back on Pax.

"Ok, as I was saying," Dee interjected with a hand up, cutting off the next round of outbursts. "Pax, this is Jules. She's the host of the show 'Ultimate Torque' and a good friend of mine. She's agreed to step in at the last minute and appear as our celebrity guest, ultimately saving your event *and* our collective asses." Dee said the last part with a pointed stare at Pax before turning an eye to Jules, who was still shooting daggers at my brother. "Jules, this is Pax Monroe. He's the Manager of Boost and going to introduce you to a crowd tonight that will open up a whole new demographic for your show and *help you* in ratings."

"Oh, so you want to penetrate a new market, huh?" Pax said with a wink. "I can make that happen for you, baby."

"Call me baby one more time and I'll walk right out of here, leaving you to explain to a club full of people why you couldn't manage to book a guest appearance tonight."

"Um, Jules," Dee said in a small voice, "*I* would actually be the one having to explain-"

"Fine by me cupcake," Pax interrupted, clearly hitting his limit at flirting in the face of rejection and abandoning his cause. "I'd rather go out there and tell all the suits we don't have a guest at all than push an uptight, wannabe gear-head on them."

"Um, Pax," I whispered, "we really can't tell any of them that-"

"Listen here, short-bus," Jules interrupted, jabbing a finger into Pax's chest. Dee and I were effectively cut out of this conversation. "The only wannabe around here is you since you're the dumbass that tried to win a street race using a prefab NOS kit while racing on standard tires." Pax's eyebrows attempted to jump off his face in shock at her comment. "Oh yeah, I've read about you, and like most people that know anything about cars, I think you're a joke."

"For your information, it was a custom kit. There's nothing prefab about me," Pax said, wrapping his hand around the finger Jules was poking into his chest. "And my NOS system is nothing compared to my dual catalytic exhaust system."

"Dual?" Jules asked breathily, to which Pax nodded. "Custom chrome piping?" Pax nodded again; they continued to stare at one another without blinking. I looked over at Dee and she shrugged, her expression mirroring my confusion at the situation.

"Code Red," Jules muttered, and Dee gasped so quietly I wasn't certain I'd actually heard it. "Where do you need me, Dee?" Jules asked quietly, staring at Pax and her finger still in his hand.

"I, well..." Dee stammered with a furrowed brow, taking a tentative step forward and placing a hand on Jules's elbow. "I'll prep you, and then we'll walk out together, ok?"

Jules nodded dumbly and smiled a goofy grin at Pax, who gave one back.

"Will you take Pax back out to mingle for now?" Dee asked me, giving me a look that asked if I knew what was going on.

"Sure," I said with a shrug, letting her know that I was rolling with the punches just as she was. "C'mon bro, let's go." I slapped a hand on Pax's shoulder and started to lead him out of the kitchens. We got halfway to the doors before he looked at me in panic.

"Phase five, bro! Phase fucking five!" Pax rushed out in a frantic whisper, his hands clenched in front of him. I gaped at him in shock as the reality of his words set in, but kept us walking toward the club while he muttered nonsense to himself. I looked over my shoulder at Dee, who had a vise grip on Jules's shoulders and talking to her with wide eyes. Jules was gaping back at her like a comatose mental patient.

By the time we hit the floor of the club, Pax had managed to pull himself together for the most part. His wide grin was in place as he shook hands and joked with guests, but his eyes shifted to the kitchen doors at regular intervals, and he was jumpier than normal. He'd been nervous going into the evening, but now he was wound tighter than I'd seen in a long time. I circulated with him for a while, only leaving him for a bit to grab us a couple of drinks. When I returned to Pax, he was telling his signature Palm Springs story to a group of people but stopped short when the DJ cut off the music to announce Jules. She walked out on stage to rowdy applause and catcalls which didn't seem to faze her but appeared to make Pax bristle.

"Jesus, Pax," I said, turning to face him, unable to seize the opportunity to repeat his words from last week back to him. "You've got it fucking *bad*!" With a huff, he shifted to look at me somberly while clapping a hand on my shoulder.

"Words cannot describe the awesome power of phase five, bro. You just have to feel it," he said, thumping his chest with his fist.

"Thank you, Pablo Neruda, for that poetic description of how badly you want to bang the woman."

"Oh brother, you don't get it," he said, shaking his head sadly. He looked back toward the stage and smiled. "But you will." I followed his gaze and saw Dee coming through the crowd toward us from the stage. Pax met her halfway to the stage and leaned in to whisper something to her. She nodded and smiled, before playfully rolling her eyes and swatting him on the shoulder as she walked away.

"I'm not usually one to pat myself on the back," she said, coming to a stop in front of me with her hands on her hips and a smug smile, "but I think I deserve a drink for pulling this off." I looked over at the VIP section where almost a dozen potential clients were gathered. Some were chatting animatedly with Jules and Pax, others were toasting with Dominic while the rest were laughing over stories with my father. Tonight, we were closing business that would have taken us months to seal.

"Fuck that," I said, gripping her hand to drag her to the bar. "You deserve ten."

We ordered a round of mojitos and toasted the night.

"How did you get Jules to agree to this?"

"It was actually easy," Dee replied, brushing her hand aside in a dismissive gesture. "I just told her that I'd owe her one."

"Something tells me that that isn't a little thing with her," I chuckled into my drink.

"Not really, actually. I'm afraid for the day she calls it in," Dee laughed back.

"Willing to subject yourself to further Jules torture, all to pull off this event. You must really want that promotion."

"I do," she said with a sigh and a nod, "I really do. And I think I deserve it."

"I agree. You've been saying it all along, and you're right; you're good at your job." She smiled warmly at me as I clinked my glass with hers before taking a drink.

"That's not it. I mean, *yes*, I am," she said with an exasperated roll of her eyes, acknowledging my admittance to what she'd been saying all along and making me laugh. "But it's more than that. I've been cleaning up PR messes for so long, I'm ready for some corporate responsibilities. Did you know," she said, swiveling on her stool to face me animatedly, "not that long ago, my job for the better part of a year was writing copy for a celebrity's twitter and Instagram feed? I would get notes back saying things like I needed to make it sound 'slightly less academic' for it to be believable that she wrote it. Which is just code for 'this is too intelligent to have come out of her dumb ass.'"

I snorted into my drink and shook my head as I laughed.

"Is it someone I've heard of?" I asked. Dee leaned over and whispered the name in my ear, to which I raised my eyebrows and nodded approvingly. "Damn, that's impressive."

"No, it isn't," Dee said with a wave of her hand. "At least it doesn't feel that way any longer. But now, I'm faced with a potential job where I'll not only create content and manage press, but also facilitate *big* decisions! I'd be part of the corporate strategy, long-term." She was bouncing slightly in her seat and gesturing wildly, her ambition and enthusiasm hard to contain. I had no doubt Dee was going to get that promotion; how could she not? All too soon, her bosses would see the work she put in for the hotel and give her the shot she was so hungry for, taking her away from me. How long would it be before she moved to the other side of the country and I never saw her again? It hadn't even been a month since she'd wandered into my life, but I suddenly found myself thinking about not having her here to talk to every day, and it made me ache. The thought was a punch to the gut, and I was surprised by how much it hurt.

But no matter how much the idea of losing Dee down the road hurt, the thought of her getting everything she ever wanted, and deserved, made me swell with happiness.

And that was it. I'd hit my breaking point and reached stage five, myself. I had to have her. Not in an I-need-to-fuck-her sort of way, but rather my entire being was calling out to her; it was taking energy to not reach out and plainly hold her. All too quickly, and in a haze that made me slightly dizzy, I realized what Pax was talking about before, because my emotions ran far beyond wanting to have sex with Dee. I wanted to consume her. I wanted to own every inch of her body and more than anything, I wanted her to know how much she already owned me.

"Are you ok?" she asked, but before I could answer, she said, "I need to go wrap up some photo-ops. See you later?"

I nodded and watched as Dee hopped off her stool and snaked her way through the crowd and across the club. With a steadying breath, I decided what needed to be done. Time was not on our side, she'd be gone soon. If we wanted to enjoy as much of what little time we *did* have together, it needed to start now.

TWENTY

Dee

The energy between Jules and Pax had reached a level that ventured on nuclear; it was the kind of icy-hot that burned at both temperatures so severely you had a hard time telling which was happening at any given moment. Pax's blunt honesty about her show, followed by Jules' outward disdain for his previous transgressions had swirled around their palpable sexual tension, and they were now flirting with a combination of innuendo, smoldering looks, and downright nasty barbs hurled at one another with maximum force. My only job left for the night was the simple task of getting the two of them through their photo-ops. However, that was proving to be an activity that required a flak jacket and safety goggles.

"I'm sure if I flashed my tits and wore skirts barely past my ass someone would give me a television show, too," Pax mumbled as they put an arm around one another to pose for a group of photographers.

"Why don't you whip out your vagina right now and test that theory," Jules said through clenched teeth without breaking her smile.

"Oh, I'm about to whip something out alright."

"Don't tease a girl with promises you don't intend to keep," Jules said as she turned to pose next to her poster and promo banner. I silently prayed that I was the only one that could hear them, standing just off to the side, and that the photographers fifteen feet away weren't picking up any of their unique brand of flirting.

After a round of group shots, photos with their props, and a gaggle of fan meet-and-greets, I was finally in a place to send them on their way. God willing, they weren't going to kill each other before the night was over. With a flurry of handshakes and pleasantries to journalists that had made an extra effort to keep this Portland media event not as weird as it could have been, I made my way to edge the of the room and took a deep breath. With my back against the wall and the wood floor thumping under my feet, I took a moment to look around at what we had created in such a short amount of time.

My eyes danced up the black and white checkered tapestries that I couldn't even fathom how Emma had managed to get in place so quickly, up across the ceiling dancing with false starlight projected on it and back down to the massive group of people dancing, drinking and discussing the event. I allowed myself a quick moment of pride and arrogance, smiled with the satisfaction that comes with pulling this particular breed of rabbit out of my hat, and decided the time had come to relax finally, maybe even finish that mojito I'd barely touched with Sam earlier.

I made my way through the throng of people crowding around bistro tables and lining the packed dance floor until I emerged from the sea of bodies to the end of the bar. With a grateful sigh I plopped down into an empty barstool that was located so far down the bar that I was practically in the kitchens, but I didn't mind. This kind of real estate was precious on nights like this, and all that truly mattered was that I was able to get off my feet and have a moment to myself. Before a bartender could even notice me or I could truly dive into people watching, a familiar smell washed over me.

His unique blend of aftershave and pheromones reached my nose before I even saw or heard him. A split second later, Sam's arm stretched out from behind me to place a palm on the bar as his strong chest gently pressed into my back. I shivered and closed my eyes for a moment at the joining of our two bodies, regardless of the clothes separating us and the feather-light pressure he was applying, I felt so close to Sam. With him still directly behind me, I felt my hair rustle as he brought his lips down to my ear.

"I need you." Sam's breath danced along my neck and collar bone with his husky whisper pushed out with enough force to still be able to hear over the loud music. I cocked my head to the side, toward his turned face, causing Sam's lips to brush along my cheek before they found home again at my ear. "Please, Dee. Can I see you upstairs?"

Sam pulled away as I turned on my barstool to face him and my breath caught in my throat as I took in the wanton need painted across his face. His eyes were hooded, his chest was rising and falling with his heavy frantic breathing; he looked possessed by something he could no longer contain. I opened my mouth to respond, but nothing came out. I just kept looking at him with a rapidly mounting need to match his. An unknown amount of time passed before I finally managed to nod simply at his request. With a cock of his head, Sam motioned for the door leading to the lobby and turned on his heel, disappearing into the crowd of people.

I waited for a beat before getting to my feet and slowly following him, understanding that Sam was attempting to disguise our leaving together; a gesture that meant he was finally listening to my advice or was at least trying to make me more comfortable. Either way, the idea made me smile as I wound my way through the tables and crowd to emerge from the club. I panned across the lobby, looking for the familiar curly hair and broad shoulders, and found Sam standing in front of the elevators with his back to me. His hands were in his pockets, and he was staring up at the lights above the doors illuminating the elevator's location. My heels clicking on the marble floor alerted him to my presence so that he turned just as I reached him. Our eyes met in an intense gaze that communicated both how much we wanted this, but also that we were both nervously heading into unfamiliar waters.

Without breaking eye contact, Sam jammed a thumb on the button and reached into his inside chest pocket and removed a black executive key card. I recognized it; I'd been given a card just like it on my first day. It was a card to the penthouse level.

It was then that I knew.

I knew what I had suspected from the moment he'd leaned into me at the bar, I knew when he pressed his lips to my ear, and I knew when I saw that fire in his eyes. We weren't going to be able to fight this any longer. Sam was done trying to resist the heat and connection we had, and as we stood waiting for the elevator to make its way down to us, he was now searching my eyes for whether or not I felt the same way. He was giving me an out. He was asking if this was ok. I suddenly felt as though I was dancing along the edge of a steep cliff that I'd been too terrified even to approach before. But in that moment, staring up into Sam's eyes and feeling the heat and inhaling the seductive smell of him, I decided to forgo peering over the edge and instead leap out with eyes closed and arms outstretched. I'd lost my will to resist, and in this fog, I couldn't quite remember why I was so insistent we fight this at all.

The elevator dinged, the doors opened, and Sam was still looking at me with questioning eyes and bated breath as I stepped across the threshold, giving him a nod and a smile as I did so. Sam slid his key card into the panel and pressed the button for the penthouse level before slipping the card back into his pocket as the doors closed. The moment the doors pressed together, Sam turned to me with such ferocity and savagery I gasped just as his lips crashed into mine and his hands gripped either side of my face. With a surging rush of relief to finally be letting these impulses loose, I quickly wrapped my arms around him and kissed him back with the same fevered passion and need. Sam brought his hands to my side and gripped my hips as he walked me back a couple of steps and pressed me into the wall of the elevator. As our kissing became more frantic, my hands took hold in his hair, and his lips slid to my neck. He lightly kissed the skin down my throat before biting the tensed section of shoulder that met with my neck, making me throw my head back with a guttural moan. Spurred by my response, Sam brought his lips back to mine, and our tongues met in a passionate dance as both of his hands gripped my ass.

Despite being pinned to the elevator wall and enveloped in Sam's embrace, I needed to be closer to him and couldn't ignore the heat and urges building in my core. I lifted my leg and hooked it around his hip, bringing his hardened cock to me even more. With a groan and without hesitation, Sam squeezed my ass, bent slightly at the waist and ran both palms down the back of my thighs as he lifted me off the ground and wrapped my legs around his waist in one, swift move. With us entangled this way, Sam spun around and pinned me to the opposite side of the elevator, once again breaking a kiss to suck and lick down my neck as I moaned in pleasure with my head thrown back and eyes closed.

The ding of the elevator as it reached the penthouse level rang out through our fog and broke our concentrated hold on one another. Panting and not breaking eye contact, Sam set me back on my feet and smoothed down the front of his shirt. Frozen in place against the elevator, trying to catch my breath and remember how to walk properly, the thought occurred to me that the spell could be broken. Sam and I had made an art of passionate, desperate embraces followed by awkward glances and quick exits. And what about tomorrow? What about when we were back in the office and had to deal with the repercussions of giving into this need?

With one hand holding the elevator open and the other outstretched to me, Sam smiled that wicked panty-dropping grin at me. "Can I give you a tour of the penthouse, Ms. Shepard?"

That was all it took; Sam's lighthearted banter was enough to shake me out of the cloud of doubt I had drifted into and bring me back to this moment.

"I would love that, Mr. Monroe," I said, taking his hand and returning his smile with a playful one of my own. We emerged from the elevator into a small foyer with a glass table in the center and a vase of crimson roses atop it. There were five sets of double doors around the foyer, each with the name of a different Portland neighborhood upon them to designate the various suites. Hand in hand, Sam led me to the door to the left labeled Mt. Tabor and used his card to open the doors.

"Holy shit!" My hand clamped over my mouth as soon as the exclamation fell out. I couldn't help it, from where I was standing on the threshold I could tell the room had one of the most amazing views of the city. I crossed the sitting room to the wall of windows and took in the expansive city laid out before me. To the right, I could make out the arching beauty of the Fremont Bridge lit up in the night sky, and I was certain on a clear day I could make out Mount Hood from these windows.

"This is exquisite," I said, touching the cool glass with my fingertips.

"My thoughts exactly," Sam said in a husky whisper behind me. He traced a single finger down my spine as he brought his lips to my neck and my eyes fluttered shut. Once more the creeping voice of doubt started to speak up in my head. For as much as I wanted Sam, would my regret be even bigger? How deep would this cut into my ability to do my job? I struggled to find my voice to tell Sam that this was a bad idea. But when I opened my eyes, Sam's reflection was in the window next to me, his eyes zeroed in on mine with laser focus.

"Dee, please," he said running both hands down my bare arms, "Just be here with me."

I spun on my heels to face Sam and could tell my movement and grin had taken him by surprise. But as I took in every curve of Sam's face and placed a hand on his cheek stubbled with a day's growth of facial hair, he smiled back, and I knew we were both present in the moment. Together we crashed into one another and embraced without hesitation, Sam's strong arms wrapping around my waist and mine entwining around his neck as our lips met. My tongue traced his bottom lip and his came out to meet mine in a sensual and sweet dance. I unhooked my arms and ran my hands across his broad chest and then up to his shoulders, relishing every hard curve of him. His hands cupped my face as mine worked the buttons down his shirt, yanking the last bit of material from his slacks and practically ripping the final button that was keeping me from his naked torso.

I broke our kiss once again to slide my hands up his chest and across his shoulders, this time removing his shirt and taking in every inch of chiseled chest and stomach, which were rising and falling with his uneven breath and making it that much more delectable. My eyes made their way from his belly button to the V of his hips and back up to his strong pecks, finally landing on his gorgeous blue eyes and smirking expression. Sam knew he was sexy, but his enjoyment of me looking at him was even sexier.

Slowly, Sam took half a step closer and placed both hands against the glass on either side of my head, looking down into my eyes with hunger as I looked back up and leaned against the window. I shuddered, but whether from the cold of the glass against my bare back or from the anticipation of what he was about to do next, I do not know. With a dip of his head, Sam brought his lips to my left shoulder as his hand slid up my right arm, traveling all the way to the base of my neck. In a swift motion, he unclasped the back of my top and let both sides drop as he dragged his tongue across my collarbone, nipping as he went and leaning back once he reached the other side.

With a gentle pull on both straps, Sam released my naked breasts from the blouse and let the satin material slink around my hips before he pushed it down my legs where it landed in a pool at my feet. He quickly fixed his mouth to my left nipple as he palmed my right. I exhaled in a pleasured whoosh as he dragged his tongue from one breast to the other and brought a second hand to my chest. My fingers tangled in his hair as I let out throaty breaths with eyes closed and every receptor in my body tuned in to his focused caresses. His lips traveled up to my collar bone and then neck before he pulled back, pressed his forehead to my own and returned his palms to the window on either side of me. We stayed like that, both topless and panting, as though we were taking a momentary pause to take each other in and the assess ledge upon which we were standing.

"If you aren't sure," Sam rushed out in a ragged breath, "just say so."

"I'm sure," I replied without hesitation, my hands ghosting down his sides and coming to rest on his ass. "I need you," I pleaded in a whisper. With that simple request, Sam resumed our kissing, wrapped his arms around me and lifted me slightly off the ground. Knowing instantly what he wanted, I brought my legs up and wrapped them around his waist, locking my ankles together as he gripped my ass and I resumed clenching his messy locks once again.

Sam turned and carried me across the room, up a couple of stairs and entered the darkened bedroom, lit only by the lights coming from the city through the expansive window. Without breaking our kiss, he released me gently as I brought my feet back to the floor. Sam's hands traveled up my naked back and down again, coming around my sides and then to the button of my slacks. With deft fingers he quickly had the button and zipper undone and was sliding both hands along the waistband. Sam was now, officially, in my pants.

With an eager grip on my hips and his tongue dancing with mine, Sam walked me backward until the back of my knees hit the bed. For a brief moment I lost my balance, but Sam's strong hold steadied me before purposefully lowering me down to the cool comforter. His hands slid around to my ass and he gripped each cheek over the top of my panties with strong hands before pushing the fabric down my legs, slipping my heels off as he pulled each leg free. Sam stood up between my spread legs and roamed my body with his eyes. His lustful gaze swept from my face to my naked breasts, down to my black panties and back

up again for another circuit. As he did so, his hands began
loosening his belt and undoing his pants. I shamefully propped
myself up my elbows to get a better view as his leg muscles
flexed as he toed off his shoes and kicked them away. He
hooked both thumbs into his waistband and tossed his slacks to
the floor, leaving him standing before me in a pair of black
boxer briefs. I watched his nearly naked body in delight as he
bent slightly to remove his socks and then came back to stand
between my legs at the foot of the bed once more.

Holding my gaze, Sam slipped a hand behind my knee
and ran it along my calf, bringing my leg up so that he could
plant a kiss on my ankle. With excruciating slowness, he
proceeded to do the same with my other leg before finally
leaning down to hover over me on propped arms.

"Before I have you," he said, pausing to bite at my neck,
"I'm going to taste you."

And with that, he moved down my body, planting kisses
on my nipples, belly, and hips, all before landing on his knees
between my legs and gripping my panties on either side. In one
swift move, Sam lifted my hips, yanked the material down and
slid them off my feet. I made an attempt to rise up on my elbows
again but quickly fell back with a thump against the lush cotton
duvet as Sam's tongue made contact with the inside of my thigh,
and his open kisses worked their way toward my center. He
danced kisses on either thigh as he slipped his arms underneath
each one, his hands taking hold of my hips just as his mouth
found its way to where I craved it the most.

"Oh god," I moaned in pleasure as his tongue swirled
and the stubble from his chin brushed against my skin. His lips
and tongue seduced my clit he slid one and then a second finger
into me and brought me to heights I didn't know were possible.
As I reached my climax and yelled out with nonsense and
guttural noises, Sam kissed his way back down my thigh and
rose to his feet.

"Christ, Dee. You keep moaning like that for me and I'm
going to lose it right here," he said, reaching to the floor and
producing a condom from his discarded pants.

I was still coming down from losing it myself, panting
and gripping the comforter on either side of me as Sam yanked
his briefs down and the most amazing cock was sprung from

captivity. With one hand unrolling the condom onto his hard dick, Sam used the other to tease and caress me as I absentmindedly ran a hand over my breast and bucked my hips slightly in anticipation. With a moan that sounded almost pained, Sam reached out and gripped my hips, pulling my ass to the edge of the bed and wrapping my legs around him. Once again, he was over me, braced on the knuckles of his clenched fists as he brought the tip of his cock to my opening. I rolled my hips to encourage him and he granted my wish by plunging deep inside of me. In unison, our heads were thrown back, and we both breathed out the sound of two people finally giving into a need that had become all-consuming.

Sam slowly pulled back out and entered me again as my breath caught in my throat, repeating the action once more as his gaze came back to mine and our eyes locked. The pressure valve had been released; we were finally giving in to this urge, and it felt better than I'd ever imagined. As he continued this slow and intense rhythm, I reached up to cup his cheek.

"Fuck me, Sam," I pleaded.

With a grin, Sam slipped an arm under my back and lifted me as he climbed up on his knees and moved us further up the bed. My back came to rest, and my legs were still wrapped around his waist as Sam rested on his forearms and kissed me hard. He reached a hand around to the nape of my neck and pulled on a fistful of hair, causing my head to be thrown back and my neck exposed for him to suck on as he plunged deep inside of me. We found a rhythm, and I began to feel the familiar pull of another climax building with each thrust of his hips and groan from his throat. My nails raked down his back as my leg hitched higher on his hip as I rocked into his movements, reaching my peak. As though he seemed to know what I wanted, or needed, Sam hooked one arm under my leg and brought it over his shoulder as the other held tight to the fistful of hair at the base of my neck, all of which brought our bodies even closer and his cock even deeper inside of me.

"Oh, god!" I panted out as I teetered on the edge of release.

"Come for me, Dee," he replied between kissed and bites along my neck. "I want you to come hard for me baby." With these words, I crashed into my climax and came with a scream of his name and a flood of euphoria.

Sam let me ride out my waves of pleasure as he continued nipping at my neck and earlobe, releasing my leg which I wrapped around his waist with my other. He released my hair and braced his weight on his forearms on either side of me as his rocking began to pick up the pace again. My hands traveled up his sides and into his hair as I lifted my hips to meet his grinding thrusts and this time our rhythm became fierce and intense. The headboard began to thump into the wall with a harder and harder cadence, as our moans and sighs became louder and less modest. I felt the muscles in Sam's back and shoulders tense and knew he was close to his own release.

I wanted this moment to last forever, but also knew that neither of us could last much longer, so before I could think twice about it, I brought my lips to Sam's ear and sucked on his earlobe before whispering, "You feel so good inside of me."

"Fuck," Sam sputtered as his body shook and his orgasm took him over. With the intensity of his climax, I felt my body tighten around him as I gave in to another wave of pleasure. We crashed over the waves together and then lay panting and clinging to each other's skin.

Coming back up on his forearms, Sam kissed me gently as he lifted his body from mine and rolled to my side. It occurred to me just then, as his body uncovered mine, that I would typically care that I was splayed out naked on the bed, panting and covered with a sheen of sweat for the first time in front of him. But strangely, I couldn't care less at that moment. Everything just felt right. This newfound peace, however, may not have been abundantly clear to Sam. He wrapped an arm around my waist and brought my naked back into his chest in a tight spooning position as he let out a sigh.

"Before you go crawling back up in your head, I just want to lay with you for a bit," he said into my hair with a voice thick with sleep. I smiled into the pillow, and as I looked out at the city through the window this time, my eyes grew heavy and my vision blurred as sleep overtook me and I fell asleep in Sam's arms.

TWENTY-ONE

Dee

I had just made my fifth mojito and was placing it on the bar when an ice cube bounced off the counter and hit my naked chest. I jumped at the cold shock and looked around Boost to make sure no one had noticed I was tending bar in the nude. I relaxed a bit, until a hand hit the small of my back and Sam's voice said in my ear, "You're my favorite naked bartender this month."

My eyes flew open with a jolt, and I was awakened from the weirdest dream ever. I blinked against the pale blue and yellow light coming into the windows as the sun was slowly trying to make its way above Mt. Hood. The dawn's early morning light was still soft enough that the room was slightly dark, and my eyes only needed a moment to adjust. I blinked a few more times and took in the surroundings I'd missed the night before.

With a murmur, Sam slid his hand from my hip and rolled over, settling with his back to me and mumbling incoherent words in his sleep. I turned and looked at his back, rising and falling with each breath as he slept, still slightly red with scratches from my nails. The latter part made me wince.

So much for rule number one.

What the hell was I doing? Twenty-four hours ago, the plan had been to start keeping my distance and playing this safe. How was this possibly going to play out? I began to imagine a variety of scenarios.

There was the one in which Sam would wake up, roll over and say, "What the hell are you still doing here?" Or then there was the reality in which he would wake up, want to leave immediately, but not before saying, "Could you please not look?" as he climbed from the bed. And for a quick moment, I entertained the possibility of us having another round of intense sex before breakfast. But that and everything else was overpowered by the more than likely soon-to-be future in which we both awkwardly looked at one another, didn't know what the hell to say, and I'd have to explain to Sam that I thought this was a mistake. I stared at the ceiling for a few minutes, trying to decide what to say and how I would react when Sam woke up, before finally deciding that the easiest thing to do would be just to leave and skip that conversation all together. I'd go home and take the weekend to figure out the perfect way to say everything I needed to say, and then have the conversation with Sam later when I could be the most composed version of myself.

I slipped a foot to the floor and let the rest of my body slink out from under the covers and to the floor. Naked and on all fours, I maneuvered around the bed collecting articles of clothing like a scavenging rat, painfully aware of how ridiculous I looked but still committed to overlooking my pathetic choice to flee. With an arm full of items, I slipped out of the bedroom, down a couple of steps into the sitting room and felt as though I'd wondered naked into the Land of Oz. The night before I'd stumbled into the suite in darkness and a fog of lust. Now, in the early morning light, I was finally able to take in its beauty, much the same way I'd done with the bedroom. As I slipped on my pants and heels, I admired the plush carpeting, amazing décor, and ostentatious kitchenette.

I realized I'd reached the bottom of the pile of clothes from the bedroom floor and was still standing in the living room topless. Panicking slightly, I spun around in frantic circles, examining the furniture in the living room, tossing the pillows off of the sofa, looking under the chaise lounge without any luck before I suddenly remembered last night.

The window.

Fully clothed now and fearing my small opportunity of escape was dangerously coming to a close, I made my way to the door and slipped out as quietly as possible. It wasn't until I was riding the elevator down to the lobby that I finally exhaled and allowed myself a moment of reflection of the past twelve hours. In a fleeting montage, I replayed Sam's hands on my skin, his needing kisses and the smell and weight of his body on my own. But each delicious memory was accompanied by a thought that brought me crashing back down to reality. The memory of how Sam's skin tasted was followed by the thought that I was deceiving this beautiful man with every day that goes by.

The feel of his body pressed upon mine.

I'm here to fire him.

The scent of his sweat and cologne and breath all mixed together.

I'm a horrible person.

The safety and contentment I felt falling asleep in his arms, unmatched by any other feeling of intimacy I'd ever felt.

This can never last.

In a haze, I walked the handful of blocks to Jules' apartments, thankful for the rare warm mornings that early September brought Portland and the freedom this walk allowed me as I cleared my head. By the time I reached the door of Jules' apartment, I knew that this weekend was going to be great; I was going to get some clarity and return to work ready to face the Monroe project, and *all* it's duties, without hesitation. All I needed was some peace and time to think.

The first thing I noticed when I walked into the apartment was the dull thumping of music that I eventually realized was coming from Jules' room. Based on the early hour and her hatred for mornings, I assumed she must have fallen asleep with her stereo on. I kicked off my shoes and went to the kitchen for a bottle of water, and that's when I noticed the mess. The kitchen counter had the remnants of a fun evening strewn across it; half a lime with a couple of unused wedges were on a cutting board, shot glasses were upside down in a row, Jules heels were in the sink, and an unopened container of hummus sat perched on the edge of the counter. With a hunch as to how this would turn out, I went back into the living room to confirm my suspicion that Jules had met someone last night and had brought him back to the apartment. Sure enough, I found men's shoes on the floor and Jules' dress from last night on the dining room table, at which point I made a mental note to scrub the hell out of its surface before eating on it again.

I was still smiling to myself as I rummaged through the couch cushions for the remote when I heard Jules' door open, and I tried to decide how best to tease her about the state of the apartment.

"Keep your legs just like- Oh, shitballs!" a familiar deep voice said from behind me. Frozen in place with my hands still in the couch cushions and bent at the waist, I squeezed my eyes shut for a moment and then exhaled.

"Pax," I said in an even tone, without moving, "please tell me that you're not standing there naked."

"No, I'm not naked, it's cool Dee," Pax said over my shoulder. A quick yelp of surprise escaped me as I turned to face Pax, who was standing in the doorway of Jules' bedroom wearing nothing more than a single black dress sock on his left foot and a pink checkered apron spread tightly around him, which just barely came down low enough to cover his nether region. As though this thought was suddenly occurring to Pax as well, he brought his hands around and crossed them in front of his crotch, one of which held a can of whipped cream. "This could not have been timed worse," he mumbled, clearing his throat and avoiding eye contact.

We stayed like that for what felt like a millennium, until Jules finally emerged from behind Pax, tying a robe around her waist and hastily making her way over to where I stood, slightly catatonic.

"Get back in bed," she commanded to Pax as she passed, causing him to turn on his heel without hesitation and disappear into Jules' bedroom, not before giving me a flash of his bare ass before he did. She made her way to me in the living room and held her hands up in a surrender pose. "Alright, I know," she started with a somewhat annoyed tone. I had no words and just stood there staring at her like an idiot. "Don't be pissed, please. I didn't mean for this to happen, it just did. That obtuse motherfucker can be charming in a strange way, and he takes orders really well."

"Was that my apron?" I asked dumbly, at a loss for words.

After giving me more highlights than I wanted, Jules filled me in on the rest of her night after the benefit and how Pax had come to be in my apron; well technically, she spared me the specifics around the apron, but that was only after I begged her to stop. The long and the short of it was that after losing a bet to Jules about carburetors or some nonsense, Pax owed her a drink and that's where things took off. Drinks led to dancing, dancing led to Pax walking Jules home, which led to a nightcap upstairs and the rest is all sexual debauchery that I chose to stop Jules from recounting before every surface in the apartment became off limits to me.

Jules seemed to be under the assumption that I'd stayed late after the event and had worked most of the night. I simply chose not to correct her and let it go for the time being. I wasn't in the headspace to go from discussing her sexual exploits with Pax, to how I fucked his brother hours ago; let alone all the 'what does this mean' and 'what are you going to do' bullshit us ladies insist on doing all the time. Giving Jules the same consideration, I decided to skip any conversation around what her hooking up with Pax was going to mean when it came to my work situation or *her* lifestyle. Those were all conversations I would let future versions of ourselves have.

After a hot shower and slipping into my favorite pair of jeans and an old concert t-shirt, I finally started to feel like myself again as I settled onto the couch with a mug of coffee. Minutes into a baking competition rerun, it occurred to me that I hadn't reminded Jules not to say anything to Pax about why I was hired at the hotel. Now that they were familiar, in a carnal sense, and Jules knew what Charles' motivations were for bringing me here, I was more vulnerable than ever to being exposed. The thought passed through my mind for a brief moment to knock on her door and remind her in hushed tones that I needed her discretion. Not only would that draw more suspicion, at the end of the day, but Jules' loyalty was also one of the few things in this world I could count on. She would never betray me to a guy, our friendship would always win out over a hot piece of ass. I smiled at the thought of how grateful I was for Jules.

"Oh, god yes!" Jules screamed from her room, interrupting my internal sentiment.

"Yeah, who's torqued *now*!" Pax boomed in reply.

"Ok, that's my limit," I mumbled to myself. There was no way I could sit through this all weekend, and it certainly wasn't helping with my frame of mind. I threw together an overnight bag and texted Jules, 'My room is off limits, but otherwise have fun. Staying at the Monroe tonight.'

Now was as good a time as any to take advantage of the Monroe perks and use one of those suites.

Again, that is...

Back at the Monroe, I checked with the front desk and was told one of the suites had been vacated this morning and cleaned. My cheeks flamed red at the thought of it being the room Sam and I were in, but the names didn't match. I settled into the Hawthorne suite and pulled out my laptop to work, which was a fruitless endeavor. I couldn't calm my mind and kept with the tennis match of thoughts, bouncing back and forth from two sides of my brain. Half of me wanting to relish in the memories of finally being with Sam, and quite honestly having the best sex of my life, while the other obsessing about how this was going to play out with Charles and the hotel, and what Sam was going to think when he found out who I was.

The obvious answer was a simple one; he was eventually going to hate me. There was no foreseeable future where I finished my work for Charles, *and* Sam and I still ended up together. The muscle memory of my personality was already crafting the course of action I would usually take in a situation like this, not that I'd ever been in this particular type of sinking ship before. Instinct said to put into motion my exit plan immediately. I could easily accelerate my strategies, suggest to Charles to make a move sooner than later, and be packed and headed to the airport by the time Sam realized what had happened, and more importantly that I had been the architect of his demise. Avoiding any and all confrontation.

There was just one problem.

I couldn't stand the thought of walking away from Sam.

He was like a drug, he had a tractor beam on me, holding me completely immobile from all of my running away tactics. Knowing that this was going to end badly, knowing that there was going to be pain, and knowing more than anything that I was going to come off looking really, really bad to Sam, I couldn't bring myself to leave.

"Oh no," I whispered to myself, looking into the shocked expression of my reflection in the window as the realization washed over me.

I was falling in love with Sam.

Just as the sentence formed in my head, there was a knock on the door.

TWENTY-TWO

Sam

Before I even opened my eyes, I could smell Dee's intoxicating scent all around me, and I was instantly reminded of our night together. Hungrily, I slid a hand to her side of the bed to cup her sweet ass, but instead found nothing more than sheets and pillows, causing my eyes to pop open. I looked around the room and didn't see a trace of her at all.

"Dee?" My voice sounded feeble as it echoed around the empty suite. I wandered around the bed and then into the living room, not seeing a single article of her clothing or any trace that she's been here. If it wasn't for the hand and ass prints all over the window, I might have been questioning if I'd dreamt the whole damn thing. She'd snuck out, and I guess I shouldn't have been surprised. I was learning that this was how Dee operated; over the past month, as I'd been spending time with her and getting to know her personality, I was realizing that when the going got tough, Dee got running.

After a quick shower, I decided the upside to spending last night in the hotel was that I could get some work done while I was here, and I was pretty sure I still had clothes stashed in my office closet. However, upon further inspection once I was downstairs, I realized that beyond a single pair of jeans, the closet only held a handful of workout clothes, running shoes and spare ties. I couldn't help but smile; in my pursuit of Dee, which I was now completely done with pretending was anything else, I'd abandoned all my dating practices and habits. Hell, last night was the first time I'd gotten laid since I'd met Dee. No way around it, I was fucked.

I slipped into the jeans, old concert t-shirt and sneakers, grateful that it was a Saturday since I'd never wandered the office in this state of dress-down. As my eyes glanced over my desk, I spotted the golf tournament packet sticking out from a stack of folders and smiled to myself, recognizing this game Dee and I had been playing for what it had been: foreplay.

Everything from that first night had been leading us here; last night was a foregone conclusion from the moment I spotted her across the bar. Even the fact that Dee had snuck out this morning and was probably in some state of anxiety right now made me smile. Being as good as she was at her job didn't come without a considerable obsession with appearances and what other people are thinking. If I didn't want to scare her off, and in an effort to make her more comfortable, knowing damn well I wasn't going to stop perusing her, I committed myself to do everything I could to be discreet.

As I rode the elevator to the lobby, I resolved myself to be the epitome of discretion with Dee. If keeping this a secret made it easier for her to be present with me, then that is what we would do, for as long as we needed to. I'd never felt this way about a woman, and I was willing to do whatever it took.

The doors opened and as I rounded the corner to the restaurant a familiar shape caught my eye at the front desk. Standing on the balls of her feet, Dee was leaning on the front desk and speaking with Anthony, our weekend concierge in hushed tones. Her back was to me, but it was undoubtedly Dee; I could recognize her shape anywhere, as well as those familiar wild gestures she made as she tried to illustrate a point. With a polite smile, Anthony handed her a familiar black executive room card.

It appeared Dee was checking back *into* the hotel, hours after sneaking out of bed with me. She was anything but predictable, that was for sure.

"Hey, Anthony," I said as I approached the desk once she'd disappeared into an elevator. He looked taken aback for a moment, probably because a second executive was at his counter on a Saturday morning. "Ms. Sheppard, is she checking into a suite for the weekend?"

Anthony blinked a couple of times and shuffled his feet as well as the papers he was holding.

"Yes, sir, Mr. Monroe," he said, clearly uncomfortable.

"Which room is she in?" I asked casually. He hesitated and smiled nervously, shaking his head before freezing in front of me, unclear what to do next. I reassured him that this wasn't a test in decorum or guest privacy, and he finally revealed Dee's suite.

Listening to the rustling noises of Dee moving around the room after I knocked on the door had my pulse quickening. As I heard her footsteps approach the door and then silence for an excruciating period of time, presumably as she gazed upon me from the peephole, the thought crossed my mind that she may not answer the door at all. But a moment later I heard the deadbolt click, and the door slowly opened to reveal her standing there in jeans and a t-shirt, which made me smile.

"Yup, I agree," I said with a decisive nod as she looked at me in confusion. I strode past her into the suite and looked around in a feigned show of observation. "When it comes to hiding places, I think *this* is second to none." Dee made her goldfish impression in a failed attempt to find the perfect thing to say at that moment, but I didn't give her the opportunity to calculate that far. "I mean personally, if it was me, and I was trying to avoid the person I'd run out on, I probably would leave the building. But this? The room next door? This is brilliant."

"Sam," she said in a low voice, clearly embarrassed and searching for what to say.

"Tell me," I continued, turning to face her and crossing my arms across my chest, "when you snuck out this morning, after what I would call one hell of a night, did you sprint out? Or did you slink along the wall toward the door? Because honestly, in my mind, it was this Pink Panther type of exaggerated tip-toe walk across the room."

Her cheeks were turning eight shades of red. She assumed I would be upset and now that I was standing here, Dee was bracing for one of our patented arguments. It was difficult to keep a straight face as she rolled her fists around in the hem of her shirt.

"I, uh, I crawled out...of the room," Dee practically whispered in shame before raising her eyes to meet mine finally. I could only hold my stance for a beat before laughing at the image of a naked Dee crawling around the bedroom. I crossed to her and cupped the back of her neck with my hand, planting a kiss on her forehead.

"Shit, you're so adorable," I said, shaking my head. Dee looked up at me in confusion. "Ok, let me make a couple of things abundantly clear," I said, brushing her hair out of her face. "Last night was on purpose. I didn't fall into bed with you

without thinking. I knew what I wanted, and I made damn sure
you knew what you wanted, too. Remember? This wasn't an
impulse for me, or for us, ok?" Dee smiled and nodded up at me
as I gently grabbed her shoulders. "Second, I get that you care
way too much about what people think and that keeping this a
secret and just between us is really important to you. So,
consider my lips sealed. No one will ever know something is
going on until we know what this is, or until you're ready for
them to know, you know?"

Dee chuckled and nodded, "Ok."

"And finally, I get you have a thing about dating
someone you work with, probably because of how messy it can
be if this doesn't work out." Dee shifted uncomfortably and
looked back down at her feet. "But I'm thinking we already got
the worst of it out of the way; we're professionals, and we made
it through that. I've been at war with Delilah and lived to tell the
tale."

Now let me be in love with Dee.

I held back that last thought and searched her eyes when
she looked back up at me, hoping she was willing to roll the dice
on this as well.

"I don't want to be at war with you," she said. "Last
night was amazing. And I don't have it in me to resist this any
longer."

"Then let go, Dee. Don't worry about what anyone will
think; it's just you and me. Unless there's something else?
Another reason you don't think this will work?" I leaned back to
take her in as I asked the question and watched as Dee once
again shifted from one foot to the other. She took in the right
side of her lower lip to chew before swapping it for the inside of
her upper lip between her teeth.

"No. No, there's nothing else," she said as she bobbed
her head. "Those are the reasons. That's why this is…hard." Her
shakiness would have been cute if it wasn't such a blatant
indicator of one thing.

She's lying.

I took a long steadying breath. Venturing a guess as to
what the fourth reason Dee had for holding back and not giving
us a chance was a dangerous exercise for me. It could be my
reputation when we met and simply because of my past. I wasn't

the purest of souls when she came into my life, met and that may be too much for her to get over. Or it could be something in *her* past; a pain I didn't even know about yet. Honestly, it could be anything. But one thing was clear, the closer this *thing* got to the surface, the more uncomfortable and sadder Dee became. For her sake, I couldn't have that.

"Ok, so there's something else, huh?" I said running my hand roughly over my face. She started to interject, but I held a hand up to stop her. "I don't care. I don't, Dee, I honestly don't. Tell me when you're ready, or never at all if you prefer. I don't need to know all of the reasons why you're scared to be with me for me to tell you that I'm not going anywhere. I'm willing to give this a chance if you are." I took her soft hands in mine and looked down at our interlaced fingers. "Can you please stop thinking ten moves down the road and just be here with me? Let's stop strategizing for a day and see what happens."

With a thoughtful nod, Dee took the step and closed the space between us before rising up onto her tiptoes and wrapping her arms around my neck. We had crashed into one other on more than a few occasions, but this time we came together in a slow, deep embrace. I hugged her body close to mine and deeply inhaled the smell of her hair as I buried my face in the crook of her neck.

"What shall we do first?" she asked as she pulled back and wiggled her eyebrows at me seductively.

I didn't even bother giving an answer to her ridiculous question. I pulled her back to me and kissed her as I started to walk her backward toward the bedroom. The closer we got to the doorway, the deeper our kissing grew and the faster our hands moved over each other's clothes, pulling on shirts and yanking jean buttons. An involuntary groan of relief came out of me as we tumbled onto the bed and I was with Dee again.

TWENTY-THREE

Sam

I'd had every intention of using our second time in bed together to take my time and really show Dee some moves that would blow her mind. But once we'd shed our clothing and her legs wrapped around my waist, I lost all sense of planning and lost myself as well. Once again, it was just a swirl of need and flesh, and before I knew it, we were laying side-by-side, panting. Last time we were together, we'd fallen asleep and Dee had snuck out. This time, instinctually, I stayed silent and didn't make any sudden movements, unsure of what she was thinking. And just as the silence was starting to play with my head, Dee's stomach let out an angry rumble, which immediately made her laugh with a lazy giggle as she rolled toward me.

"I suppose after the past fifteen hours I've worked up a bit of an appetite," she said as she propped herself up on an elbow and crossed her legs. I chanced a look down the length of her naked body, from her beautiful breasts painted with the slightest sheen of sweat, over the supple curve of her hip and down the length of her smooth legs to the point of her toes.

"Well, then I suppose we should feed you," I said as I rolled onto an elbow and mirrored her pose. "What can I get you from room service? I hear this hotel has an amazing restaurant," I said.

"Won't ordering for two raise some questions and unwanted attention?" Dee asked, furrowing her brow in contemplation.

"Delilah," I sighed with mock seriousness, as I placed a hand on her naked hip, "I hate to break this to you, but you're not *that* big of a deal around here. No one knows who you are, except for those of us on the management team that you're personally torturing."

Dee reached over her head to grip a pillow and with a quickness brought it down over my face with a thud. "I haven't even begun to torture you, Mr. Monroe," she said as I wrestled her onto her back and pinned her hands above her head. The flush of her cheeks, her breasts against my chest and the gorgeous authentic smile on her face, all combined to make me want to ravage her again.

As my eyes swept across her cheekbone again and came to rest on her big beautiful eyes, I realized she'd been watching me watch her, a gleam in her eye that was playful and sexy. I dipped my head and kissed her lips gently, enjoying the sensation on her soft skin on my own. And as I slid a hand down her side to land on her hip, she pulled back ever so slightly to whisper, "Food first." With a laugh, I rolled off her and grabbed the robes from the back of the bathroom door, tossing one in her direction as I winked and headed out to the living room for the room service menu.

I convinced her to order food from downstairs, contingent on me being out of sight when the staff brought it up to the room. Shortly after, we were seated at the table on the terrace, sharing small plates and enjoying the rare Portland sunny day while chatting and laughing. All at once a feeling washed over me that while this was all so comfortable and I was utterly at peace, everything was also different. As Dee was telling me another story from her college days with Jules, it occurred to me the strange new sensation I felt with her.

The sexual tension was gone.

In its place, was a comfortability unlike any I'd ever felt before. If I thought the tension and electricity had been addictive, this new contentment was off the charts. My mind kept wandering, looking for the word to describe how this all felt; sitting together on a Saturday afternoon, eating crostini while tucking an errant strand of hair behind Dee's ear. As she guffawed while telling a self-deprecating story about a 20-year old version of herself, whom I would have fallen for just as much as I was falling for the present version, it occurred to me.

Happy.

That was the word. Simply and purely, I was happy.

"Dee, I get that it's a bit backward to ask you this now, after last night together…and again this morning," I said as I slipped her hand into my own and enjoyed the pink color that brightened the ridges of her ears, "but will you please allow me the honor of taking you out on a date tonight?"

She laughed, most likely a little relieved, and said, "Of course. What did you have in mind?"

I knew she only had casual clothes with her, and for a moment I considered having a dress from a nearby store sent up as I made reservations at a local high-end restaurant for us. However, I systematically checked off way too many plot points from *Pretty Woman* and thought better of it. We had spent the last couple of weeks in suits and dresses and elegance, maybe now was the time to let this casual authenticity be the name of the game.

"I don't know," I answered honestly. "But I will be back here to pick you up at seven. And I'll still be wearing this," I said with a tug on my t-shirt as I watched her eyes darted around in her usual Dee way.

"Ok," she said with a decisive nod. I stood and kissed her before turning and leaving the suite. I spent the entire elevator ride to the lobby planning and seconded-guessing nearly a dozen ideas. This was unlike any other date I had planned before, and so none of my usual plays would work, nor did they even feel appealing. Dee and I knew each other so well already, we were already so far past the first date get-to-know-you nonsense, not to mention we'd already had sex. Any sort of elaborate plan to impress Dee just seemed so ingenuine. Instead, I thought about what I wanted out of tonight, what did I want for Dee? And then it hit me.

A few hours later, I found myself once again knocking on the door of Dee's suite. She opened the door with a smile and nervously slung her purse over her shoulder.

"No bag," I said. "Isn't necessary since we aren't going far." She eyed me warily as she slid her room keycard into her back pocket and deposited her bag on the entry table.

"I think the last time I wore jeans and a t-shirt on a first date I was in high school," she said as she grabbed my outstretched hand and crossed the threshold into the hall.

"I bet you were the cutest girl at the roller rink that night."

"Wow," she said with a shake of her head, "How old *are* you?"

"Oh, come on, skating rinks were still *in* when we were teenagers…right?" I asked, suddenly unsure of the coolness of my youth. Dee shook her head again with a soft laugh. "At least I didn't say discotheque."

"Yes, Sam," she laughed, "you get points for not referencing discotheques."

I led her by the hand past the elevator and heard her breath hitch when I opened the door to the stairwell. I offered her nothing more than a smile as we started to climb the single flight from the penthouse level to the roof. I punched in the administrative four-digit code into the keypad, and the lock clicked, swinging the door open.

"Oh, wow," Dee whispered as she stepped past me to take in the private garden and patio on the roof.

"This was something of a pet project for my mother a few years ago," I said as Dee wandered around the garden, smelling late season blooming plants and examining trellises and arbors adorned with ivy and twinkly lights. "We have a yoga class up here for guests during the summer. Emma organizes a few small events up here, too."

We came upon the circular wooden deck in the center where I'd had the restaurant crew set up a small table for us to have dinner, as well as an accompanying dry bar. Soft jazz music was playing from unseen speakers. Dee turned and looked at me with the most amazing smile and adorable look of shock.

"I know that discretion is important to you," I explained as we walked up to the deck. "And I wanted to give you the privacy you needed to enjoy yourself tonight. God knows, I'd personally love to drag you all over town and let the world know that I managed to convince the most beautiful woman in the world to accompany me for dinner," I said as I slipped an arm around her waist, pulling her to me so I could kiss her temple and smell that intoxicating hair. "But I will settle for a close second of being able to have her all to myself for an evening."

Dee beamed up at me, and my heart tightened at the look she gave me. Making this woman smile like this was becoming the most important thing I did every day.

"It's gorgeous," Dee said, gesturing around before looking at the two cloche covered plates on the candlelit table. "Did you cook as well?"

I laughed as I led her past the table to the dry bar set up beyond it, "I do a lot of things well, and while cooking isn't one of them, you may know that mixology is." Dee slid onto a patio stool while I stepped behind the bar, leaned on both palms and said, "What can I get you?"

The move had the desired effect, and Dee's cheeks turned a crimson as she found herself in a recreation of the moment we'd met.

"I...ugh," Dee stammered, looking up at me with a broad smile.

"Trick question," I cut her off as I started grabbing ingredients and glasses. "I'm not letting you order this time."

"But I-" she said, rising up to lean over the lip of the bar to look at what I was doing.

"I'm going to tell you the story," I said, with closed eyes and a dramatic pause and sigh, "of Slick Sammy." Based on the widening of her eyes, I assumed Emma or Pax or both had eluded to the nickname when explaining to Dee why the hell I was bartending the night we met. I also sensed, based on the hardening of her jaw, that she was apprehensive about stories from my past and the sexual deviancy I'm sure she thought was in them. Now was probably a good time to tell her what my plan was, so I came back around the bar and cupped her face in my hands and stared hard into those beautiful eyes. "I want you to know me, Delilah. That's what this night is all about. I want you to have the space and environment to be with just me. And I want you to know who I am. And if I'm being honest, I want you to replace all the bullshit stories you have in your head with the man that is standing in front of you."

"Oh, Sam," Dee said, reaching up to grab my forearms as I leaned over to kiss her delicately. "I do know you, I feel like I know you so well. But that being said," she said as she ran her fingers through my hair, "you *have* to tell me this story."

With a laugh and then a dramatic flourish I walked behind the bar.

"The story of Slick Sammy. In my undergraduate days, as a young collegiate man at the wise old age of twenty, twenty-one, I began to learn the fine art of mixology." I grabbed a shaker and spooned some ice into it as I spoke, gathering ingredients and making a big showing of mixing as I told Dee the story. "I worked nights and weekends at a bistro downtown, learning the chemistry behind bartending, but what became strangely apparent to me, was that the more I learned about bartending, the easier it was for me to guess someone's drink. It was weird. Not only could I size a person up and figure out what their usual order would be, but I could also guess what order would also make a customer particularly happy. Now, a more sophisticated person might hear that and think there is a phycological or sociological effect taking place; I, however, decided this was a spectacular way to meet girls." I punctuated the last point by flipping the cherry liquor bottle in my hand and rolling a peach down my forearm before catching it, enjoying the entertainment Dee was gleaming from this. "As stories of my gift spread, and I began to get a name for myself as an alcohol-psychic, it was only a matter of time before I became something of a dating consultant, helping young men dazzle women by anticipating and pre-ordering their drink order for them. Hence the ridiculous name, Slick Sammy."

"This story toes the line between being James Bond-ish and a little date-rapey," she deadpanned.

"Now, when we first met, you were drinking a dirty martini," I said as I held up an empty martini glass for consideration, ignoring and yet loving her complete lack of admiration. "For courage, you admitted. But this is certainly not your drink. It's bold and powerful, just as you are, but it's too simple. You, my dear, are not a simple woman. And then there is your fun drink, the mojito. While you're a sweet and zesty lady," I said with a wiggle of my eyebrows, "this is not your drink either. You're so much more low-maintenance than this."

"Wait," said Dee with a chuckle and a confused shake of her head, "I thought I wasn't simple, and now I'm not complicated?"

"You're a particular kind of complicated," I said holding up a finger to stop any more interruptions on her part. "You're a unique cocktail of complications and low-key simplicity, slight craziness and refreshing loveliness." I set an empty champagne flute on the bar in front of her and poured the fruity concoction into it as she examined it skeptically.

"I'm a mimosa?" she asked, poorly hiding her disappointment.

"You're a peach bellini. Peaches are luscious and universal but can be bruised so easily if you don't know how to care for them. And prosecco, to me, is an approachable beverage, wine. But it's bubbled, making you taste wine in a way you've never had it before. To me, this drink is a blending of things we all think we know but are presented in a way that are wholly unique."

As Dee hesitantly turned on her stool and took a sip of the sparkling beverage, I came around the bar to stand in front of her.

"Mmm, it's delicious," she said, licking her lips.

"You're delicious." I bent to kiss her sugared lips, tasting the sweet peach flavor on her tongue as her head tilted back and I leaned into her deeply. As she gripped the back of my shirt and moaned, I steeled myself to pull away before she dropped her glass and we got carried away. "Let's eat."

We sat at the table and ate an unbelievable meal put together by our restaurant's chef. When I managed to get Dee to be brave enough to take this relationship on dry land, and not hide on rooftops any longer, we would have to eat downstairs at the chef's table in the kitchen. It was an experience I knew she would love, and I smiled to myself with the realization that I had begun planning future dates together. I couldn't remember the last time I'd planned ahead with a woman like this.

Nearly an hour later, the food was long eaten and the second round of peach bellinis sat in front of us as we talked. Stories about our childhoods gave way to talk about our careers. Dee had crisscrossed her legs and tucked her feet underneath her, leaning her elbows on the table as I told her about my time in Japan, interning for a hedge fund firm. Knowing my CV backward and forwards at this point, she obviously knew I'd been pre-law and then went on to get my MBA, but she'd seemed a bit surprised to hear about my penchant for mergers and acquisitions.

"It was just such a fun swirl of all the things I was good at," I said with a smile, wistfully thinking back to those 14-hour work days that I wouldn't trade for anything. "On the business side, you're consulting with owners and executives, connecting two companies that might not have come together before, working the legal side of the deal. Made me want to move to New York and take the first junior man position I could land and never look back."

Dee leaned back against her chair and furrowed her brow slightly.

"What?" I asked.

"I'm curious about something." She cleared her throat and sat up a little straighter. "Mergers and acquisitions. Corporate law and contract negotiations. International business. None of those things go into running a single hotel location in Portland."

"Is there a question in there somewhere?" I asked with a lazy smile, knowing where she was probably going with this.

"Do you *really* want to take over for your dad?"

"It's a fair question." I just wasn't expecting it to be put so pointedly. "I mean, sure, I'd love to be doing those things every day. Maybe even traveling the world to do it. But the hotel is *family*."

"No, it's the family's *business*," Dee corrected. "It's not your family. If you didn't work at the hotel, you wouldn't lose your family, Sam."

"I know that, but it's just always been the plan. I've always known that one day I would take over for dad and run the hotel. And I know dad is just testing me, not giving me the reigns completely until he knows I've really cut my teeth," I said feebly, knowing how weak the whole thing sounded.

"Your father is waiting for his MBA son with an international internship with Japanese venture firms, to *cut his teeth* before giving him the mid-level business?"

"Easy killer," I said, holding my hands up in mock surrender.

"I'm sorry," she said, her cheeks blushing slightly. "It just seems like you're giving up an awful lot to take over a job you don't even want."

"Well, hopefully, this expansion project will mitigate some of that. Give me a little taste of the old days, a little bit of acquisitions, some contract negotiation sprinkled in."

"Sure," she said, with clear doubt in her voice, "maybe." It was obvious she wasn't convinced, doubting that this one hypothetical project in the future would be enough to leave me satisfied with the highest leadership position at the hotel. And if I was being honest with myself, she was probably right. This often felt like a waste of my talents, and more often than not, something I was settling for rather than choosing. A promotion from GM to CEO wasn't going to change much of that. But my dad was relying on me; this was the game plan, and I knew that before even stepping foot on a college campus. I found it sweet Dee was so concerned with my happiness and satisfaction. But the conversation had started to harden some of her edges and work-Dee was slowly creeping into this conversation.

"Enough work talk," I said, standing from the table and reaching a hand out for her own.

"More tricks up your sleeve?" she asked, slipping her hand in mine and rising to her feet. She was in a state of comfortability and authenticity; I couldn't have been happier. It was as though after twenty-four hours of peeling layer upon layer of ourselves away, we were finally standing in front of one other, just us. No bullshit.

"No tricks tonight, darling. Just you. Just me."

"I don't want this night to end," she said, bringing her arms up around my neck and lacing her fingers into my hair. She scrunched her nose up and added, "I get how cliché that is to say, but it's true, Sam. I just want this night to last forever and for tomorrow to never come. Can we live on this roof?"

"We can try, but it's September in Portland. You're not from here, so let me just inform you, this son of a bitch is going to be soaking wet for months soon."

Dee laughed, and I reveled in the feel of her body shaking against mine. With a rub of her back and a smack on her ass, I led her back to the stairwell door and down to the penthouse floor. We walked back into the suite, and I could tell Dee was looking for another curveball but found her room the same way she'd left it.

"Did you really think I would have someone sneak in here to set up a surprise of some kind when the whole theme of tonight has been discretion and making you comfortable?"

"You never know," she said, turning to face me after scanning the living room and appearing satisfied that I didn't have a string quartet stashed behind the curtains. "We never seem to stop surprising one another."

"Touché," I said, crossing the room and making a show of toeing off my shoes, "but aren't you tired of surprises?"

"You have no idea," she said, kicking her shoes under the side table.

Dee was initially surprised that my plan was for us to curl up on the plush sofa and watch a movie together. She seemed to fight the idea of an authentic, casual night together until the bitter end. But eventually, around the half-way mark of *The Shop Around the Corner,* I felt her sink into the crook of my arm as her ankles crossed on the table. I tossed the throw blanket over the top of us and watched Dee as she watched the movie. I took in every piece of the scene with all my senses, trying to capture it all in my memory forever. The sound of her laughing softly and sighing with empathy as Jimmy Stewart and Margaret Sullavan bumbled through their love affair. The smell of her hair. The sight of our fingers intertwined, her thumb absentmindedly rubbing soft circles on my wrist. And then there was the feel of the weight of her head on my chest, not post-coital and in exhaustion, but rather in comfort, intimacy, and most importantly, trust.

She was right, it would be amazing if tomorrow never came and we could just live in this night together, forever. Once upon a time, I would have chosen last night as the evening for us to live in forever; the night of lust and passion and sweaty skin pressed against one another and hurried embrace. But now that I was in it, I realized that I would choose intimacy and authenticity with Dee over anything else. This is where I belonged; she had suddenly become home to me.

When the credits began to roll, I realized that at some point Dee had fallen asleep. Her mouth was slightly open with her soft breathing, and her head had grown heavy without my noticing it. With care and deliberation, I reached up and turned off the lamp, casting the suite into darkness only lit by the city lights coming through the windows. I sat up and shifted her body into my arms such that I could lift her. With her head once again on my shoulder and her legs draped over my opposite arm,

I stood and carried her to the equally dark bedroom. I laid her on the soft sheets with her head on the pillow and pulled the feather comforter over her legs, tucking it under her arms. I took one last look at her gorgeous face and her sleeping form before turning to leave. I'd just made it to the door when I heard her soft voice.

"Sam? Don't go."

I hadn't realized how sad I was to leave her until she called out for me to stay. I turned and silently went to the other side of the bed, slipping under the covers and meeting her in the middle of the mattress in an urgent embrace. Our legs tangled together and her head was once again on my chest, my arms were tight around her and we both exhaled loudly with the relief of our bodies being together again.

I had every intention of staying like that. If we had fallen asleep fully clothed, jean-clad legs wrapped around one another, and her soft breath on my neck, I would have been happy. More than happy, I would have been entirely content and slept like a baby. But Dee had other plans.

Slowly, her hand drifted under my shirt and across my belly, sending goosebumps down my arms as her tiny fingers ghosted from one side to the other and she tilted her head up to plant a soft kiss on my neck. It wasn't rushed or needing; it was loving and tender. I closed my eyes and took in a deep breath, steadying myself under the weight of what I realized I was feeling. I had fallen in love with Delilah. Heart, mind, and soul, she owned me and probably had for a while, but the difference was that now I knew it and the feeling washed over me in a terrifyingly blissful wave. I wanted Dee, I always wanted Dee, but I also wanted to worship her.

I rolled and caught her mouth to mine, kissing her deeply as I slowly ran a hand down her back to land on her ass with a gentle squeeze. As she lifted her leg and wrapped it around my waist, I ran my hand down her thigh, pulling her body closer to me, as if that was possible. It faintly registered as I deepened our kiss with an arm around her leg and other around her shoulders that I had her completely captured in a tight embrace, trying to eliminate space between us that did not physically exist. But as she brought her arms around my chest and pulled me closer with her hands on the back of my shoulders, it occurred to me that

she felt the same way. Our need was different tonight; we both
needed to be enveloped by the other.

I pulled back just enough to look down into Dee's eyes.
Even in the pale light coming from the city outside, I could tell
that there was a gorgeous flush across her cheeks and her bright
eyes were blazing with passion. Her lips were slightly parted as
she softly panted to catch her breath, just as I was. I wanted to
say so many things right then; when our eyes met, and she
looked up at me like that, I couldn't even catalog all of my
thoughts, but it did register in my conscious that each one
sounded crazier than the one before it. I'd scare her if I told her I
loved her right now, not to mention I didn't even know what that
meant. And what's the love-equivalent sentiment to say at that
moment? I struggled for words, shaking my head slightly and
closing my eyes to steady my brain's onslaught.

It was then that Dee's soft hand landed on my cheek. I
opened my eyes as she brought another hand up to hold my face
in front of her, while her eyes held mine steady. And then ever
so slightly, she nodded and smiled. She knew. She knew the
tornado of thoughts going on in my head and was letting me
know it was ok. Damn, is this what it was like in Dee's head all
the time? This shit was exhausting and confusing; I was amazed
she got anything done every day. Dee smiled tenderly at me, and
I rested my forehead on hers with a soft exhale of relief.

"Be with me," she whispered. My head jerked up at her
use of my words from earlier and the cute smirk on her face
made me fall in love with her even more. I took her advice to be
present in this moment and brought my lips hungrily back to
hers. I'd figure out what to do with the intensity of my feelings
for her, and I'd work out telling her I loved her at another time.
Right now, I was going to be in this moment and do what I
wanted with the beautiful woman underneath me. And what I
wanted to do was something I'd never done before.

I was going to worship every inch of her.

Methodically and with care, we peeled away each other's
clothes, taking our sweet time as we did. My mouth followed the
hem of Dee's shirt as I lifted it, littering kisses along her
stomach and chest as I brought it over her head, my tongue
coming to rest within the crook of her neck, softly licking and
sucking at her flesh. Jeans were shed, clothes tossed with a

flourish as we unwrapped the naked gifts waiting for us until finally, it was her and I, skin-to-skin, tangled together. Dee's legs slid up and wrapped around my waist, giving her leverage to buck her hips and open herself to me. I smiled at her urgency and took a breath as I fought the voice in the back of my head telling me to give in to temptation.

"Not yet," I whispered with a laugh as she groaned in frustration when I pulled away. I came up on all fours, knees planted on the mattress between her legs and hand splayed next to her ribs. I allowed my eyes to slowly trace up and down her body, taking in every curve, every dimple, every freckle. I was tempted to reach over and turn on the lamp so that I could see her better, not just to ogle her beautiful form, but to also commit it all to memory. The thought was hard to dwell on, but I had no idea how long I had Dee and if these moments together were fleeting, I didn't want to remember them in darkness and frenzied lust.

I ran my hands up her arms, taking my time to let my thumbs and fingertips play across the soft flesh inside her forearms before folding her hands together above her head. With deliberate precision, I placed kisses back down, tracing from her wrists to the inside of her elbows and down to her shoulders, stopping there to lift my head and kiss her deeply before moving on. I zig-zagged my way down her body, taking in every inch I came in contact with; the slope of her breasts, the feel of her nipples, the crater of her belly button and the freckles above her hips. With hands and lips and breath, I greeted and paid homage to every little piece that made up the whole of her body.

When I came to rest between her legs, I took my time in a way I never had before. I wasn't there for foreplay; my focus was to please her and make her feel the love I couldn't express verbally. Dee's hips began to rise off the mattress, and her fingers dug into my scalp with ferocity the closer she got to her climax. I reveled in her pleasure and got harder the more she came. I kissed up her thigh, giving her a minute to catch her breath and come back down before starting to worship her all over again. And just as I shifted to plant kisses on the inside of her other thigh, the bed shifted as Dee came up on her elbows and looked down at me. I met her eyeline and she crooked her finger at me, motioning me back up to her. I knew what she wanted, and if I was being honest, I was barely hanging on myself.

I crawled back up the length of her body, kissing her neck and then lips as she wrapped her legs around my waist and laced her fingers in my hair. With a familiarity as though I'd done it a thousand times, I positioned myself at her opening and slowly plunged into her, groaning as her warmth encircled me. All concept of time and place and consequence and reality were gone; for all I knew, Dee and I lived in that moment forever. I languished each movement, taking deep long thrusts and being careful to never let my mouth leave her skin as I attempted to pour every ounce of emotion I had into our physical connection, in hopes she would understand, somehow, that this was different for me and I was with her in a way I'd never been with any other woman before.

With excruciating focus, I held off from coming until I could feel her reaching her own ledge and getting ready to crash over, and that's when I hooked an elbow under her knee, opening her deeper to me and plunging deep inside her. With a yelp and a guttural moan, Dee's fingers dug into the flesh at my shoulders as her heels ground into my lower back and she came with ferocity. Her reaction was the little push I needed to fall over my own edge of reason and growl into her neck with my own finish.

We lay there panting, Dee feebly clinging to me as I hovered on top of her, held up on shaking elbows and knees. Just as I thought I would collapse, Dee's arms encircled my torso and brought me down to her, guiding me to her side and laying me next to her in the sweetest of motions. Her head came to rest on my chest and hand began caressing my stomach as she curled up to me and covered us with the comforter. I wrapped my arms around her tightly and kissed her head, vaguely registering that she was saying something as I involuntarily freefell into a content sleep.

TWENTY-FOUR

Dee

The faint smell of Sam's cologne hit my nose, and I
smiled, shifting backward to fit even closer inside his embrace.
His arm was draped over my hip, and his breath was warm
against the back of my neck, steady with the rhythmic breathing
of his sleep. I peeled my eyes open and took in the gorgeous
pale blue light of the sky; the sun hadn't completely risen over
Portland yet, and the city looked so perfect in this early light.
Everything seemed perfect at that moment. It was hard to
believe it had only been days because suddenly, being with Sam
felt like the most natural thing in the world. He'd asked me to
put aside any reservations and concerns I had in order to be
present and give this all a shot, a request he probably would
have thought twice about if he'd known my reasons for
hesitating.

I cringed slightly and squinted my eyes at the thought of
what I was keeping from Sam. If the thought of telling him the
truth was hard to imagine *before*, telling him now that I was here
to help his dad fire him felt unimaginable. Every scenario I
dreamt up about telling him, finding some way to come clean,
ended with us parting ways and all hope of ever being together
destroyed. I let myself feel optimistic when Sam shared that
running the hotel isn't even what he really wanted to do, but
then I realized that even if it all worked out for the best, he
would never forgive the false pretenses I'd been operating
under, especially now that we'd spent the weekend together.

What were my options?

I could get Charles to rethink the management change, a
prospect that became more and more possible as Sam got in line
with Charles' corporate strategy, but then Sam would be in a
career he doesn't really want. He could walk away from the
hotel and come with me to New York, but probably only to end
up hating my guts for passively dashing his hopes of fulfilling
his family destiny. Any scenario ended in resentment and pain.

And despite my better judgment, I had put those thoughts on a shelf and slipped into the weekend with Sam like a warm bath. Our day together had been wonderful, but our evening had been unforgettable. Never in my life had I felt so *seen* by a man. It was an understatement to say that Sam had gotten to me; it was accurate to say that I was falling irretrievably in love with him.

The thought first occurred to me when we were sitting on the terrace, sharing plates of food while he gently massaged my foot. We'd been trading stories and making each other laugh, but it was a moment of silence in particular that had resonated. With a contented sigh, Sam had tilted his head back to the sky to soak in the warmth of the day, eyes closed to the sun and a small smile dancing across his lips before lifting my foot in his hand and placing a soft kiss on my ankle bone. He'd grabbed his fork right after and speared a shrimp while asking me something about where I grew up. The question was lost on me, and I had to have him repeat it because at that moment a singular thought was cascading over me.

I was in love with Sam.

I had no intention of telling him, especially knowing that ours was a relationship destined to be over just as quickly as it had started. Whenever my mind wandered to hypothesizing *how* this was all going to come to an end, my stomach dropped a bit, and the air left my lungs. But Sam's words about being present would ring in my ears, and I would shake off the thought and just enjoy the moment. I guessed Sam knew our future as well; he may not know why I was here, but there were a dozen other reasons why a happily-ever-after was unlikely between us. And I could tell he was making an effort to keep our impending end out of his mind as well, which is why I'd tried to keep him in the moment with me, just as he'd coached me to do with him. And afterward, as I crawled into the crook of his arm and snuggled into the place that was quickly becoming my favorite place in the world, the emotions just bubbled to the surface, and despite myself, I'd told him I loved him. Thankfully, by all accounts, it appeared I had shared the sentiment just after he had slipped off to sleep. Or at least I was hoping. Telling him I loved him, while true, was just going to make this harder when the moment of truth came, and everything crashed to the ground. As I watched the sky warm with the colors of the rising sun, I steeled myself with the reality that lay before me. I would soak up every moment I had with Sam. I would be present and enjoy all the happiness and memories I could. And when the day inevitably came, I would put on my big girl panties, face his anger and resentment, and accept our separation.

I was just grateful that today was not that day. The clock had not run out yet for us to simply enjoy each other's company and be together uninterrupted.

And because the universe loves irony, Sam's alarm began chirping at that moment. He startled awake with a shake and gripped my hip reflexively. For a moment, I thought I may have my days mixed up and panicked that it was Monday already.

"Sorry," Sam mumbled as he turned on his back to reach his phone on the nightstand and click off the annoying bleat of the alarm. He rolled back to spooning position and gave my naked body a squeeze, nuzzling the back of my neck with his nose and sighing.

"Why the hell do you have an alarm set for...," I lifted my head to check the digital clock on my own nightstand, "5:45AM on a Sunday?"

"You're joking, right?" Sam's voice was heavy with sleep, the deep gravel of just waking up combined with a gruffness. The indignancy of his tone, however, made me quickly self-reflect. Was he religious and church-going and I'd somehow missed it? Doubtful. Had I agreed to an early morning jaunt after imbibing a couple of those deceptively smooth peach bellinis? Plausible. What the hell was he talking about?

The silence stretched on for what felt like forever.

"I'm golfing in a charity tournament today," he said, rolling onto his back and rubbing his face roughly. "I need to get home and change before being in Hillsboro by eight."

We laid like that for a long pause before I couldn't take it any longer and erupted into laughter. The fact that this event was cutting into my weekend with Sam, and that I had to be witness to his wake-up routine for it, was nothing short of hilarious to me.

"Think that's funny, do you?" Sam asked, trying to hide his own smile and pinching my side playfully, making me laugh all the harder.

"I'm sorry, it's not funny," I said, composing myself. "It's karma, that's what it is. Here I am, wanting to have a proper morning with you, and I'm the one who sabotaged it."

"Well, technically the shrew did," he said before kissing my cheek and rising from the bed. "That woman's a ballbuster."

"You know we're the same person, right?" I drawled out as I watched his naked ass as he walked away and into the bathroom.

He stuck his head back out and added, "No, you aren't." And with a wink, he disappeared again and shut the door. I was just starting to doze back off to sleep when he reemerged, looking more awake now as he collected his clothes from the floor. "No…please…don't get up, honey," he deadpanned sarcastically while zipping his jeans and looking at me sprawled out under the sheet. "I insist, you should stay in bed and sleep some more."

"Does it *look* like I'm getting out of this bed any time soon?" I punctuated it with a wiggle of my legs. He slipped his shirt over his head as he came around to my side of the bed and sat down.

"You *should* stay in bed, baby," he said as he tucked a strand of hair behind my ear. I was quickly getting used to these little terms of endearment. "You're going to need your strength this week," he whispered just before leaning down to kiss my lips softly. "I plan on fucking you every chance I get." He kissed me deeper this time, our tongues colliding and a shiver going down my spine. Last night had been so tender and wonderful, but the idea of him ravaging me with ferocity made my belly clench with anticipation and excitement. He pulled away and said, "I have to go. I'll call you later," but just as he reached the bedroom door, he abruptly turned and quickly returned to my side. "One more," he said in a rush as he bent at the waist, captured my lips in another deep kiss and palmed my naked breast for good measure. With willpower *I* certainly didn't have, he separated us and left the suite.

I laid there panting for a bit, staring at the ceiling and replaying last night, and this morning, and Friday night, all of it in my head, over and over. The previous two days were on a loop in my mind, and I could feel the heat in my cheeks as I replayed key moments. One thing was for certain, and that was that sleep was no longer in the cards for me. I leisurely showered and ordered breakfast to the room. Eventually, once I thought it wasn't too early to text, I sent a message to Jules asking if the coast was clear and I was safe to come back to the apartment. I figured at the very least I would grab more clothes for the week and make use of the hotel room, but no matter what, I wanted to make my arrival well-known before crossing the threshold and risk seeing Paxton's bare ass.

Just as I was finishing my coffee on the terrace, staring at the empty chair Sam occupied just yesterday and inwardly cursing myself for setting up that ridiculous golf tournament, my phone beeped with a message from Jules.

"P just started breakfast. Will likely turn into sexual escapades in the kitchen. Give me a couple of hours?"

I would be giving her *more* than a couple of hours, just to be safe.

With nothing but time on my hands, and being that I was already in the building, I decided to head down to my office and get some work done. Mae had been on me about a stack of press releases that needed approval, so I dug into those first. The sun was just starting to stream through my windows with its full mid-morning intensity when a gentle knock on my open door startled me in my seat. I looked up and standing in my doorway was Emma. Her casual appearance made me take pause, but then I remembered my own t-shirt and jean-clad appearance and that it was Sunday in the office after all.

"Hey!" I said cheerily, only realizing then how much I'd needed company with the quiet of the office.

"Hi," she offered meekly, and it was then that I realized how *off* she looked from her usually brightly colored and perky self. Not only was she in black yoga pants and a simple coral hoodie, but she was sans makeup and lacking her usual Emma spark.

"Are you ok?" I asked, standing to cross the office to meet her at the door.

"Oh yeah," she offered meekly, "just tired."

I stood in front of her and took in the sad look in her eyes and said, "Do you want to sit down?"

"Sure."

"What's going on, Emma?" I asked as I sat in a chair next to her.

"I was trying to find Dominic," she said, gesturing behind her at the offices with a flip of her hand. "He's not answering my calls or texts, thought maybe he was buried in work and I'd find him here. But nope. He's probably off somewhere, ignoring my messages."

"Actually, I think he's with Sam at the golf tournament in Hillsboro."

"Aha, that would explain it," she said, without so much as a change in facial expression or body language. "I'm sure that golf course has zero cell reception and would completely explain why he hasn't gotten a single text or call from me." Emma's sharp tone and dripping sarcasm were odd and off-putting.

"Emma, is everything ok? Are you and Dominic ok?" I didn't want to pry, but I was picking up that something was seriously bothering her and she needed to talk.

"This isn't really a PR problem," Emma said with a shrug, "so I wouldn't expect you to give a shit."

"I'd like to think that we're friends, too," I said meekly. I'd never experienced angry, aggressive Emma. It was surprisingly scary.

"Are we? Because it doesn't seem like it," she said, picking at her nails and staring into her lap. "For a moment there it looked like we were going to be friends, but now it just seems like you're focused on what I can do for the hotel. My worth is wrapped up in my role in *whatever* this whole thing is," she said as she gestured to my office around her, clearly indicating my place here with the company. Emma was having a spectacular mope, and it looked like she was determined to find the droopy perspective of everything. I could relate; I've been in those dark places where everything seemed lackluster. Maybe I could help her with this by showing her how I coached myself out of this particular funk.

"Emma, you did something *amazing* for the hotel; you do know that, right? In the blink of an eye you put together Friday's event, and it was a huge success. I've been sitting here all morning swimming in work because of the good press we're getting from it. You nailed it! And I think you're just being self-conscious about the whole thing, which is making you thirsty for reassurance about other stuff. Dominic loves you and is *not* avoiding you. And yes, of course we're friends! You're loved, honey." I reached out and squeezed her knee to punctuate my last point. Her closed-lip smile and slight head nod was not the enthusiastic and classic Emma response I was looking for, but I understood that she may need some time to come out of the funk she had fallen so deeply into by now. "You should go shopping! Get some ideas for a whole new clothing line. Can you imagine how amazing it would be if next spring we kicked off a fashion week event with your return to the design world?" I offered with what felt like over-the-top enthusiasm. I just wanted to get classic Emma back and knew that I was being an over-zealous cheerleader to get it.

She nodded and shifted her bag from one shoulder to the other as she stood; I assumed I was making her uncomfortable with all the praise and decided to back off and let her go.

"Sure, I guess you're right," she said, turning for the door, her eyes still sad despite her smile.

"Emma," I called after her, "Everything is going really well." I couldn't help the beaming smile on my face, and I wanted her to feel the optimism I was feeling. She didn't know I was here to fire Sam so she wouldn't understand my flood of enthusiasm at coming up with a new plan to change that future, but I still wanted her to join in on my excitement. "All of you are doing so amazingly well, and this image rebranding is not only ahead of schedule but going better than I ever hoped. Charles is going to be over the moon with these results and what it means for your family's business. You should be proud, Emma."

"Right," she chuckled softly and looked at her shoes, "I guess if Sam Monroe can clean up his act and look shiny and perfect for the press, none of us have an excuse." She looked back up at me, and there was a new shine in her eyes. I wasn't sure what she meant precisely; it sounded like more self-deprecation but her whole demeanor seemed to change, so if she was happy, I wasn't going to stand in the way.

"Exactly," I offered back with a playful shrug.

"I'll see you tomorrow," Emma said as she finally crossed the threshold and made her way across the office to the elevators.

"Go do something fun with your Sunday!" I called after her, one last ditched effort to rile up the Emma I knew and loved. She didn't offer a reply or even a look back, instead just lifted a hand in a lazy wave over her shoulder as she turned the corner. I stared after her for a long while, eyes glued to the hall she'd turned down, both wondering if she would return so we could talk some more, and also wondering if anything I'd said had helped. Tomorrow I'd make a point of taking her to lunch or out for coffee, hoping she would be in a better place and ready to talk then. For now, I had to focus on getting through the rest of the day resisting sending texts to Sam like a love-crazed teenager. I also needed to steel myself for our first day back at work together after all that had happened.

And while I was nervous for Monday to come, had I known then what was in store for me the next day, I probably would have fled the Hotel Monroe and never looked back again.

TWENTY-FIVE

Dee

I woke up a full hour before my alarm, which I'd set for way earlier than usual. Not only was I anxious to see Sam, but I was also even more concerned about our first day back at work together. To say our relationship had changed since Friday night's Boost event was a drastic understatement. However, what was front-of-mind for me today was the idea of meeting with Charles. I'd sent out a meeting request the night before, hoping that in my sleep I would put together the words that would succinctly execute my plan.

My hope was that I could get Charles to agree that firing Sam wasn't a top-tier priority for the rebranding of the hotel; a tough sell since I'd been the one to insist upon it being within the first thirty-days' objectives and a major milestone for our cause. But if I could get him to hold off, somehow convince Charles that leaving Sam in place for a bit longer was in the best interest of the hotel, I could then work on convincing Sam that this wasn't where he wanted to be. At the end of the day, we both knew that the CEO position of the hotel was not what he ultimately wanted with his career. But Sam was never going to admit that, not as long as he thought he was crucial to Charles' retirement plans. If I could get Sam to admit he wanted to do something else, and time it just right, Charles would respond with enthusiasm, and I could make this work without Charles knowing of my intentions, or Sam knowing that I was here to fire him, *or* corporate knowing I had completely compromised this assignment. It was going to be the most vigorous tap-dancing of my career, but thankfully everything else at the Monroe was falling into place so I could focus all my energy on this for a couple of days.

I took my time getting ready, went down to the coffee shop on the corner for a latte rather than hitting the bistro in the lobby, and still made it to my office an hour and a half earlier than usual. The corporate floor was quiet at this hour, early

morning sunlight coming up next to Mt. Hood through the
eastern facing windows, making one side of the floor far brighter
than the other. I strode past Mae's empty desk and into my
office, enjoying the quiet before an otherwise complicated day.
As my laptop booted up in its docking station, I stood at the
window watching the waking city beneath me and drinking my
coffee.

The excitement was rising in me at the thought that I had
an actual chance of pulling this off. I just might be able to
complete the assignment, get the promotion, help the hotel,
make Charles happy, and get the guy. It would take some work,
but by god it was doable; I just had to stay focused.

"Hello, beautiful," a voice said from behind me. Sam
was standing in my doorway, hands in his pockets, leaning
against the doorframe with the warmest smile I'd ever seen on
him. As my stomach clenched in excitement, I realized how
much I'd missed not seeing him for a whole day. Shit, I was
becoming one of those women I hated.

I missed him? *Seriously?*

But it was true; his absence had been felt in everything I
did, and now that he was standing in front of me, I let out a
physical and mental sigh of relief.

"You're here early," I said, placing my coffee on my
desk. I started to cross the room to him and stopped, my foot
leaving the floor and returning once more. Sam sensed my
hesitation and confusion about how we were supposed to behave
in the office and took a step inside, closing the door behind him.

"There, how's that?" He stayed planted across the room,
two paces in front of the door he'd just closed, unmoving once
he hands went into his pockets, demonstrating restraint. True to
his word, Sam was exercising discretion and letting me lead. I
crossed to him and wrapped my arms around his neck, pulling
him in for a kiss and relishing the feel of his arms snaking
around my waist once more. His kiss was passionate and
comfortable at the same time; I was beginning to love this
intimate place we were sinking into together.

"I couldn't sleep," he said pulling back just enough to
look down at me but still holding me close. "I thought I'd come
to see if you were just as anxious to see me as I was to see you.
And boy was I right!"

"How was your golf tournament?" I asked, not letting him get too full of himself.

"I spent the day with the most mind-numbing partner, listening to him prattle on about his soon-to-be-ex-wife and their nasty divorce, oh and I'm sore as hell today. But hey, at least I'm sunburned, too!" he said with mock enthusiasm.

"Poor baby," I said with a rub of his arm. "Do you need to take a sick day?"

"If I'm taking the day off, you are too, and we're going upstairs," Sam said with a wiggle of his eyebrows before kissing my neck. His necking grew more passionate and quickly led to more kissing and ass grabbing. I had no idea how long we'd been standing there making out like teenagers when I heard Mae moving around as she settled herself in her desk outside my door. At the first sound of her arrival, Sam and I both pulled back and silently looked at each other for a moment.

"Do *you* have a creative idea for why I would be in a closed-door meeting with you at this hour?" Sam asked, clearly hoping I had a plan for when we opened the door and Mae, not to mention whoever else was within eyeshot of my office door, saw Sam emerge.

"I uh, well, I mean it stands to reason that..." I drifted off, staring at the door, trying to come up with something that would make sense to Mae, who owned my calendar and knew damned well I didn't have an early day, let alone an early meeting with Sam.

"Ok, good plan, I like it," Sam said, stepping back and straightening his tie and suit jacket. "But how about we try it my way? Follow my lead."

Before I could argue, Sam crossed the room in a quick stride, threw open the door with a bang and crossed the threshold. As he got one step out, he turned back to me with a fabricated fire and intensity that resembled the intensity we'd had with one another weeks ago.

"I mean it, Delilah, this is *not* over." His tone rang heavy with his faux rage, but his eyes were playful, and his lips came together in a small pucker, sending a subtle air-kiss so quickly you'd miss it if you blinked. He turned and stormed across the office, mumbling 'shrew' as he did for good measure. As soon as the doorway was clear Mae's head appeared with wide eyes and mouth open in shock.

"What *happened*?" she asked with concern so deep I felt guilty at playing her in our little façade. "I thought you two were doing so much better lately."

"Well, that's the job, I guess. Never ends." Mae thankfully didn't question my vague answer and left me to get settled.

A few hours later, I headed to the restaurant downstairs and met Charles at a table by the window. The location of our meeting had been his choice; the man clearly had one foot out the door and couldn't be bothered to sit behind his desk any longer. He was even wearing the uniform of an executive in transition into retirement; he was sans tie, and his button-down dress shirt was untucked over a pair of dark jeans and canvas loafers. Everything about his appearance, right down to the slouch in his posture as he sipped from a cup of coffee and lazily stared out the window screamed, "I don't want to be at work today."

"Hi, Charles." I took a seat and set my tablet off to the side. I was there to work, but I wanted to keep him as relaxed and comfortable as possible.

"Well, if it isn't the witchy woman!" He sat up in his seat and beamed at me, clearly pleased with our progress so far. "Friday's event was amazing! I don't know how you pulled that together so fast, and the shuffle with the celebrity appearance on the fly, I'm impressed. We should have hired someone like you a long time ago; I'd probably be on a boat in the Caribbean by now if I had."

"I can't take all the praise. Mae has done some phenomenal work, and Emma practically killed herself getting this all executed on time."

"Modesty," he said, waving his hand in front of him as though dismissing a ridiculous notice. "No time for that. Take the praise and accolades because it is followed closely by me asking where we are with the rest of our initiatives."

"Right," I said, placing a hand on my tablet but not yet opening it up. "Before we jump into updates and such, I'd like to chat with you about something. Specifically, your, well I suppose *our*, decision to remove Sam from his leadership role." Charles' expression was unmoving, giving me absolutely no indication as to his reaction to this new topic. "We have our fair share of initiatives ahead of us and holding off on turnover at the executive level would most likely make all of that easier. I say all this because it seems that Sam has made some changes to his...erm, *behavior*, and I think with him being more compliant with what we're trying to do, image-wise, we can hold off on making that change until we are closer to a sale date."

I felt like I was standing in Times Square naked. Surely Charles could see right through my flip-flopping and any minute was going to put together that I was retracting my position on firing Sam because I was sleeping with him.

"I'm glad you brought this up," Charles said, leaning on his forearm and taking a sip of coffee that seemed to take years. "I've actually been thinking about this for the last week or so, and I agree."

Yes!

This had been easier than I thought! Now that I'd bought some more time, all I had to do was coach Sam into telling his father he wanted out, and the whole thing would resolve itself beautifully.

"I can't believe I'm going to say this," Charles said wistfully, "but it's a testament to how good you are at what you do; I don't plan on removing Sam at all."

No!

"My one hesitation with leaving Sam at the helm was this reckless behavior, his complete disregard for the image of the hotel; but now that's no longer an issue. I can't imagine any better way to retire than by handing over the business to my oldest son to run."

Shit. Over-correction. He's going way too far with this.

"Well, Charles, as nice as that is," I stammered, trying not to sound too panicky, "let's not forget that financially and operationally the end goal here is to sell the property. And I don't know if-"

"But *is it*, though?" he interrupted. "*Should* it be, still? If
Sam and Dominic really come together and create an expansion
plan that would work, why *couldn't* we keep the business in the
family?"

Oh shit.

He was getting excited now. The more Charles spoke,
the more animated and enthusiastic he got about this newfangled
game-plan he was forming. A game plan that not only pitted
Sam in a CEO position he did not want, for the rest of his career
no less but also wholly undermined the corporate objectives my
bosses had sent me here to accomplish. My moment of self-
congratulatory celebration quickly faded into me standing on the
sidelines in horror as everything I built was going up in flames. I
had to stop this.

"Let's not get ahead of ourselves," I said feebly, unsure
of how I was going to talk him out of this new epiphany. "For
the time being, I would recommend not making any major
announcements to the firm that you're reconsidering selling. It
will make you look a little wishy-washy, and the last thing you
would want to do is have to go back on that and start the
valuation process all over again." Charles nodded in somber
agreement, and I internally let out a huge sigh of relief. "We still
have some items to accomplish that need to happen no matter
what you decide, so why don't we focus on the next 30-days.
We'll get you to a great place so that no matter what you decide
you'll be set up for success. And *then*, we'll come back to the
conversation about Sam's position and whether to sell."

"That sounds reasonable," Charles said.

Somehow, I made it through the rest of our meeting with
a modicum of composure. And as the elevator took me back
upstairs, I paced like a caged animal inside the little box. There
had to be a way to still bring all the pieces together without
losing too much face, but I was starting to lose track of all the
chess pieces. I'd stalled Charles, so with a hope and prayer that
he sat tight for the time being, as promised, I could work on
Sam. If I still worked the job-satisfaction angle, got Sam to see
that he would be happier somewhere else, he could leave on his
own. And then, with no other alternative, Charles would get
back on board with the sale. I would just have to figure out how,
when the time came, that Sam didn't mention that any of it was

my idea to his father; that would seriously jeopardize my standing with the firm. Simultaneously, I would need to ensure that Charles didn't divulge to Sam that he had originally planned on firing him, with my help; that would seriously jeopardize our relationship for sure.

I stopped pacing and took in a long breath as I stared at my reflection in the steel doors.

"Why are you doing this?" The question left my lips in a whisper before I even had time to register the thought. I was exhausted and for a fleeting moment considered coming clean and just telling Sam everything. But if I did that, this whole illusion would be shattered, and things would never be the same between us, and I was really starting to love how things were developing between us. As much of a longshot and complicated maneuver as it would all be, I had to try at least to make this work.

I swung by the breakroom for fresh coffee before making my way to the conference room for the weekly sales meeting. My head was still swirling in a fog of strategy and contingency planning, so it was a good thing I was only in this meeting as an observer, simply there to jot down any mentionable factoids in the coming press releases and media blurbs. But as soon as I walked in, I knew it wasn't going to be that simple. Sitting at the head of the table, reclined in his chair and looking sexy as ever, was Sam. His suit jacket was gone, and his sleeves were rolled up his forearms, his traditional mid-afternoon look on a busy day. He laughed at something Dominic was saying and then looked up to see me standing in the doorway. With a slight and subtle tilt of his head, so minute I wasn't even sure he did it, he indicated the seat to his left for me to sit down.

This was going to be our first meeting together since *being* together, and I had no clue how it was going to go. I silently crossed the room and nodded politely when various members of the team greeted me, except for Dominic of course. Even as I took the seat directly across from him, he did not glance in my direction once. Clearly, still not my biggest fan.

"Dee, how are you?" Sam said casually. I turned to meet his eye and he was cool as could be, not a crack at all in his demeanor. He was really pulling this discretion and secrecy thing off. I, however, the PR and image consultant, could not for the life of me remember how I usually sat in a chair, or what in god's name I did with my hands during a meeting. I smiled meekly as I shifted nervously in my seat and then became completely still when I felt Sam's leg come in contact with my own. In a simple and delicate move, he had extended his leg and brought his shin to the back of my calf. Nothing sexual, nothing overt, just a small move to let me know that he was there. It worked perfectly; I relaxed into my seat, anchored to him.

Sam cleared his throat and started the meeting. The team took turns updating the group, talk went on for a while about new markets and leads generated from Friday's event. I absentmindedly made notes on and off throughout, but mainly focused on trying to not outright stare at Sam as he worked. He was focused and direct and smart as hell. He called his employees on their shit but still managed to motivate and inspire them at the same time. And one look around the table was all you needed to see that they respected and liked him. Sam was a fantastic boss.

I'd never really taken the time to sit and watch him work for any length of time; I was usually multitasking in this meeting, that is when I hadn't asked Mae to come in my stead. But now, it was all I could do to not lean in on my elbows and gawk at him as and Dominic discussed the closing of a major partnership deal with an airline. Despite all of my incessant talk of discretion, and against any sensible reasoning, I slowly moved my leg upwards, running my calf along his shin and back down again, before looping my ankle underneath his and rubbing small circles.

Sam's body language didn't give away a thing, and his eyes never left the contract he was reading, it was only the slight tick that played at the corner of his mouth that made me know he appreciated the move.

"Right," he said, clearing his throat as he returned my motion with a shift of his foot, "until this contract is finalized, I want this kept completely under wraps." He looked up to meet my eyes with a piercing look. "Are we clear on that, Delilah?" he said tersely.

Oh, you want to play?

"Not at all," I replied in a clipped tone as I set my pen down. "I think releasing some sort of PR about us being 'in talks' with an airline could generate a lot more buzz for the hotel. I don't see why that would be an issue." I raised an eyebrow in challenge.

"And *I* don't want to appear overly confident to the client when they read that in the trade journals. I don't see why *that* isn't obvious," he said aloud as he kept playing footsies with me.

"We wouldn't name the airline by name," I said flippantly. "Who knows, we could get other companies reaching out, trying to edge out the competition."

"That's a bit overly optimistic, isn't it?" he said with a sigh and an eye roll. "You may know PR, but you clearly don't understand sales and negotiation, so I repeat, keep your department out of this until I'm ready to make an announcement."

The room was getting tense, and everyone around the table was shifting with uncomfortable silence, once again not sure how to behave when Sam and I got into it. Everyone except Dominic, who was watching us like a tennis match, his eyes bouncing from one to the other as we spoke. Meanwhile, I was getting hotter and hotter. This charade, the hiding, the knowledge that those minuscule little eyebrow raises Sam was giving me through this discourse was aimed at egging me on and playing with him. It was foreplay like I'd never experienced, and I was starting to shift in my seat with anticipation.

"Your job is to close deals; my job is to keep interest in the hotel so there are new opportunities waiting once that contract is signed."

"No, that's this team's job," he said motioning around the table. "*Their* job is to generate new leads and create opportunities. *Your* job is to write pithy press releases to brag about us once we're done."

"I think we should take this conversation offline and not waste the group's time with this any further," I said. I could care less about the PR strategy on this one; if he didn't want the word out yet, that was fine. But I couldn't keep going like this without some sort of tell coming across.

"Agreed," Sam said, shuffling the contract aside and looking back at his notes. "We'll get in a room later and bang this out."

I had to bite the inside of my cheek to keep from reacting to that. Thankfully, there wasn't much left of the agenda past that point, and soon everyone was gathering their things to leave. Sam and I stood and faced off for a second; I could tell by the look on his face he was just as turned on as I was.

"Your office?" I said in a clipped tone, trying to maintain composure. Sam gestured for me to lead the way and I strode out of the conference room toward his corner office with a desperation that hopefully came across to anyone observing as professional irritation. His assistant eyed us cautiously as I entered his office without a word and Sam said, "No interruptions please," in a gruff voice before closing the door. His stern demeanor melted as the door closed and as it clicked shut a smile broke out on his face.

"Look, I'm sorry if I-"

I didn't let him get out his apologies for taking our flirtation to a whole new level. I couldn't handle the tension any longer and pounced on him like a tigress let out of her cage. In one large step, which felt more like a leap, I crossed the space between us and wrapped my arms around him. Before he could even react, my lips were on his, and I was pulling him to me with ferocity. It didn't take Sam long to recover, and his posture went from rigid and shocked, to intense and flesh-hungry as well. I was bent backward slightly as he leaned in to deepen our kiss and pull me closer with one arm around my back and the other hand snaking up my neck to grab the nape of my neck. As he stood upright and took me with him, my feet left the floor and I clung to him even tighter, continuing to kiss him as we tried desperately to keep our frantic breathing quiet.

"Fuck, I've never been so turned on," he whispered roughly in-between kisses. I wrapped my legs around his waist and pressed him hard to me with a pull of my heels on his ass; I was trying to close a nonexistent space between the two of us which resulted instead in us just grinding our hips together even harder, sending lightning bolts through my body.

"Fuck me," I whispered into his ear right before sucking his earlobe into my mouth and then kissing his neck. He pulled back slightly to meet my gaze, most assuredly to make sure I was serious. After all my blustering about keeping this a secret, Sam had to be thrown through a loop at my request. I pressed

my forehead to his and ground my hips once again, a quiet moan
releasing in my throat, feverish desperation building inside of
me. Sam pressed on the back of my head and brought my lips
back to his, in part probably to keep me quiet. Without breaking
our embrace, he walked us around to the back of his desk and
pushed his chair to the side, setting me down on the cool surface
of the desk and standing between my legs, looking down at me
with hooded eyes and lips parted. I immediately went to work on
his belt, and he didn't need any more invitation than that to get
to work on my skirt. His strong hands ran up the sides of my
legs, under the hem of my pencil skirt, pushing it upwards as he
went. He reached my hips and hooked a finger in each side of
my panties as I lifted myself up with flat palms on his desk,
allowing him to slide them down and off in one fluid motion. As
we worked fast and silently, shirts unbuttoning, pants unzipping,
not once did we break eye contact. I couldn't look away from
Sam's intense stare just inches away, and my gaze still didn't
falter as he roughly gripped my ass and slid me to the very edge
of the desk. But as he finally thrust inside of me I couldn't help
but tilt my head back, eyes closed tightly at the intensity. I
wrapped my legs around him, leaned back on one arm and
gripped the collar of his opened shirt as he used his grip to bring
me to him over and over again.

This was not the soft lovemaking from a couple of nights
before. This wasn't even the passionate release that we'd
experienced that first night we'd finally come together.

Sam reached up and grabbed a fistful of hair at the base
of my neck, pulling my head back even further in the process.
And as he clamped his mouth down hard on my neck and my
nails dug deep into the flesh of his shoulder, I realized what this
was.

This was rough and powerful and charged with so much
ferocity; neither of us relenting to the other, no one willing to be
dominated and so instead two alphas locking horns and crashing
together.

This was the Shrew and Samuel fucking. And we needed
this.

My release quickly built up with that thought, and before
I knew it, my body tensed, and Sam clamped his lips over mine
to catch the moan I was having trouble trapping in my throat.

Moments later, his fists tightened on me, and he shuddered with his own climax.

As reality slowly started to creep in around the edges, I began to realize the pornographic tableau Sam and I were frozen in as we both fought to catch our breath as quickly and quietly as possible. I prayed we hadn't been too loud; it certainly didn't feel like I was capable of being any quieter than I'd been.

Sam pulled his head up from where it had been resting on my collarbone; our faces so close I could feel his ragged breath just as he could probably feel mine. And as our eyes met we instantly both broke out into matching grins.

"What the hell, Sheppard?" Sam whispered in mock indignancy.

"Sorry, guess I don't have this whole discretion thing down as well as I thought," I said. "Your PR rep is going to be pissed."

"I'm actually more worried about my *HR* rep at this point," he said, glancing downward at his pants pooled on the floor below his naked legs. We both chuckled quietly, and I placed a hand on his cheek absentmindedly. Sam turned slightly and placed a chaste kiss on my palm as I did so, making me smile even more. He helped me to my feet and we both got to work at reassembling our own clothing, silently taking note of ourselves from head-to-toe, before turning back toward one another and giving each other's ensembles an appraising glance.

"Shall we make this a recurring meeting, then?" Sam asked with a wink.

"Is that your way of asking me to go steady, Mr. Monroe?" The question left my mouth before I could even think about it and I immediately regretted it as I felt the air sucked out of the room. I'd doused our post-coital light-hearted banter with a seemingly passive-aggressive attempt at the whole 'where is this going?' conversation. I didn't even *want* to have that conversation yet! After my meeting with Charles that morning the last thing I wanted to do was jump the gun on a commitment conversation with Sam. Not to mention, this was Samuel Monroe! Surely, I was not the first woman to roll in bed with him and start asking for long-term plans. I was such an idiot.

"Yes." I snapped my head up from reexamining the hem of my skirt in faux fascination at his matter-of-fact and direct answer. "That's what I want."

"What?"

"I want you." Sam was standing in front of me as calm and relaxed as I'd ever seen him. He shrugged casually and said, "I want this. And by this, I mean us." He nodded to the desk with his head and smiled ruefully before adding, "Don't get me wrong, I want *this* too, and encourage you to at least consider the standing meeting calendar invite you're going to receive later today, but more than anything... I just want you, Dee."

I knew there was much to consider, but at that moment, I just let myself bask in the feeling of being seen and wanted by this man who made me feel more alive than I ever had before. I stepped to him and couldn't stop the smile that beamed from me at his words.

"I want you, too," I said just before kissing him. It was a feeble reply and all I managed to say. But before I could spend any more time considering what to say next, Sam's intercom buzzed loudly. We both jumped, and I took a flying step backward like I'd been electrocuted. Sam rolled his eyes at my response and made a production of pushing the button and demonstrating where the sound was coming from like I was a paranoid schizophrenic.

"Yes, Leslie?" he said.

"I'm so sorry to bother you," she said nervously, "but Mae is here looking for Ms. Sheppard. I wouldn't interrupt, normally, but she says it's an emergency."

I furrowed my brow in confusion and looked up from the intercom to Sam, who shrugged with similar confusion. An emergency? Mae knew better than to ring that alarm unless it was crucial. I smoothed the front of my blouse down absentmindedly as I came around to the front of Sam's desk and nodded for him to give the green light as I picked up my tablet.

"Send her in." A second later Mae opened the door looking panicked and afraid.

"What's going on?" I asked, and as she looked from Sam back to me with unsure eyes, I added, "It's fine, you can tell me here. What is it?"

"It's Emma," Mae rushed out. "She's been arrested."

TWENTY-SIX

Dee

Mae's words landed like a bomb in Sam's office and for the first time in my professional career I was frozen in place and completely unsure of what to do. My first instinct was to launch into damage control mode; save Emma's image, save the hotel's reputation, prevent as much bad press as possible. But Emma was also my friend and I wanted to be there for Sam. I couldn't do both. I couldn't launch into work mode, bulldozing through the press and working with police to mitigate the shit out of this situation while still being in girlfriend mode at the same time. Maybe one day I would know how to do that, but not today.

I looked at Sam behind his desk and was heartbroken at his demeanor. His frown was deep, and he ran a hand forcefully over his face in concern and frustration. We both had a pretty good idea why Emma was arrested and were probably both trying to figure out how we got here out of the blue. His eyes met mine, and I tried everything I could to silently convey to him that I was there for him and wanted to do what I could, what I *needed* to do.

"Go," he said with a collaborative nod, as though reading my thoughts. He wanted me on this just as much as I did.

"I'll keep you in the loop," I said as I grabbed my things and gestured for Mae to follow me. Sam nodded solemnly as he reached for his phone on his desk, presumably to start contacting Dominic and the family for information. "Please tell everyone to decline all press and send all inquiries my way," I said as I made my way to the door.

"'No comment.' We know the drill," Sam replied without sarcasm or wit, but instead as a rallying cry of a fellow comrade. We were finally fighting on the same side, but the moment was bittersweet with Emma's relapse being the catalyst.

"Tell me everything we know," I said to Mae as we rushed across the floor to my office.

"She was arrested in Pioneer Place. Security picked her up in the lower level and escorted her to the street where police were waiting. I'm hearing there are multiple stores making shoplifting claims, but I haven't verified that. We also don't know what there is in the way of security tapes yet. Local news has a blurb about it on their website, but I haven't found anything else yet. I'm assuming they'll run with a story during their 6PM broadcast, but until then, the web story just says that she has been arrested and no other details are available." We made it to my office, and I started packing my things into my bag while Mae caught her breath in the doorway.

"How did we hear about this? Charles? Legal?"

"No, it just happened, I don't even know if *they* know yet. I only found out because Levi called. He said one of his freelance photographers had pictures and was shopping them around to reporters running the story this morning. He said he tried to reach you directly, but you weren't answering his texts."

It was only then that I realized I must have left my phone in Sam's office.

"Ok, reach out to Charles and let him know what's going on and that I'll meet him and the lawyers at the courthouse. Hopefully, she'll be arraigned quickly, and we can get her out of there before there's too much press. Field any calls for the time being and send an email out to executives that there has been an *incident* with Emma and should they be contacted in any way they should say 'no comment' and refer the call to you."

I left Mae with her marching orders and rushed across the floor back to Sam's office. Leslie didn't even bother to try to stop me from opening Sam's door, probably at her wit's end with the breakdown in her system today. Sam was standing where I'd left him behind his desk, one hand on his hip and the other holding his phone to his ear. His brow was furrowed, and he nodded as he listened to the caller on the other end. I latched the door silently and bent to look for my phone on the floor.

"Hang on one sec, dad." Sam pressed his phone to his chest and held mine up in front of him.

"Thanks," I whispered as I crossed to him and took the phone.

"Dad's on his way to the courthouse with Gavin," he whispered back.

"I figured," I said with a nod, assuming the family attorney had been Charles' first phone call. "I'm on my way to meet them there now. Hopefully, they can get her out of there while I distract the reporters with a statement of some kind." Without even thinking about it, I lifted up on my toes and pecked his lips with a kiss before turning to leave.

"Hey," he called quietly after me. "Give 'em hell, baby." He gave me a smile before turning toward the window and resuming his call. I blushed and felt the deepest warmth spread over my body, while also having a renewed sense of purpose. I strode to the elevator and then out of the hotel, ready for battle.

The courthouse was a complete madhouse. Local reporters from all sorts of news outlets had gotten wind of the story, as well as a handful of gossip rags, bloggers and websites. The event at Boost had only just happened days prior, so the hotel and the Monroe family were still topical in local news. The timing of this was spectacularly unfortunate because there were more eyes on Emma than ever. I managed to find Charles waiting in the wings with Gavin, and they were able to catch me up on what had transpired.

Emma had been arrested for shoplifting from multiple stores throughout the plaza. One store, in particular, had alerted security, who then proceeded to follow her and call the police. But because the overall worth of all the things she stole could add up to a hefty sum, Gavin was preparing for more than a petty theft and shoplifting charge and something more in the neighborhood of grand larceny.

"Where's Dominic?" I asked, looking around the busy halls for Emma's stern and forceful protector. Charles and Gavin quickly shared a look before Gavin went back to his phone.

"Well," Charles said, leaning down to speak ever so quietly, "I actually have conservatorship over Emma. I have for about four years now. She will have to be released into my custody. Dominic is waiting at the house with the rest of the family, and her doctor will be joining us too."

I was shocked. I had no idea Emma was under a conservatorship; it had never come up, and no one had ever shared it with me. For all of our sharing and secret airing as a group, I was suddenly reminded that, at the end of the day, this was a family with secrets just like any other.

It was decided that I would prepare a statement and organize the press for a briefing just after Emma's release. While I held their attention with the dangling of vague non-facts, Charles and Gavin could slip out a side exit and get her home unnoticed. Writing said press release turned out to be a challenge, addressing charges and arraignment details that hadn't happened yet. I held in my hands one speech with roughly six different themes, depending on how the afternoon proceeded. It was like a high-stakes choose your own adventure book. Eventually, Emma's docket was finally called, and she was charged with theft in the first degree, a felony, and released to her father on a hefty sized bail. And as they ushered her out of the building, I took my place in front of the cameras and microphones to tell the press my convoluted web of half-truths and empty sentiments.

Events are still being made clear....working with local law enforcement...the Monroe's continue to be pillars of the community...et cetera et cetera.

After a half an hour of questions from the press, the conference ran out of steam and the reporters dissipated, scurrying off to make some sort of sensationalized narrative out of my doubletalk. And as the crowd cleared, Levi wandered up to me with a smirk and a loud slow-clap.

"Bravo, Delilah Sheppard. That was some impressive spin. I'm assuming you shuttled the poor girl right out of here under our noses while all that was going on?"

"But of course," I said with a curtsey and a smile. We took seats on a bench in the now nearly abandoned corridor and stared out the window at the setting sun.

"How you doing kiddo?" he asked, putting an arm around my shoulders.

"Long day," I said with a sigh.

"Oh, come on, a shoplifting heiress is a walk in the park for you, even *if* you like her the way that you do."

"It's not just Emma, although I am really worried about her," I said, stopping there before getting too close to divulging her diagnosis.

"What's happening?" Levi asked with genuine concern. "I shouldn't have to tell you 'off the record' for you to know you can tell me anything."

"I know," I laughed. "I just wouldn't even know where to begin." I rested my head on Levi's shoulder, and a long, comfortable silence stretched out in front of us. He was simply waiting for me to continue, whenever I was ready. "Have you ever felt like you no longer recognize yourself? It's as though you make one allowance with yourself, and then another, and another...repeatedly moving the line you refused to cross, one inch at a time...until eventually you look behind you and can't even see where you started?"

Levi let out a low whistle. "Damn, girl. Where was this kind of writing in your sorry ass press conference? Ow!" he said as I poked him in the ribs and sat up to look at him. "What do you want me to tell you, Dee? Have I ever had a crisis of self? I'm a gay Hispanic man. Yes, I think I can get behind what you're talking about and wrap my brain around having to redefine one's self, take a second look at all those things you *thought* you knew about yourself. Yes, I've been there. But that's where the growth is, honey. You can't map out your life and expect to stick to *that* map forever. Things change, people change; you have to change with it."

I sighed and smiled up at him, "How did you get so wise?"

"It's a gift."

With a kiss to his cheek, I started to gather my things. "I need to get to the Monroe's."

"Ok," he said with a subdued smile. We hugged and made promises to connect soon, and after I started to walk away, Levi said, "Dee, if you need anything, or if you're ready to *really* talk to me about what's going on, you know how to find me."

I blew a kiss and waved before turning the corner toward the parking garage. I was thankful for Levi but just wasn't sure what to tell him. I didn't know how much I was telling anyone about Sam and me, let alone this professional game of pickle I'd gotten into with Charles and my firm. I decided it was better to clean up the clutter in my head before unleashing it all on him.

     I spent the ride up to the Monroe's home in the hills consumed with worry about Emma. I had no idea how she was doing after her whole ordeal since I hadn't been able to speak to her at the courthouse. Not only had she been through an incredibly rough day with being arrested and spending a good chunk of time in jail, but she had also experienced a massive setback with her disorder. When she'd shared her condition with me, she'd said she'd gone a long while without a relapse. I couldn't even imagine what was going on that had led to this today.

     My rideshare pulled up to the expansive house, and I gathered my things to head up the long driveway to the front doors. I rang the bell and seconds later Sam threw the door open, looking both irritated and relieved.

     "Hi," I managed to say while trying to read his intense expression.

     "Hey," he said, softening a bit. "You're walking into the middle of a shit storm, be forewarned."

     I could hear tense voices over his shoulder and crossed the threshold into the foyer.

     "If this is a family thing, I can come back or just-"

     "No, I think you should stay," Sam said, eyeing the hallway that appeared to lead to wherever the voices were coming from. "You're in this now." He smiled weakly, giving me no indication what the hell that even meant. I followed him down the hall and into a large living room at the back of the house. Emma was on the couch, her knees pulled up to her chest and a blanket wrapped over her shoulders. She stared at the floor in front of her as everyone moved around the room and spoke. Dominic wasn't too far away, maintaining a protective stance next to her as he spoke in clipped tones to Charles, who stood opposite him while Rachel leaned against the back of the couch. The room fell silent when Sam and I walked in. Emma looked up and our eyes met, causing my heart to break with her vacant expression and red-rimmed eyelids.

"You!" Dominic shouted, causing Emma and me to jump in unison at the outburst. He had a finger pointed at me and rage in his eyes. "You get the fuck out of here before I *throw* you out."

TWENTY-SEVEN

Sam

I watched Dee stride out of my office in a rush to get to my sister at the courthouse, while blushing under the term of endearment I'd laid upon her; it was adorable. She was continuing to surprise me at every turn, and today's sexcapades were no different. I genuinely was trying to keep my promise for discretion and secrecy, but it was starting to look like that was less and less of a priority to Dee. And when it appeared she was coming out of her shell, I seized the first opportunity I could to tell her that I wasn't seeing anyone else on the side. I'd yet to organically find a way to work into the conversation that since we hooked up, I'd been, and intended to stay, exclusive. There just never seems to be the right lull in conversation to work in the remark, "Hey, just so you know, I'm *not* fucking other women, presently." So, when she afforded me the window, I leapt through it. My intention was for her to know that I'd changed and that I was taking this seriously; I needed her to know those things while she worked out whatever was happening in that busy mind of hers.

"Son? You still there?"

"Sorry, dad. Yes, I'm here."

"Why don't you head over to the house; your mother is there now. Who knows how long this will take; we'll just meet you at home," my dad sounded tired. No, he sounded resigned. None of us wanted to see Emma in this situation again. A relapse was always a possibility, but we had all fiercely denied to ourselves it would happen. And these situations were always so hard on mom and dad.

"Hang in there, dad," I said softly. "Dee is on her way to the courthouse to meet you now. I'm guessing she's going to run as much interference as possible, that way you can get Emma out of there."

"That's good. Until we know what we're dealing with and what's going on with Emma, I don't want to deal with all that noise."

"I'm fairly confident that she or Mae will be sending out communication to the team, just in case the press reaches out for a comment. I'll make sure to check in with Mae and have a word with some key people around here before I leave. I'll also give the front desk a heads-up as well, just in case we have reporters show up."

I was attempting to show dad that I was finally playing ball and supporting Dee's every move, not to mention his initiative for branding, image, and good press. I needed him to know that while he worked out whatever was happening in that busy mind of his.

After checking in with Mae and swinging by a few folks' offices for brief conversations about her memo, I made my way to the lobby to chat with the concierge and staff. Unsurprisingly, Dee had done the same thing on her way out, and they were already prepped. As I left downtown and drove through The Pearl, I gave my navigation the voice command to call Pax, and after a couple of rings, his voice was coming through my car's speakers.

"What up?" he barked.

"Catching you at a bad time?" I wasn't supposed to know about him and Jules. Because knowing *that* would mean that Dee had told me, and as far as anyone was concerned, since Friday's event I'd only seen her in a meeting or two today.

"Nah," Pax said, with an impatient huff. "Just working out."

"Sure," I couldn't help but say with a smirk. "Listen I wasn't sure if anyone reached out to you or not. Emma was arrested this morning."

"What the fuck?" Pax exclaimed with pure shock and awe. "Why? For what?" Always the optimist, Pax completely dismissed the possibility of Emma's relapse, and the thought didn't even occur to him.

"Shoplifting."

There was a long pause, during which I heard a slightly muffled sound, presumably Pax whispering a quick recap to Jules.

"She's sick again?" Pax asked meekly, sounding like the baby brother I remembered from childhood.

"I don't know what's happening, Pax. They picked her up this morning in Pioneer; she hasn't been arraigned yet. Dad's at the courthouse with the lawyer and Dee's headed there, too. I'm going to go meet mom at their house, and I got a text from Dominic that he'll meet us there with Emma's doctor."

"I'm on my way," Pax said in a rush, the sound of clothes and rustling getting louder.

"Drive careful, take your time. It's probably going to take dad a while to get her home," I said, attempting to slow his panicked roll. With some sort of inaudible grunt of acknowledgment, Pax hung up.

I pulled into my parents' large driveway and noticed Dominic's car, as well as a second car I didn't recognize, presumably Emma's psychiatrist. Mom met me at the door.

"Hi sweetie," she said, giving me a warm hug and burying her face in my chest for a quick second of comfort give-and-take.

"How's Dominic?" I asked, looking over her head into the living room where Dominic was pacing the floor, staring intently at his phone. Emma's doctor sat calmly on a couch watching him, speaking to Dominic in low tones every few passes.

"He's on edge, for sure," mom said. "It's all been theoretical for him up until this point, now he's facing Emma's syndrome head-on. We'll see if he's ready for it," she said, hinting at what we were both thinking. This was a make or break moment for their relationship; he was either going to step up, and they'd get through this together, or it would be too much, and they would ultimately fall apart.

"Well, we'll help him, too. Give him some pointers at all this stuff."

For the next couple of hours, we tried to pass the time as calmly as possible, but every ding or chirp of a phone sent everyone's spine straight as an arrow while we silently waited to see if there was news. Pax showed up not much later and threw out a machine gun burst of questions to the room that unfortunately none of us had the answers to, making Dominic tenser than ever and bristle at the helplessness of the situation.

Dr. Bradshaw diffused a lot of the particularly tense moments, placating Pax, soothing Dominic, comforting my mom, and eventually giving me a rundown of what he had in mind when Emma got home.

"She's going to be dealing with a lot of emotions right now, but the most prevalent is usually shame and embarrassment after an episode. We need to make sure we're giving her some space and not pouncing on her for explanations and information," the doctor explained, looking pointedly at Dominic. Mom and I nodded, knowing the drill and remembering how Emma usually was after a spell. She tended to shy away from human contact, avoiding eye contact and refusing to be with any of us for days. "I have a suspicion that she's off her meds," he continued, "I'd like some time to talk with her in private, about both the medication as well as everything that fed into and triggered today."

As if on cue, we heard car doors in the driveway and the front door opened shortly afterward. Dad came in first, and a sullen-looking Emma followed behind. She had her grey hoodie zipped all the way up, and her makeup was smudged around her red eyes, evidence of a day of tears. Before I could completely register her appearance, Dominic rushed forward into the foyer and scooped her up into a hug.

"Way to give her some space," I grumbled under my breath as I ran a hand over my face in frustration. But surprisingly, Emma wrapped her arms around him tightly and burrowed her face into the crook of his arm.

"I'm so sorry," she rushed out.

"It's ok, honey, it's ok," Dominic soothed back.

"I didn't mean it, I'm so sorry." Emma was just gushing apologies and indistinguishable nothings at Dominic, who just shushed her and rocked her back and forth. It was like nothing I'd ever seen after an episode. I looked over at mom, who shrugged and smiled, just as pleasantly surprised as I was.

Dad joined us in the living room and put an arm around mom, kissing the top of her head while she rubbed small comforting circles on his chest. After a moment, Dr. Bradshaw stood up and cleared his throat softly. Dominic nodded at him and started to lead Emma into the living room.

"Let's give them some space," I said to Pax and my folks, who nodded and followed me into the kitchen. Shortly afterward, Dominic joined us, leaving Emma with the doctor, and exhaled deeply as he leaned his elbows on the kitchen counter and let his face fall into his hands.

"You did good, brother," I said, clapping a hand on his shoulder. He looked up at me and nodded, knowing what I meant. Mom busied herself with pulling food from the fridge and setting out snacks for everyone, while Pax disappeared out back to make a phone call, my guess was to Jules. After what felt like an eternity, Dr. Bradshaw entered the kitchen alone with an expression that gave away nothing. Dad, Dominic and I stepped forward, practically forming a huddle around the poor man.

"I was right, she stopped taking her meds recently, so first things first, we need to get her back on those," he said softly.

"Did she say anything else about what happened? What caused this?" Dominic was desperate for answers, an explanation for *why* Emma slipped back into an episode he'd prayed he would never have to see.

"Who is Dee?" Dr. Bradshaw asked.

The three of us tensed and stood up at attention, myself more than Dominic or dad.

"Why?" Dominic demanded before anyone else could speak.

"Well, Emma mentioned some events that have transpired over the past few weeks, things that have placed a significant amount of pressure and undue stress on her, a couple of conversations with this Dee person in particular, and I was just curious her connection to the family."

"She's the new public relations representative for the hotel," dad said matter-of-factly. It was abundantly clear that his mind was churning this new information quickly, it just wasn't clear where his thoughts were taking him. What conversations had Dee had with Emma that could have led to this? What was Emma talking about? While on the one hand, I could understand the pressure of Dee's new approach and changes to the hotel, I also knew that she and Emma were friends. Not to mention, she was a lot of things, but even the shrew wouldn't knowingly push

Emma to the brink of a breakdown. But one look at Dominic
was enough to know that he wasn't so sure of that at all. His jaw
was clenched, and his whole demeanor just seethed with rage.

"Before you say anything," I said to him pointedly, "let's
make sure we have our facts straight."

"Oh, believe me," Dominic sneered, "I'm going to get all
of the information." And with that, he turned and stormed out of
the kitchen in the direction of the living room, and thankfully
my mother followed closely behind. Dr. Bradshaw sighed
heavily and looked back and forth between my father and me.

"Listen, you know I can't say anything specific; my
conversations with Emma are privileged. But I *can* tell you that
she knows going off her meds was a mistake. She's in
agreement about restarting her medication regiment and was
completely amenable to all my suggestions for therapy and
treatment going forward, with the exception of considering a
local group once a week. She's still maintaining that she needs
to go to Seattle once a month to help with anonymity. If it comes
up in conversation, please reiterate to her that these groups are
anonymous in nature and built on the premise of discretion."

"Of course," dad said solemnly. "Is there nothing else
you can tell us about the Dee situation?" It was on his mind, as
well.

"I think you should talk to Emma about the last couple of
weeks, and what's been occurring for her. The Dee stories will
flush out."

"What I'm asking doc, is if you think I need to keep this
woman away from my daughter."

"Dad!" I said before I could stop myself. Was he
seriously taking this to mean that Dee was toxic?

"What I'm saying," Dr. Bradshaw said slowly, choosing
his words carefully, "is that Emma has taken conversations she's
had with this Dee person to a place that is damaging to her. And
whether or not that is Emma's doing, or Dee's doing, it is
completely up to Emma."

"That's not answering my question."

"You need to treat Emma like an adult. We all need to
treat Emma like an adult. She needs to make her own decisions,
establish her own relationships, and deal with what relationships
do to her, just as everyone else does."

Dad took in a slow breath of air and nodded. For lack of knowing what else to do, I shook the doctor's hand and thanked him. As hard as it was to hear, we were all guilty of shielding and protecting Emma in a way that crippled her from being able to process the world around her all by herself.

We wandered into the living room where Dominic was sitting with Emma on the couch, speaking in low tones, while my mother looked on from the opposite side of the room. Clearly wanting to give them their space without leaving her daughter completely alone with the boyfriend navigating this situation for the first time. Upon our arrival, Dominic sat up straighter and put an arm around Emma protectively.

"I don't want that woman anywhere near her," he said to us over the top of Emma's head.

"Dominic," Emma whispered.

"Why don't we take a beat, relax a bit, and just talk," dad said as he crossed the room to my mother, taking her hand and guiding her to join him on the love seat. There was a long silence. Dominic was holding his tongue out of respect for my dad, while the rest of us waited for Emma to find her words. She fidgeted in her seat, staring at her crossed feet underneath her, and played with the sleeves of her hoodie.

"I don't know what to say," she mumbled, clearly embarrassed and wanting the attention off of her.

"Would you like to go shower and rest?" dad asked. "We can talk about this in the morning if you think you'd be more up for it then." Emma nodded and started to rise as dad added, "That puts all discussions off until tomorrow." He was looking directly at Dominic, "We will not sit down here and discuss what's best for Emma without her present."

"Then I have something to say," Dominic said, gently pulling on Emma's hand for her to sit back down. I tried to maintain my patience and reminded myself that he cared for Emma and was just trying to protect her.

"I think we need to start by closing ranks and eliminating the outside element." He was speaking to me directly, and I wondered if he was playing to my desire for the crown or his assumptions that I hated Dee and wanted the firm out of the hotel. "Until things calm down, I think it's best if Dee wasn't around. We can let the firm know we want to put things on hold, and when the time is right, we can have them send someone more...*qualified.*" Dominic was clearly trying to keep his composure, but the rage was boiling just under the surface, and his degree of indignancy was really starting to piss me off.

"Eliminating the *outside element* means sheltering Emma from the world and anyone outside of this room," I said. "I don't think that's what she wants or needs right now. Instead, why don't we all just wait for her to feel comfortable talking about it, and when she does, she can tell us what she needs."

"Suddenly you're on neutral ground when it comes to Dee? Real nice," Dominic said sardonically.

"What is that supposed to mean?"

"It means clearly this professional farce you've been putting on for the last couple of weeks is just that, a charade. You haven't changed one bit; your loyalty and ethics are securely housed in your dick." My mother gasped, and Emma's head jerked up to look at Dominic in anger. Pax chose that moment to reenter the room and looked at me with a questioning stare that said he was ready to go to bat for me if I needed it. I shook my head and sighed; if Dominic needed to yell at the rain and take his bullshit out on me, that was fine. Let him purge his frustration and anger so we could get on with helping Emma. And clearly, he was just warming up. "I remember not that long ago you preaching to any one of us who would listen that Dee was bad for business and we should keep things within the current team. And now that she has not only created one of the biggest PR messes the hotel and family have ever had but is also directly responsible for your sister having a relapse and being in the trouble she's in, I'd think you'd have all the evidence you needed to make your case once and for all. But here you are, defending Dee. And why? Because you're fucking her."

All eyes swiveled in my direction for confirmation, and when I didn't dispute it, my father's head fell into his hands in blatant disappointment. Pax, meanwhile, extended his fist to me for a bump.

"How would you even know-" I started to ask Dominic.

"It was so obvious today," he cut me off, "the two of you playing grab ass in that sales meeting like a couple of horny teenagers."

"Ok, I've had just about enough of this." It was my turn to interrupt and shut that noise down. "First of all, you're exaggerating, don't you think? I'll kindly ask you to turn down the hyperbole, just a bit. And second of all, my personal relationship has nothing to do with my stance on this. Dr. Bradshaw simply said that Emma's interactions with Dee have contributed to her breakdown; that is *not* code for 'this is all Dee's fault.' I get that you're upset Dominic, we all understand how hard this is to see and how useless you feel standing on the sidelines when Emma is hurting. But a witch hunt for someone to lay blame on is a waste of time."

At that moment there was a light rap on the front door, and I knew instinctively that it was Dee before I even opened the door. She looked so hopeful and concerned. My heart went out for her and the hornet's nest she was walking into, and I also steeled myself to stand by her side, personally and professionally.

"You're in this now," I said as I lead her back to the living room where everyone was still waiting.

"You! You'll get the fuck out of here before I *throw* you out." Dominic shouted.

"That's enough," dad said, rising to his feet. "This is *my* home, and you will not be throwing anyone out of it. And I'll kindly ask you to calm down son before I actually throw *you* out."

Dee stood rigidly next to me, frozen in shock and fear. I gently reached out and took her hand, squeezing before she could pull away. "They all know," I said, looking down into her wide eyes.

"I agree with Sam," dad said. "I think we all need to-"

"You people are all deranged!" Dominic said, standing up and making Emma jump in the process. He took a step into the center of the room to address dad and me more forcefully, and as he did so, mom went to sit at Emma's side. "Charles, just sell the damn hotel and be done with this already! I've been telling you from the beginning that I am your best bet to take over, and I think this proves it," he said, gesturing to Dee and myself.

"You're going to sell the hotel?" I asked dad, the wind knocked out of me a bit.

"Why else do you think he hired that firm? Why else do you think he would *suddenly* need to make a major overhaul to the hotel's PR and brand?" Dominic asked me incredulously.

I looked down and Dee who was already looking up at me with a concerned look that verged on panic. "You were here to help him sell?" I dropped her hand and shook my head in confusion, "Why wouldn't you two tell me?" I asked, looking between her and my dad.

"Because she was also here to fucking fire you!" Dominic exclaimed, frustrated that I wasn't catching on faster. I rolled my eyes at Dominic's outburst and the way in which he was taking this way too far. There was no way *that* was true. But as I looked back down to Dee and she returned my confusion with a pleading look of regret and pity, I knew instantly that he was right. She had come here to fire me. The whole reason Dee was in my life, was to help my father remove me from our family business.

"It was before I met you," she said meekly, "It was just the job." She reached out to touch my arm, and I instinctively pulled away.

"It's true, son," I heard dad say as I continued to search Dee's eyes as I made heads or tails of this news. "That was originally part of my plan with Dee, but things have changed, *you* have changed. Just this morning she was telling me that she thought we should put that whole idea on hold. We agreed we were going to not making any decisions right now and-"

"Hold on," I said, holding a hand up to stop my father, "You told him *today* that he should keep me onboard?" The color drained from Dee's face. "After you spent the weekend trying to convince me I would be happier if I *left*."

There was a long pause, and all eyes were on Dee now, as she swallowed hard and looked back and forth between my father and me.

"Well, I-"

"Why would you ask me to keep my son in his role and give him the business, while also coaching him to *quit*?"

"I never actually said you should give him the business when we met today, just that you should consider waiting-"

"To fire me."

"No, well yes, in a way."

"So maybe fire me, maybe not. But the priority was always to help him sell the hotel?"

"Not anymore," she pleaded.

"Oh, really?" dad asked, crossing his arms and cocking his head to the side. Clearly, she had led him to believe something different.

"Well, yes, I mean that is why I'm here, officially. But in terms of my priority today-"

"Oh my god," Dominic sighed, standing there with his own arms crossed, shaking his head in disgust. "You are so full of shit." Dee looked hurt at his comment and furrowed her brow in frustration.

There was a long pause as we all stared at her, watching her try to find the right words to say, when my dad finally said, "Dee, I think you should go. I'll call the firm tomorrow morning and follow up with you afterward, but I think it's safe to say that we're done here."

Dee looked up at me, and her eyes were glossy with tears. I knew her well enough now to know that she was doing everything she could not to cry; she was trying to save as much of her dignity as possible and not look any worse than she already did. But as she silently searched my own eyes for answers, I thought back to all of our conversations and interactions since she'd been here, with an emphasis on this last week. It was as if our relationship was being hit by a figurative bus and my mind was replaying every moment from the beginning. The bar, the conference room, the dance, the bedroom. It suddenly all looked different now.

"He's right," I said quietly, "we're done here."

TWENTY-EIGHT

Dee

I was in shock. I stood rooted in place, staring up into Sam's face hoping I had just hallucinated his words after the long, emotional day we'd just had. There had to be some way I could fix this, a way I could explain and make him, and everyone else understand. I racked my brain for the best place to start, but before I could come up with anything, Sam said, "You should go."

All at once, the blood rushed from my face, and I felt both numb and raw at the same time.

I wanted to scream.

I wanted to rage.

This whole thing was spiraling out of control faster than I could even process and everything was slipping through my fingers. Everything I had been working toward, everything I wanted, and everything I didn't even *know* I wanted until it was too late. It was all turning into wisps of smoke and dissipating before my eyes. I chanced a look around the room, despite my deep shame and embarrassment. Emma and Rachel were both looking at me sadly, as though they knew this was the last time they would ever clap eyes on me again. Dominic was still glaring at me but had softened just a bit with the smugness of his victory, while Charles had a look of deep disappointment that made me want to sob. It wasn't until I looked over at Pax, my gentle giant of a friend, with his arms crossed and his eyes glued to the floor, unwilling to even look at me that I realized this was an insurmountable mess. There was no coming back from this. And if there was even a glimmer of hope that perhaps that was too extreme of a prognosis, one look back up at Sam confirmed it all. It was over. This was all over. I set my jaw with all the strength I had and willed myself to keep the tears at bay until I got outside.

I walked out in silence and let the door latch quietly behind me as I closed my eyes and took a shaky breath. With

equally shaky hands, I pulled out my phone and ordered a car
through my ride-sharing app, a small squeak coming from me in
despair as the arrival time displayed nearly twelve minutes from
now. This was a neighborhood of large houses and long winding
driveways; I'd wait down at the street, but that still didn't give
me the satisfaction of running from this place as fast as I could.

I took a jerky step across the porch and down the first
step as the tears started to come. Each foot took its place on the
next step further away from the front door, and farther from the
people inside I cared so much about, and with it I saw in my
mind's eye their faces and felt their disappointment. Emma's
sadness and fear, Rachel and Charles' disappointment, Pax's
feelings of betrayal. It all cut through my chest like a hot knife,
and I felt like I couldn't breathe. And then there was Sam. He
was more than disappointed, he was heartbroken. I hadn't just
let Sam down, I had crushed him, made him feel as though it
was all illusion and that none of what we felt, or anything that I
had said, were real. As it fully washed over me that Sam
believed I was a monster and it was all a manipulation, I covered
my mouth hastily and let out the sob I'd been holding back. I
had become the very thing I'd accused him of being back in that
conference room on day one. I had used him and let him believe
it was all real when I'd been the one deceiving him from the
start.

Sam had never hidden who he was or what he wanted, he
was always straightforward and honest with me. Meanwhile, I
couldn't think of a single day, since that first night in the bar,
that I hadn't misled, manipulated or outright lied to him. I
reveled in his affection and declarations of endearment, basked
in the attention, and selfishly drank up all the love he had to
give, all of which were stolen moments that I had no right to
take.

I was a thief and a liar.

By the time I reached the end of the driveway, I was in
complete hysterics. I took a few steps off to the right,
positioning myself next to the buzzer outside the gate so that
there would be no way my driver would miss me and
accidentally ring the house. Headlights appeared in the distance,
and as the car approached and my phone chimed with the alert
my ride was here, I frantically wiped my face and tried to stop

my hiccups and involuntary gulps for air. Regardless, I was certain I looked like a crazy woman as I climbed in the backseat and mumbled a weak hello to the driver.

As we rode down the hill and into The Pearl, my mind wandered to Charles and the conversations he must be having with Sam right now. Surely, they were piecing everything together, comparing timelines and conversations, getting a sense for the when and where of my deception. I let my face fall into my hands as new waves of humiliation and regret washed over me. What were they saying right now? Was there *any* chance they could see the pattern and figure out my good intentions.

Probably not.

They weren't good intentions. They'd never been; it was all selfish intentions. I'd wanted it all. I wanted the professional glory, the kudos, and praise from Charles, and the happy ending with Sam. If they'd ever truly been pure intentions, I would have come clean to Sam about why I was there in the first place. I would have let him decide for himself what he wanted to do and sacrificed our budding romance for his happiness and contentment. It would have at least occurred to me that I wasn't just playing with his relationship within the family business but messing with Sam's relationship with his *actual* family.

Or you could have quit.

I could have just walked away from this clusterfuck of an assignment the moment I realized Sam was important to me. I could have helped him as a girlfriend, instead of manipulating him like the PR robot that I am. It would have been so easy to ask for a reassignment. Why didn't I just step away and let this all go so I could be there for him? I fell in love with the man and completely ignored the fact that he was at odds with his father and in turmoil over what he thought was his destiny. How could I be so self-centered and obtuse?

At the very least, I could have let Charles continue with his plans and not thrown a speed bump in our conversations, just to appease my own confusion about Sam. There were a dozen ways I could have handled the past month, specifically the last few days, that would have been for the good of the hotel, or Charles, or Sam. And I did none of them. I took the convoluted road that put everyone else's needs behind my own and made a mess of everything, just for the chance to get what I wanted, with the least resistance and in the easiest way possible.

What's wrong with me?

Just as I started to feel like I couldn't breathe, and the back of the car was closing in on me, we pulled up in front of Jules' building, and I climbed out to feel warm droplets of water on my skin. I stood on the sidewalk, gulping in the night air and staring up at the sky as I watched the rain fall from seemingly nowhere. The air smelled of concrete and asphalt freshly kissed with rain after months without, and the streets bustled with people hurrying to destinations they did not plan on reaching through falling rain.

Autumn had finally arrived in Portland.

I turned and made my way into the building, riding the elevator up and coming to stand in front of Jules' door. It was only then that I realized I wasn't supposed to be here; I'd packed a bag and told her I was going to stay at the hotel. In what felt like a lifetime ago, I'd happily agreed to stay in my suite so she and Pax could be here, in *her* home. My things were there, in Charles' hotel, in the room Sam and I had shared. My hairbrush and toothbrush were currently sitting in the bathroom; my worn-out concert t-shirt was still laying across the bed where I'd left it this morning as I'd rushed to get dressed. My sneakers were under the coffee table in the living room, where I'd fallen asleep on Sam's chest watching movies the night before. It suddenly occurred to me that all my possessions were currently sitting in a darkened hotel room, surrounded by the echoes of my happy weekend with Sam, and I couldn't handle it any longer. My eyes clouded over with tears and squinted tightly shut as heavy sobs overtook my whole body. I leaned against the door frame and didn't even recognize the noises that came from me as I collapsed to my knees and cradled my head in my hands.

I had no idea how much time had passed until it finally registered to me that Jules' arms were tightly around me and she was murmuring reassuring words as she sat next to me on her doormat.

"Come on, honey," she whispered, coaxing me to my feet. "Come on. Let's go inside."

I grabbed her hand tightly and squeezed, lifting my head and finally meeting her eye for the first time since arriving on her doorstep in a puddle of tears and emotional breakdown. Jules was looking down at me with a mixture of concern, pity, and confusion.

"I ruined everything," I whispered. "I hurt everyone." And as authenticity finally crossed my lips, I exhaled and closed my eyes closed, causing large solemn tears to cascade down my cheeks with the motion. Just as I was ready to curl up in a ball again, Jules' hands firmly planted on my cheeks and lifted my face to meet hers.

"You're not alone," she said as our eyes met again. I nodded with a sad smile and gripped her wrists. She helped me to my feet and led me into the apartment. Without a word, she walked me to my guest room and helped me to bed, covering me with a heavy duvet and another fluffy blanket. "Do you want me to stay?" she asked as she sat on the side of the bed, brushing the hair from my forehead. I shook my head no as I grabbed her hand and kissed her palm. It was all I could think to do to show my appreciation. With a small smile, she got up and went to the door, turning the light off as she did and whispering, "I'm right outside." It wasn't long before my eyes burned from both exhaustion and crying and I couldn't keep them open any longer. As I listened to the sound of rain hit my window I let the darkness turn into a restless sleep.

I spent the night having frantic dreams in which I was chasing Sam so that I could explain everything to him or looking for him in a maze of hotel hallways and doors. I'd awake from a dream panting, my heart racing, only to remember where I was and what had happened, bringing more tears and waves of embarrassment and shame. I'd throw the covers over my head, force myself back to sleep, and it would start all over again.

By the hue of the light coming through my windows, it was just after dawn when I awoke the final time, deciding that I'd had enough of trying to rest. I climbed from my bed and started removing yesterday's wrinkled work clothes, trying not to focus on the slight smell of Sam I could still catch on my blouse. I threw on yoga pants and a hooded sweatshirt and wandered into the living room, where I found Jules asleep on the couch, her cell phone face down on her stomach and the TV muted in the background. I took in her appearance and smiled, grateful for her, for her friendship. I tried to soak up the moment as much as possible since I knew there was a chance that she wasn't going to like me very much soon. While Jules was in on some of what I was up to at the Hotel Monroe, she didn't know everything. And when she did finally hear the whole story, she may have a hard time separating herself from it since she and Pax were now seemingly a couple.

Just as I was about to turn back toward my room and let her sleep longer, Jules' eyes fluttered open, and she jerked awake when she saw me standing there.

"Everything ok?" she asked sleepily, clearly not quite awake yet but still with the presence of mind to worry.

"Yeah, I'm good, sorry to wake you," I said, coming over to slide under her feet and sit on the couch. "Were you out here all night?"

"I thought you may get up at some point and want to talk," she said with a yawn. "After all, you *did* go to bed at 8PM, like a fourth grader. I figured you'd be getting up at some point, craving wine or ice cream, and wanting to purge and tell me about it. I must have eventually fallen asleep."

"Unfortunately, this was more of a 'have fits of crying in-between nightmares' sort of purge," I said with a sigh.

"Mmhmm. The sobbing on the doormat should have been my first clue," she said with a playful smile, nudging me with her foot. "Pax called after you went to sleep, filled me in a little bit." I could feel my face turning red; just the thought of Pax retelling last night's events made me feel embarrassed and horrified all over again. I wanted to ask what he said, but hearing Jules retell it may have actually made it sound worse. I simultaneously wanted comfort, but without having to share what a horrible person I was and watch the microscopic twitches and reactions on Jules' face as I told her.

There you go again, being selfish.

The thought made my eyes prickle with tears again, and I sighed in frustration, sick of being so sad and broken I couldn't even control my damn tears.

"Ok," Jules said with a nod, sitting up and running her hands through her gorgeous hair that looked even more amazing after a night of sleeping on the couch. "I think we need to go down to the bakery on the corner, get some coffee and a copious amount of decadent pastries that are fancy enough to help us

ignore we're having dessert for breakfast, and you tell me
everything, from the beginning."

And so, we did.

We donned the Portland early morning uniform and
headed out in hooded sweatshirts, flip-flops, me in my yoga
pants and Jules in her leggings, both with our hair tied in messy
knots. We wandered down the block to the bakery attached to
the French bistro that served amazing food but was closed at this
early hour, asleep after a night of dinner dates, candlelit dinners,
and a plentiful supply of wine. As the bistro went to sleep, the
bakery began her day, opening at 5AM to serve espresso and
warm pastries for the morning crowd. With lattes in hand and
Jules carrying a box with more eclairs, croissants, and
profiteroles than I cared to admit, we made our way back to the
apartment and arranged ourselves in a picnic on the floor around
the coffee table. And as we did all this, I told her everything.

I told her all the details of my assignment and my
conversations with Charles. I told her about the past weekend. I
told her about Sam, everything about Sam. How we had spent
the weekend together, how I'd fallen in love with him, and how
I ultimately took it upon myself to manipulate him and his dad
to make that situation come out perfectly for all involved,
namely myself. I shared my conversation with Emma on Sunday
before her relapse, racking my brain for what could have
contributed to her stress and where I'd gone wrong. And
eventually, I gave her the play by play of the night before, right
down to every word Sam and Charles said before I left.

And when I was all done, Jules let out a low whistle and
shook her head slightly.

"Wow," she said with a mouth full of éclair. I had zero
read on her and could not for the life of me figure out what she
was thinking. Her expression had remained unchanged, and she
was looking at me with the same clean expression she'd had the
whole time I'd been talking. I gestured for her to go on,
encouraging her to elaborate. I didn't necessarily *want* to feel
worse, but at this point, I had to hear what she thought. It was
almost as though *not* knowing was making me feel even more on
edge. The flood gates were open, I just needed to hear it straight
from everyone how much they hated me.

"Well, you definitely made a fucking mess," she said, taking a sip of her coffee.

"I know," I said despondently, waiting for the flailing to commence and bracing for her words of reproach.

"What do you want me to say, Dee?" she said impatiently.

"I want you to tell me how pissed you are!" I said defensively, frustrated I had to spell it out for her. "I want you to tell me how bad this is and how bad I've made everything between us."

"Oh my god, you *must* stop this. You've got to get over your obsession with what everyone else thinks! You just sat here and told me how you destroyed your career and devastated the man you're in love with, and you're worried about whether or not *I'm* mad at you?"

"Ok, yes, I do have more pressing things to worry about, but you're with Pax, and that may make you more inclined to hate me over this."

"First of all, give our friendship a little more credit than that, and secondly, and most importantly, who gives a shit if I'm mad at you about this, Dee? Stop trying to collect evidence that you're a victim here. Just suck it up and admit you screwed up royally and it's on you to fix it. But let me be clear, you did a bad *thing*, you're not a bad *person*. The more you dwell on that, the more you make this about you." I sat unmoving, just taking in every word of her outburst. "Look, I love you, and this whole looking good thing you've got going on is nothing new in your personality. For Christ's sake, you made a damn career out of it. And for years, I haven't said anything," my cheeks bristled with embarrassment at the thought that she had been carrying this unspoken judgment of me around for a decade, "but honey, you *must* stop trying to make everything perfect and control every little thing. You don't give people any space to be themselves when you do that. And while that may work in your job, and there's an argument that it doesn't even work *there*, it definitely doesn't work in relationships."

There was a long pause, and I could feel the pink still in my cheeks. "How long have you been holding on to all of that?" I asked with a smile.

"Oh, I don't know, since the day I met you."

"I know," I said with a sigh. "It's on me to fix this, and I get everything that you're saying."

"I don't think you do," she said calmly, taking a drink from her coffee. "But you will. Someday." She stood up and started clearing away our breakfast picnic, which was probably for the best since I had no idea how to respond to her last comment. Part of me wanted to argue that I *did* understand her point, but a voice of doubt was telling me that maybe I didn't, and I'd end up making a fool of myself by arguing with her. I decided to drop it and go take a long, hot shower.

When I emerged from the bathroom and began dressing in my room, a ding from my phone alerted me to a voicemail. As I opened the screen, I saw that I had several voicemails, many texts from Mae, and dozens of emails. With a sigh and a knot in my stomach, I started with my texts to Mae. I apologized for being incommunicado this morning and let her know that there were some new developments with Charles and I would reach out to her later when I had more details; for the time being, I asked her to just keep things on course. I was pretty sure I was being fired, but I didn't want to alarm Mae until it was all definite and I knew what was next for her. Next, I moved on to my voicemails. The first was from Charles with a timestamp of earlier when we'd gone for breakfast and I'd left my phone at home.

"Hello Dee, I just wanted to chat with you this morning about the events of last night and where we go from here. I'd prefer to chat with you in person before I speak with Victor at your firm, but Mae informs me you aren't in the office yet this morning." I cringed at that last part, mortified that Charles was expecting me to show and I wasn't there. I'd just naturally assumed I was done and he didn't want me there. The idea of me looking like a no-show today made the pit in my stomach even deeper.

The second message was from my boss in L.A, and another one right after that had come from Charles, both while I was in the shower.

"Delilah, it's Victor. I just had a very distressing call with Mr. Monroe. I'd like to speak with you immediately. Please call my office as soon as you receive this."

"Dee, it's Charles again," Charles' voice in his second message was much more morose. "I'm so sorry. My call with Victor just ended. We agreed it was best if he sent another publicist up to finish our project plan and complete the sale. I'm sure he'll be reaching out to you directly, and I wish I'd had a chance to speak with you beforehand." There was a long pause, during which Charles took a deep, steadying breath and my eyes prickled with tears. "I really did enjoy working with you Dee. And I can't even begin to tell you the impact you've had on my son. I know last night did not end well, but for what it's worth...I've never seen him like this. You're good at what you do, Dee. This just got too...convoluted. I guess you were right from the start, family and business are a messy combination. Best of luck, Dee."

My breath caught in my throat at the thought that this message was the last communication I would have with Charles, and in a panic, I replayed his message from the beginning, just to hear it all over again. I got dressed and braced myself for my call to Victor. It went pretty much the way I had expected it to but was nonetheless horrible and embarrassing. Charles asking for a new publicist was really all that was needed for me to be pulled off the assignment. It was Charles' hesitation to sell, or at the very least make any leadership changes, that ultimately led my boss to decide that I'd gone beyond failing to get the promotion and had also cost the firm revenue, leading to my termination. The new PR rep was coming in to not only take over but also clean up my mess. And because things were so off-course with Charles' motivations to use the firm at all going forward, Mae was to be reassigned, and a whole new team was being brought in to dazzle the Monroe's. Now my mess was bigger than me, affecting Mae and her career.

I felt miserable.

I reached out to Mae and told her to take the rest of the day off. I was vague, and I'm sure confusing, but I didn't want to have this conversation over the phone. I'd work on what I wanted to say and meet with her in the morning. Now I just had to figure out how to get to the office and hotel suite to get my stuff without seeing anyone. For a moment I thought about asking Jules if she would go retrieve my things, but based on our earlier conversation, I was betting that was going to be a solid 'no' from her.

"I'm headed to the studio," Jules called from the living room. I popped my head out and bid her farewell.

"Thank you for this morning. And last night. And oh, my goodness, thank you for Friday! I can't believe I forgot to say that," I said, really starting to hate this persistent feeling of disappointment in myself.

"You've had some stuff on your mind," she said, finishing a text and slipping her phone into her bag. "Don't worry, I expect you to shower me with gratitude and listen to all of my gratuitous sex stories about Pax, once you're not such a hot mess."

"Deal," I said as she walked out.

I had a whole afternoon to kill since I'd decided I would wait until after the work day to go for my things at the hotel. I skimmed through my emails again, hoping to see something from Sam, but there was nothing but business as usual emails; reporters asking for comments, a handful of things from Mae for review, updates and questions from marketing about communications going out, but nothing from Sam. There was a glimmer of hope when I saw Pax's name, but it was just one of his weekly accidental reply-all emails sent out to the whole company.

I wandered aimlessly around the apartment, unsure of what to do with myself. I couldn't remember the last time I'd been out of work. And then like a lightning bolt it hit me; I was so focused on getting my things from the office and hotel, but then what? I couldn't stay in Jules' guest room forever. This was always supposed to be a temporary thing, but a temporary thing leading to New York. I was supposed to be packing my things in the fall, but not this soon and certainly not without anywhere else to go. What in the world was I going to do? It occurred to me that I should start brushing off my resume. The pragmatic side of my brain started formulating a game plan, figuring out next steps. I would have to get a new job and doing so would be a challenge with a lack of references from *this* one. And then I would have to start all over in another city, which was certainly something I'd done a million times, but this time the thought of it felt more exhausting than exciting.

I took another lap around the living room and smiled as I passed Jules' bookshelf and the various photos she had in frames. I hadn't noticed until now that many of them were of us over the years. I picked up a small wooden frame with a picture of us at graduation and ran a finger over the glass, marveling at the enthusiasm and glee of those two girls, ready to conquer the world. What I wouldn't give to wake up as that naïve, wide-eyed girl and get to do it all over again.

A knock at the door jarred me from my thoughts so hard I jumped and almost dropped the frame. I laughed at my skittishness and put it back in its place before crossing to the front door. But once again my breath caught, and I was jolted with a shock when standing before me was Sam, holding my overnight bag in his hands.

TWENTY-NINE

Dee

"I thought you might want your stuff," Sam said solemnly, holding up my bag between us like a bomb. I reached out tentatively and took the offending bag from his hand, and as soon as I did, he brushed past me into the apartment in a flurry. "I assumed you were going to hide out here and get your shit later. When mid-afternoon rolled around and there was still no sign of you, I got tired of waiting around to confirm how right I was."

I shut the door softly and set the bag down on the floor, moving slowly and silently since I had absolutely no idea what to say or how to react. I hadn't had a chance to rehearse what I would say to Sam when I saw him again; truth be told, a small part of me wondered if I would *ever* see him again.

"To be clear," he continued, stepping into the living room and then turning to face me. His forehead was wrinkled with the deep furrow he was pulling off with his eyebrows. "I *get* why you didn't show up to work this morning; dad all but fired you in his living room last night. But why exactly *I* have not heard from you at all today, is beyond me."

Now my brow was furrowed as I tried to search for the answer to his question. Why *hadn't* I reached out to him today? After all, I owed him multiple apologies for what I'd done, and I cared about him enough to feel that he deserved to hear those apologies. So why had I stayed silent? The answer was obvious the second I posed the question to myself.

I was embarrassed and had no idea what to say.

What's the perfect way to apologize for what I'd done? How could I make him understand how bad I felt but yet how well-meaning my intentions had been, without upsetting him even more? And if that wasn't possible, which it probably wasn't, I was terrified of hearing him say all the horrible things he now thought of me.

But doesn't he deserve that, too? You owe him the opportunity to say to you all the ways you hurt him.

"For fuck's sake!" Sam's outburst made me jump out of the headspace I was in. "You *do* realize that you're not actually speaking out loud, yes? You are just standing there, shifty-eyed and silent. Do you have *anything* to say to me? Or should I just go?"

"No," I rushed out in a panic. Now that he was here I didn't want him to leave; there was a chance I'd never get an audience with him again. "I want to talk, I just have no idea what's the right thing to say."

"Dee," he rubbed a hand over his face in frustration, and I blushed with the thought that I was already screwing this up. "I don't give a shit about the right thing. I care about the true thing." His words hung in the air between us. "Will you please, just *talk* to me?" He was practically pleading. I'd crushed and manipulated this man, and here he was standing in my living room, begging for me to talk to him. My eyes prickled with tears and I realized in that moment that he was asking me to do what Jules had been asking me to do just hours before. All at once, I became completely aware of the wall I had built up around myself over the years, and how claustrophobic it was suddenly making me. The awareness took my breath away for a second, and I put a steadying hand on my stomach to try and remain calm. I was entirely on an island of my own building, having never fully shared myself with Sam, or anyone, for as long as I could remember. The pressure was pushing hard on the levy in my soul, and I suddenly felt like I could just burst.

"You know what," Sam said in frustration as he strode past me toward the front door, "forget I even fucking asked."

"What the hell was I supposed to do?!" I bleated out before I could stop myself.

The one thought that had been rolling around in the back of my mind since last night, the one thought I didn't want to entertain because I knew how wrong I had been overall, quite literally came screaming out of me. There was a brief moment of silence, during which Sam turned and met my eye, taking in my change in posture and expression.

"It was an unwinnable situation, and I was fucked no matter what I did!" I said with my hand splayed in front of me.

Sam started to speak, but I took a step toward him and said, "No, please just listen." I cut the space between us by half but was still speaking way louder than I needed to as the waterfall of thoughts and emotions cascaded from my mouth. "I have worked *so hard* to get where I am; you have no idea the depths of shit I have waded through to get a shot at corporate PR. I've dealt with more than my fair share of perv musicians, coked-out heiresses, and adultery committing politicians just so I could work my way up to lead a communications team somewhere finally. This bullshit assignment was supposed to be my launch pad to my dream job. All I had to do was come here, clean up the hotel's press, help Charles transition in a new CEO, and hold his hand through the hotel's sale. That's all that stood between me and my dream job. That's it! But what do I do? I fall in love with the guy I'm here to fire." I sucked in a breath, and it registered to me that I'd just shared with Sam that I loved him in the *worst* way possible, by practically screaming it at him in accusatory anger. But I was on a roll and not about to stop there. "There I find myself, trying to make the dream job still happen, while not ruining my chances with the dream *guy*. Rock and hard place, that's where I fucking set up camp. So, excuse the shit out of me for attempting to save both things I wanted, and *believe me*, I get that I did it poorly."

"You think I don't understand the conflict between personal and professional dreams? You think *I* can't understand what it's like to be stuck between that rock and a hard place? This isn't about you trying to win an unwinnable situation, Dee. I would understand and sympathize if it were. No, this is about you choosing to lie and manipulate whenever and where ever you can. That's your go-to move. You do it in your personal life just as much as when you're the Shrew."

"Enough with the damn Shrew nonsense!" I exclaimed, instantly feeling better for having finally said something about the nickname. "If I were a man, you and your buddies would just refer to me a 'tough as nails' or 'hardnosed' rather than some Shakespearean term for a no-bullshit-tolerating female character. I let this Shrew shit go on way too long; it's sexist, and you're better than that."

Sam glared down at me for a beat and then smiled slightly as he sighed, "Ok. You have a point; thank you for saying something," he added pointedly with narrowed eyes at the last bit. "But the fact remains that you don't give any of us, the people you work with and certainly the people in your life, the space to be ourselves. And it's becoming apparent to me that you don't even give *yourself* the space to be real."

"What is that supposed to mean?"

"You're so worried about what people are going to think. God forbid anyone anywhere has a negative thought. And in the process of worrying about all that, you disappear," he said, waving his hand in front of me. "Anything original or inherently *Dee* starts to become transparent as you mold your whole being around controlling the situation."

My first reaction was to feel defensive, and I had the urge to argue, but instantly I could feel my cheeks burning crimson as I gave what he said consideration. "Do I really do that?" I hadn't meant to ask the question out loud.

"Think about that first night we met. How long would you have sat on that date if I hadn't been there? Why not just say, 'Hey, thanks man, but you're not my type,' and move on? Because it's an uncomfortable conversation? Because he wouldn't have thought well of you afterward? You were willing to make yourself physically ill just to avoid being straight with the guy. Doesn't this obsession with making sure everyone's reaction happens just the way you want it to get exhausting after a while?"

"Of course it does!" I sighed and buried my face in my hands, finally absorbing what he was saying, which wasn't too dissimilar to what Jules had been saying. "Of course it does," I repeated softly, more to myself. "I've made such a mess."

"Yeah. You have," Sam said matter-of-factly, crossing his arms in front of him.

"Ok, if you could tone down the smugness just a bit that would be nice," I said, getting ruffled at his elite attitude. "Sure, I fucked up, but let's not forget why I was brought here in the first place."

Sam laughed sardonically. "Losing the moral high-ground and so all bets are off, huh? Fine, let's just get this all out on the table now. Yes, you were hired to clean up *my* PR mess. A mess I made by fucking lots and lots of women." I winced at the declaration as though I'd been slapped. "That's a fact. I can't go back in time and make that reality go away. But there are two other facts you need to know, Dee. One is that I have never hidden who I am or the choices I've made, from you or anyone else. Regardless of whether or not I'm proud of, or regret, the choices I've made, I'm upfront and honest about them."

"Do you think that makes it any easier for me?" I blurted out. "Great, so you're honest about sleeping with every hot piece of ass that comes your way. That's supposed to make it easier for me to deal with the fact that everywhere we go I'm wondering if the waitress is leering at you because she thinks you're hot. Or is it instead because she's remembering when you were *inside* of her?"

"Who cares?" he exclaimed in raw frustration. "Why does it matter, if at that moment I'm standing there *with you*?"

"Because... Because..." I was searching for the logical answer and the rational point that would win me the argument, but instead, so many emotions were boiling right at the surface, and I'd apparently opened a gate that I could not shut again. "Because I'm jealous! Because I *hate* that you've been with so many women. And I hate even more that you've been so flagrant about it and now the whole world knows."

"Wait, just to be clear, you're not just upset that I've been with other women, a fact I cannot undo, but you're also upset because people know about it... yet another thing I have *zero* control over in the present."

"Yes! And I know that makes me sound like a crazy, jealous person, and I get how irrational I'm sounding right now, but it's how I feel. Once I fell for you, it wasn't about the hotel's reputation any longer. Instead, it was my heart I was protecting by being guarded and-"

"Deceptive, manipulative."

"Don't interrupt me! Yes, I was deceptive and manipulative, and I'm sorry!" None of the things I had envisioned telling Sam, that I was in love with him, or any of my apologies, were ever supposed to come out in a rapid-fire argument, but here we were.

"You *do* sound like a crazy person, but at least it's all honest." There was a long pause as we looked at each other and I realized that I too recognized the difference he was talking about. This certainly felt like more of an unveiled conversation for a change. "The second fact you need to know," he said, picking up where he'd left off, "is that from the night we met, I haven't been with anyone else. And the moment I realized I was in love with you, it became a conscious choice for me to not be with anyone else." My heart leapt into my throat with his admission. "There's nothing else I can do or give you when it comes to other women, other than the choices I'm making *because* of you."

It was as though a bomb had gone off in the living room. My ears practically rang from the reverberation my understanding created.

This went beyond my need to be liked, or need to look good, and stretched passed my inclination to control people's reactions; this had everything to do with my lack of being in the moment. I was never just *there* with him, without bringing the past or the future into the room. Sam had tried to illustrate that point to me numerous times, I suddenly realized. And more than that, I couldn't remember the last time I was just present to what was happening around me, to me, for me...and not letting in all the voices that distracted me from what was real right then. I couldn't think of a single example. My head was *always* just so loud. I was always thinking about how I looked and what the other person was thinking. By playing chess with people and always thinking two or three steps ahead, it meant that I was never, *ever*, just enjoying the space I was standing in.

All of a sudden, it came crashing down on me the realization of what that must have been like for Sam. What had it been like for him to be with someone he *knew* wasn't with him completely? What was it like to be with someone and know their mind was in a dozen places other than just this conversation or moment or embrace? Sam must have felt like he was getting half of me all the time, and suddenly my heart broke even more. His experience of me thus far had been that of one sitting with a ghost.

"How could you fall in love with me?" I was literally dumbfounded by his admission of love in the midst of his explanation of how I'd been with him. Or *hadn't* been with him, more appropriately. But my musing must have landed as self-deprecating pity because Sam rolled his eyes and geared up for quite the retort. "That came out wrong!" I rushed out before he

could say anything, and this misstep took us too far down the
rabbit hole. "What I meant to say, was that I get how lonely and
dismissive that must have felt, being with someone so distracted
and...selfish." It was an ugly word, but once I tried it on out
loud, it completely suited me.

"I'm not going to stand here and reassure you, Dee. And
I don't need your pity; that's not why I came here."

"Why did you come here?" It was a genuine question. In
all of my self-preserving panic and gusto, I suddenly realized I
had no idea why Sam was here, and what he was looking for
from me. The question seemed to throw him off a bit, and for a
moment he looked taken aback, almost as though he'd forgotten
the answer himself.

"I came here because I needed you to know some things
before you cowardly slink off into the sunset." He was pissed, as
he had a right to be, and he wasn't entirely wrong either; I don't
know if I would have had the guts to face him before leaving
town.

"What else do you want me to know?" I wanted to make
sure I'd given him the space to say everything he needed to, no
matter how hard it was for me to hear. I was ready for whatever
else there was to lay on me. I wasn't going to let him feel
unheard any longer. I braced for a second helping of Sam's take
on my flaws and faults.

"This is over." I reeled back a bit at his comment, not
expecting that. "Look, last night was charged, and we were in
the moment, and I wanted to end this...*right*. I wanted to get
closure."

"You're here to break up with me *officially*?" I wasn't
mad. I wasn't indignant. I was just genuinely shocked at where
the conversation had led.

Sam shrugged apologetically and said, "I don't want
anything unsaid between us. This is a mess, but I still think it
would be good for both of us if we at least had a clean break. Or
at least some semblance of-"

"An ending."

"Right."

I was mortified. I wanted to crawl into a hole and
disappear forever. Here I'd been trying to apologize and make
Sam understand what he meant to me and how I wanted to fix

things, when this whole time he'd been here to end things
altogether. He'd patiently been humoring me while I prostrated
myself, just waiting for the right moment to jump in and tell me
I was dumped. I simultaneously understood and did not blame
him, while also wanting to rip his face off.

"Ok, so you've said your peace," I said. "If there's
nothing else, I think I've had about all the closure I can handle
for one day." I strode past him and to the front door, which I
opened and held for him to walk through.

"Dee, come on."

"No, you know what. I think I'm done. Fired and
dumped in one afternoon is about all I can take, on top of
whatever I did to mess up Emma's life." Sam took a step toward
me and started to speak, but I held up a hand to stop him. "Look,
I listened to all of your notes on my personality, which I will
take under advisement and try to fix before the next poor soul
comes along and gets chewed up by the lying machine that I am.
I may be at fault, I may have been wrong, but I don't have to
stand here and listen to the long version of why you don't want
to be with me. I think I have the general gist. Thank you for
sharing and loving me, for what little time it lasted."

Sam stepped up into the doorway, staring down at me,
his scent rolling over me and my body ached to lean into him. It
would be so easy to reach out; just inches in front of me was that
strong chest that could comfort and hold me, like no other place
I'd ever been before. But I held back from leaning into him as I
remembered that I'd messed this all up and that chest was no
longer my safe place. It would be someone else's in no time.
Before long, another woman would find security in those arms
and home on that chest; most likely a woman that wouldn't take
it for granted and destroy all chances of a future. I blinked
furiously as I felt the tears coming; I was getting sick and tired
of crying and I sure as hell didn't want to do it in front of Sam
and put him in the position of giving me obligatory pity.

Sam grabbed my hand and looked down at it, examining
my fingers while lost in thought. "Promise me," he said, barely
over a whisper, "when you find that future guy, you'll fight with
him the way you did with me today." It was then that I realized
he was thinking the same things I was. We were both coming to
grips with the fact that this wasn't going to work and we would

end up with other people, and it was breaking both of our hearts. "You're amazing when you let yourself off the leash," he whispered before planting a kiss on the top of my hand and turning to leave without meeting my gaze. I shut the door quickly before I lost my nerve and ran after him, begging for another chance, pleading that he not let all these transgressions destroy us. But I was stopped every time by the knowledge that he was right; this was over.

I had a gaping hole of sadness when it came to Sam, but what else was there left to say? I was ashamed and embarrassed for how I'd left things with Charles, but what else could I do about that? All of these mistakes I'd seen coming, and in some way knew could land me right here where I was standing. While I was sad and upset, in a small way, I was resigned to my plight. Sam wanted out, and Charles wanted me gone. Both facts hurt, but neither were surprising or wrong or anything I would fight to correct. They were right in how they felt, I had knowingly deceived them and couldn't fault them their anger as they realized it.

It was in that moment that a lightning bolt figuratively clapped over my head and I realized the one conversation I *had* to have at that moment. The only person I needed to speak with more than anyone. I yanked my phone from my back pocket and dialed quickly, already heading to grab my shoes and purse before the ringing even stopped, and a voice met me on the other end.

"Hello?"

"It's me. Can we meet?"

THIRTY

Dee

Emma agreed to meet me at the Monroe offices after hours. She'd been curt on the phone, giving nothing away about her state of being or how she was doing. When I asked that we speak face-to-face, there had been a long, unbearable pause before she finally agreed. She asked that we meet somewhere private and I suggested the offices since I would be there late cleaning out my office. Sam may have brought my bag of things from the suite, but I still had an office to box up. And since I was already planning on doing it after everyone had gone home, it seemed our shared desire for privacy was kismet.

I was halfway through packing my last box when Emma appeared in my doorway. Her hands were rolled in the hem of her t-shirt and shifted from one ripped jean-clad leg to the other.

"Hey," I said, setting the box aside, "I was getting worried you were going to stand me up." I sat in one of the chairs in front of my desk and motioned for her to take the other. It occurred to me as she silently entered and sat that we were seated in the same position as the last time we were alone together, although angry Emma was replaced with someone that seemed very shy and timid. She wasn't speaking, but she was here, so I resigned myself to say what I wanted her to hear and be fine with whatever answer, or lack thereof, I received. "Look, Emma, I want you to know that if I said or did *anything* to-"

"I'm so sorry!" Emma blurted out as she covered her face with her hands. "I didn't mean to get you in so much trouble."

I chuckled at Emma's childlike response and shook my head, "You didn't get me into trouble."

"I was talking to my doctor about how I've been feeling lately," she interrupted, looking up and grabbing my hand in hers as she started in. "And I mentioned that it was stressful being confronted with all of these secrets I've been hiding. I mean, I don't really notice them on a regular basis, that is until someone says, 'whatever you do, keep *those* a secret!' And so, every day I'm walking around, not only thinking about all of these new things I should make sure no one ever finds out about but also thinking about my condition all the time and what an *embarrassment* it is." The way she spat out that last part confirmed to me that I did, in fact, have some apologizing to do. "When I came here the other day, I was just so deep in my funk and nothing – I've stressed this multiple times today – *nothing* would have gotten me out of it. But in telling that story, somehow it got all convoluted, and everyone thought you were the reason I messed up." Emma had been staring at our joined hands this whole time and finally lifted her watery gaze to meet mine. She was banged up and tired, but it was Emma sitting there, the girl I'd fallen in friend-love with way back in the beginning. I smiled and rubbed her hand.

"Emma, you don't owe me an apology." I sighed, not even sure where to start. "The mess and trouble that I'm in, I got myself here all on my own. I manipulated Charles, lied to Sam. Basically made a mess. But I'm so sorry I made you feel like you had to hide who you are." Emma's gaze shifted a bit uncomfortably. "I mean, I get that I *actually* told you, and everyone else, to hide who they really are…" I stood up and gestured out my door in frustration. "I pretty much just stormed in here, told everyone they needed to repress and conceal everything real, and insisted they pretend to be fake versions of themselves. That's my job, apparently! I'm in charge of rolling into town and stripping away the authenticity and integrity from everything and everyone."

"Ok then," Emma said, lifting her eyebrows at me, "I wouldn't put it that way on your resume, exactly…"

"Seriously, I'm the architect of dishonesty!"

"Sick wrestling name."

I couldn't help but laugh with Emma.

"I didn't really get you fired?" Emma asked meekly.

"No, I got myself fired." I steeled myself for whatever her answer may be and asked, "I didn't really say something that made you relapse?"

"Are you kidding? You were there, it took a lot more damage than that to lead me to do *that*."

"Regardless, Emma. Here you are, dealing with something *real*, an actual condition and the history that comes with it, and I stroll in here, put all this pressure on you to hide that and be ashamed of it and think that who you are is an embarrassment! I owe *you* the apology, and I'd honestly understand if you chose not to accept it."

"I accept your apology, mostly because I think you need me to," she said with a chuckle. And just like that, we were back to how things had been a week ago. I sank back into the chair next to her.

"I'm going to miss you."

"Wait," Emma said, looking around my office, "You're really leaving?"

"That's typically what one does when they've been fired. I mean, I could hang out for a while, but I'm sure after a day or two security would escort me out. This way I get to take my stuff with me."

"No, I mean, you're not going to fight this?"

I shook my head in confusion. "Fight what?"

"Fight being fired! We need you."

"I think your dad and Sam would disagree."

"I don't! I think everyone would agree you've been instrumental in getting the hotel on track and thriving."

"That's not what's up for debate, Emma. I was let go for misleading your dad. No one cares about the projects you do when you're seen as a manipulative liar." I tossed a coffee mug into the box with more force than I'd intended and noted Emma's look of concern. "I'm sorry, it's just been a long fucking day. In the span of 24 hours I've been shit-canned, dumped, and made to realize that my entire way of being is at odds with any kind of happiness."

"Well, in 24 hours I've been arrested, publicly scorned and humiliated." We stared at each other in silence before both smiling and shaking our heads. "Welcome to the club?" Emma said with a laugh. "How ironic is it that the PR goddess has a shameful dark side."

"We all have that side," I said, sliding a lid on the box. "If I've learned nothing else over the years, after working with all different types of people, covering up all different kinds of secrets, it's that at the end of the day…we're all capable of bad press."

"Huh. You'd think if it were the one equalizer, we wouldn't be so keen to hide it all the time," Emma said with a scoff, reclining in her chair. And with that musing, an epiphany hit me so hard I practically stumbled backward.

"Oh, shit."

"Dee?"

"I have to go."

"What? Why?"

"You're an absolute genius," I said, leaning in to kiss her cheek as I slid into my coat. "I have to go talk to your dad. Do you know where he is?"

"It's Tuesday night, they're at Ardino's."

"Right, thanks. I'll talk to you later," I called over my shoulder as I rushed out to interrupt Charles and Rachel on their weekly date night. I knew it was intrusive and would probably look crazy, but I didn't care. I had to share my idea and clean up as much of my mess as possible.

Despite being a Tuesday night, the restaurant was booked to the max with a dinner rush. I made my way up the steep staircase in the entryway and into the tight hallway that held the hostess station. Before she could stop me, I made a motion to indicate that I was looking for someone and turned the corner into the main dining room. I spotted Charles and Rachel right away, tucked into a corner table next to the window.

As I approached their table, I started to feel my nerve waver a bit, but I steeled myself to keep walking. I couldn't look any worse or any crazier than I already did, so I had nothing to lose. The worst that would happen would be Charles telling me it was a stupid idea and asking me to leave. Charles was speaking as I walked up and stopped suddenly when our eyes met.

"Hello," I said meekly, my voice getting drowned out by the loud noises of the restaurant. "I'm sorry to intrude," I said to Rachel. "I needed to talk to you, to both of you, and it just couldn't wait." Rachel gestured at one of the empty chairs, and I took a seat in front of them, swallowing hard. "First of all, I want to say again that I'm so very sorry for misleading you and for lying. I never intended to interfere that way with your relationship with Sam, my intentions were honestly to help. But regardless of what I was trying to do, I understand if you're left feeling manipulated. To be honest, in the beginning, I felt like this assignment was a bit of a cakewalk. I came here planning on going through the motions and steamrolling this to the outcome I wanted, as fast as possible, because a promotion was waiting for me on the other side. I came in with my textbook approaches, tried and true strategies, and never really took the time to get to know you. Any of you," I said looking over at Rachel, who was smiling warmly next to her husband, who was giving me his signature blank stare until I was finished speaking. "The truth of the matter is, I fell in love with your son. If I'm being completely honest, I fell in love with him right from the beginning. And I've had a lot of trouble keeping my head on straight since. All in all, you've gotten the worst of me, professionally, during the most important part of your family business' existence. And I'm very sorry about that."

Charles raised his eyebrows and exchanged a look with his wife, "Well," he said, clearing his throat. "Thank you for that. I appreciate your honesty and sincerity. Although, I don't think all of that changes where we are now. And at the very least, it could have waited for tomorrow?"

"There's another reason I'm here, actually." I took a deep breath and for one millisecond took pause in how I was jumping into a huge life decision without even thinking about it. I had no idea how this would go; even if Charles agreed and liked my idea, this could spiral into something I had no clear vision of executing. I was leaping without a single look, and it felt freeing. "If you still want to sell the hotel to the property company and move forward with the original plans, you should stay with my firm. My old firm, I mean. They really are the best and are probably putting someone on a plane as we speak to come up here and finish what I started, probably a hundred times better since that person will be focused and not in love with Sam, at least I hope not." I chuckled nervously and moved on before I could digress further. "But, if you're interested in keeping the hotel and trying something a little different, I have an idea for you."

"Delilah," Rachel said with a note of apology in her voice, leading me to think she didn't even want to hear what I had to say. "That's very sweet of you, and I'm sure whatever you have in mind is all fine."

"But with everything that's going on with Emma," Charles interjected.

"Which she has explained in detail was *not* your doing," Rachel added pointedly.

"I just think the family and the business are going to take a time-out on the whole PR thing."

"Exactly!" I said, with an enthusiastic tap of my fist on the table. Over the next half an hour I laid out my ideas for Charles and Rachel, and when I was done they exchanged one of the longest looks and telepathic conversations I'd sat through yet. Just when I thought I was going to jump out of my skin, Charles turned to me and said, "I love it."

I let out a sigh of relief and smiled. "Fantastic, I'll get started first thing tomorrow."

"Well, before you do," Rachel said, "we should probably talk about the Sam piece of this plan."

"Don't worry," I said, jumping in to put her concerns to rest. "I promise you that I will be nothing but professional. I'm certain Sam and I can find a way to put our personal lives aside and not let this breakup get in the way of us working together."

"No, dear," Rachel said, once again putting on her motherly apologetic face.

"We'll need to do all of this *without* Sam," Charles said. "He left for New York this evening. And in a week, he'll be headed to Japan."

"What?" Loud static played in my head for a solid minute as I tried to process what he'd just said.

"We had a good, long talk last night," Charles said, leaning back in his chair and looking relaxed and non-business like for the first time since I'd arrived. "In all honesty, it's probably *because* of you that we got so much out in the open last night. After all the chaos settled down, we sat out back, smoked a couple cigars and talked about what he wants, what he *really* wants."

"Sam's going to meet up with some contacts he has from his MBA days," Rachel offered in explanation. "He's going to see about getting set up with a hedge fund, working in acquisitions and international finance."

"Apparently, it's what he's always wanted," Charles said, taking a sip from his wine.

"Yeah, it is," I said, smiling to myself at the realization that Sam was getting what he wanted after all. The irony that it all worked out and happened the way I'd wanted *because* I failed so miserably was not lost on me. And despite the initial punch to the gut that came with the news, and the sadness I was still working through, knowing I wouldn't see Sam again, I still couldn't help but smile.

"Are you ok, dear?" Rachel asked.

"I am. I'm happy for him. I want him to be happy." And I meant it.

"We'll work on the whole leadership piece of your idea, but otherwise, I'm on board," Charles said, finally giving me a smile and a wink. It was like no time had been wasted, and I was back at his round table, plotting a course for the hotel. Only now, I was actually doing what I should have done from the beginning: I was putting his family and the hotel first.

"Looks like I've got my work cut out for me!" I said, rubbing my hands together as I stood and gathered my coat and purse.

"I'll call Victor tomorrow and fire them. The rest is up to you," Charles held up his glass in salute. "You've got three weeks."

"You won't regret this," I said before bidding them goodnight, apologizing again for interrupting date night and heading out.

As I started my walk back to Jules' apartment, I allowed myself a brief moment to process my sadness about Sam. He was gone, and it was really over. But, at the end of the day, this new plan was for the hotel, and Charles and Emma, and the integrity of the job I should have done from the very beginning. Even if I never saw Sam again, I was going to pull this off so that I could walk away from Portland and the Monroe family with pride. I pulled out my phone and dialed Levi's number.

"Suit up, bitch. I've got a job for you."

THIRTY-ONE

Sam

I pulled up to the valet stand in front of the hotel with a pit in my stomach. It had been nearly a month since I'd been here, since I'd seen my family, since I'd been in a room with Dee. The last few weeks had been non-stop, and I'd felt happier with my career than ever before. And it had all started with an honest conversation with my dad. It felt like a lifetime ago that we'd sat down to have our heart-to-heart.

Dee had just left after the explosive confrontation with the family, and I was left standing in my parents' living room, realizing that for the first time in a long while, I'd fallen in love with a woman and it had all crumbled around me faster than I ever thought possible. I was standing there, searching for the words to describe, even just to myself, what this feeling was. I couldn't put into words what was happening to me, that was until my mom crossed the living room and gave me a hug. In the frozen silence of our living room, mom walked over and put her arms around my waist, and I fought back the urge to shed a tear. Here I was a grown ass man and my mommy hugging me at this moment reduced me to near-tears. And that's when the word to describe this feeling occurred to me; I was heartbroken.

"You'll get through this, baby," she whispered. I gave her a squeeze and kissed the top of her head before excusing myself and heading out back. I walked around the garden for a bit, thinking about Dee.

"Can I join you?"

Dad's voice made me jump as I was standing in the middle of the patio gazing out at their view of the city.

"Emma doing ok?"

"Oh yeah," he said, coming to stand by me at the railing. "She went up to bed. I sent Dominic home to cool off and get his head straight."

"That guy's a hothead, that's for sure."

"Just where Emma is concerned. It's love," Dad turned to me and smiled, "I'm guessing you know something about that."

"I never get tired of looking at Portland from up here," I said, turning back to the blanket of stars laid out below us. I didn't know what else to say to dad's comment.

"Did I ever tell you that we bought this place because we could see the hotel from here?" dad asked, pointing to the lights I knew to be the Monroe. "Your mother and I were about to put in an offer on a place in Lake Oswego. It was twice as big and sat on much more property than this. Even had a pool."

"Because you need that in Portland," I said sarcastically, making my dad laugh. He reached into his pocket and pulled out two cigars and handed me one. It was then that I knew we were about to have the conversation that was long overdue for the two of us. We were about to discuss the shit Dee had been scheming for us to work out organically on our own.

"We were just about to put the offer in when our agent told us about one more property she wanted us to see before we decided." Dad paused long enough to light his cigar and then reached over to light mine as he continued. "Your mom was so annoyed that day. She was pregnant and about to pop with Emma. You and Pax were in every summer camp this town had to offer, and so after dropping you off at the zoo that morning for camp, we met the agent here, knowing full well we were going to tell her to get the paperwork started on the other place. Your mom and I came through the house, took one look at this view and just knew. I'll never forget the look on her face when she stood where you're standing and saw the hotel down there in the distance. She said to me, 'Charles, we can watch our future from here.'"

I looked over at him when he stopped talking. Dad was gazing at the cigar in his hand, and his brow was furrowed in emotion as I'd only seen once or twice in my life.

"I never thought we would end up selling the thing, kiddo," he said quietly, and my heart ached at the sadness in his voice.

"Dad, I'm sorry I let you down."

"No. You didn't let me down, Sam. I let you down. I'm so proud of you, and if I'm being honest, I knew on some level you were meant for more than running a hotel. I was being selfish, forcing all this on you."

"There's nothing wrong with running a hotel, pop."

"No, there isn't. But there *is* something wrong with wasting potential, and I'm not letting you do that anymore."

"I hardly think running a multimillion-dollar hotel is a waste of potential."

"Maybe," he said, taking a drag and puffing out cigar smoke, "but it's a waste of yours. And that's all I give a shit about."

I took a long steadying breath and turned to my father. "Dad, I'm not happy."

"I know," he said with a sigh. "While I may have been intending for you to take over for me one day, I never asked myself whether or not you wanted that for yourself. So, what *do* you want for yourself?"

"I want to travel. I want to help other businesses get off the ground, people with big ideas and no idea how to execute them, I want to help them. I think I want to start my own hedge fund."

Dad and I looked at each other for a beat before he started to chuckle. "Think about it, take all the time you need, don't feel like you need to answer me right away." I laughed too and then he said, "Sounds like you've been giving this some thought lately."

I nodded.

"Sounds like someone may have been giving you a little push into thinking about this lately."

"Yeah," I said with a scoff, taking another pull of the cigar, "like a move in a chess match."

"Oh, come now, you don't actually believe that girl was doing anything devious. Misguided and reckless, sure. But I don't believe for a second that she was purely out for personal gain, let alone out to hurt you or any one of us."

"No," I said, acknowledging what I already knew. "I'm certain that wasn't the case either."

"You're in love with her." It wasn't a question.

"I am." There was a long, comfortable silence while we both sat with that reality, father and son, discussing love for the first time. "The problem is, I don't think we can ever come back from this. She's shown me who she is, time and time again, and tonight just confirmed it all, in stone. When in doubt, Dee does not rely on honesty." I looked out at the city I loved so much, the city that embraced its uniqueness the same way I did. And I thought of Dee, and her LA ways and rigid conformity to appearances. "I just don't think I can be with someone who is never really there."

"Dee just needs to figure out who she is and work through what's holding her back in life," dad said, clapping a hand on my shoulder. "And I dare say the same can be said about you. So, let me ask you, where would you start? What's the first step?"

"I'm not sure what you mean."

"Let's assume the hotel was handled and hypothetically you could be in two places at once. While one of you managed the Monroe, what would the other be doing to start this new career?"

"Well, um," I was flummoxed. I hadn't thought this far into the hypothetical future. I'd been so consumed with *how* I would get out of managing the hotel, I hadn't given any thought into what I would do next. "I suppose my first move would be to reach out to the firm in Tokyo I interned with, maybe even visit in person. They have offices around the world, and I still know some people there. Tapping into those contacts, and maybe even some of my NYU alums on Wall Street would be a great place to start, help me figure out the road ahead."

Dad listened and nodded along as I spoke, and when I was done, he turned to me, smiled, and said, "Samuel, I love you with every fiber of my being, and all I want for you is to be happy. So, I say this to you with love. You're fired."

"Dad, come on, be serious."

"I am serious, kiddo. You're done. I want you to get out there and do all those things, and so much more. It's time to cut the anchor that is the family business and sail out into the world. I'm sorry I've waited this long to set you free."

"But dad, where does that leave the hotel?" And suddenly it occurred to me what his plans where. "You're really going to sell it?!"

"No," dad said with a sharp shake of his head and dismissive wave of his hand. "That was going to be the plan, but your mother and I have thought better of the idea. As much as I appreciate and care for Dee, her 'action plan' and everything her and the firm have put together for us around the sale of the hotel have felt so alien to who we are as a business." I gave dad an I-told-you-so face, and he chuckled. "Not the PR stuff kid, that is all sound. You needed to lock that shit up, and we've done nothing but benefit from the positive attention in the press lately. No, I'm talking about the corporate bureaucracy and cloak and dagger approach. The first thing Victor and his team recommended was a confidential GM search and replacement. That's not us; we're a transparent family, and a transparent business. I'm sorry, Sam, I shouldn't have gone for the idea. It's just that I was at my wit's end, what with the business failing and all of the bad press…"

I could tell that my father was in turmoil over the whole decision and it made me confront how much I must have tied him in knots and left him with no choice.

"It's ok dad, I get it," I said, taking my turn at the shoulder clapping. "You were backed into a corner, it actually makes sense to me that you started looking for a lifeline. Wait, so it wasn't Dee's idea to fire me?"

"No, the decision had been made before she was assigned to us. Dee was just sent here to figure out when was the best time and then help me pull the trigger." After a second or two of silence, dad started to laugh. "Don't worry, that won't be my wedding toast for you two."

"Dad, come on," I said, shaking my head. "You and I both know that's not going to happen."

"We'll see," he said, to which I rolled my eyes. "I wouldn't count that girl out just yet." He was staring out over the city again, smiling to himself like a kid with a secret.

"But honestly, dad, who will run the hotel if I up and leave?"

"Don't you worry about that. I ran the Monroe for decades, I think I can jump back in and take over the day-to-day," he said.

"I don't doubt that, dad. It's just not a big picture answer."

"I know; I'm pretty sure between the two of us we can come up with a plan that makes sense. You're going to New

York and Tokyo, not the moon. Before you leave tomorrow, we should sit down and talk about communication."

"Tomorrow?!"

"Yes," dad said seriously. "You're getting on a plane and starting this plan of yours tomorrow. I've aided and abetted you putting your life off for too long."

"And you're compensating by shoving my ass on an airplane?"

"Bon voyage, bucko." He held up his glass to toast.

We both laughed, and I felt a sudden surge of freedom and release. I was finally setting out to chart my own course and make my own destiny; I no longer had the albatross of taking over the family business around my neck, and it wasn't until I appreciated the freedom of that release did I finally acknowledge the weight of that burden. With a deep breath of fresh air, my shoulders slumped with the relief from the weight of it all. Dee was right, I had been flattened by the hotel. But my relief hit a crescendo and then quickly came back down to reality.

"I know you can run the day-to-day dad, obviously you can. But you were supposed to be rounding the corner toward retirement, not turning around to work 60 hours a week. What's the end game here, if not to sell and cash out?"

"We're going to work on that, don't you worry. Between you, me and Dominic, I'm confident we can iron out a game plan that works for everyone."

"Dominic? Really? The guy that just lost his shit in your living room and blew up at my... at Dee. The guy who we both agree is a hot head?"

"Meh," dad said shrugging. "He's a hot head, and he has his faults. But I trust him. He says what he means and does what he promises. That feels like a pretty solid foundation to build from. And regardless of what happens with him and your sister, I think he has the integrity to keep running things with an even hand. And it's not like I'm handing him the keys to everything. As I said, we all need to figure out what this looks like, as a team. As a transparent, communicating team."

"Sounds good, dad."

"Just promise me one thing."

"Anything."

"Before you leave, you go see Dee."

"Dad, come on," I whined. "There's nothing left to say, it's over."

"Maybe," he said, stubbing out the butt of his cigar and turning to me fully. "Maybe it's all over, and this is the end. But if you're in love with her, if you *ever* loved her, you do not end things by muttering a final dismissive sentence in your parents' living room, in front of an audience no less, before sending her out into the night alone." Guilt panged in my chest at the imagery. "My only request, before you embark on this great new chapter of your life, is to go get closure with Dee."

And so that's what I did.

Six hours later I was on a plane to Seattle where I would catch a connecting red-eye flight to New York. We took off along the river, and I watched the Portland skyline twinkle and shrink in the distance as the plane turned north. I thought about all the things, and all the people, I was leaving behind. I finally had the freedom I'd been dreaming of professionally. In the blink of an eye, I had detached myself from the hotel that had been weighing me down while still keeping my relationship with dad intact. It may not have been the way she intended it to happen, but Dee had done the impossible and made both sides work. And in a twist of irony, here I was winging my way back to New York and Tokyo, and all I could think about was the woman I was leaving behind in Portland. It was going to be work to get over Dee, and I was hoping time and distance would be enough to do that. Not seeing her any longer, while painful, was for the best.

Or at least I thought. That first 24 hours in New York had been busy. I reconnected with contacts, had a couple meetings, dinner with a prospective employer, drinks with old friends. And while I was back in my element, seeing friends and working deals, Dee was on my mind everywhere I went. It appeared I could no longer be in a conference room without expectantly looking up to see if she was walking in wearing one of her sexy skirts or suits. Every click of heels on tile, whether I was in a restaurant or hotel lobby or office building, made me turn my head at the sound.

Two days later, my Dee detox was going better; I was thinking about her just a little less every day. With my flight to Tokyo in the morning, I was set to have a video meeting with Dominic and dad to go over the growing items on their transition list. From what I'd been able to tell from emails, dad had slid back into the GM role and quickly brought Dominic in to shadow his work. It wasn't much of a stretch for Dominic; while leading sales and marketing, he hadn't been completely removed from the hotel's operations. Plus, he was wicked smart and business savvy so the handoff of the GM role would be relatively low-maintenance. It was the future of the hotel that was the question.

I clicked on the video conference link, and that all-too-familiar conference room appeared on my screen. Dominic, who was sitting alone at the table typing away on his laptop, looked up when my face appeared on the flat screen on the wall and he shut his computer.

"Sam, how are you?" he asked as he rose from his chair and stood in front of the table, closer to the camera and screen.

"I'm good, buddy. How are things there?"

"Going well, Emma is doing loads better. You should see her, you wouldn't believe that it's been less than a week."

I smiled that his first thoughts were to update me on Emma.

"She bounces back. I know it's scary in the middle of it, but she's resilient and always finds her way back."

"Yeah, about that. I'm sorry I overreacted the other day, Sam. I was out of line, and I don't know what came over me. I just got so scared, and that made me so irrational. That's not usually like me, I hope you know that."

"Of course, this was a different kind of situation. You love her," I said, echoing my dad's take on the situation.

"I do. And that element made me act completely outside of myself with you guys. You're my employers and coworkers, and I just lost it."

"Trust me, I get it." I thought about elaborating, but Dominic's nod and knowing look told me he knew exactly what I meant. All bets are off when the heart is involved.

"Well, thank you for allowing me my momentary lapse and not letting it interfere with this transition. I'm really excited about the things we have planned for the hotel, and I'm grateful you're willing to help."

"Of course, why wouldn't I be? I'm surprised you would even doubt it." Dominic gave me a curious glance as he turned to go back to his seat at the table. "Is dad not joining us any longer?" I asked, noticing that we were past our meeting start time, which was not like dad at all.

"He is. He had a meeting with Dee just before this, so I'm assuming that ran long."

"Dee?!" I must have heard him wrong. My Dee detox was playing games with my brain's chemistry, I *had* to have imagined he said her name. Dominic froze at my outburst, panic dancing across his face. And as his eyes darted frantically to the conference room door, desperate to escape what he clearly deemed an awkward situation, I knew right then that I'd heard him correctly.

"You don't know?" he asked in astonishment. But before I could answer him, I watched the conference room door open and dad stride into the room with a pep in his step that I hadn't seen in a while. He looked like a guy in the middle of a workday at a job he loved.

"Sam!" he beamed as he set his things down across from Dominic and pulled the chair out to sit. "How's the trip? Getting excited for Tokyo tomorrow?"

"Fine. It's fine," I said impatiently, suddenly not in the mood for small talk at all. "Did you say Dee?"

Dad and Dominic shared a look.

"I didn't know he didn't know!" Dominic rushed out as dad let out a big sigh and sat down.

"I wanted to tell you on our call today, face-to-face. There are a lot of pieces to this, and I worried if I sent an email, as soon as you read that I hired Dee back you would stop reading and react."

"You hired her back?" I asked incredulously. "I thought we weren't selling the hotel! The last conversation we had, you and I agreed to iron out a plan for transitioning the GM role in a way that would keep the hotel in the family. What the fuck happened to transparency?" I pinched the bridge of my nose, wondering if rather than going to Tokyo tomorrow I should instead hop on a plane back to Portland.

"Glad to see I can still predict what my kids will do," dad said with a smug grin to Dominic, who looked slightly uncomfortable with the start of this meeting. "For the most part anyway," he said winking at me. I could feel my brow furrowing in deep frustration at how playful and caviler he was being. "Calm down, Sam, we're not selling. What you and I talked about it is still the plan. Dee's helping us execute it."

"To be clear," Dominic offered, probably noting my confusion, "Charles hired Dee, *independently*, not her firm."

"Right," dad said. "I probably should have specified that. Let me explain."

And then dad told me a story that completely erased any work I'd done to get over Dee, and made the ache I felt to be with her utterly renewed. After I'd left her that day, Dee had gone to my parents and pitched a entirely new idea. She had told them that the firm was their best choice for moving forward with the original plan of sale, but she wanted to represent the Monroe and execute a whole new branding idea.

"We're giving the hotel to Emma."

"I'm sorry, what?" I blurted out, making dad and Dominic laugh. Maybe I really did need to go home.

"Not actually," Dominic corrected, clearly trying to keep Charles' glee and giddiness on track. "We are making her the face of the hotel. She's going to be the spokesperson for the Monroe, so to speak."

"It's really quite brilliant," dad said excitedly, getting up from his chair to grab a bottle of water from the table behind him before strolling around the room as he spoke. "Dee's idea is to embrace our bad press, our uniqueness, fully. Not only are we going to build a brand around the idiosyncrasies that make up the Monroe family, but also this town as well. We're going to be the hotel for Portland, a place dedicated to the city, and the idea that authenticity is what makes us great."

Dad had clearly been buzzing on this new plan, and it was caffeinating his very soul; I'd never seen him this invigorated at work.

"We're going to get out a bunch of new marketing materials; billboards, magazine ads, radio, TV, all highlighting

Emma as the face of the hotel," Dominic explained. "We're going to use the stories about her, that we cannot stop even if we wanted to, and use them as a springboard for this new campaign."

"Steering into the skid," I said.

"Exactly!" dad exclaimed.

"How does Emma feel about this?" I asked Dominic since he seemed to be the level-headed one in the room at the moment and I trusted he would give it to me straight.

"She's onboard," he said with a decisive nod. "Her first response was understandable apprehension. But once Dee and dad shared with her the whole idea, the notion that she would be embracing who she is to the world, Emma was really excited."

"I like it," I said. "It really is a great idea. But what does Dee propose we do about all of this new branding we've been putting out for the past month? We're going to stop those messages and rebrand the *rebrand*?"

"That was our concern as well," Dominic said. "The last thing we want is to appear vacillating and indecisive."

"Right. We'll look like we don't even know who's in charge over there," I added, making both of them laugh.

"Dee's solution to that was…" Dominic and dad shared a look. "Interesting."

"Her solution is actually what sold the whole idea for me, both the new campaign, as well as hiring her back," dad said as Dominic nodded in agreement. There was a long pause before dad turned back to me and said simply, "She wants us to blame it all on her in the press."

"Come again?"

"Dee's idea is to basically put out messaging and branding that tells the story of the Monroe family going to an LA firm for image advice, hiring a publicist, and everything going to hell," Dominic said.

"'We tried to put a stopper on the crazy, and it just made it spill out more!'" Dad said, holding up air quotes around the slogan.

Dominic rolled his eyes, "Emma suggested that one, but Dee and I agree there are more tactful ways to say it." My heart clenched at the sudden image of Dominic and Dee brainstorming and strategizing around a conference table. Not in my wildest dreams would I imagine anything romantic would happen between them, but that was *our* thing, and I suddenly missed home and wished I was there. "Essentially, Dee's persona is going to be portrayed as something we tried, and Emma's new image is going to be the result."

"It's brilliant," I said, leaning back in my chair and taking it all in. Dee was making herself, even if it was just her likeness, look like the villain in order to make Emma and the rest of the family embrace themselves. "What's the plan of attack on this?"

Dad and Dominic walked me through Dee's execution plan. Media was going to start rolling out as soon as the end of the week with a variety of plays on authenticity and a splash of Portland love. All of it would be advertising the anniversary ball, which would be held to raise money for OCD and mental health crisis centers.

"Dee has a great plan for that night," dad added at the end. "Her and Emma have been working around the clock."

"The theme is 'be true to thine self,' and it's going to center around embracing the secrets we hide in order to look good," Dominic added.

"Well, fuck me," I muttered to myself as I rubbed my cheek absentmindedly. It appeared that everything was falling into place back home at warp speed, and it all started roughly around the time I boarded the airplane to leave town. Not only was the hotel going to experience the most genius rebrand and revitalization it had ever seen, but it was being done in a way that left everyone, most importantly Emma, feeling comfortable in their own skin. And let's not forget the big takeaway from all of this: Dee suddenly had more integrity than I'd ever known her to have. I broke out of my mental fog, and it registered that my dad was giving me a squinted look. The last thing I wanted him to think was that I was doubting the new Dee plan he was so enthusiastic about. With a smile, I said, "What do you need from me?"

"Well," Dominic said, returning his attention to his laptop where he was undoubtedly looking at a detailed agenda, "there are a handful of items I'd like to run through with you."

"Before we dig into that," dad interrupted, holding a hand out to Dominic and looking at me. "Son, I also want to announce the night of the anniversary gala that Dominic will be taking over as GM."

"Of course, stands to reason," I said. With Emma as the face of the hotel, it only enhanced Dominic's place at the head of the table.

"And I'd also like to announce the future *ownership* of the hotel as well." He glanced back and forth between myself and Dominic, who clearly did not know this would be on the agenda for today.

Welcome to the club, dude.

"I have some ideas on how to structure it, and I'd like the three of us to work through that."

Dominic looked at me, and I nodded. "Let's do it."

And so, a roadmap was formed, and within the hour Dominic had action plans and project timelines in all of our inboxes.

Over the next two weeks, while meeting with investors and contacts in Tokyo, I began to remember who I was outside of the hotel. I was reoriented with the investing world and reminded what it was like to nurture an idea and help all kinds of businesses at once. My Japanese was a little rusty, having only used it in basic conversation for the last few years, rather than contract negotiation. But just like everything else, it was like riding a bike and came back to me faster than I thought it would.

Shortly after I got settled in my corporate housing in Tokyo, I got a video call from Emma at what I estimated to be around midnight in Portland. I answered in a panic, hoping it wasn't another crisis, but burst out laughing when the image that popped up on the screen was Emma's left hand pressed against the screen of her phone so I could just make out the blurry edges of what I guessed to be an engagement ring. Based on her squeal of delight in the background, I assumed I'd guessed right.

"Congratulations!" I said. Emma pulled her hand away, and my heart swelled at the look of pure happiness on my baby sister's face. She was happy, and it showed. For the next half hour, she went into excruciating detail about where and how

Dominic asked, and how surprised she was, and how perfect the ring was and her ideas for the big day.

"I just couldn't believe it," she said once again. "I guess he bought the ring a while ago and then my whole episode happened and now all these new plans for rebranding, he said he almost wasn't going to go through with it. Can you believe that?!" She rolled her eyes, and the comparison made me laugh. Poor Dominic, three weeks ago this plan probably seemed so simple and romantic.

"Well, good for him for mustering the courage to do it in the middle of all this craziness," I said.

"Dee had a lot to do with it."

"Really?" I asked, surprised since there wasn't a lot of love lost between her and Dominic. But then again, things were moving at a lightspeed pace back in Portland; I was starting to question everything I knew about the team I'd left.

"We're all trying to live by this mantra her and Mae have put into everything we're doing."

"Which is?"

"'Fuck what everyone else thinks.'" Emma giggled.

"How very PC of the PR team," I laughed, trying to imagine Dee saying that in a meeting.

"Oh yeah, she's all about it. Every time I start to second guess what people will think about my photoshoot ideas, or Pax is thinking about starting a Fast & the Furious karaoke night, or anything... Dee will say, 'Does it make *you* happy?' and when you tell her it does, she says, 'Then fuck what everyone else thinks.' It's become somewhat of an anthem around here."

"What is *happening*?" I asked, more to myself, as I ran a hand over my face.

"I know it must seem like she's morphed into a whole new person to you," Emma said, getting serious and once again zeroing in on exactly what I was feeling. "That's not really the case, though. You're hearing about it in bursts and fits every few days. If you were here, you would see that it's gradual. I don't mean that as a dig, big brother. I'm glad you're off getting comfortable with who *you* are, too. It's just that for us here, it's an organic thing. Every day she just becomes a little more relaxed and a little more herself. It's like watching someone shed a layer of armor piece by piece. She's just getting comfortable in her skin." I smiled at my sister and told her how proud and happy I was she was my family. "Yeah, yeah," she said, dismissing my sappiness. "Tell me about Tokyo!"

We caught up for a while; I told her about the people I was meeting, the deals I was striking, the food I was eating. And she shared her photo shoot and recent morning radio interview Dee had escorted her to for the new campaign. As expected, Dee had taken amazing care of my sister and Emma was loving every minute of this particular spotlight.

"Ok, before I let you go so I can call more friends and family and tell them I'm engaged, I have a question."

"Isn't it almost 1AM there?"

"And?" she asked, rolling her eyes and laughing.

"Right, carry on."

"I would like for you to be at the anniversary gala." I started to speak, but Emma quickly held up a hand to stop me. "I know it's a lot to ask you to come all the way back just as you're getting stuff settled out there. And I know it's complicated with the whole Dee thing. But I would really like to have you there."

With a sigh and the inability to say no to my sister I said, "I'll see what I can do."

"That's all I ask!"

And with that promise, she was off to call everyone in her contacts list. I sat at my desk in silence, turning to look out the window at the city bustling below me. I didn't want to disappoint Emma, so of course, I would make an appearance. I'd just have to steel myself between now and then to be ready to run into Dee.

Intermittently over the next two weeks, I would exchange emails or video conference with dad and Dominic. Being sixteen hours ahead, most of the meetings were either very early in my day, or well into my evening. And with every call, each time that conference room would pop up on the screen, all work I'd done since the last conference to get Dee out of my brain evaporated and she was right back at the forefront of my mind. I found myself walking around markets thinking about our day together at the farmers market in Portland. Every restaurant I went to I would inadvertently decide whether or not I would bring Dee there, should we ever find ourselves in Tokyo together. She was everywhere I went. And even if I managed to make it a day without picturing her, or being reminded of the exact smell of her hair, I would jump onto one of those fucking video calls, see the conference room, and invariably hear her name spoken a dozen times by people that spent hours with her every day. Dee was becoming a very present ghost in my life; a whisper of a memory I was trying to forget, but yet discussed every day.

And just when I wondered if I was ever going to get her foggy image out of my mind, her crystal-clear image finally appeared on my screen.

It was just before 6AM my time, and I was due to meet with dad and Dominic about our changes to the expansion plans. I hadn't showered yet, but this certainly wasn't the first meeting we'd had while I sipped coffee with bedhead in a t-shirt. I clicked on the link for the conference and snorted into my coffee mug as the live feed opened on my screen. It appeared I had joined just as a previous meeting was ending. I caught a glimpse of a couple sales guys leaving and Mae following behind them just as they were exiting the conference room. Dominic was leaning back in his chair laughing, and across the table, there she was.

Dee was standing, gathering papers and stacking them on the closed leather case I recognized as her tablet. She looked completely the same and yet completely different, all at once. Her hair was gathered in a loose, messy knot with pieces of it falling here and there in a way I'd only ever seen on the weekends when we were alone. She wore a white dress shirt with the sleeves rolled up and untucked from the jeans she was wearing. Never before had I seen Dee look like this at work. But it was still, most undoubtedly, *her*. She was shaking her head in laughter, presumably at whatever had Dominic guffawing, and the sound of it tickled my ears and gave me goosebumps. Her smile, her eyes, the shape of the slope of her back as I looked at her in profile; it was all the same. She was relaxed and freer than I was used to seeing, wearing a different uniform at work for sure, but it was my Dee without a doubt. And the air of confidence and tranquility she managed to exhibit in just a few brief moments was enough to bring all of my feelings rushing back to the forefront.

Dominic looked up to see me on the flat screen and sat straight up in his chair, making a commotion as he did so and causing Dee to jump.

"Hey man!" he said, looking nervously between the two of us. "Sorry about that, we ran a little long. Charles should be here any minute."

Dee had turned to look at the screen, and the webcam somehow managed to capture the deepness of her blue eyes all the way across the world as we just looked at one another in silence. I felt my mouth open to speak and then close again, bringing the slightest smirk to Dee's face. And after what felt like minutes and was most likely only moments, dad rushed in the room.

"Sorry I'm late," he announced as he strode in.

"I was just leaving," Dee said as she scooped up her things and headed quickly to the door. Just as she reached the doorway, she turned and said, "Bye, Sam."

And then she was gone.

Dad and Dominic started talking, taking turns saying things that just sounded like noise in my head as I stared at the top left corner of my laptop screen where I'd watched Dee walk through the door.

"Sam?" Dominic asked for what I guessed to be the second time based on his tone.

"Sorry," I said, shaking my head and trying to refocus. I looked down at my notepad to orient myself for the meeting and just couldn't muster the energy any longer. "Dominic, I'm sorry, I know we have some stuff to cover today, but can my dad and I have the room?"

Dominic looked over at dad who was already nodding his agreement. He shrugged and closed his laptop, letting us know he would be free if we wanted to reconvene later, and shut the door behind him. Dad remained sitting in his chair, tapping a pen slowly on the pad in front of him, smiling up at me.

"Dad," I started with a steadying breath. "I'd like to rework the ownership plan."

"I thought you may," he said, his smile getting bigger.

And that brings us to tonight. A week after that video call with dad, I boarded a plane and flew back across the Pacific Ocean to be at what can only be described as my sister's debut. On the drive in from the airport, I'd spied multiple billboards advertising the Hotel Monroe featuring Emma. My favorite had been the adorable picture of her after just taking a large bite of a VooDoo donut and wiping her mouth with what looked to be a page from the Wall Street Journal. Although that was second to my all-time favorite image of the campaign, which featured Emma sitting at a board room table surrounded by women that appeared to be Dee facsimiles dressed in black suits and slicked backed pony-tails. And while the top half of the photograph was Emma staring into the camera nervously while they all spoke in her ear, the bottom half of the photo showed under the table, where the black slacks and black heels flanked either side of Emma's pink tutu and flip-flops. Dee had done an amazing job; the imagery alone was enough to sell the anti-establishment sentiment of Portland.

After a quick trip home to clean up, make sure the house sitter hadn't let the place go to hell, and change my clothes, I was on the road to the hotel and parking in front of the valet station. As I turned the corner in the lobby to head to Boost, there lining the walk to the front entrance was a series of six-foot by six-foot poster boards, splashed with brightly colored photos of the people I loved. A quick glance down the line told me right away that this was a photographic telling of Emma's journey, albeit it a comedic one. And to my surprise, unlike the billboards and print materials being used for official advertisement, Dee was playing the role of herself in each photo.

The first photo was centered on Dee, standing tall at the head of a conference table, looking down disapprovingly at everyone. She was in a dark suit, and her arms were crossed as she furrowed her brow in exaggerated anger. The next two were comedic plays on my siblings pretending to get on board with her plan, Pax in a business suit that was two sizes too small, making him look even more uncomfortable and out of place as he stood in front of a PowerPoint presentation chock-full of graphs and charts. Emma was in a dark suit made to match Dee's, her hands tied in her lap and a police report sticking out the top of a shredder.

When I got to the fourth and final photo, I actually let out a deep laugh. Dee, clad in her suit and with wide and wild eyes staring into the camera, was duct-taped to a chair with a gag in her mouth. To her right stood Dominic, a roll of duct tape in one hand while smashing her laptop with the other. On her left, Pax dancing around a makeshift fire on the floor while burning speeding tickets and wearing a racing suit. And above them all, standing with two planted feet on the desk and her palms planted on her hips like Peter Pan, stood Emma, grinning at the chaos below her.

It was perfect.

I stood taking in every facet of the picture, mesmerized by the freedom of everyone in it, even Dee portraying a comical version of herself. I was so immersed in the picture I jumped when a hand clapped on my shoulder.

"Well look at what the fucking cat dragged in," Pax said. I turned and smiled at the sight of my brother standing in front of me; he wasn't one for video calls or emails, so all we had had over the last few weeks were scattered texts and pictures.

"How are you, brother?" I asked as I gave him a hug.

"Oh, I'm amazing. While you were in China-"

"Tokyo."

"Ok, fine," he said rolling his eyes. "While you were in whatever Chinese city you were in, Boost has done nothing but explode."

"I've heard," I said. "I'm happy for you Pax. And I'm sorry I didn't get a chance to say goodbye before I left."

"It's cool. I know you needed to go do your own thing. You've been trying to make yourself fit into this specific dad-shaped position for years. I'm glad you finally struck out; road less traveled, right? I'm just sorry about you and Dee."

I nodded solemnly, appreciative for his support but not sure what there was to say. It was then that I noted his black on black suit and tie. While everyone in attendance seemed to be dressing down and embracing Portland's casual culture, suddenly my brother was dressed to the nines.

"Nice suit!"

"Thanks," he beamed, straightening his jacket. "It's part of my truth."

"Your truth?"

"Oh yeah, it's the theme for tonight," he said just as we crossed the threshold into Boost and my mouth fell open. I didn't recognize the place. "This whole 'be yourself' campaign that Dee has been working on," Pax said with air quotes. "Tonight's event is specifically centered around the idea of it all culminating in people being their true selves. See, over there?" Pax pointed to the far wall of the club which appeared to have been painted with chalkboard paint and was covered in writing. "People are writing their secrets and who they truly are. We're going to keep it as sort of an art feature that's always there."

And that's when I saw her.

Dee was at the opposite end of the bar in the most dazzling red dress. You couldn't help but notice her as she maneuvered between people, shaking hands, smiling and laughing and looking light as air.

"Have you talked to her since you left?"

"No," I said, not taking my eyes off Dee as she introduced Emma to someone in the crowd. I was mesmerized by the easiness of her being.

"It's gotta be tough, man," Pax said next to me. "But it's cool you came tonight. Not just for Emma, but for all of us. It's a packed house, I'm sure you can get through tonight without having to talk to her at all if you want."

"I'm not here to avoid her," I said to Pax. "I'm here to get her back."

THIRTY-TWO

Dee

"Thank you, everyone. These past three weeks have been amazing and what we're celebrating tonight is the culmination of what everyone has put into this project. We kick off a new era for the Monroe Hotel tonight," I said, dabbing at a tear in the corner of my eye with my knuckle.

"Oh my god, are you *crying*?" Pax said laughing, and everyone else joined in with him, including me. The whole executive team was gathered in the bar, seated around a collection of bistro tables, just as we'd been a month ago before Pax's Boost event. Today, we were having our final meeting before breaking so everyone could go home and change before our anniversary celebration and rebrand unveiling.

"I suppose I'm more excited than I thought."

Dominic, who had been standing next to me, took a step closer and put an arm around my shoulders. "We all are," he said with a squeeze. I leaned my head on his shoulder briefly in acknowledgment of his support, taking a moment to marvel at the fast evolution of our professional relationship and friendship. A month ago, if you would have told me that we would have linked arms and joined forces to create a whole new roadmap for the Monroe family, I would have thought you were crazy. But here we were. Over the past few weeks, Dominic and I had put our differences aside and dedicated all our energy into the 're-rebrand,' as we had taken to jokingly referring to it. In the beginning, it had been rocky. We were still reeling from Emma's incident, and I was adjusting to being in the Monroe offices without Sam, not only working with someone new on operations but working with someone who openly did not like me. But once Dominic wrapped his head around my ideas, and how at the end of the day it was all aimed at empowering Emma just as much as the hotel, his icy demeanor melted, and things quickly became amicable. And as it tends to be with most things, time and exposure proved to be the answer to making things click.

I'd grown to respect Dominic and his experience. He was unlike a lot of the executives I'd worked with in the past, in that he was completely transparent in everything he did, a rarity for sure. His calendars were public to his whole team, he spoke openly and honestly with everyone; if Dominic said he liked something, you knew he was telling the truth. What you saw was what you got where Dominic was concerned, whether he was screaming at you in your boss' living room or telling you in a conference room full of people that your ideas were inspired, you always knew where you stood with him. There was no subtext. Ultimately, the stars had aligned with Charles' plans for transition and my new branding ideas, making Dominic the perfect choice to lead the new Monroe. He was also the best pairing for me to work with at this particular crossroads in my career, not to mention *life*.

But I still missed Sam. Every day I waited for the ache to go away, just a little. I assumed that eventually, with time, little by little I would start to get over him and miss him less. And yet, every morning I woke up thinking of him, and even if I managed to have a reprieve in my day where for one brief moment I got lost in my work and forgot the heartache, invariably his name would come up in conversation or in an email, and it'd start all over again. It was hard to get over a breakup with your former coworker and boss' son, plain and simple.

But life goes on, and about a week after Sam left, I decided I needed to at least fake it until I made it. Maybe if I went through the motions of moving on, made an effort to do all the things one does when they've found peace after a breakup, the emotions would follow.

I found a great apartment not too far from the hotel, which would get me out of Jules' guest room, but still close enough to see my best friend as much as I wanted. That was, whenever she wasn't spending her time with Pax. The two of them had been fairly inseparable since that first weekend together after the Boost event. In just a matter of weeks, Jules was powering through milestones in her relationship with Pax, some of which I'd never seen her do with a boyfriend before. She'd met Charles and Rachel, having dinner with them at the

house after the Emma situation had died down. And Pax had
even been to her set a few times, watching her film segments
and meeting her whole production team. Pax had become such a
mainstay at her house, part of me was sure that he would be
moving in just as soon as I got myself out of there.

"Before we all disperse," Charles said at the table next
to us, bringing me out of my reverie and back to the present, "I
have an announcement to make. Not even our fearless PR leader
knows about this one yet, so Dee, please forgive me this last
surprise before we embark on a new frontier." I smiled at
Charles before making a show of nervously biting my nails, but
it was mostly theatrics since I had a sinking suspicion what his
announcement was about. There was just one lingering item
regarding leadership that we'd yet to address in our press
releases. "This news will be going out publicly next week, but I
wanted to tell all of you now since we're family."

I looked around the collection of people in attendance,
some actual family members, like Pax and Emma, some soon-to-
be-family like Dominic, and then the rest of us, managers and
VP's over various departments, working for Charles and the
Monroe family with just as much passion as if we *were*, in fact,
family.

"As you all know, Dominic has transitioned into the GM
role officially and starting today will lead all operations for the
hotel. Samuel completed his transition and exit this week, and I
will be officially stepping down from any official role this
evening. Taking over Dominic's position leading our sales team
will be Mike Griffin, let's all give him a round of applause." The
group hooped and hollered for Mike, who waved awkwardly,
still finding his place in these leadership meetings. "And lastly,
as for the lingering question of ownership." The group quieted
down quickly; most employees, regardless of their level, were
anxious to know the fate of the hotel. Dominic and I had been
vocal about dismissing the rumors that Charles was selling, but
that was always followed up with the question: 'then what *is*
going to happen?'

"These past few weeks, Sam has been traveling the
globe, meeting with investors and contacts, networking,
basically figuring out his place in this world, both personally and
professionally." Charles glanced my way, and I fidgeted in my

seat. "And as time and distance both have a tendency to do with such matters, clarity came to Sam in a way that just makes perfect sense for all of us. This past week, Dominic, Sam and I have been working with our legal team, as well as some handpicked angel investors Sam encountered during his travels, and we have established Monroe Holdings Incorporated! For now, the Hotel Monroe in Portland is the only property under the MHI umbrella," Charles said with a chuckle, tipping his hat to an acknowledgment of his grandiose language, "but soon, roughly five to seven years by our planning estimations, this hotel will be the flagship property in a portfolio of locations."

Applause and relief rang out from the group. For some, it was relief that their jobs were safe, for others it was that the hotel would stay within the family, and for a select few, it was the celebration that the Monroe brand would be expanding. But for me, it was the knowledge that Sam had found the answer to everything he wanted. This was a beautiful solution for him; he would be leading an international company, overseeing expansions and acquisitions, while staying in touch with the business, and family, that tethered him to this world. It was perfect, and my heart leapt for him.

"As for some of the nitty-gritty logistics that some of you may be wondering about," Charles continued. "Samuel will be President and CEO of MHI and Dominic will report into him, as will all GM's of future properties. We're still working on where our first new location will be, but I can tell you that whichever location we choose, the hotel will be a love letter to that city, just as the Monroe now is to Portland." Charles turned fully to me and said, "The idea of embracing the place you call home, giving guests a glimpse into what it's like to be a local, and giving locals a place to call their mascot, was nothing short of inspiring. Thank you."

Tears prickled my eyes again, and I nodded to Charles in appreciation for his kind words.

"As for me," Charles said with a deep sigh and a smile, "I will be a silent partner in MHI, which means two things. First, Sam and the people he assembles as his executive team will be making all of the decisions for MHI. And second, and most importantly, I will be retreating to a beach somewhere with my lovely wife, collecting my checks there. So finally, once and for all, I bid you all bon voyage."

The laughter and applause were thunderous as everyone rushed to hug Charles and wish him well. I stayed in my seat, clapping and feeling happy for Charles, but still frozen in place. Dominic elbowed me in the arm, and when I looked up at him, he was unsurprisingly studying my reaction.

"You ok?" he asked.

"Of course! That's all such great news!" I said automatically, in a voice way too high and with a smile way too big. Dominic arched an eyebrow at me, and I let my shoulders slump, remembering the motto around here of authenticity. "I just feel even further away from Sam than I did before," I said as Dominic sat in the seat next to me. "I would love nothing more than to be able to congratulate him and give him a hug and tell him how happy I am that he found what he was looking for..."

"If that's all you wish for, you can have it. He's going to be here tonight."

I sucked in a sharp breath and nodded. "I assumed as much. But you know that's not what I mean," I said with a knowing smile and Dominic nodded. "No sense in wishing for what can't be, I'm just going to focus on what I *can* do, and that's finish the most amazing campaign I've ever put together."

"Look, tonight's going to be a whirlwind," Dominic said, scooting forward and speaking conspiratorially to me. "The next time we're in this room together it's going to be wall-to-wall people, a packed agenda, and hopefully reason after reason to celebrate."

"Here, here!" I cheered on.

"I just wanted to say, while it's just you and I sitting here, and life hasn't taken off on the express path I think it's going to for each of us," Dominic grabbed my hands on the table and squeezed, looking me in the eye as he did so, "I wouldn't be here without you. I could take a week to explain to you the many ways in which that's true, but just know, that in my very being I *know* that you're the reason I have the life I'm about to have. And I thank you."

Before he could see what was coming and refuse, I leapt from my seat and wrapped Dominic in a hug. "I have to hug you because you're making it sound like we're not going to see each other anymore and that makes me sad," I said into his neck.

"We will," Dominic said, patting me on the back. "If for no other reason than my soon-to-be wife will stalk you to the ends of the earth if you refuse to be in our wedding."

With a laugh, I left Dominic to celebrate with the rest of his family and made my way to the lobby. I turned and glanced back at the group gathered in the middle of the empty nightclub, and my heart swelled, both with pride and a touch of sadness. While tonight was gearing up to be a colossal success celebrating a monumental feat, it probably *was* going to be the last time I saw most of them. I didn't want to rain on Dominic's parade, but once things settled back into a routine, with him running the hotel, everyone executing on their roles, and now Sam in this new MHI position, there wasn't much room for me at the table. And that was ok, even if it made me sad. This was Sam's family; I wasn't going to force myself into the mix. And when it came to the Hotel Monroe, my job was essentially done. I was here to rebrand; that and damage control were what I was best at, and there wasn't really a place for me here professionally any longer.

"Dee!" Mae had caught sight of me leaving the club and left the group to catch up with me. "Sorry," she said, falling into place next to me, "I didn't see you leave. Where do you need me?"

I turned to face her full on, making her stop short and look surprised. "I was going to tell you tonight, and that's just because I wasn't going to be able to make it until Monday morning when Dominic and I were going to meet with you," I said in a rush. "But now I can't even wait until tonight." I grabbed her hand and gave it a squeeze. "You've been amazing. Not just this past month, getting all *this* put together," I said gesturing at the huge photographs flanking us in the wide hallway. "But before that. When we first got here…and when everything went to hell." I felt a knot in my throat and swallowed hard, trying to stay cool. But it was hard to stay impartial about Mae's loyalty.

When Charles had accepted my proposal and fired the firm, hiring me directly instead, it left Mae in an odd place. Technically, she was still employed by the firm; their intention

had been for her to report to the new publicist, and when the
firm's contract was terminated, she was expected to report back
to the LA office for a new assignment. I'd given her complete
transparency about what had happened with Sam and me and the
family, and that I had been fired, *and* that I had effectively out-
pitched Victor and gotten hired on independently. It was a long
lunch, to say the least, but I wanted Mae to have all the facts
before the firm called and filled her in on her new assignment
and location. And that's when she surprised me.

"Then I quit, too," she said with a nod of her head and
taking a sip of her coffee. It was as though she'd decided to
order to dessert, rather than quit her job.

"What? No, that's not what I meant. I was just saying-" I
stammered.

"You're my mentor," she said matter-of-factly. "You
stay, I stay."

I'd been so moved, and to be honest, looking back, I
don't know how I would have gotten through the last month
without Mae. She went beyond protégé and had become a full-
fledged PR pro.

"Oh boy," she said, pulling me back to the present.
"Where are we going now?" She rolled her eyes in mock
indignation.

"*We* aren't going anywhere," I said pointedly, raising an
eyebrow at her. "I talked to Dominic, and he agrees with me that
they need an in-house publicist to manage PR and
communications for the hotel. He also agrees with me that
you're the best person for the position." Mae opened her mouth
to speak, but I cut her off and kept going. "Neither of us is under
the illusion you'll be in this role forever, it's a stepping stone for
sure. Personally, I expect to hear you were recruited by a big
firm within a few years. But it's going to give you the chops and
exposure you need to really launch into what you want."

"But what about you?"

Classic Mae, standing in the face of a promotion and job
offer, she's worried about what happens to me.

"I'm going to be just fine. I have absolutely no clue what
I'm going to do next, and I love it." I shook her hand in mine to
bring her back to the present. "This job is yours, and you're
going to be amazing."

"Thank you so much," Mae said, launching herself at me in a hug that almost bowled me over. "I won't let you down."

"I know," I said softly, patting her on the back. "Now go sync up with Dominic; you're running the agenda tonight."

Mae's eyes went wide with excitement, and she hugged me once more before dashing off back into the club, passing Pax who was making his way toward us. He stepped aside to let a frantic Mae brush past but not without taking his eyes from mine.

"Is this where Dorothy is saying goodbye to everyone before going back home to Oz?" he asked as he closed the distance between us and gestured around the corridor.

"What are you talking about?"

"I'm not an idiot, Dee. I only play one in the press." He came to stand in front of me and crossed his arms over his massive chest as he took in all the photographs around us. "You know," he said thoughtfully, "you did something I never thought would be possible."

"Got you into a race car?"

"Pffft, no," he said with a dismissive scoff. "That was going to happen even if I had to steal one someday. So, yeah, I guess, you got me into one *legally*." He rolled his eyes in faux exasperation. "No, you brought this family together." He looked down at me, and I couldn't help but feel proud under his appraising smile. "All the Monroe kids have their dream jobs, even Sam, which is really saying something since that guy can be a moody motherfucker. And somehow, we all have that, *and* the hotel is going to live on in the family, and mom and dad are happy and retiring. You managed to bring everyone together. You not only saved the hotel, but you also saved my family. And it's not just because I'm sticking it to your best-friend that I know that you managed to do it all by sacrificing a lot yourself." I chuckled at his crudeness and brushed at a tear playing at the corner of my eye. "It's not lost on me that to do all this," he said, once again gesturing around him dramatically, "you had to lose a little bit of yourself and give up some big things."

He was right. I'd given up my career, or at least what I had *thought* I wanted it to be, and I'd let go of love. But regret and sorrow were the last things I felt when it came to those choices; I'd do it all over again in a heartbeat because it had

made me…like *me*. For the first time in my life, I felt aimless
and alone and absolutely happy in my own skin.

"Wow," I said with a sigh and a solemn nod. "Jules has
made you wise beyond your years."

"Are you kidding? Plugging into that woman every night
upgrades my whole system."

"Oh, dear god," I said, wincing and rolling my eyes at
what I knew to be a comment designed to get a reaction.

"Seriously though," he said. "I get that you're about to
pull a Mary Poppins tonight."

"I thought I was Dorothy in Oz…"

"You're going to do what you need to do tonight, smile
at all of us being happy together, and walk out that door into the
night, disappearing down a foggy street like she did."

"Well, technically, Mary Poppins flew off with her
umbrella."

"Jesus, you're such a nerd," Pax said with a roll of his
eyes.

"You're the one referencing Mary Poppins. And Wizard
of Oz!"

"The point is," he said, "I get why you probably want to
walk away from the hotel and the family, but I'm rubbing his
chin in thought, "that came out all threat-like. What I meant to
say is, whether you like it or not, I'm going to be in your life.
No…I mean-"

"I get it," I said with a laugh. "You're saying you're not
scarecrow because we're not actually parting ways?"

"The fuck?" Pax looked absolutely lost.

"I'm glad you and I are still going to be family," I said
with a sigh and a smile.

"Bitchin'," he said as he broke out into his own smile
and hugged me.

As I finally made it to the exit to head home and get
ready for tonight, I thought about how apt his comparison was,
not only the Dorothy-like goodbyes but also my plans to leave
while everyone was happy and distracted. I hadn't decided yet
how that applied to Sam; I was still wrapping my brain around
actually seeing him and how I'd manage to keep myself in
check, rather than the if's and how's of telling him goodbye.
Again.

I arrived at the hotel later that night and stood on the opposite side of the street for a long while, enjoying the late autumn breeze and taking in the sight of the entrance. Banners with Emma's photograph hung in the windows of the hotel. Inside, our funny photoshoot lined the corridor leading into the club, but outside, whether you were a passerby, press, VIP, or a hopeful attendee waiting in line to get a spot in the packed event, you saw Emma's face smiling out at you in a variety of poses with the hotel emblem.

"Shouldn't you be in there, bossing people around?" Levi's voice in my ear made me jump, and I laughed despite myself.

"Shouldn't you be inside in the press box, pestering people and sexually harassing Pax?"

"I'm actually not covering tonight," he said straightening his black tie and smoothing his crisp white shirt. "The magazine has an associate reporter inside getting the basics; we don't have to stress too much on a scoop tonight, thanks to you." Levi beamed down at me. He was right about that. We'd given Levi the exclusive on Emma's story after the arrest, not only because I trusted him to report it well, but also because I wanted him to cover the re-rebrand. If I was going to prostrate myself and be the villain in the Monroe PR story, you better believe I wanted it done with some class. And Levi had undoubtedly delivered.

"What's next for you, Ms. PR badass? Skipping town now that you're not needed?"

"Not this time."

"Well, please allow me this honor of escorting you into your main event." Levi held out his elbow, and I hooked my arm in his.

We made our way through the front, navigating the folks gawking at the poster boards in the corridor and emerged into what was the perfect setting for tonight. Emma's event staff had transformed the place in a way I could never have imaged. The tapestries were gone and in their place were mesh white sheets with projections of images of newspaper headlines. I caught a couple real ones, such as 'Hotel Heiress Arrested' but others that were so fantastical you knew they were fake, like 'Sasquatch Spotted at Salt & Straw.' The lights were fanciful shades of neon, and a vintage disco ball spun overhead, casting glittering lights down on the people in attendance below.

"Can you believe this shit?" Pax asked as he emerged from the crowd and met us at the entrance. "It's like walking into a fucking Batman movie!"

I laughed and hugged him back as he lifted me in an embrace.

"Pax, you remember my friend Levi," I said, gesturing as he set me back on my feet.

"Oh yeah," he said, nodding and shaking Levi's enthusiastically outstretched hand. "You're the reporter that did my sister's story. You drink for free tonight. Hell, you drink free forever dude." Pax cupped Levi's shoulder and gave it a squeeze for emphasis before taking his leave and heading through the crowd.

"If you don't mind," Levi said, face flushed and teeth bared in a wide grin, "I'm going to follow that beautiful man to the bar and take advantage of my new VIP status." We hugged and promised to meet up soon for brunch, Levi rushing to take his leave as quickly as possible.

As I made my way through the crowd, I was greeted by multiple coworkers and introduced to their spouses and partners, shook hands and exchanged pleasantries with the various members of the press I'd come to know over the past couple months, and even ran into some of the local business owners I'd met as we'd been partnering up. For a woman who rarely set down any roots, I was starting to feel awfully planted in Portland.

"Have you signed the wall?" Emma asked enthusiastically, coming up behind me and not even bothering with a hello.

"Not yet," I said, glancing up at the impressive chalkboard wall. I would have loved to take credit for it, but it was actually all Emma's idea. "I'll go do that now. Have fun, I'll come find you when it's time." She nodded and bounded off into the crowd, looking as though she was ready and willing to chat with anyone interested. And right on cue, as she was less than ten feet away, a young girl came up gesturing for a selfie with Emma, which she naturally obliged to with gusto.

I turned toward the wall and stepped toward it, looking up and down the length of wall covered with all sorts of the different truths written in multiple colors of chalk, in print large and small, confessions ranging from a couple of words to blocks of text. It was moving to see people's public expressions of truth.

I should have called her.

I think I'm hot even though I try to act humble.

I wished I'd called my mom more before she died.

I can't believe I wasted so much time with him.

I regret not traveling.

I don't really like bike riding, but my girlfriend loves it and I'm afraid to say anything now.

I chuckled at the last one as I grabbed a piece of chalk and walked further down the wall, and just as I was going to write in an empty space just above my head, I saw familiar handwriting. I knelt to bring the text eye-level.

I steal shit.

I ghosted a touch over the text, which Emma had punctuated with a heart, and swallowed hard against the lump in my throat. Emma was inspiring me more and more every day. Staying in my crouched position, I brought the chalk to the board and wrote.

I'm dishonest.

I leaned back and looked at my words for a moment before scoffing at myself and erasing it with the butt of my hand. If Emma could be blatantly honest, any one of us could, and *should*. With a cleared off space, I put the chalk to the wall again and wrote.

I push everyone away and am afraid I'll always be alone.

I stood and looked down at my words, happy with my truth and relieved to have gotten the thought out.

"I wouldn't worry about that," a silken voice said in my ear, causing my eyes to close as goosebumps spread out across my skin. I would have loved a steadying breath before turning around, but I just didn't have it in me. Impatiently, I spun on my heel and looked up into those familiar hazel eyes.

"Hello, Sam."

THIRTY-THREE

Dee

"Hi," Sam said so quietly I almost didn't hear him.

We were locked into a stare that was becoming impossible for me to break. Sam was looking at me like he was seeing me for the first time; I didn't know if I was reading too much into it, but it seemed like his stare was full of lust and passion and love. I had to remind myself that this was the man that dumped me and hopped on a plane to the other side of the world only a few weeks ago. Because at this moment, as he was looking at me like I was the only person in the room, and I had no idea what to do with that. What did I choose to do? I stood there, standing so close to him I had to tilt my head to keep eye contact and could smell his cologne and shampoo in alternating wafts.

There was so much to say. There was weeks' worth of thoughts that I wanted to share with him. I'd been daydreaming about this moment forever, and here I was, standing in front of him, and all that noise in my head evaporated as I just stood, gaping at him. Sam continued to look down at me and arched a brow at my silent stance.

"I have no idea what to say," I blurted out. Sam laughed and rubbed his chin absentmindedly, looking around the room.

"Yeah, me either. So how about we dance?" He didn't wait for my answer, he turned and grabbed me by the hand, leading me out to the floor. Before I knew it, he had spun me around and pulled me into an embrace like a dizzying sex trap.

For one short moment, I reeled against the realization that I was being held within Sam's embrace and leaning into his strong body. But I glanced up at the banner of Emma billowing over the stage, her mischievous grin and cute wink, and I was reminded that there was power in being true to yourself.

"I fucked up so bad," I said as he twirled us around the floor.

"I did too," he said, looking down at me. "No, really," he said in response to my look of confusion. "You were never malicious; it's not like you were out for complete personal gain regardless of who it hurt. You were just trying to get a win for everyone, I get that. And for all my talk and self-bravado about always being myself, you were always upfront about who *you* are. I knew going into this that managing appearances was your gig, I shouldn't have been surprised when you did it to me."

"But that's just it," I interrupted, "I let it all get out of hand. There should be a line; *you* should have been the line. This was never going to work with so many lies between us. Everything you said that day was true; you were right, and as hard as it was to hear, I *needed* to hear it. More than anything, I want you to know that I heard you loud and clear."

"Apparently," Sam laughed as he looked around the club. "This whole idea was really inspired, Dee, I'm sure you know that. I don't doubt you've been hearing it nonstop the last few days, but I want *you* to know, that I get what all this really means." Sam's words and warm smile touched me deeply. He understood that this was all part of my process of letting go of who I had become and starting fresh. This was my mea-culpa to the family. It was my way of telling him I was trying to change. "What's next for the amazing publicist Sheppard? I heard you gave Mae the job of running things here."

"I did. She's more than ready. Plus, I don't think I'm a day-to-day manager type, I've learned that about myself."

"You're more of a swoop in and shake things up kind of gal?"

"Exactly. Parachute in, make everyone miserable, and then leave." We both laughed. "No, what I mean is, this has been so much fun, I think I want to do it all the time. I'm thinking about looking for something focused on rebranding and special projects. There's a firm in town that's already approached me; I guess they like my honest approach to advertising, said it was very 'Portland' of me." Sam threw his head back in laughter.

"Am I right in guessing that you're sticking around?"

"Yup, I got an apartment and everything. I'm officially one of those annoying Californians that you locals like to bitch about."

"Yuck, you guys are just the worst," Sam said, smiling down at me and brushing a bit of hair behind my ear. It was such a simple and intimate gesture, I almost thought he might kiss me. "Listen, I wanted to ask you something."

I tried to control my face and keep my excitement and expectations as low as possible. I didn't know for sure if he was going to ask to start seeing each other again, but my heart leapt at the possibility.

"There you are!" Mae said as she came through the dancing crowd, the determined, no-nonsense look on her face made me almost take a step backward. "You're due on stage in three minutes to introduce Charles. He speaks for six minutes, introduces Emma, who speaks for another four minutes, and then the band strikes up at exactly midnight, ringing in the official 'new day' of the Monroe. But all of that goes to shit if you're not taking the podium in exactly," Mae glanced at her watch, "two and a half minutes. Honestly, Dee. You organized this, I didn't think I was going to have to manage you, too." And with that, she turned on her heel and stormed off, presumably to yell at someone else.

"Jesus. Was I like that?"

"Let's just say, it's clear she's your protégé."

"I have to go," I said, dropping his hand and starting to step away.

"Damn straight you do; I wouldn't mess with Mae right now."

"Talk later?" Sam nodded, and I took my exit.

To Mae's relief, I took the podium two minutes later, thanking everyone for coming, acknowledging the press in the room, and then introducing Charles, who delivered the speech I had prepared for him. We'd agreed that tonight's event would be a benefit for OCD groups, in an ongoing effort to bring awareness to the disorder. After sharing a few words about the impact of OCD and mental illness, for both the sufferer and their family, Charles quickly pivoted to his praise of Emma, telling her story to a room full of people that had all heard it before, but never seemed to tire of listening to it. At the end, Charles officially announced the passing of the torch to Emma and brought her out on stage.

To a deafening round of applause and cheers, Emma floated across the stage, waving out to the crowd as she took her place behind the podium.

"Thank you, Portland. I must say, I've called Portland home my entire life, but it isn't until now that I've truly felt at home." More applause. "We are a city defined by what makes us different, and I can't imagine a better place to stand here in front of you and be myself."

Charles was applauding with the rest of the crowd and leaned close to my ear, "I saw you dancing with Sam earlier."

"Oh," I blushed and smiled awkwardly at the remark, "just catching up."

"Did he ask you?"

"What?" Charles mistook my surprise at his inquiry about Sam as my not hearing him over the noise and gestured for us to retreat further backstage.

"Did he ask you about the job?"

"What job?"

"Looks like I'm ruining his surprise, but I'm an old retired guy, I can do what I want," Charles chuckled at his own joke, clearly enjoying this new role in life. "Sam told me yesterday that he wants to hire you to be the lead PR and advertising strategist for MHI. You'll be in charge of basically doing this for each property MHI opens," he said, gesturing out at Emma and the crowd. "Like I mentioned this morning, we want each hotel to be a distinctive homage to its hometown, and Sam thinks we should do that loud and with a splash for each opening."

"Wow," I said, speechless. What an amazing opportunity and *exactly* what I wanted to do. So why wasn't I happier.

Because I thought he was asking me back to him.

I winced at the pettiness of my thought.

"Something wrong?" Charles asked, catching my expression, or more than likely reacting to my lack of reaction.

"No, it sounds perfect for me! I just hope our history won't be a problem, working together, I mean."

Charles smirked and shook his head, "I seriously don't think that's going to be a problem for Sam." And then he laughed.

It was clear that whatever Sam had shared with Charles had made it crystal clear that there was nothing left between us. Charles' reaction to what he clearly thought was an absurd concern said it all. That was ancient history. Sam had moved on.

Maybe it was for the best. This was a life-changing opportunity for me, a dream job served up on a silver platter, practically at the moment I'd redefined what that dream actually looked like. This time apart, these last three weeks, had probably given Sam the space to move on, and it was about time I did the same.

Emma's speech ended and in a New Year's Eve style countdown, she led the crowd through counting the last ten seconds to midnight, and when the clock struck twelve, the band started up behind her and Charles made his way back onto the stage to hug Emma as pink and silver confetti rained over the club. This was where I was planning on making my exit. That had been the plan, anyway. As everyone cheered and rejoiced at the new day, I had planned on quietly slipping out the door. But this new opportunity with MHI changed things. With reluctance, and admittedly a bit of embarrassment at my previous assumption, I made my way back down into the crowd to find Sam. I'd let him make his proposal, and I'd accept, and the two of us would start our own new day, as coworkers. I just needed a minute to prepare for that conversation and steel myself so that I didn't let on that I was disappointed. And as I was doing that, my phone vibrated in the pocket of my dress.

It was from Sam: Meet me in the conference room.

"Sure thing, boss," I said under my breath.

I made my way upstairs to the abandoned executive floor and toward the only lit room. Sam was standing at the window, hands in his pockets as he stared out over his city. His jacket was flung over one of the chairs, and his white dress shirt was bright in the window's reflection. I stepped into the room and the sequins from my dress danced the light around the room and across the window. Sam's eyes met mine in the window's reflection just before he turned.

"Thanks for meeting me up here," he said as he stepped away from the window. "I wanted to ask you something and-"

"Your dad already told me," I blurted out.

"He *what*?"

"He told me about the job. I'm sorry, I should have let you finish, I just wanted you to know that I know," I rambled as I came around the end of the table to stand in front of him. "Charles told me about the PR job with MHI, and I think it's wonderful."

"Oh," Sam was taken aback.

"If you want to go ahead and ask me, I mean, *officially*, that's fine. I'd like to hear what you have to say about the role, and you know, now that I'm thinking about it, I have some thoughts and ideas of my own. Questions, too. We should discuss everything and make sure we're in sync before officially moving forward."

"Ok, but Dee-"

"Don't be mad at Charles, ok? He was excited and honestly, I think a little tipsy. Sidebar, someone is *really* enjoying being retired. I know he stepped on your toes by telling me about it, but in all honesty, I really needed a little bit of time to process it before talking to you. You see, now that I know that you're over me, over this," I said in a rush, gesturing between us as I started sharing things I hadn't meant to say, "I just needed to wrap my brain around putting all of that away and focusing on just being coworkers again."

"Wait, he said *what*?" Sam was shaking his head, clearly trying to catch up with my manic train of thought.

"He didn't have to say anything; his reaction to my concern about us working together when there's unfinished stuff between us said it all."

"Ok, but-"

"And I'm not going to lie, for a brief moment I was really bummed, ok not *that* brief of a moment... because I thought you were going to ask me *something else* downstairs," I rolled my eyes at my own ridiculousness. "Look, this may be finished for you, but I've failed miserably at getting over you. I made minuscule steps at progress and then your name would come up in conversation around here, or your big dumb sexy head appeared on the fucking wall," I said with a dramatic gesture at the darkened flat screen. "So, yeah...I'm not there yet, but I will be."

"No, Dee-"

"Please don't reconsider giving me this job," I said frantically as I took a step closer to him, worried that all of my oversharing had just cost me the opportunity. "Despite all this personal stuff, I know I'd be really, *really* good at it. And if you can look past all this," I said with a gesture around my head, "I know I'd make you and MHI proud. In the span of a month, I've had a horrible breakdown but some wicked breakthroughs! All that's left for me to do is catch up to where you are, emotionally, and we'll be-"

My words were cut off as Sam reached out and quickly pulled me to him, crashing a kiss down on my lips. I froze in shock and complete confusion and then thought that on the off-chance this was a goodbye kiss, I should enjoy every bit of it. And so, I leaned into him and did nothing else but savor his lips and the warm, safe feel of his arms around me.

"Holy shit," Sam said as he pulled away and helped me stabilize my footing. "Does your new commitment to honesty also come with a side-effect of not taking a fucking *breath* when you talk? Will you let me speak now? Please!"

I pursed my lips in embarrassment as it occurred to me he'd been trying to chime in this whole time.

"Thank you," he said as he rubbed his forehead and sighed. "Ok, first of all… Christ, I don't even know where to start, you had so many points during that maniacal rant I'm having a hard time prioritizing which one to address first." He sighed and dropped his hands. "Yes, I want to hire you. I think you'd kick ass at leading MHI's advertising and PR, that's obvious," he said with a frustrated shrug before taking a deep breath. "But that's not what I was going to ask you downstairs. I wanted to ask you… what I *am* asking you, is if I can take you to dinner."

I felt my mouth open to speak, but nothing came out as I furrowed my brow in complete confusion. I had no idea what that even meant, but I thought it best to let him finish before firing a machine gun burst of questions at him.

"I've been complete shit at getting over you, too," he said, throwing his hands up in exasperation. "Everywhere I went, everything I did, everyone I talked to, all I could think about was you. I'm just as much in love with you today, Dee, as I was when I got on that fucking airplane. Actually, honestly, probably more." He shrugged in a 'what are you going to do' sort of fashion and sighed again. "And so, I want to take you out to dinner and have a proper first date and start this whole thing over, from the beginning. Let's put the man-whore and the shrew on a shelf and forget about them. But not us, not this," he said, making the same gesture between us that I had done. "Let's give this a real chance."

The world seemed to shift beneath my feet as I realized what was happening. Tears pricked at the corners of my eyes at the thought that I was getting a second chance at the love of my life.

"I would love that," I rushed out in a whisper, relief and elation coursing through me. And at that moment we both took a step forward, closing the distance between us and coming together in a tight embrace. I could hear Sam's soft sigh into my hair as he held me. "I just have one request," I said into the crook of his neck before he leaned back and looked at me inquisitively. "Can our date be *outside* of this hotel?"

Sam's laugh shook both of our bodies. "Absolutely," he said as he brought his forehead down to touch mine. My arms tightened around him as my eyes closed in contented bliss while the city lights danced outside the window next to us.

And there, standing in the same conference room where our war had once begun, Sam and I rang in a new day together with a passionate kiss, and nothing left unsaid.

The End

ABOUT THE AUTHOR

Candice Franklynn grew up in Northern California, where she graduated from the University of California, Davis with a degree in Communications. After far too many years of working her tail off in the corporate rat-race, Candice gave up her days of conference calls and board meetings for the excruciating bliss of writing. She's called the Pacific Northwest home for over a decade, currently residing outside of Portland with her loving husband, adorable three children, and overly-hyper two dogs.

Bad Press is Candice's debut novel.

Made in the USA
Middletown, DE
15 September 2019